"Leah," the voice whispered near her ear.

Her name echoed around her, growing fainter and fainter until it disappeared in the haze.

If only she could stay in this place forever. Cocooned in softness. Warm and comforted.

"Are you all right?" Kyle's face floated in front of her.

She drifted closer to the surface. Broke free from the murky depths. Her head ached. Her eyes burned. And the pain that had sent her into oblivion returned with a vengeance.

Kyle squatted in front of her. "Are you in pain?"

Could she reach out and smooth that frown from his face? But where were her hands, and why didn't they work? Why was she on the floor? Nothing made sense.

"I'm taking you to the hospital. You need to see a specialist." Kyle's tone brooked no argument.

Leah tried to protest, but he set a gentle hand on her head to keep her from getting up. Then he lifted her. Cradled in his arms, Leah leaned her head against his chest the way she had in her dreams.

Was she still dreaming? If she was, she never wanted to wake up.

The
AMISH
MIDWIFE'S
SECRET

ALSO BY RACHEL J. GOOD

The Love & Promises Series
The Amish Teacher's Gift

The
AMISH
MIDWIFE'S
SECRET

Love & Promises
Book Two

RACHEL J. GOOD

FOREVER
NEW YORK   BOSTON

Copyright © 2018 by Rachel J. Good
A preview of *The Amish Widow's Rescue* copyright © 2018 by Rachel J. Good

Cover design by Elizabeth Turner Stokes
Cover illustration by Trish Cramblet
Cover copyright © 2018 by Hachette Book Group, Inc.

Forever
Hachette Book Group
1290 Avenue of the Americas, New York, NY 10104
forever-romance.com
twitter.com/foreverromance

First Edition: November 2018

Forever is an imprint of Grand Central Publishing. The Forever name and logo are trademarks of Hachette Book Group, Inc.

The publisher is not responsible for websites (or their content) that are not owned by the publisher.

The Hachette Speakers Bureau provides a wide range of authors for speaking events. To find out more, go to www.hachettespeakersbureau.com or call (866) 376-6591.

ISBN: 978-1-5387-1128-6 (mass market), 978-1-5387-1129-3 (ebook)

Printed in the United States of America

OPM

10 9 8 7 6 5 4 3 2 1

To Martha, the Amish midwife who delivered my children at home

and

To the babies who have recently brought much joy into my life: Leland, Easton, and Sienna

Chapter One

The phone rang as Kyle Miller was rushing out the door. He didn't recognize the number. Probably a telemarketer, but just in case it was work related, he hit the answer button, tucked the phone between his ear and shoulder, and shoved one arm into his coat before saying, "Hello."

Slamming the door shut behind him by hooking it with one foot, he repeated his greeting. Definitely an automated call. He should hang up now, but he was busy shrugging his other arm into the sleeve. If traffic was heavy, he was going to be late. He sighed loudly.

A voice on the other end quavered. "Kyle?"

It sounded like a human, but some of those telemarketing firms managed to make their robocalls sound real. "Yes?" he answered cautiously. He wasn't interested in a time share or a free cruise or...

"Kyle, it's Dr. Hess. I have a question for you."

Dr. Hess? Name doesn't sound familiar. Not one of the doctors I work with at the hospital.

"Yes?" he said again as he clicked open his car door and slid into the seat.

"I'm not sure if you remember me, but you and your brother used to visit my office. And I took care of your parents when…"

The words hit Kyle like a fast, hard gut punch. He froze with his hand on the car door but couldn't move to close it. Old memories came flooding back. Memories he'd pushed below the surface. Memories he'd hoped never to dredge up again.

His "I remember" came out shakily. Why would the doctor be calling him? Had something happened to his brother? He hadn't spoken to Caleb in years. A flood of guilt hit him. If Caleb had been hurt or was dying, could he go back and face him? And what about the twins and…and Emma. No, he never wanted to see Emma again.

"Is everything all right? Has something happened to Caleb or—?"

"No, no, I didn't mean to alarm you. This isn't a medical emergency. Well, it is in a way. But it's my own emergency."

It dawned on Kyle that he'd been sitting there unmoving. He'd forgotten all about being late for his shift. He yanked the car door shut and started the engine. Flicking the phone button on the steering wheel with one hand, he pocketed the phone with his other, then yanked the gear shift into reverse to back out.

"I have some friends at the hospital who've been keeping tabs on you," Dr. Hess continued. "They've been telling me you'll go far in the field."

"Thanks." Although if he were honest, the thought of someone checking up on him gave him an uncomfortable feeling. Had Caleb asked their old family doctor to spy?

Kyle whipped his car into traffic and pressed his foot on the accelerator to shoot around a slow-moving truck. The minute he did, old memories haunted him. One memory in particular he wished he could erase. Speeding had destroyed his life and cost him everything he'd always wanted. He lifted his foot and let the car glide to a safer speed while Dr. Hess prattled on about his retirement dreams.

Biting back a sigh, Kyle tuned out the old man's words as he maneuvered through heavy rush hour traffic. He regretted not grabbing a cup of coffee to wake him up, because the drone of Dr. Hess's words was lulling him to sleep. Surely, the doctor hadn't called a relative stranger to discuss his future plans. Kyle wished Dr. Hess would get to the point.

"So I considered shutting down the practice, but I'm one of the few doctors in the Lancaster area who still makes house calls. People have come to expect it. That's where you come in."

"Me?"

"Yes, you. Seems to me you'll be needing a place to work now that you're done with your residency. I'd be happy to turn my practice over to you if you'd help me out for the next year or two. I'd like to cut back to part-time hours."

Kyle slammed on the brakes before he ran a red light. "Take over your practice?"

"Yes, I thought Esther and I could move to the retirement village she's been talking about. You could live in the house so you'd have the office right there."

Kyle pictured the huge old farmhouse set on a country road with the office attached to one side. It was a far cry from his future aspirations, which included working at a major medical center in a large city. Country life wasn't for him.

"It's a great offer," he said, planning to let his old family doctor down gently. "I'll, umm…"

"Esther and I prayed about it, and we both felt led to give the practice to you."

"Give?" Kyle said faintly.

"Yes, *give*. We have plenty of money to buy a home in the retirement village and live comfortably. With no children of our own, we thought it would be nice to help another young doctor starting out. The mortgage is paid off, and you'd only be responsible for the bills once I leave the practice."

Kyle pulled into a parking space at the hospital. *The man is giving away his practice and his home?* "That's a mighty generous offer. I, umm, need to get in to work now. If I don't, I'll be late. But I'll think about it."

"Don't just think. Pray about it."

Kyle choked back the negative retort that sprang to his lips. You wouldn't catch him praying. "Um, yes. I have to go, but I'll let you know my decision." He said a hasty good-bye and ran for the staff entrance.

Having just completed his residency and still drowning in med school debt, the offer was tempting. And it would allow him to repay another huge debt. A debt that had haunted him for years. An unpaid debt to an Amish community.

But it would mean returning to a place he'd left years

ago and to which he'd vowed never to return. A place where he'd have to face all the demons of his past.

* * *

Leah waited for Dr. Hess to get off the phone. Usually his wife, Esther, acted as receptionist, but the doctor was sitting in the outer office, which meant Leah couldn't help overhearing his conversation.

"You're finally getting some assistance?" she asked when he hung up.

Dr. Hess laughed. "Esther convinced me it's time to retire, but I can't go until I'm sure I have a good replacement who will do everything I do."

"Someone like that may be hard to find."

"True, but I'm hoping to convince a recent med school graduate to move back to the area. He grew up around here, and his mother—" Dr. Hess ran a hand through his silver hair. "Esther tells me I ramble too much, and she's right." He leaned forward, all attention on her. "What do you need today, Leah?"

"I have an expectant mother I'm worried about, but she refuses to come to the office. She says she can't leave the children. I suspect it's money." Leah held out some ten-dollar bills.

Dr. Hess waved them away. "I have more than enough money. I can certainly afford to do some free visits."

"Yes, but—"

The doctor interrupted her. "What's her name and address?"

Leah gave him the information and tried once again to give him the money, but the doctor refused it.

He rose and picked up his medical bag. "I'll head over there now."

"Thank you so much. I'm praying for a healthy delivery for her." Leah followed him to the door and out to the parking lot. "I must admit I'm curious about this new doctor. You said he was from the area?" As a midwife, she'd have to work closely with him.

Dr. Hess stopped beside his car. "His name's Kyle Miller."

Leah gasped. "Caleb Miller's brother?"

With a quick nod, Dr. Hess slipped into the driver's seat. "I'm hoping everyone can let bygones be bygones."

The Amish community had forgiven Kyle, but having him back in their midst as a doctor might dredge up old hurts. And for Leah, it meant confronting a secret she thought would stay hidden. A secret she'd concealed for years.

Chapter Two

The rest of the week, Dr. Hess's offer haunted Kyle. Could he go back to that sleepy town in the middle of nowhere? Leave behind his dreams of a fellowship in rare diseases? Even more worrisome, could he live and work among the Amish, especially if it meant facing the ones whose lives he'd destroyed?

The doctor called on Friday, just before Kyle flopped into bed, exhausted after extra hours on call. "Son, I'm not trying to pressure you, but I wondered if you'd thought about my offer."

Kyle mumbled something noncommittal. All he wanted to do was sleep.

"According to Dr. Patel, you have three days off in a row starting next Wednesday. I'd like to buy you a plane ticket to fly here for a visit. It would give you a chance to look over the practice, see what I do, and discuss possible arrangements if it's something you decide will suit."

Kyle had been planning to catch up on sleep and dirty laundry. "I don't know if—"

"I realize it's a major commitment. That's why I'd like you to come for a brief visit."

Kyle hesitated. How could he refuse? Dr. Hess and his wife had been there for him and his brother, Caleb, during their agonizing decision to remove their mom from life support after the car accident that had already taken their dad's life. Esther had mothered them for months after both funerals, ensuring they had clean clothes and meals and occasional motherly hugs.

"You probably have a lot to do." Dr. Hess's voice wavered, adding to Kyle's guilt.

"I, umm, I'll book a flight."

"I'm happy to pay. I know how expensive medical school is, and I'm asking you to do me a favor on your precious time off."

"It's all right." Kyle yawned. "I'll swing it." Money was tight, but he didn't want to be beholden to Dr. Hess. If Kyle decided staying in the Amish community was too painful, it would make turning the doctor down that much harder.

"I apologize," Dr. Hess said. "Sounds like I'm keeping you from some much-needed sleep. Good night, and I'll see you Wednesday. Let me know when your flight gets in, and Esther will pick you up."

"Thanks," Kyle managed before another yawn overtook him. Soon after he shut off his phone, he fell into a deep sleep. But his last thoughts before he drifted off were of Emma... and the baby...

* * *

Memories continued to trouble Kyle as the days ticked down to Wednesday. Several times he almost canceled his flight, but he hated to break a promise or let the Hesses down, so on Wednesday morning, he headed to the airport as planned.

After a brief flight, Kyle walked out into a frigid October day. He preferred the warmer North Carolina weather.

Esther Hess was waiting by the curb when he walked out the door. She'd aged since he'd last seen her, but the wrinkles creasing her face formed deep smile lines. "I'm so glad you decided to come." She motioned for him to get into an old-fashioned black car sporting black bumpers, grill, and hubcaps. Not fashionable ones, but ones whose chrome had been blackened with a paint-brush. She smiled at his confusion.

"It's a Black-Bumper Mennonite car. They believe the silver is too gaudy and showy. They also dress plainly and have some of the same practices as the Amish."

At the word Amish, Kyle winced. "Are you and the doctor planning to join a Black-Bumper church?" If they were, would Esther need to exchange her matronly flower-print dress, which fell to just below her knees, for a calf-length black dress that some conservative Mennonites wore?

Esther smiled. "We may be Mennonites, but we're not quite that strict. We bought the car secondhand because it was an excellent price. I kept everything black to remind me to stay humble."

A few people in the airport parking lot pointed and stared, making Kyle glad he didn't know many people in the area anymore.

"Martin's promised to give up the practice as soon as God sends someone who'll do it for him. It may be selfish of me"—Esther shot him a sideways glance—"but I'm hoping he's found that someone in you. Forty years is a long time. He deserves a break."

"He certainly does." *That doesn't mean it needs to be me. I certainly wouldn't be anyone's answer to prayer.*

As Esther drove, Kyle almost drifted off to sleep. Not only because he was physically drained, but because coming back here had hit him hard emotionally.

The jangle of a phone startled him.

"Would you mind answering that?" Esther asked. "It's Martin's ringtone."

Kyle mumbled a groggy hello.

Dr. Hess's jovial welcome boomed through the phone, and Kyle held it away from his ear.

"Glad you arrived safely. Could you ask Esther to come to Enos Fisher's?"

"We'll be there shortly, Martin," Esther called out. She smiled apologetically at Kyle. "I was hoping you'd get a bit more rest before Martin dragged you around on house calls."

"It's all right. I'm used to it. The lack of sleep, I mean." He'd never done house calls. That would be a first.

As Esther wound her way out into the country, the neat brown squares of harvested fields resembled giant patchwork quilts, like the multicolored ones flapping on some clotheslines they passed. Kyle's heart sank. He'd forgotten how isolated some of these farms were. And the outbuildings reminded him of parties at an Amish barn and...

He released a sigh as Esther bumped down a dirt lane toward a neat white farmhouse surrounded by rows of chopped-down cornstalks. Behind a wooden fence, cows lowed in the field, and when he opened the car door, the crisp fall air carried the earthy scent of farmland. Kyle inhaled deeply. The familiar sights and sounds made his eyes misty. Though he and Caleb had grown up *Englisch* and had lived in town, they'd spent time on friends' farms, and Kyle had visited one Amish house more times than he could count.

He shook off the nostalgia. Being here with the doctor meant he needed to appear professional. He pasted on a neutral, businesslike expression.

Esther stepped past him and hurried onto the wooden porch. "Yoo-hoo," she called through the screen door.

A little boy of about four, with a bowl haircut, pushed open the door. His black pants and suspenders signaled they'd come to an Amish home. Kyle's stomach clenched. Not only his first house call. His first time entering an Amish home since...

"We left the door open so you could come in." The boy's eyes widened as they traveled up Kyle's height. "You're tall."

"Yes, he is." Esther stepped into the living room. "How's baby Aaron?"

His older sister, who appeared to be about eight, came up behind him and smiled shyly. She wore a long dress and had her hair twisted on the sides and pulled back into a bun. "He'll get better now that Leah's here. She brought some ingredients to help *Mamm*. They're in the kitchen."

"Oh, good. Did you stay home from school today?"

The young girl shook her head. "I only came home during lunchtime to watch Aaron while *Mamm* and *Daed* meet with Leah."

Esther motioned for Kyle to follow her down the hall. "You'll get to meet Leah, our midwife-in-training. The two of you will work together on high-risk preg— um, high-risk cases." She leaned over and whispered so the children couldn't hear. "Amish women never mention they're expecting, especially not to men and children."

Kyle frowned. "I'd think it would be obvious."

"That may be, but no one talks about it. I hope you'll respect that."

Once again, Esther acted as if he'd already agreed to take over the practice. They crossed the threshold to a large, spacious kitchen with a hand-hewn wooden table capable of seating ten. Dr. Hess sat on one of the chairs, waiting patiently as several women and girls bustled around.

Whew! Onions and cayenne pepper stung Kyle's nose and eyes. The odor didn't remind him of typical Amish cooking. A young woman who appeared to be in her midtwenties and about eight months pregnant stepped over to the stove carrying what looked like a piece of nylon stocking.

"Are you ready for this, Leah?" she asked an attractive Amish girl stirring a pot on the stove.

"Not quite. Could you hand me the herbs and essential oils?"

The young mother obliged, and the girl—Leah?— took the pot off the stove before adding some ingredients to the mixture she was stirring.

A small girl who couldn't have been more than five

staggered into the kitchen, carrying a heavy bundle wrapped in blankets. "Here's Aaron, *Mamm*."

She was holding a baby? Sucking in a breath, Kyle rushed across the kitchen floor to rescue the dangling infant. Before he reached them, Dr. Hess turned around and held out his arms.

"I'll take him." The doctor slid a hand under the baby. He didn't seem at all perturbed that the girl could have dropped the child.

Kyle's heart banged against his chest at the near accident, but the expectant mother only smiled and thanked the little girl for bringing her brother to the doctor. The girl had called her *Mamm*, so she and the baby must both belong to this woman.

"This baby is yours?" Kyle could barely keep the shock from his voice. "He's only about a year old."

"Eleven months," the mother corrected, her words soft and gentle.

Eleven months? And she was about to have another soon. Kyle almost asked when her next baby was due, but recalling Esther's caution, he clamped his mouth shut.

After the little girl partially undressed the baby, Dr. Hess lowered the stethoscope to the infant's chest. His face grave, he slid the chest piece around several times. Then, while propping the baby's chest against his hand, he touched the stethoscope to various spots on the baby's back. He rewrapped the child in blankets and beckoned for Kyle to take his place on the chair.

"See what you think." The doctor set one hand on the baby to keep him from rolling off the table and held out the stethoscope with the other.

The look in his eyes challenged Kyle. Was this a test of competence? His nervous fingers closed around the earpieces. Overcoming his squeamishness about using someone else's equipment, he fumbled to insert the ear tips and then set the diaphragm against the infant's tiny chest. The crackling, bubbling, and rumbling coming through the chest piece as the baby wheezed left no doubt of the diagnosis.

To keep from blurting out the answer, Kyle fiddled with the earpieces as he waited for Dr. Hess to reposition the baby. Kyle had no need to listen to the child's back, but to look professional, he finished the exam. His eyes sought Dr. Hess's before he announced, "Pneumonia."

Dr. Hess nodded.

"I know." Leah, who'd been stirring the smelly mixture in the pot, motioned for the mother to hold out the nylon bag so she could spoon the mush into it. "That's why we're making this poultice." With a quick motion, she wrapped the nylon in a towel and hurried to the table.

She practically elbowed Kyle out of the way as she reached for the baby. With deft movements, she placed the stinking mixture on the baby's chest, quickly re-dressed him, and swaddled him in warm blankets. "This should help."

"Help?" Kyle's eyes burned from the sharp stench rising from the infant's body, and he choked. "That child belongs in a hospital."

"Hospital?" Leah shot him an incredulous glance. "How could his *mamm* be with him? She shouldn't be jolting all that way to the hospital, and who'd care for the children?"

Kyle couldn't believe his ears. "Children under age two are at the greatest risk—" He broke off when Dr. Hess jiggled his arm. Snapping his mouth shut, Kyle waited for the doctor to speak. This was still Dr. Hess's case, after all. Just because he'd allowed Kyle to offer a diagnosis, it didn't mean Kyle should take over.

"I'll put the baby in the cradle." Leah looked at the mother, who nodded.

Dr. Hess held out a hand to stop her, and Kyle released a pent-up sigh. The doctor would explain the need for hospitalization. Instead he gestured toward Kyle. "Before you go, Leah, I'd like you to meet Kyle. I'm hoping to convince him to take over my practice."

Leah ducked her head and mumbled a brief greeting. She refused to meet his eyes, which might be just as well, because his face likely would reveal how upset he was about the home remedy. Pneumonia wasn't something to fool around with, especially not in infants.

"Kyle, you'll be working closely with Leah. She's in training to be a midwife, and she makes many effective herbal remedies."

Kyle managed to say, "Pleased to meet you," but he wasn't sure how true that was.

Dr. Hess might trust Leah's homemade brews, but when Kyle graduated from medical school, he'd taken an oath promising his patients' health would always be his foremost consideration. So how could he stand here and let her smear a stinky concoction on a baby's chest when that child should be taken to the hospital?

He could never allow anyone to harm a baby. Never.

Chapter Three

*K*yle. Leah's arms tightened around the baby, and her heart quickened. She averted her gaze because, if she met Kyle's eyes, he might read the guilt in hers. Or worse yet, remember the part she'd played that dreadful night. After he'd left town years ago, she'd buried her fear that he'd discover the truth. Now he was here in this kitchen, close enough to touch. Leah struggled to control her trembling, to put the past out of her mind, to concentrate on the darling baby in her arms.

Although she avoided meeting Kyle's eyes, she couldn't help noting his pursed lips. He appeared to be pinching back a retort, and his nose had wrinkled when she'd put the onion poultice on baby Aaron's chest. She suspected Kyle's expression wasn't only a reaction to the strong smell. Definitely not a good sign. The last thing they needed was a doctor who didn't understand Amish ways.

His half-hearted greeting proved he felt as wary of her as she did of him. Having Kyle Miller back in the community would be difficult enough, but having to work with him during deliveries would be torture. Any moment he might glance at her and...

The baby emitted a phlegmy cough, and Leah tipped him upright and patted his back to ease his breathing. Beside her, Kyle's body tensed as if he wanted to snatch Aaron from her. Leah swished past him before he could make a move and headed for the cradle in the back bedroom.

When she reached the room, she shut the door behind her to give herself some time to recover. Her breathing was as labored as the baby's. Kyle hadn't looked at her closely. If he did, would he remember that time their eyes locked and both their worlds changed forever? Leah didn't want to take that chance.

From the brief glimpse she had of him, Kyle looked too slick and polished to return to a small farming community. Why would he even want to come back after what happened? Although the Amish would never hold his past against him, few in their area would visit his office or invite him into their homes if he refused to accept their way of life.

As much as she wanted to see Dr. Hess enjoy retirement—he worked much too hard—Kyle Miller was the last person she'd want to take his place. The first chance she got, she'd recommend that Dr. Hess find a different assistant. Seeing Kyle again made her realize she couldn't work with him. Not only did they have totally different ideas on how to handle illness, but being around him sent waves of guilt over her. Kyle might never remember what she'd done, but the shame of that night was burned indelibly into her memory.

Rather than settling baby Aaron in the cradle, Leah sank onto the nearby bed and cuddled him close. For years, she'd yearned to have a family of her own, but holding babies like this had been her only chance to hug little ones. Blinking back tears, she patted Aaron's back as he coughed. Now that she'd started dating Ben, she'd begun to hope someday he'd be her husband and they'd have a family. That possibility could become a reality...if only they could start agreeing on things.

Ben didn't want her being a midwife, but Leah was determined to show him she could make their relationship and her career work. So far, they'd crossed a few hurdles and managed to stay together. The fall months would be busier than usual with weddings, babies, and illnesses, making it a challenge to find time to be together.

"Leah?" Dr. Hess's voice boomed through the house, and she jumped, startling baby Aaron, whose thin wail came out choked.

She lifted him to her shoulder, breathing shallowly to avoid getting a strong whiff of the onion, and rubbed his back. "Be right there," she called back as she waited for Aaron's spate of coughing to subside. When he'd quieted, she propped him in the cradle to make it easier for him to breathe. She had no desire to subject herself to Kyle's withering looks or take a chance he might recognize her.

When she entered the kitchen, Kyle's clenched fists and tight jaw made it clear he was holding back anger. Anger he probably wanted to direct at her for disregarding his advice about the baby. She hoped Dr. Hess would explain about Amish ways. Kyle, though, didn't look as if he'd listen.

Leah nibbled on her lower lip. She had no right to judge him. She herself had been guilty of the same fault. She wanted her own way too. She'd ignored his advice about taking the baby to the hospital, believing her poultice was the correct solution. Talk about *hochmut*! If she hadn't been so prideful, she would have considered Kyle's recommendation as well as his feelings. Instead she'd not only dismissed it, she'd pointed out how wrong he was. Leah's conscience insisted she apologize, but the stubborn part of her refused to give in.

Before her better side could convince her to do the right thing, Dr. Hess rose from the table and beckoned to Kyle.

"We'd better get going. I have a lot to do and plenty to show you." The doctor picked up his black leather bag and smiled at Leah. "Kyle's only here for three days, but when he comes back, I'll make sure to get the two of you together so you can get to know each other."

Kyle looked as if that were the last thing he'd ever want to do. Not that she blamed him. Maybe being here had made it clear this job didn't suit him. Perhaps she'd never see him again, which Leah would consider a great blessing.

* * *

Kyle held his tongue until the front door closed behind him and the Hesses. "You're leaving that baby here?"

Dr. Hess slowed and put a hand on Kyle's arm. "The

Amish around here prefer chiropractors. They rarely consult a doctor unless it's a medical emergency."

"Like this baby?"

Dr. Hess sighed. "I know most people would rush that child to the hospital, but the Amish don't do things the way we *Englischers* do."

"If the parents plan to ignore what you tell them to do, why do they bother to call you in the first place?" In his worry for the baby, Kyle's words came out more sharply than he'd intended.

"Actually, the parents weren't the ones who contacted me. Leah asked me to check the baby. She was convinced he had pneumonia."

"The midwife diagnoses people?"

Esther chuckled. "I don't imagine all midwives do, but Leah's different. She's been running her family's natural products store for years. She has an extensive knowledge of herbs and alternative medicine."

Kyle's fear for the baby's health boiled over and spilled out into his words. "So she not only diagnoses diseases, she recommends quack remedies?"

"I wouldn't call her treatments 'quack.' In fact," Esther said, "she's quite knowledgeable. By the time Martin gets called in, she often has the cases pretty well in hand."

"Esther's right." Dr. Hess flashed his wife a loving smile. "One other thing you need to know is that the Amish come to me for a diagnosis, but most of them ignore the prescriptions I write."

Kyle stopped and stared at him. "What's the point of going to a doctor if you're going to ignore the advice?"

"They mainly want to confirm the diagnosis. Then

they'll get products at Leah's family's store to treat whatever I tell them they have."

"That's crazy."

Dr. Hess reached his car, opened the trunk, and set his bag inside before he turned and pinned Kyle with a look that pierced his soul. "I believe in honoring God by doing my job and leaving the rest up to Him."

Kyle squirmed and looked away. God had ignored his pleas for his mother's life, so it seemed foolhardy to trust Him—or the Amish midwife—with patients' lives.

When Kyle didn't answer him, Dr. Hess continued, "You might be surprised at how well the natural treatments work. Some of the remedies the Amish use might seem odd."

"Yes, indeed," Esther said. "Like BEMER treatments or reflexology or—"

Her husband held up his hand. "Maybe we'd better not overwhelm the boy with that information right now." He and Esther exchanged glances that seemed to convey deep messages between them.

Esther's lips quirked. "You're right, Martin. We don't want to scare him off."

She needn't worry about that. If he hadn't already planned to turn them down, his encounter with the Amish midwife would have been enough to change his mind. Hearing the patients would ignore his advice only confirmed his decision.

Dr. Hess opened the passenger door and looked at Kyle. "Why don't you ride with me so we can discuss some of our plans?" He turned to his wife. "If you'll be all right, dear? You just took that long drive to the airport."

"Of course I will. Don't worry about me, Martin. I'm not tired."

"I just want to be sure you're safe." He moved closer to her, took her hand, and squeezed it. "You're precious to me."

Esther beamed up at her husband. "I pray God will watch over all of us as well as the Fisher family, especially the unborn baby and little Aaron."

He bent and planted a gentle kiss on her forehead. "Till we meet again."

Kyle turned away, a lump blocking his throat. He had no idea how long those two had been married, but they acted like young lovers. His heart longed for a relationship like that. A relationship he'd never have. Once he'd loved someone with his whole heart, but anger and carelessness had destroyed both their lives.

"Are you ready, Kyle?" Dr. Hess's words startled him from his grief.

After he and Dr. Hess got into the car, the doctor turned on the engine but motioned for his wife to pull out ahead of them. "That way we can keep an eye on her."

"You don't trust her driving?"

After turning a shocked glance in Kyle's direction, Dr. Hess said with a touch of sternness, "Esther's a wonderful driver. You've ridden with her, so you should know."

"Yes, she is. But when you said you were keeping an eye on her, you were worried—"

"Cars can break down. Drunk drivers can cause accidents."

The word *accident* stabbed Kyle, and he winced.

"As a doctor, I've realized how fragile life can be. And if it's in my power, I want to protect my wife."

Kyle pressed his fingers against his eyelids to ease the stinging. He certainly knew how fragile life could be.

Dr. Hess continued, "I consider every moment with Esther as a gift."

His throat tight, Kyle asked, "How long have you been married?"

"We'll be celebrating our forty-sixth anniversary this spring." Dr. Hess kept his gaze trained on the rutted lane as they bounced along. "Which means I'm no longer a spry chicken. That's why I need some help in the practice. Esther's been by my side all this time, but we had to be apart for many holidays, anniversaries, birthdays, and other special occasions. And I can't count the number of dates I've broken."

After they pulled out onto the main highway, Dr. Hess stayed right behind his wife, even though she drove well under the speed limit.

"When you're the only doctor in an area like this," he continued, "you make a lot of sacrifices. Esther's made all of them and more. She deserves my full time and attention now. That's why I'm ready to hand over the practice to a deserving young doctor." He shot Kyle a look.

I'm not the deserving young doctor you're looking for. But Kyle couldn't bring himself to blurt that out and destroy Dr. Hess's hopes. Instead, he deflected the conversation. "I still can't believe you're giving your practice away. Why would anyone do that?"

"I have my reasons." Dr. Hess gripped the steering wheel even more tightly. "I did tell you the main one when I called."

Yes, something about God. A reason Kyle had quickly tuned out. But there had to be more to it than that. Later, Kyle would press him to discover the other more plausible reasons. Perhaps his business wasn't doing well, or it was deeply in debt. No one just gave away a thriving practice.

Chapter Four

The next morning, while Dr. Hess talked on the phone, Kyle paced the waiting room. Nothing had changed in the reception room or offices since he'd been here last, except the walls had recently been painted and the old-fashioned wooden spindle-back chairs sported new cushions. The dark mahogany paneling on the lower half of the wall gleamed, as did the reception desk.

Kyle mentally updated the room with a counter and plastic partition for the receptionist rather than the old-fashioned desk. He also added some bright modern seating for adults and some beanbag chairs for the children instead of the small wooden chairs surrounding the scarred maple table. The multicolored beads on a wire frame and *Highlights* magazines scattered around had been there since he was three, or maybe even before that.

He shook himself. *What am I doing planning changes for an office when I don't intend to take the job?*

But he couldn't stop the feelings of nostalgia as he sat in one of the old wooden chairs lined up along the wall. His mom had sat here, as stiff and upright as the chair backs, while he and Caleb paged through the children's magazines. Esther Hess had ushered them down the hall to one of the small examination rooms, where they waited for Dr. Hess.

Fearful of getting a shot, Kyle had clung to his mother's hand until the doctor reassured him he didn't need one that time. The times he did, Mom let him squeeze her hand and then hugged him after it was over. Dr. Hess always pulled a lollipop from the pocket of his white coat. He wouldn't be surprised if the doctor still did that. Most doctors had given up the practice, preferring to hand out stickers or small plastic toys.

Memories of Mom warmed him inside. She'd been so loving and caring. He still couldn't believe she was gone. Those last horrible days Caleb tried to prevent him from seeing her, afraid it would be too traumatic. He couldn't get his brother to understand that he wanted to be with Mom as she endured her last painful hours hooked up to machines that fed her and breathed for her. He wanted to hold her hand the way she'd held his.

"Kyle?" Dr. Hess emerged from his office at the end of the long hall. "We need to make a house call in Gordonville."

"I thought Thursday was your day off." The office was closed, and Esther had stayed in the house after breakfast to work on a baby blanket she was knitting for a local women's shelter. Dr. Hess had invited Kyle for a tour of the office, but when the phone rang, he'd rushed down the hall to answer it.

With a shrug, Dr. Hess escorted him back into the house for their jackets. "When you're a doctor, days off are rare. If someone needs me, I have to go."

Esther sat in an armchair in the living room, a Bible in her lap. On the table beside her, two balls of yarn lay next to shiny knitting needles with rows of green and yellow stitching on them.

"Sorry to disturb your devotions, dear," the doctor said. "Just got an emergency call. Not sure how long we'll be."

"Oh, Martin, on your day off?" She held up a hand to stop her husband's spluttering. "I know, I know. You need to help." She turned grateful eyes to Kyle. "I'm so glad you're willing to help Martin. You'll be a real blessing."

Kyle punched his balled fists into his pockets and bit back a response. He managed a half-hearted smile. "We'd better go."

Dr. Hess nodded. "I switched the office line to ring in here in case of an emergency, but I hope this will be the only call today."

"I hope so too, but if anyone calls, I'll ring your cell." Esther stood and hurried over to her husband, who wrapped his arms around her.

When they began to kiss, Kyle turned his back and concentrated on buttoning his coat. Knowing he'd never find a love like theirs left a hollow emptiness in his chest. He'd plugged that hole with nonstop studying, constant work, and general busyness. Some of the women at the hospital, both doctors and nurses, had expressed interest in him, but he'd brushed them off. He had no time—or room—in his life for relationships.

"Let's go," Dr. Hess said as he reached around Kyle for the doorknob. "Miriam said her husband took a tumble and couldn't get up. She's afraid he may have broken something."

Gusts of frigid air slapped them in the face as they exited the house, and Kyle hunched over to ward off the cold. He wrestled the car door open and managed to get inside before the wind slammed it shut. He shivered until the heater blasted out enough warmth to ward off the chill.

Dr. Hess drove down country roads and back lanes past farms and barns. As they approached a familiar turnoff, the car slowed, and the doctor clicked on his turn signal. Kyle's whole body went rigid. A short distance down the road, Dr. Hess tapped the brakes when he reached a long driveway. The tightness in Kyle's stomach now constricted his throat. *No!* They couldn't be going here.

How many times had he pulled into this driveway? How many nights had he sat out here watching for the light to go out in Emma's bedroom, counting down the minutes it took for her sisters to fall asleep? For her to slip out to meet him? How many times had he waited impatiently for the front door to open? For her to come tripping across the lawn, all dolled up in *Englisch* clothes?

The last time he'd visited this house, he'd come to beg Emma not to marry her Amish fiancé. He'd walked away with a broken heart and vowed never again to fall in love.

The minute Dr. Hess parked the car, he hopped out and grabbed his bag, but Kyle clutched the door handle. He couldn't bring himself to open the door. The doctor tapped on the window, and Kyle jumped, his tense nerves making him skittish. When Dr. Hess beckoned him, Kyle forced himself to step from the protection of the car into one of his worst nightmares.

Dr. Hess was already scurrying along the walkway toward the front door, his old-fashioned black overcoat flapping in the wind.

Kyle's feet stayed rooted to the first stone block of the walkway. If he didn't hurry, the doctor would go inside without him. Then he'd be forced to stand on the doorstep to knock, and he'd have to confront whoever opened the door. At least if he caught up to Dr. Hess, he wouldn't have to enter alone, and maybe he'd be camouflaged by the doctor's bulk. Or maybe not. Kyle towered over the doctor by about six inches. He rushed to the porch and arrived breathless just as the front door opened.

A woman, her face scrunched into worried lines, never looked up. Instead, she took one glance at the bag in the doctor's hand and motioned for them to come in. "Thank the Lord, you're here. Reuben's in a lot of pain."

Kyle had never stepped over the threshold of this house. Although Dr. Hess followed the woman, Kyle hesitated. The woman who'd answered the door seemed unfamiliar. Definitely not one of Emma's sisters; he'd recognize both of them. He'd only met the rest of Emma's family once. So much had happened that fateful day perhaps her parents wouldn't recognize him. He hoped not. Sucking in a deep breath that did little to calm his jittery nerves, Kyle padded down the hall after the doctor and stood to one side, trying to remain unnoticed, his attention riveted to the man on the floor. The man who could have been his father-in-law.

Eyes glazed with pain, Reuben Esh lay sprawled on the floor in an awkward position. He'd gained a great deal of weight since Kyle had last seen him, which would make it difficult for him to move. Emma's mother sat beside him on the floor, holding his hand.

Dr. Hess knelt beside Reuben and began his examination, while Kyle tried to blend into the shadows in the doorway and prayed the doctor wouldn't ask him to confirm the diagnosis.

As a doctor, it was Kyle's duty to treat any patient who came to him. Yet he'd also been taught to keep a professional boundary between himself and his patients. Not treating friends or family members would prevent his emotions from clouding his medical judgment. Did the parents of the girl you once loved count?

His face grave, Dr. Hess met Reuben's eyes. "I'm going to call for medical transport to take you to the hospital."

Reuben grasped Dr. Hess's hand. "If you help me up, I'll lie down for a few hours. I'll soon be feeling better."

Dr. Hess shook his head. "I'm pretty sure you've broken your hip. You need to go to the hospital for an X-ray."

"I have too much work to do. I'm behind on orders in my cabinet-making shop. With the shop closed so often next month for November weddings and all the Christmas orders coming in, I can't miss any days of work."

"Sorry, but if you don't get your hip fixed, you could be crippled." Dr. Hess reached for his cell phone.

Reuben stopped him and tried to struggle to a sitting position. "At least give me a few hours to see if I can walk on it."

Dr. Hess set a hand on his chest to restrain him. "Trust me—this is not something you'll walk off."

Emma's mother leaned over him. "Please listen to the doctor."

Reuben tried to push the doctor's hand away. "I can't lose time now. There's no way Jakob can handle all the work on his own."

"Let Zeke and Abe help him," Emma's mother begged. "They're old enough to do some of the routine tasks. You've taken them to the shop since they were small. I want you to do whatever Dr. Hess says."

Dr. Hess adopted a stern tone. "Reuben, you know I wouldn't recommend this if I didn't think it was absolutely necessary."

His lips pinched together, Reuben glanced from the doctor's stern look to his wife's pleading one and back again. Then he lay back down and closed his eyes. "Do whatever you need to do, doc. I'll cooperate. God must have a purpose in this, so I'll trust Him."

"And we'll trust Him for your healing," Emma's mother added.

"I'll be praying too." Dr. Hess pulled his phone out of his pocket and dialed.

Kyle shifted uneasily in the doorway at all this talk about God. Everyone discussed God as if He were an important part of their lives, the way Kyle's parents used to do. They'd taught him to believe in God when he was small, but now that he was in the medical field, he'd learned to trust science and rational facts. Losing both of his parents in one week had taught him never to trust in a God who could allow the people he loved to suffer and die.

Dr. Hess clicked his phone shut and groaned as he struggled to his feet. "It's a bit chilly on the floor. Perhaps you could cover him while we wait."

"I have a quilt right here." Emma's mother rose and crossed the room to pick up a quilt that had been draped over the sofa. Her back appeared more bowed than it had years ago. "I tried to put this on him earlier, but he insisted he was fine."

Before she turned around, Kyle stepped to a spot where the door hid him from the family's view.

A few seconds later, Dr. Hess peeked around the corner. "I'm sorry I forgot about you. Would you like to take a look?"

Kyle shook his head. Surely the doctor had heard the rumors.

Dr. Hess stared at him. "Are you all right? You look pale."

"I, um..." Kyle ducked his head and gestured toward the room where Reuben lay.

Light dawned in the doctor's eyes, and he put a hand on Kyle's arm. "I'm sorry. I didn't mean to put you in such an uncomfortable situation. I was so focused on helping a patient, the past slipped my mind."

"Yes, well..." Kyle cleared his throat. "I could go out and wait for the transport. I can direct them in here."

"Good idea," Dr. Hess said. "And again, I truly am sorry. I should have mentioned the patient's name and given you a chance to opt out. Esther will have my head when she finds out."

Kyle started down the hallway, but Dr. Hess followed him, and when they reached the front door and were out of earshot of the family, he laid a hand on Kyle's shoulder. "You know, son, there comes a time when you need to make peace with your past."

Too sick inside to answer, Kyle only nodded. The doctor had only heard the gossip about the accident. Only Emma's family knew the truth. As soon as they finished here at the Eshes', he'd tell Dr. Hess he couldn't take this job. He couldn't come back to this town and relive that agony. He should have never come back at all.

Chapter Five

After fixing breakfast for her parents and giving *Mamm* a massage to ease her MS pain, Leah hurried down the passageway from the kitchen to their natural products shop and flipped the sign to OPEN. A short while later, the bells on the shop door jangled, and Leah looked up from her inventory of the vitamin bottles. Her friend Ada stood in the doorway, looking frazzled.

"Are you all right?" Leah had lost count of the bottles, but her friend's problems were more important.

"I don't see how I'll get everything done."

With assisting the midwife, helping people in the community, working at her family's natural products store, and squeezing in time to see Ben, Leah'd had little time to help with Ada's upcoming wedding. "I'm so sorry. What do you need me to do?"

Ada waved away her question. "You have enough to

do." She gestured toward the vitamin bottles on the counter. "I didn't mean to take you away from your work."

"This can be done any time." Leah stepped around from behind the counter, took Ada's arm, and ushered her toward the door that led into the house. The bell on the door would jangle if customers entered the shop. Leah fixed two cups of herbal tea and handed one to Ada. "This is a secret blend I'm working on to calm anxiety."

Ada took a sip. "It's delicious, but does it work?"

"I guess we'll find out. If it does, I'll package it and sell it in the shop."

After a few swallows, the tension lines on Ada's forehead eased, and she leaned back with a sigh. "I don't know if it's the ingredients or the warmth of the tea or sitting down to relax for the first time in weeks, but I'm already feeling calmer."

"Good. I hope the tea is helping. Now, what's causing your stress?"

Ada appeared close to tears. "I don't see how I can get everything done in the next few weeks."

"Take a breath," Leah advised. "It'll all get done, and if it doesn't, it's not the end of the world."

"The worst part is, we're both so busy Josiah and I barely spend any time together."

"The two of you will have plenty of time with each other soon. Once the wedding is over, you'll be together in the same house every day."

Leaning her head against the ladder-back chair, Ada closed her eyes. "Yes, I need to remind myself this is only temporary."

"Unlike my situation with Ben." Leah regretted the words as soon as they left her lips.

Ada's eyes popped open, and she fixed Leah with a tell-me-everything stare.

Leah shrugged. "Not much has been happening because I've been so busy. He has time during the day between milkings at the dairy farm, but I have to work here. And most days, I'm either studying, visiting patients, accompanying Sharon on deliveries, or working long hours at the store."

"But I thought your *daed* agreed to fewer hours for the store."

"He did." Leah couldn't prevent the deep sigh that escaped her lips. "But with some unexpected bills for *Mamm*, he changed his mind and took a full-time woodworking job in town, so I need to work his hours as well as mine."

Ada shot her a sympathetic glance. "I'm sorry. That doesn't make it easy for you and Ben."

"No, it doesn't. Ben wants me to give up the midwifing so we can have more time together." That wasn't his only reason, though. Once she was his wife, he'd expect her to stay home to care for their own children.

"But you love being a midwife. And all the young *mamm*s in our buddy bunch have said how wonderful you are at deliveries."

Leah picked at a fingernail so she wouldn't have to meet Ada's gaze. Sharon, too, had told her she had a gift, but she shouldn't be prideful. The church frowned on *hochmut*, which was one of the reasons they didn't allow higher education. Leah had never confessed to anyone how much she longed to continue her midwife training and be certified like Sharon.

"Are you all right? You seem a bit down. Not your usual cheerful self."

"I'm just tired." And discouraged. With both *Daed* and Ben pressuring her to forget the career she loved along with the long hours she'd been working and her doubts about Ben and now the worry that Kyle...

"That's not the only thing bothering you. Not with the look that just flashed across your face." Ada set her elbows on the table, propped her chin in her hands, and fixed Leah with a stare that made her squirm. "There's something you're not telling me."

Leah opened her mouth to deny it, but instead the story about yesterday tumbled from her lips. She explained how Kyle seemed frustrated by their Amish ways, but she didn't mention her secret. She finally ended with, "What if Kyle takes over for Dr. Hess? How will I ever work with him?"

"If it's God's will for Kyle to be here, He'll work everything out."

Though Ada's words were true, they didn't calm Leah's fear that someday Kyle would look at her and remember. And when he did...

Ada took a final sip of tea and pushed back her chair. "I should go. I have so much to do, but it was great talking to you, and the tea was wonderful *gut*. So relaxing. You definitely should package it for the shop."

One more thing for her to-do list. Leah rose and picked up the cups. She set them in the sink and then crossed the room to hug Ada.

The shop bell jangled, and Leah broke their brief embrace to rush down the hall. "I'm so glad you came by," she called as she hurried into the store. All thoughts of Kyle fled when she saw who had entered.

Ben stood at the counter, and Leah stopped and ran

a self-conscious hand over the band of her *kapp* to be sure it was securely in place. Ben placed a high priority on neatness and decorum, so she tried hard not to appear disheveled around him. With quick, nervous gestures, she smoothed down her black work apron. She took a deep breath, but her "Hello" came out as a gasp.

With a slight frown, Ben surveyed the empty counter and then turned to her. "I thought the store opened at nine."

"It did." She gestured toward Ada who'd emerged through the door. "I took Ada into the kitchen for some tea."

"I see." Ben shook his head slightly. "But what if someone came in while you were visiting?"

Why did he always make her feel so defensive? "I listen for the bell." She smiled at him. "That's why I came out to greet you."

"I guess." Ben didn't sound convinced, but as she kept beaming at him, his expression softened. "I'm glad to see you."

"I'm happy you stopped by. Let me say good-bye to Ada, and then we can talk."

Ben's smile faded slightly. "I can't stay long. *Onkel* and I are heading to the horse auction. He..."

Ada waved and headed for the outside door. "I'll see you later."

"Let me know how I can help," Leah called after her.

"You have enough to do." Ada pulled her coat around her and pushed open the door. A blast of frigid air blew into the shop, and the door slammed shut behind her.

"She's right, you know," Ben said when Leah turned

around. "I worry about you trying to handle so much, and I wish we had more time together," he said wistfully.

"I do too." Leah moved behind the counter and slid all the vitamin bottles back into a group so she could resume counting, but she kept her attention on Ben. "When do you leave for the auction?"

"Trying to get rid of me?" he said in a teasing voice, but the worry in his eyes revealed he wasn't kidding.

"Of course not. I'm always glad to see you," she assured him, although she did wish she could get some work done in the store.

"I'll be meeting the driver of the horse trailer shortly, but I wanted to see if you'd like to go out for a pumpkin latte after the shop closes at four." His eyes twinkled. "I know how much you like those."

"That sounds *wunderbar*!" Imagining inhaling the spicy aroma of the steam made Leah's mouth water. The local store only carried the pumpkin flavor from early October through the end of November, making it an extra-special treat.

"I'll stop by to pick you up. That should give us some time to talk." Ben turned toward the door. "I wish I didn't have to go, but I can't keep Herb waiting. I'm so glad we'll finally have some time together this afternoon."

"I am too." Leah gave him a cheery wave as he exited. "See you later." Spending an hour or two with Ben would hopefully help smooth things over between them.

Grateful for that, Leah prayed for a quiet morning to get the stock inventoried and items shelved before tomorrow's huge delivery. *Daed* had prepaid for the order before *Mamm*'s big medical bills had come flooding in. Leah hoped they'd have enough money to cover both.

* * *

Mamm spent most days in bed now that her MS had gotten worse. Leah had just carried *Mamm*'s lunch tray upstairs when her cell phone rang. At least *Daed* wasn't here. He disliked her having a phone, but Sharon had given her one, insisting she needed it so expectant parents could call her. So far, Sharon had been the only one to ring her. As soon as she answered, a man's panicked voice said, "This is Enos. Hannah said to call you. She needs you to come."

"Are you sure? It's way too early."

"I know." Enos's voice shook. "But she says it's time."

Leah squeezed her eyes shut. Hannah had lost two babies close to term. Leah prayed this wouldn't be another. She struggled to keep worry from coloring her words. "Sharon's on the way?"

"She didn't answer. I left a message, but she hasn't called back. I can't wait. I need to get back home to Hannah."

"Yes, do that. I'll try Sharon again." Leah pictured Enos running down the lane from his neighbor's phone shanty to comfort Hannah.

As soon as she hung up, Leah dialed Sharon's number. The phone rang and rang. After each ring, Leah's concern rose.

A woman's voice kicked on saying Sharon was not available and to leave a message. Leah hung up and redialed. Sharon always had her cell phone with her, and she usually answered on the first ring. Or the second. Leah's worry changed to full-blown panic. She couldn't deliver a premature baby on her own, especially not if . . .

She had to leave. She couldn't let Enos and Hannah handle this on their own. Fingers shaking, she dialed Dr. Hess's office. Esther answered right away, and Leah babbled about the situation, her tongue getting tangled as she tried to explain.

"Calm down, dear," Esther soothed. "Now, let me get this straight. Enos and Hannah's baby isn't due for another month, right? And Sharon isn't answering?" She paused. "The doctor and Kyle are on a house call in Gordonville, but I'll send them over as soon as they're done."

Leah had forgotten about Kyle. The last thing she wanted was to do a delivery—any delivery—with Kyle there. A premature baby would be even worse. "Thank you, but—"

"It'll be fine, dear." Esther must have misunderstood her hesitation. "Babies usually take their time coming."

Not always true for Amish babies. Many mothers didn't send their husbands to call the midwife until they were close to delivering.

"Why don't you go out and stay with her, though, until the doctor gets there? And don't worry. Sharon may already be there by the time you arrive."

Leah hoped so. She thanked the doctor's wife, explained the situation to *Mamm*, bundled up against the cold, flipped the shop sign to CLOSED, and rushed out to hook the horse to the buggy. Praying Sharon had gotten Enos's message, Leah wrestled her huge midwife bag into the carriage and galloped toward the Fishers' farm.

* * *

Dr. Hess's phone rang. "It's Esther."

Kyle had been heading out the door but paused with his hand on the doorknob when Dr. Hess said the name Leah. That was the midwife. He hoped she hadn't made someone ill with her concoctions.

"Already?" Dr. Hess's voice rose in alarm. "Is she sure it isn't Braxton-Hicks?" He listened for a few moments. "Where's Sharon? It's not like her not to answer her phone." After a brief pause, he added, "Kyle and I will head over there as soon as we can. We're waiting for the medical transport to pick up Reuben Esh. I'm pretty sure he's broken his hip."

"You took Kyle to the Eshes'?" Esther's shrill question blared from the phone. "Did he know that's where you were heading?"

"No, and it didn't occur to me to tell him. My only thought was to help a man in pain lying on the floor." He glanced over at Kyle. *I'm so sorry*, he mouthed, his eyes mirroring his regret. "Yes, I've apologized, and he took it quite well considering the circumstances."

Esther lowered her voice so Kyle couldn't hear the rest of her conversation, but she must have been berating her husband, because he replied, "Yes, dear, I'll try to think about things like that next time. I do tend to focus on the job and forget about everything else." He finished with an "I love you too," so Esther must have forgiven his forgetfulness.

After he hung up, Dr. Hess looked worried. "I wonder why Sharon isn't answering her phone. Leah's alone for a delivery, and the baby's coming early. Amish moms often wait until the last minute to call, so there's not much time. We'll have to head over to the Fishers' as soon as we get Reuben off to the hospital."

"The Fishers'? Isn't that where we went yesterday?"

"Yes, it is."

"The baby with pneumonia," Kyle said flatly. "The one who belongs in the hospital."

"I suppose she might let us admit him," Dr. Hess mused, "if the newborn needs to go to the hospital for preemie care."

Kyle stopped himself from a sarcastic comment. If they could get that little boy to the hospital, it didn't matter how it happened. His main concern right now was not leaving Leah alone at a delivery. "Didn't you say Leah was *learning* to be a midwife? She's not certified?"

"No, and she can't be."

What? "If she isn't competent enough to be certified, what's she doing at a delivery alone?"

Dr. Hess smiled. "I didn't mean she couldn't qualify for certification. She's actually pretty skilled for only practicing a few months. Sharon's been the area midwife for almost thirty years now, and she says Leah's the best assistant she's ever had."

At Kyle's puzzled look, Dr. Hess explained, "The Amish believe that everyone should be equal, and they don't want their children exposed to worldly things, which means they don't believe in higher education or certifications."

Kyle shook his head. He knew their schooling went only to the eighth grade, but he hadn't realized they couldn't be certified. Why do all that work without getting the credentials and recognition to go with it? It made no sense.

Dr. Hess glanced at his watch. "The medical transport should be here soon. Why don't you stand inside the storm door to wait? It's awfully cold outside. And I'll go back to stay with"—he hesitated—"the, um, patient."

Avoiding the name didn't make it any easier for Kyle. At least he wasn't in the same room, worried the Eshes would recognize him. Despite all the letters of forgiveness they—and everyone else in the Amish community—had sent, Kyle still lived with the blame. At the time, those letters had made him so angry he'd crumpled them up and thrown them away. He had a hard time believing the messages were genuine, and he never felt he deserved them. If he were in the Eshes' position, he'd never forgive someone who'd destroyed his daughter's life. And he could never forgive himself.

Dr. Hess had only gone partway down the hall when the medical transport pulled into the driveway.

"They're here," Kyle called after him. He went out to meet them and usher them toward the living room, but he hung back as they crowded around Emma's father. Hoping Reuben wouldn't notice him, Kyle flattened himself against the wall as they took him out. He waited until they were close to the vehicle before exiting the house.

But as Reuben was being lifted inside, he glanced in Kyle's direction. His eyes widened, and he lifted a shaky finger to point directly at Kyle. *You*, he mouthed.

Kyle shrank against the front door, pinned by guilt and shame. Yet the look in Reuben's eyes was not condemnation. He stared steadily at Kyle as if trying to convey a message. A message of sympathy and sorrow.

Reuben's lips formed the words *I'm sorry*, just before the transport doors shut.

His hands clenched into fists, Kyle thrust them deep in his pockets, shivering in the freezing wind as the vehicle pulled away. The sick feeling in his stomach intensified. Reuben blamed himself for Emma's rebellion and the tragic consequences that followed. But the only one at fault was Kyle himself. His carelessness and anger had led to the accident.

Chapter Six

Arriving at the Fishers' *haus*, Leah drove her horse close to the barn. She had no idea how long she'd be here, but he'd need shelter. As she climbed from her carriage, Enos burst from the back door and loped across the yard.

"We were waiting for you," he said. "I'll take care of your horse so you can care for Hannah, but first let me carry in your bag." He lifted the heavy bag from the front seat.

"*Danke.*" Leah rushed to keep pace with his swift steps. When she held the bag, she staggered, but Enos lifted the tote full of supplies as easily as he hefted bales of hay.

Along with phones, Sharon had insisted they both have bags with all the necessary supplies for a delivery. Leah was grateful she'd agreed. Neither of them had anticipated her doing a delivery alone, though. At that thought, the lukewarm oatmeal she'd gulped down earlier turned into a hard ball of fear in her stomach. She prayed Sharon or Dr. Hess would arrive before the baby did.

They reached the back porch, and she sucked in some air. The frigid wind needled her lungs, but she managed to push out a question between short, sharp breaths. "How's Hannah?"

Not even slightly winded by their run, Enos winced. "She's in a lot of pain."

"Already?"

He ducked his head as he reached for the doorknob. "*Ach, vell*, she's been up most of the night. She tried to ignore the pains at first because it was too early. She's close to ready now."

Most of the night? Leah was used to Amish women waiting until they were close to transitioning before calling the midwife, but this time, it could be dangerous.

The door flew open, and Hannah's oldest daughter, Maria, stepped out on the porch to hold the storm door so they could enter. She tilted her head shyly in Leah's direction, then turned to her *daed* as the door banged shut behind her.

"I put the pots of water to boil on the stove. And the others are dressed in their coats and ready to go. I'll take them to *Aenti* Sarah's now." Maria shepherded the four-year-old and six-year-old toward the back door. "And I changed Aaron's diaper, gave him a bottle, and propped him up. He's still having trouble breathing."

Enos nodded and set Leah's bag on the sparkling-clean kitchen table. "*Gut, gut.* I'll come to get you soon.

Behave yourselves, now. And be sure to help Sarah with the cleaning and pies for church."

"We will," Maria promised as she led the others out onto the porch.

Despite the tension in her stomach, Leah smiled at the girls. She prayed they'd have a lovely surprise when they got home, but her roiling stomach warned her of danger. Especially if she had to handle this delivery alone.

"Hannah," Enos called, after the door had banged shut behind the children, "Leah is here. I'll unhook her carriage and be right back."

Hannah's tired *danke* barely carried from the back bedroom.

Leah unzipped her bag and hastily pulled out a few basic supplies. "I'll go back to her."

With murmured thanks, Enos rushed for the door.

Using some of the boiling water to wash up, Leah called after him, "Did Sharon answer?"

"*Neh*, and I didn't want to leave Hannah alone for too long, so I didn't try again." The door slammed, and Enos was gone.

Dear Lord, please help Sharon and Dr. Hess to answer their phones, Leah prayed as she raced down the hall.

No sound came from the bedroom. Leah always marveled at how most Amish women barely made a sound during labor unlike the *Englischers* she'd heard when Sharon took her to the local hospital for observation. Groans, screeches, and crying came from the delivery rooms. Perhaps some of the mothers' distress was caused by being forced into such an unnatural position, lying on their backs.

Hannah, like most other Amish mothers, still paced the room. Leah drew in a breath. If she hadn't gotten on her hands and knees yet, maybe delivery wasn't imminent. Hannah bent over, panting and clutching her abdomen.

"Can I check you?" Leah asked gently once the contraction had passed.

Hannah nodded and moved toward the bed with its plastic sheeting and freshly washed, but worn, bedding. Leah's hands shook. She'd never done an examination alone. She tried hard to remember everything Sharon had taught her, but she didn't need any of her training. The baby's head was already crowning.

Enos clattered through the back door, and Leah yelled to him, "The baby's almost here."

A rush of water in the other room indicated he was washing his hands. Enos had been fastidious whenever she and Sharon came for Hannah's monthly checkups, but Leah needed him now. He had more experience with deliveries than she had. He'd been with his wife through six other deliveries, including the two babies she'd lost. Leah prayed this wouldn't be another.

Enos must have had the same thought, because worry lines framed his eyes and mouth, but he smoothed his face into a reassuring smile as he hurried toward his wife. After a loving look at Hannah, he climbed on the bed to support her while she pushed. His quiet words of encouragement helped calm Leah's nerves and shaky hands. With a whispered prayer, she prepared to do her best, but this delivery was now in God's hands.

* * *

Dr. Hess wove the car down the bumpy lanes and chattered to Kyle, seeming not to notice the lack of response. Kyle let the words wash over him as soothing white noise, but he took in little of what the doctor was saying. Kyle's mind was still on Reuben's face.

The last time he'd seen Reuben, he'd been blindsided by the news of the baby and Emma's rejection. Every time he thought of that day, of Emma's agony as she pushed her way past her amnesia and recognized him, Kyle's heart clenched into a knot so tight his chest ached. He'd brought her nothing but pain. Knowing that had kept him from ever getting close to another woman. He couldn't bear to think of inflicting anyone else with such agony. He'd become a doctor to atone for his guilt. But nothing he did could ever erase his past.

Fall leaves swirled in the gusts that shook the car. Scarlet, russet, pumpkin, and maize drifted into a carpet covering the ground, leaving behind stark, bare branches silhouetted against the sky. He'd first seen Emma at this time of year, and he'd lost her on a freezing winter day. Kyle squeezed his eyes shut.

One of his friends had convinced him to go to a party at an Amish barn. Emma had defied her family during *Rumspringa* by wearing *Englisch* clothes and breaking all the rules her Amish parents set. They'd both been young and foolish teenagers when they fell in love, but he'd offered to marry her. Instead she'd insisted on leaving and returning to the Amish. He'd lost his temper and driven recklessly. They'd skidded on the ice and crashed.

He'd walked away from the accident with minor injuries, but Emma...

He still couldn't bear to think of that night. Of her bleeding on the snow. Of his inability to help. She survived, but they'd both lost something precious that night.

Emma's recovery took years. And her father blamed himself for everything.

Kyle had seen Emma one final time a few days before her wedding to another man. He'd begged her to forgive him. She said she had, but then she'd walked off into someone else's arms. His insides twisted as fresh pain welled up.

Friends kept telling him to let go, but for Kyle, reliving the anguish was a penance. A reminder never to lose his temper. Never to do anything to damage someone else's life. Never to give in to love.

"Are you all right?" Dr. Hess reached over and laid a comforting hand on Kyle's shoulder. "I'm sorry I took you to the Eshes'. I wish I'd thought about..." His voice trailed off, and Kyle felt sorry for him.

"It's not your fault." The visit had taken him back. Back to a painful past. "I'm mainly just tired." But that wasn't the whole truth. The last thing he wanted to do, though, was to make this kindly old doctor feel worse.

"I apologize for your tiredness too," Dr. Hess said. "Listen, if you'd rather rest while I help Leah, just tilt your seat back and wrap up in that afghan back there." He gestured toward a knitted blanket of multicolored squares that matched the fall colors outside the window. "Esther has made a few of those over the past few years for me to keep in the car, but I often end up giving them away or using them to cover patients." His lips curved into a fond smile. "She doesn't mind. She keeps knitting replacements."

"She's a good woman." Kyle knew that firsthand. Esther had offered continual support in those dark days before and after his mother's death.

Smile lines creasing his eyes, Dr. Hess turned down the Fishers' gravel driveway. "Yes, she's a giving person. I'm so grateful God provided such a wonderful helpmeet." After putting the car in park and turning off the engine, he turned to Kyle and fixed him with a serious stare. "If you wait for the special person God has for you, you'll be as blessed as I am. A loving heart is the most wonderful attribute you could ask for in a wife."

Kyle tried not to wince. He wasn't in the market for a wife and never would be. Falling in love was too painful. Besides, he'd given up on God, so God definitely didn't have a special person for him.

Dr. Hess hopped out of the car and grabbed his bag from the trunk. Kyle unwound himself from the car the way he wished he could unwind the tight cords surrounding his heart.

He followed the doctor, who walked into the house without knocking. Dr. Hess called out a *hello* as he charged down a back hall. No one answered, but he kept going past several bedrooms. Before they reached the last one, a thin, reedy wail stopped Kyle dead. A baby in distress.

Dr. Hess hurried toward the sound, but Kyle froze. Too many memories rushed over him—another baby whose cries had been silenced the night his world had been ripped apart.

The doctor's booming voice jolted him back to reality. He needed to get in there to help. They'd come to save a preemie. A child whose life might be hanging in the balance. Kyle forced himself to head toward the room.

Leah settled a small, still-damp infant upright against his mother's chest.

Although he still worried about her home remedies, Kyle's estimate of Leah's competence rose. Had that been instinctive, or did she know about kangaroo care for preemies?

The Amish man who sat on the bed beside his wife set a large, calloused hand on the baby's back before Leah swiftly covered the baby with a pile of blankets. After she rubbed the baby's head dry, she tucked a tiny knitted cap over a headful of black hair.

Leah turned to Dr. Hess, and her wide, generous smile took Kyle's breath away. He jerked his gaze from her face. Never again would he make that mistake. She had an appealing, fresh-faced sweetness that called to something deep within him, but falling for another Amish woman would only lead to heartache.

What was wrong with him? Lack of sleep and nostalgia over Emma must have overtaken his groggy brain. Why else would he be thinking such thoughts about a woman he'd just met?

When she glanced at him, her gaze quickly skittered away. Yet her eyes stirred a long-forgotten memory deep within his soul. He shook his head to clear away the mist fogging his brain.

"His one-minute Apgar was seven," Leah said, drawing Kyle's attention to the tears sparkling in her eyes. She ran down the list of stats quietly so the parents couldn't hear, but Kyle barely registered her words. "Appearance: slightly blue—one; Pulse rate: greater than one hundred beats per minute—two; Grimace: cry on stimulation—two; Activity: some flexion—one; and Respiration: weak cry—one."

He was impressed with her assessment. For a midwife-in-training, she sounded very knowledgeable.

"Kyle can do the five-minute Apgar," Dr. Hess said, and elbowed Kyle when he didn't respond. "What do you say? Would you like to do the Apgar?"

Kyle tore his gaze from Leah. "Of course." He tried to sound businesslike and avoid looking into her eyes again. "Is it almost time?"

Leah glanced at her watch. "Ten more seconds."

Kyle moved to the bed and awaited the signal from Leah. He completed the five quick assessments and covered the baby again to keep him warm. "Still a seven."

Leah pursed her lips. "I hoped it would be higher."

"It's a bit low," Dr. Hess said, "but it falls in the normal range. And with him coming several weeks early, it's a major blessing."

Kyle broke in. "Yes, and that's likely why he has jaundice. We should get him to the hospital and under UV lights immediately."

"I'd already noticed his skin is slightly yellowish," Leah said. "I planned to move the cradle to that window"—she gestured to her left—"where he'll get the most sunlight."

Dr. Hess nodded, and Kyle glanced at him as if he

were crazy. "You're going to call an ambulance or something and take this preemie to a hospital, aren't you? He should also be tested for—"

Holding up a hand, the doctor stopped Kyle's frantic rush of words. "I don't see the need. He seems to be breathing on his own quite well." The doctor took Kyle's place by the bed and began his examination. "His lungs sound normal, so perhaps the due date was a bit off."

"What about the jaundice?" Kyle struggled to regain normality in this alternate universe, where all the usual procedures and cures had been upended.

Leah dragged the cradle from the parents' bedside to the window. Sunshine streamed through onto the cradle. She stood and faced Kyle. "Is that better?"

To tamp down the strange magnetism that overtook him whenever he glanced in her direction today, Kyle turned to Dr. Hess, waiting for him to say the baby should be hospitalized. Instead, the doctor's lips curved into a half smile. "That should work."

What? Kyle wanted to shout at them both that they shouldn't take chances with an infant's life.

"Don't worry." Dr. Hess stepped closer and laid a hand on Kyle's arm. "I'll keep an eye on the baby. If he appears to need medical intervention, I'll recommend it." He leaned closer and added in a low voice, "Remember what I said yesterday?"

Yes, Kyle remembered the Amish often preferred home remedies to prescriptions, but there must be a way to encourage them to consider other options. This young midwife-in-training could be the key. People listened to her. If he could convince her of the importance of hospitals and medicine, he might be able to help this community.

Wait a minute. Surely he wasn't considering taking this job. No way could he come back to this area to live. Too many memories. Too much heartache. But the thought of working with Leah was definitely tempting.

Chapter Seven

Leah tried not to let Kyle's reactions influence her. The frown wrinkling his forehead when she put the cradle in the sunlight made it clear he'd disagreed with her decision. Now he was gazing at her thoughtfully. She had to admit he was quite handsome when he wasn't glowering.

Leah shook her head to dislodge the wayward thought. She had no business thinking like that. Besides, if he spent time around her, sooner or later he'd glance into her eyes and realize...

"He's trying to eat," Hannah said, raising Leah's spirits and driving thoughts of Kyle from her mind.

"Thank the Lord!" Leah had been so nervous about her first solo delivery, especially one she'd been expecting to go wrong. Joy bubbled up inside. She beamed as Enos wrapped an arm around Hannah and held her close while she fed the baby.

"Yoo-hoo." A loud voice echoing down the hall was soon followed by Sharon's bouncing steps. "Sorry I didn't answer your call. I was delivering the Heises' baby." She stopped in the doorway to take in the scene. "Well, well, well, Miss Leah, it looks like you did a fine job on your own here."

Although she was grateful for her mentor's approval, Leah couldn't take credit for a successful delivery. "God was gracious. And Enos and Hannah have had plenty of experience."

"So everything went well?" Sharon gazed from one to the other.

"Very well," Leah assured her, "although the baby does have jaundice. Dr. Hess thinks the due date might have been off, because his lungs are functioning properly."

"Highly possible," Sharon agreed. "We've had that trouble before, haven't we, Hannah?"

Her eyes brimming with tears, Hannah nodded. Leah's heart went out to her. It must be painful to remember the babies she'd lost, even while holding her precious newborn.

Sharon examined the room. "Looks like you've already prepared for the jaundice, Leah. I'm so proud of you for handling everything so well."

A muscle in Kyle's cheek quivered, and Leah suspected he was holding back a retort. She returned her attention to the happy couple but said to Sharon, "I'm not done yet. I still have a lot of cleanup to do. I'll wait until Hannah's done feeding the baby, though."

Once the baby had eaten, Enos rose, tucked the covers around his wife, and kissed her forehead. "You rest now,

Hannie," he said. "I'm heading to Sarah's to get the children. I won't be long. I know you're in good hands with Leah and Sharon."

After Enos left, Dr. Hess stepped into the hallway to call his wife and tell her about the baby. Esther loved each new baby that arrived. Leah could only imagine how heartbroken she must be to have none of her own.

Sharon assisted Hannah down the hallway to get cleaned up, but Kyle remained where he was as Leah diapered and dressed the baby. Her usual smooth movements became jerky under his watchful eyes. If only Dr. Hess would finish his call and take Kyle back to the office with him. Taking deep breaths to calm her nerves, she cocooned the newborn in blankets and laid him in the cradle before changing the sheets.

She had to walk past Kyle with the bundled-up bed linens. He stepped aside, but her arms, filled with linens, brushed against his sleeve. He jolted back as if she'd burned him, and he draped the coat he'd taken off earlier over his arm as if to protect it from any more unwelcome contact.

Leah shriveled up inside. He disliked her so much he'd been repulsed by an accidental touch? She wouldn't let him see how much that hurt. She lifted her chin and strode through the doorway, acting as if she didn't care. Yet her arm still registered the warmth of his skin and the hardness of his muscles under the tan wool sweater that stretched tightly across his broad chest. If he were Amish and she weren't dating Ben, Leah might have sneaked another look, but she had no interest in anyone who wasn't with the church.

After soaking and rinsing the sheets in lukewarm

water, Leah ran them through the wringer washer and hung them out on the line. She hoped they'd dry before nightfall in this chilly weather, because all laundry needed to be off the line by then. She hurried back to the bedroom with the fresh sheets Enos had left on the kitchen table and stopped short.

His back to the door, Kyle had gone down on one knee beside the cradle to pick up the whimpering baby. He cradled the newborn in his arms, cuddling it close and crooning, "There, there. Mommy will be back soon. It's not easy coming into this cold world after being so snug and warm, is it?"

He stood and rocked gently from foot to foot until the baby quieted. "I wish they'd take you to the hospital, little one. You should be sleeping under UV lights, and your brother needs to be staying there too."

His heartfelt sigh touched Leah, and she blinked back a tear. He genuinely cared about both babies, and he seemed to have a magic touch with them. The newborn in his arms had quieted quickly.

Kyle knelt by the cradle, lowered the baby in, and tucked the blankets securely around the now-sleeping child. Instead of getting to his feet, he stayed where he was, one hand resting on the baby's rising and falling chest, and Leah's heart fluttered. What a wonderful father he'd make. And a great doctor.

If only she could persuade him of the benefits of natural remedies, they could work together as a team...

What was she thinking? All along, she'd been hoping he wouldn't take Dr. Hess's place, but now she wasn't sure. But if he stayed, she'd need to confess her part in the horrific accident that had injured Emma.

Years ago, she'd asked Emma for forgiveness, which Emma graciously gave, but it had never erased her guilt. Leah had never had a chance to apologize to Kyle because he'd left town right after the accident. Now, though, she had to do it. As soon as the right opening presented itself.

So far, he hadn't recognized her, but many people blocked out traumatic memories. Even if he had, she couldn't be dishonest or live with the uncertainty that he might remember.

Kyle rose, and Leah backed into the hallway so he wouldn't know she'd been watching. She waited a minute before carrying in the sheets. Kyle still stood by the cradle, but he turned as she entered.

"Need help with those?" he offered.

Too choked up to speak, Leah only nodded. She'd misjudged him. Not only did he care about children, he wasn't haughty like some of the doctors she'd encountered at the hospital when she'd taken *Mamm*.

Kyle helped her spread the sheets on the bed and tuck them in. Leah had just finished straightening the quilt when Sharon helped Hannah back into the room. Kyle stepped aside as Sharon tucked Hannah into bed and Leah made sure Hannah had everything she needed on the bedside table.

Once Hannah drifted off to sleep, Leah carried her equipment to the kitchen to sterilize it and pack it back in her bag. Dr. Hess and Kyle stayed in the room, huddled over the sleeping baby, and Leah wondered if he was trying to convince the doctor to take the baby to the hospital. She had faith in Dr. Hess's powers of persuasion.

When everything was properly sterilized and packed,

she and Sharon sat at the kitchen table to fill out the required paperwork. Leah wished she'd brought her notebook in from the carriage to record details of the birth. She'd try to remember to fill it out later tonight. She and Sharon had completed the record keeping and started on the birth certificate when Enos returned with the three older children. He led them down the hall to see the new baby.

A spate of coughing came from the other back bedroom, and Leah jumped up from the table. In all the excitement of the delivery and the new baby, she'd forgotten about Aaron. She raced down the hall and skidded to a stop when she spotted Kyle, but her foot slipped on the polished wooden floorboards, and she crashed into his rock-solid chest. He gripped her arms to steady her, and her skin tingled under the touch of his fingers. This time she was the one who jerked away, and she kept whispering Ben's name under her breath until the strange sensations ended.

"I, um, was going to check on the baby," she said once she'd caught her breath and her rapid heartbeat had slowed slightly.

"So was I." Kyle looked as flustered as she felt. He stepped back and motioned for her to precede him.

Leah's eyebrows shot up. He didn't intend to block her from the room? She'd been expecting censure rather than politeness, so his response threw her off balance. Smoothing down her black work apron to calm herself, Leah walked past him into the room.

Dr. Hess stood by the cradle, his stethoscope pressed against baby Aaron's chest. He looked up when they entered. "Not much change since yesterday."

"I'll cut up fresh onion." Leah hurried from the room, her perverse emotions wishing for a few more moments in Kyle's arms. She returned with another stocking filled with onion and cayenne, ingredients that made her eyes water, and a small sippy cup of fresh pineapple juice, which she held out to Dr. Hess.

"What's in that?" Kyle asked.

"This has onion and cayenne pepper and—"

"I know that. I meant in the cup."

While Dr. Hess held Aaron, Leah removed the old poultice and replaced it with the new one. "The cup is filled with pineapple juice."

"Pineapple juice?" His surprise was evident.

"Fresh pineapple juice is great for coughs." Leah had recommended it to Enos and Hannah yesterday. She waited for Kyle to dispute that.

"I suppose," Kyle said. "I've not seen studies proving it's effective for coughs. It does contain bromelain, though, which reduces swelling of the nose and sinuses, so it might reduce some symptoms."

Leah was so surprised to have him partially agree with her she almost dropped the cup. She longed to retort, *I know. I also recommend it for hay fever*, but she managed to bite her tongue. He'd attempted to be nice, and she should reciprocate. "I like finding natural cures that can be used instead of conventional medicine."

Slight frown lines appeared between his brows. Perhaps her comment hadn't been conciliatory. Leah sighed inwardly. If she'd already offended him, she might as well continue. Maybe, though, she could offer an explanation he might accept. "Because many medicines are derived from plants, I prefer to go back to the original sources and use those plants so they aren't combined with chemicals."

"I suppose that makes sense."

She couldn't believe Kyle had agreed with her twice in this short conversation.

Dr. Hess shifted baby Aaron in his arms. "Why don't you feed him the juice, Leah? I'll wash up and peek in on the new baby. Then I should probably get Kyle back to the house."

Leah took Aaron from the doctor's arms and settled on the bed. She expected Kyle to follow Dr. Hess, but instead he remained standing near the doorway. She tried to ignore him, but her hands were unsteady.

As she lifted the cup to Aaron's lips, deep, thick coughs racked his tiny body. Holding him upright against her, she patted his back until they subsided. Kyle's frown deepened.

"That child should be in the hospital and so should the newborn." The words burst from Kyle's lips. "You're endangering both of their lives. If you're as interested in healing as you claim, you'd never suggest keeping them here at home."

So much for their temporary truce. "What about Hannah? She'd have to travel all that way to the hospital, and if she stayed with the baby, she'd have to leave her other children here, and…"

"You'd put a mother's convenience over her baby's life?"

"If the babies truly were in danger, I'd be the first to recommend taking them to the hospital. Plenty of babies get over jaundice and pneumonia without going to the hospital."

"And some don't get over it." His words rang around the room like a death knell.

"I understand you're a doctor, but hospitals aren't always the best solution."

"They're much safer than treating sick children and having preemies at home."

"The baby isn't a preemie. He was only a little early."

"You didn't know that before the delivery, though, did you?" Kyle's voice rose.

That was true. "You're right. I didn't, but everything turned out all right."

"Yes, it did, but there's an equal chance things could have gone wrong. Very wrong."

The anguish on Kyle's face tugged at Leah's heart. "That's always a possibility," she said softly. "It could happen with any birth, whether at home or at the hospital. We can only leave that up to God."

Kyle's face darkened. "Leave God out of it."

"I can't leave God out of anything. And as for birth, it's a natural process." Leah wished she had the textbook Sharon had given her so she could show him the actual statistics from countries around the world, but at least she remembered the overall stats. "Studies have shown that a greater percentage of planned home births use less intervention and have fewer deaths compared to hospital births."

"That depends on what studies you're looking at," Kyle said. "Just remember most people who choose home births have low-risk pregnancies. Almost all high-risk pregnancies use hospitals."

Leah disliked admitting he did have a point. "That's true." Her textbook had pointed that out too. "Still, women have been delivering babies for centuries before hospitals existed."

"And look at the mortality rates before there were hospitals. Many of those babies died."

"Perhaps they did in earlier times, but that's not true now."

"If home births are so great, why are more and more Amish women in this area having their babies in hospitals? Maybe because it's safer?"

"Perhaps they've been trained to think that way." Leah didn't want to concede he was right. "It might also be because there aren't enough trained midwives or doctors willing to serve as backup for emergencies."

"Of course there aren't," Kyle shot back. "It takes a lot more time to do house calls, and there's always the chance of a malpractice lawsuit."

"The Amish don't believe in suing people."

As if she'd poked a hole in his pride, all the bluster and fight leaked out, leaving Kyle deflated. "I know," he mumbled.

Leah cringed inside. She hadn't meant to hurt him or remind him of his past. She'd only been trying to make her point and defend her profession. No wonder God warned against *hochmut*. Pride destroyed so many relationships. In this case, Kyle wasn't the only one to blame.

* * *

Kyle muttered an excuse to get away as quickly as he could. As much as he enjoyed sparring with Leah and seeing her face light up with that fierce fire when she defended a cause she believed in, she'd hit him in a vulnerable spot.

He, of all people, should know the Amish didn't sue. Anyone else would have taken him to court, not only for medical bills but also for pain and suffering. If they had, he'd be paying off those bills for the rest of his life. Kyle had vowed that once he'd paid off his med school loans, he'd start sending money to Emma's family and to their church community anonymously, because the members had helped her parents foot the bills. If he took over for Dr. Hess, he'd be able to do that sooner, but being back here had been painful. Every day he'd wonder if he'd be called on to treat someone who knew about his past or, worse yet, someone from his past. Now he had one more reason not to accept Dr. Hess's offer. His growing attraction for the midwife. The farther he stayed from Leah, the better.

As much as he hated disappointing the Hesses after all they'd done for him and his family, he couldn't live in this town with all the memories. That brought him right back to the talk he needed to have with them. He'd be flying out of here tomorrow night, and they still believed he'd be taking over the practice. He owed it to them to let them know they needed to find someone else. He couldn't keep them hanging like this. It wasn't fair.

He crossed the hall and stood in the doorway of the room where Dr. Hess was talking to the new father.

Enos knelt beside the cradle and laid a gentle hand on his sleeping son's head. "We're going to call him Caleb after my *onkel*."

A wave of sadness flooded over Kyle. When he was small, that had been his favorite name in the whole world. He'd adored his older brother, Caleb, and followed him everywhere. Now the name only brought sickness and sorrow. If only his brother hadn't joined the Amish, they'd still be best friends. If Kyle hadn't dated Emma, Caleb never would have met and fallen for Emma's older sister, Lydia. His brother had left his *Englisch* life behind to marry her, something Kyle could never do.

Kyle missed the closeness of their early years, but he wanted nothing to do with his brother's new lifestyle. Even worse, Kyle could never visit him, because he and Lydia lived next door to Emma and her husband.

Kyle had retreated so deep into thought he jumped when Dr. Hess called his name.

The doctor crossed the room and laid a hand on his arm. "Are you ready to go?"

Kyle pulled himself from the painful past.

"I'm sorry," Dr. Hess said. "You must be exhausted. Let's head back."

Kyle was glad the doctor had mistaken his reverie for tiredness. Yes, he'd had a hectic schedule before he'd flown here, but the main reason for his tiredness had been coming here. This trip had been emotionally battering. Everywhere he turned, he collided with upsetting memories.

When they got to the front door, Kyle reached around Dr. Hess to open it. The wind almost tore the door from his hands. Overcast skies signaled a storm was brewing. Leaves whipped through the air as Kyle, bent against the gale force of the wind, led the way to the car, using his body to shield the elderly doctor from the gusts and pelting leaves. He wrestled the doctor's door open and held it as Dr. Hess climbed inside. Then he rounded the car, fighting the wind. After a tussle, Kyle managed to open the car door, slide in, and catch his breath. Thankful to be inside, he sank back against the seat, buckled his seat belt, and closed his eyes while Dr. Hess drove the rocking car down the driveway. Kyle's mind churned even more than the wind.

As they drove home through the gale, Kyle not only worried about the babies, but he had an added concern about Leah's safety. Despite their disagreements over the best treatments, he couldn't help thinking about how small and slight she was. She barely came up to his shoulder. How would she get home in her buggy in this windstorm? The gusts battering the car felt as if they might be strong enough to overturn a buggy.

"How do buggies withstand a storm like this?" Kyle asked Dr. Hess.

The doctor smiled. "They're sturdier than they look. You might be surprised."

"But look at the way the car is shaking."

"If you're concerned about Leah, she'll probably stay at the house for several more hours. Midwives usually help the family for a while after a birth. Let's hope this windstorm dies down by then."

Kyle nodded, but thinking about her heading home later made him anxious about accidents on the road after dark. And speaking of his anxieties...

Taking a deep breath, he turned to the doctor. "I'm also worried about the newborn and little Aaron. Even if the natural remedies are helpful, both children would be better off in the hospital. I wish the Fishers would take your advice."

Dr. Hess smiled. "There are times when I'd agree with you. Sometimes it seems Leah has more influence on the community than I do, but her advice is usually sound. She won't steer people in the wrong direction."

"But don't you think jaundice and pneumonia both need hospitalization?"

"Not necessarily." Dr. Hess's tone remained unconcerned. "Although I wish the Fishers would consider it, plenty of children recover from both without going to hospitals." Dr. Hess took a hand from the steering wheel and laid it on Kyle's arm. "The Amish believe in trusting God for the outcome. Perhaps rather than worrying, we should follow their example and pray for the children."

Kyle pinched his lips together to hold back his retort. He had firsthand experience praying for his mom to survive. God hadn't answered that prayer, so how could he trust God for these little ones?

The rest of the ride, Kyle remained silent. Leah had said the Amish believed any outcome was God's will too.

Thinking about Leah brought back her smile, her sparkling eyes, the joy shining on her face as she held the baby and little Aaron. He jerked his thoughts from those images. The last thing he needed was to let a fleeting attraction distract him. Coming back here had been a mistake. An even bigger mistake would be to allow himself to fall for another Amish girl.

Chapter Eight

Once Kyle had departed with Dr. Hess, the tension level in the house decreased, at least for Leah. Following a quick check of Hannah and the new baby, Leah looked up when Sharon stuck her head into the room where Leah was helping Aaron with his juice.

"I'm heading out now. You'll be all right here, won't you?" she asked. At Leah's nod, Sharon continued, "You're going to be a wonderful midwife, Leah. Mark my words."

"I hope so. Doing it alone was frightening. I don't know what I'd have done if they hadn't been so experienced. And if we hadn't had God's help."

"That's the most important thing. Whatever the outcome, it's always in God's hands."

"Yes, that's such a comforting thought." Although she'd sometimes silently railed against God's will, Leah believed with deep certainty that God had a greater purpose she couldn't always see.

After Sharon left, Aaron finished most of the juice, and his breathing grew less raspy. Leah took him into the kitchen and, with Maria's help, fed him a little, but his appetite seemed lackluster. He drifted off to sleep in her arms, so Leah tucked him back in the cradle. She scrubbed up again before she went in to Hannah and the baby. The last thing she wanted to do was to carry germs to the newborn.

Enos stood when she entered. "If you can keep an eye on Hannah, I'll go out and do the milking."

A tiny cry erupted into wails as Enos headed out the door. Leah rushed over to pick up the newborn. She rocked him gently in her arms and whispered, "Hush."

"It's all right," Hannah said weakly. "I'm awake. You can bring him over here so I can feed him."

Leah carried the precious bundle to the bed and lowered the baby into Hannah's arms. "I hope you got a little rest. Enos said you were up all night in labor."

"Yes, but this makes it all worthwhile." She cradled her tiny son. "Besides, with little ones, getting a full night's sleep is rare."

"I'm sure it is." Leah had no idea how mothers managed to function on such a small amount of rest. After losing sleep a few nights a week during busy times with Sharon, Leah struggled to keep her eyes open during the day. All she had to do was wait on customers and count packages and money. How would she handle it if she couldn't sleep much for months?

As soon as Leah made sure the baby was eating well, she headed to the kitchen to help Maria start dinner. Staying busy kept her mind from her arguments with Kyle. Between the odd sensations he generated—the touch of his fingers still lingered on her arms—and her fear he'd recognize her, Kyle had left her nerves on edge. Although it was evident he cared about babies, he would insist on his own way. They could never work on deliveries together without generating sparks—of two different kinds.

By the time Enos came in and washed up, the meal was ready, and all three girls were seated at the table. Although Enos invited Leah to join them, she shook her head.

"I'll just get the sheets off the line and check on Hannah once more before I go." *Mamm* and *Daed* would already have had dinner. Leah took care of breakfast and lunch, but her older sisters alternated bringing the evening meals.

The sky had already darkened by the time Leah headed for the door to gather the bedding. She hoped the neighbors—or the bishop—hadn't seen the laundry hanging on the line after dusk. Perhaps if they realized Hannah had just had her baby, they'd be a little less critical, but the Amish community followed many unwritten rules, and one of those rules included taking down their wash before nightfall. The wind ripped the screen door from her hands, and she could barely close it. The still-damp sheets flapped wildly, slapping her face. As she unpinned them, gusts almost tore them from her hands. Leah wrestled the sweet-smelling bedding into the laundry basket and carried it down to the basement, where she hung up each piece. After a quick check on Hannah, the baby, and Aaron, Leah donned her cape and black bonnet and braved the wind to head out to the barn to hitch up the horse.

Icy gusts penetrated the blankets she wrapped around herself, and the sides of the buggy shook as her horse plodded through the almost deserted back lanes. One advantage of fighting the winds was not thinking about Kyle.

Leah tensed and swerved onto the shoulder when a car roared up behind the buggy, then whipped around her, leaving the buggy shaking even more than the wind had. Leah stayed on the shoulder of the road for the rest of the ride home. Ordinarily, the slow drive and lack of street-lights out here in the country allowed her to enjoy the scenery, but tonight the wind's freezing fingers made her urge her horse to move faster.

After she pulled into the parking lot of the shop, Leah released a grateful sigh. Without any further direction from her, her horse trotted around behind the store and to the barn. She opened the barn door and un-hooked him. Once she'd cared for and fed him and the other horses, she pulled the buggy into place and shut the doors.

Hunching her back against the cold, she struggled to unlock the shop door, her stiff fingers fumbling with the key. Once she succeeded in opening the door, she tussled with the wind until she slammed the door shut behind her. Glad to be out of the cold, she rubbed her hands together to warm them while she bent to pick up the mail that had been shoved through the slot. Several handwritten notes lay on top of the envelopes and cata-logs. Leah set the stack of regular mail beside the cash register. She could deal with that tomorrow, but she'd better check to be sure no one had had an emergency while she was gone.

Two notes were from *Englischers* who had stopped by around noontime to pick up their orders. She should have thought to call them before she left for the Fishers' so they wouldn't have had to waste their lunch breaks venturing out in the cold. The third one was from someone with a sick baby who needed her help as soon as possible. Leah hoped they hadn't been waiting long. She'd grab a quick bite to eat and run a few herbal remedies over to them right away.

She picked up the last note, and her stomach sank at the familiar bold, black printing. *Ben's writing.* After putting off so many dates because she was busy, she'd missed another one today. Even worse, she had no way to reach him now to apologize. His family had no phone shanty nearby. If she left a message on the answering machine at one of his neighbors' houses, he wouldn't get it until tomorrow. Most farmers were in bed by now.

With trembling fingers, she unfolded the paper:

> *Leah, I stopped by to pick you up as planned. I was really looking forward to seeing you, but the shop was closed. I waited in the cold. I'm wondering if you want to reschedule or…*

The next part of the note was scribbled out. It appeared Ben had written several different endings to the sentence and changed his mind. He'd finally settled on:

> *…maybe we need to talk. I'll try to stop by tomorrow afternoon if I can get away. Ben*

Dropping the note onto the counter, Leah sank onto the stool and buried her head in her hands. Ben's note added a huge weight to the heavy burden of guilt already weighing her down. She'd not only forgotten him, but he'd sat outside in that cold, biting wind, waiting for her. How did you apologize to someone for forgetting a date, not once, but twice? She'd hurt him by doing this when he first started courting her. Could she blame it on an emergency delivery again?

Yes, she'd been solely focused on her fears about delivering a preemie. That was completely understandable. What was her excuse after the baby had been safely delivered? Why had being at the Fishers' driven everything else from her mind? She hadn't remembered her date with Ben, not even when she pulled into the driveway a short while ago. Maybe she didn't belong in a relationship. Not if she couldn't keep her mind on the man who was one day to be her husband.

Like other Amish women, she hadn't made the commitment to court Ben lightly. Unlike the *Englischers* who dated around, in her community, agreeing to court someone meant you'd most likely marry. Leah expected to keep that promise. That is, if Ben still wanted to date her after she'd hurt him this way.

* * *

As they sat around the dinner table that night, Kyle choked up watching Dr. Hess seat his wife at the table and take her hand for prayer. Then when Esther reached across the table for Kyle's hand and the doctor gripped his other one, Kyle drifted back in time to the family dinner table, where his parents insisted they hold hands while Dad prayed.

Although Kyle lowered his head slightly out of respect for their beliefs, he couldn't bring himself to close his eyes. Not only did he have no right to pray, but participating would add to the flood of memories swamping him. He missed the days when he had the simple belief that God would take care of him and those he loved.

After the doctor and his wife raised their heads, the lump in Kyle's throat made it hard to swallow, let alone contribute to the conversation. And each time Dr. Hess gave his wife a secret smile or she gazed at him adoringly, a sharp pain pierced Kyle's chest, a longing for what they had, a home filled with love and a supportive partnership that lasted a lifetime.

Esther passed around hot potato salad with dill dressing to go with the ham her husband was carving. "We had several calls today. No emergencies. I scheduled them for tomorrow morning in the office."

The juices from the ham oozed out onto the serving plate, making Kyle's stomach rumble. The scent of cloves and cooked pineapple adorning the crisscross cuts of crackly ham skin scented the room. "Everything smells delicious," he said, heaping his plate with potatoes.

"Fill up," Esther encouraged him. "I'm sure you probably don't get many home-cooked meals."

"You're right about that." Kyle often missed meals, and when he ate, he usually grabbed hospital cafeteria food. On days off, takeout or leftovers were his go-to.

Dr. Hess served his wife and then placed a generous pile of ham slices on Kyle's plate. After the doctor filled his own plate, Kyle dug into the food. The tang of vinegar, mustard, and red onion added the perfect touch to the flaky potato chunks and complemented the smoky taste of the ham. Green beans and homemade zucchini bread completed the meal.

"Well, Leah did a wonderful job today on her first solo delivery," Dr. Hess said.

Kyle froze with a forkful of potatoes almost to his mouth. He'd hoped fleeing from the Fishers' house earlier meant erasing the Amish midwife from his mind, although if he were honest, she'd intruded on his thoughts quite a bit since. He'd made a mistake touching her in the hallway today. The softness of her skin . . .

Esther beamed. "She'll make a wonderful midwife. Sharon needs help, and so do you." She turned a tender gaze on her husband, which he returned. "Leah has already given so much to the community with her remedies."

Kyle wasn't so sure about that, but he held his peace. No sense in arguing about a situation he had no control over. Also, he needed to put that midwife out of his mind, which was easier said than done.

He'd be glad to get back to his hospital duties, where the nonstop work would drive her and all the memories of the past from his mind.

Later, Esther dolloped large scoops of ice cream onto the warm apple crisp for dessert. Neither the doctor nor his wife seemed to worry about their diets. Kyle tried to make healthy choices, even in his takeout or cafeteria meals. Ice cream was a rare indulgence. He wondered if Leah's natural glow and trim figure came from eating organic foods. Would she frown on his eating habits?

He had to admit he'd like to squabble with her over that. When she felt strongly about something, her eyes lit up with a fierce, determined look. This time, he'd do it just to tease her, because he suspected they'd both agree health foods were best.

Kyle had spooned in his last bite of tart apple crisp with creamy, melted ice cream. He leaned back in his chair with his eyes closed to savor the taste.

"Thank you for a delicious meal, dear," Dr. Hess said as he pushed back his chair and reached for the dishes. "Why don't you relax in the living room, Kyle?"

Although Kyle offered to help, the doctor and his wife insisted they enjoyed doing the dishes together every evening.

"It's our time to talk," Esther told him. "Many nights we don't get that opportunity."

Kyle wandered into the living room and perused the bookshelves. Books about faith were shelved with a few outdated medical dictionaries and magazines. Nothing to hold his interest. Kyle paced back and forth but couldn't help overhearing the low murmur of conversation coming from the kitchen.

"I want to head to the hospital this evening to check on Reuben," Dr. Hess said, "but I'll leave Kyle here."

"I still can't believe you took him over there today. I hope that reminder of the past doesn't change his mind about coming here."

Dr. Hess sighed. "I know I'm getting forgetful in my

old age, but I never thought I'd make a mistake like that."

"You're not old, honey. You're the perfect age." Esther's remark was followed by kissing noises.

Kyle moved to the piano in one corner of the room and tapped a few keys to drown out the sound. Maybe it would also alert them to the fact that he could overhear.

"Do you play, Kyle?" Esther called. "Feel free to entertain us with some songs."

"Sorry, but my only experience with music was a required class in college. I don't remember much. My parents never encouraged us to play instruments."

"Of course, they wouldn't have." Esther sounded quite sure of that.

How did she know that? Even he himself hadn't known about his parents' Amish heritage until his brother made the decision to join the church. His parents had left the Amish faith and had been shunned by their family. Never once during their growing-up years did Kyle suspect they were hiding that secret. He'd believed that both his parents were orphans. They'd raised Caleb and him as *Englischers*, although they were much stricter than any of his friends' parents and never allowed TV, radio, or instruments in their home.

Esther poked her head into the living room. "But they sang beautifully."

"You heard my parents sing?" They had sometimes sung songs as a family from an old hymnal, which Kyle only recently discovered was the *Ausbund*, an Amish hymnal. But they wouldn't have been doing that in the doctor's office.

Esther's eyes rounded, and she clapped a hand over her mouth. "I, um…"

Dr. Hess's voice boomed from the kitchen. "Esther, dear, we need to get these dishes finished so I can leave."

Her cheeks red, Esther ducked back into the kitchen. "Sorry, Martin." Her voice dropped to a whisper. "I didn't mean to—" A rush of water drowned out her next words.

The gushing stopped, and Dr. Hess's quiet question penetrated the wall between the rooms. "You don't think he'd remember that, do you? He was so young."

Remember what? Did Dr. Hess make a house call? Why would his wife come along, and how would they have heard my parents singing?

Kyle sank onto the couch and squeezed his eyes shut to block out the images floating before them, but they kept coming. His parents singing, his mom humming as she worked, their family devotions every morning…

When he tuned back into the conversation, Dr. Hess's whisper carried into the living room. "Would you be able to keep Kyle occupied while I head to the hospital?"

"Should I talk to him about the practice and our proposed timeline for moving?"

"That sounds like a good plan." A cupboard door banged open and dishes rattled. "Please be careful what you say, though."

"I know, Martin. I won't make a mistake like that again." Esther's whisper was barely audible. "I wish we could tell him the truth."

Clanging silverware covered most of Dr. Hess's answer. Kyle distinguished only two hushed words: *promise* and *secret*.

What in the world was going on? And what did it have to do with him?

Chapter Nine

Leah opened the store the next morning, dealt with the mail, placed some weekly orders, stocked a few shelves, and completed the inventory in one aisle. She'd just finished taking lunch up to *Mamm* when the two *Englischers* from the previous day arrived within a few minutes of each other.

"I'm so sorry I wasn't here yesterday," Leah said as she fetched their orders. "I had an emergency delivery."

The blond swished her shoulder-length hair back from her face. "No worries. I don't know how you manage to run a store when you're a midwife."

The older woman behind her sniffed. "Yes, your family should get someone else to cover for you when you're gone."

Leah winced as she sorted through the bags on the To-Be-Picked-Up shelves. Working in the shop should be her brother Joel's job, but he'd rebelled during

Rumspringa and had never joined the church. He'd fought with *Daed* and wanted nothing to do with the family or their Amish community. *Daed* had insisted on Leah taking Joel's place at the store. Her heart was with midwifery, but she needed to help her family. She'd only been supposed to work part-time hours, but with *Mamm*'s MS keeping her in bed most days and *Daed*'s full-time job, she'd ended up running the shop single-handedly. They'd discussed closing it, but too many people in the community depended on their products.

The phone rang soon after the customers left. Sharon's breathless voice came over the line. "If you can come over, I'm going to turn a breech baby. It would be a good learning experience for you."

"I'd love to be there. Where are you?" Leah jotted down the address. Then she locked the register and hurried to the door. She screeched to a halt. *Ben.* She needed to leave him a note. She wished he wouldn't come all the way over here only to find her gone, but she had no way to contact him.

Grabbing a piece of paper, she jotted a quick message:

Ben, I'm so sorry to have missed you yesterday. Sharon couldn't be reached so I was needed at the Fishers'. Sharon called and wants me to meet her at another patient's house today. I should be back by early evening. Leah

After folding the message shut, she printed his name in bold letters and taped it to the door. She set the return time to five p.m.—something she'd forgotten to do yesterday—and turned the store sign to CLOSED. Then she rushed out to her buggy and took off for the Groffs' house. She hoped she wouldn't be gone that long, but Sharon liked her to stay after all observations and deliveries to discuss what Leah had learned and what she could improve on next time.

She'd been hoping to learn to turn a breech baby. Sharon had described several different procedures a few weeks ago while Leah took some general notes. She'd also read about it in the informal booklet Sharon had put together for her assistants, but actually seeing it and participating was the best way to learn.

* * *

Kyle rejoiced that today was his last day in Lancaster. They had a busy schedule planned, and the doctor's long list of appointments wouldn't give them time for any in-depth talks. Kyle planned to confine all their interactions to discussing patients and symptoms rather than talking about his future plans or about God.

He'd been on edge since his conversation with Esther last evening. He'd survived their mealtime prayer, but he wanted to avoid a discussion about religion, so he steered the conversation away from talk about God for the rest of the evening. Although references to God peppered Esther's conversation, she hadn't asked any pointed questions about what he believed. She evidently assumed they shared the same faith.

As the evening progressed and she explained what she and Martin had planned for him, Kyle's reluctance to disappoint her grew with each passing minute. They'd both worked hard for so many years, so they deserved to retire.

Esther leaned forward in her chair. "I can't tell you how much this means to me. I'm excited that we can give the practice to you because your mother—" Her rapid flow of words stopped abruptly. "That is, well"— she seemed to be floundering to finish her sentence— "she was...um, a wonderful woman. A very wonderful woman. It was heartbreaking when she passed on. We always wanted to do something to help you. And Caleb, of course."

Esther rattled on without pausing for breath. "We also chose you not only because you used to live here but because Martin knows you were a wonderful student and thinks you're the right person to trust with his practice."

Kyle stared down at his clenched fists. How could he say no to them after all they'd done for him? And he'd be turning down a chance to pay off his med school loans and Emma's medical expenses. He'd been shocked to discover the Amish didn't believe in having insurance. Instead, Emma's family, with the help of the Amish community, had paid her extensive medical and rehab bills. His carelessness had depleted their funds. Funds that could have been used to help other families in need. Although they'd insist he owed them nothing, his conscience wouldn't allow him to escape financial responsibility. It might take years, or even decades, but he'd determined to pay back every penny.

When he didn't answer, Esther filled in the silence with rapid chatter. "We don't want you to feel obligated, of course, if this isn't where God is leading you. Martin and I have been praying, and I'm sure you've been doing the same, but we'll support whatever decision you make with God's guidance."

Participating in the conversation increased Kyle's feelings of being a fraud. He hadn't been praying and had no desire to do so. Maybe he could tell the doctor God was leading him elsewhere. To a fellowship at a big city hospital. Their hopes would be dashed when he said no. Especially Esther's. She anticipated spending time with Martin, doing many of the things they'd always hoped to do together, but they'd both accept his answer as God's will.

Kyle couldn't bring himself to lie to them, though. If he told them the truth about losing his faith, she and the doctor would probably hammer him with Scripture verses to bring him back to God. Might they change their minds about giving him the practice if they knew he'd lost his faith?

After he'd gone to bed last night, Kyle tossed and turned, weighing all the pros and cons, but despite the many reasons drawing him to stay, many more were urging him to leave. The long hours and hectic schedule of med school had kept him too busy to dwell on his mistakes, failures, and losses. In the same way, a challenging fellowship might prevent him from agonizing over the past. The slower-paced lifestyle here would force him to face his previous actions—and his guilt.

Yet he still hadn't come up with the courage—or the words—to tell the Hesses his final decision. It might be easier to say no to Dr. Hess when they were alone in the car, driving to the airport tonight. With darkness surrounding them, he wouldn't have to read the sadness in the doctor's eyes. And he wouldn't have to see Esther's hopes dashed. Besides, darkness made it easier to hide lies and guilt.

"Kyle?" Esther's soft voice startled him back to the office, where he'd joined Dr. Hess for the day. "Would you be willing to drive my car to the Stoltzfus Natural Products Store to pick up some prenatal vitamins for a patient who'll be coming in later today? She can't afford them, so we'll pay for them. Have them put the items on our personal account."

Still groggy after his sleepless night, Kyle took the list, money, directions, and car keys she handed him. Was there no end to the Hesses' generosity? He'd seen Esther lower charges for doctor visits for several uninsured people today, they handed out medicines they'd paid for as free samples, they bought items for a needy mother, and they planned to turn their practice over to a virtual stranger. What would motivate that kind of giving?

The cold wind outdoors drove the last of the cobwebs from Kyle's fogged brain. Didn't Leah's family own a natural products store? Most likely this was the same one. After all, how many of those stores would be located in this rural area? He hoped Leah wouldn't be there. He had no desire to spar with her again. Or did he? Last night at dinner, he'd imagined arguing with her would be fun.

When he turned into the parking lot, a huge delivery truck blocked the entrance. Kyle swerved around it and parked near a side fence. Hunching into his coat, he crossed the parking lot and rounded the delivery truck to find the driver pacing the sidewalk.

Kyle headed toward the glass entrance door.

"Wouldn't bother if I were you," the driver said. "Nobody's here."

"But it says it's open from nine to six today." Kyle glanced at the sign and checked his watch. "It's only three."

The driver pointed to the CLOSED sign and the clock, with its hands pointing to five o'clock. "Evidently, she doesn't plan to get back until five. What am I supposed to do?"

"Five? I was supposed to pick up a few things."

The driver stamped his feet and blew on his reddened hands. "They knew I was coming today. We prescheduled it. I have other deliveries to do, and I need to get this order off the truck so I can reach the boxes for my other delivery."

Kyle longed to get out of the wind, but he felt sorry for the man. "Can you leave the packages by the door?"

"I sometimes do, but this order has a bunch of glass bottles filled with liquid. They could freeze and shatter."

"How many are there? Would they fit in the car over there?"

The driver looked at him like he was crazy. "Sure, man, I'll just load the boxes into some stranger's car."

Oh, right. Kyle should have thought of that. "I'm Dr. Hess's assistant, and I'm running errands for his wife." He held out the list Esther had printed on an office notepad.

The man's suspicious look didn't change. "I do deliveries for the doctor, and I heard he was getting an assistant. I also recognize Mrs. Hess's car. It's rather distinct." He snickered a little but then returned to his judgmental stare. "How do I know you didn't steal it?"

"If you know the Hesses, you could call them and ask."

"Guess if I don't, I'll be stuck out here on the road for another two hours tonight." He slid through the numbers on his cell, clicked on one, and held the phone to his ear. "Nobody's picking up."

"Maybe try one more time?" Kyle had no idea why he was being so persistent. This delivery wasn't his responsibility, but maybe hanging around the Hesses was restoring the charitable part of himself he'd buried years ago.

Yes, and you have a soft spot for the girl who works here. Maybe you're hoping it'll give you a chance to see her again.

Kyle shook his head to dislodge those thoughts. Leah got under his skin, and the only thing he wanted to do was confront her about her dangerous practices.

Liar, his conscience whispered.

Beside him, the driver had reached Esther and was questioning her. A short while later, he clicked off his phone. "Mrs. Hess promises she'll see that Leah gets the delivery, and she vouched for you."

Fighting the wind, Kyle helped the man pile the boxes into the roomy old trunk and onto the car seats. By the time they were done, boxes were stacked ceiling high on the floor and across the backseat, except for a small opening he could peer through. They filled the bench seat next to Kyle so tightly he could barely squeeze into the driver's seat.

After everything had been wedged inside, the driver made Kyle print his phone number on a form and took his driver's license information. Then he shook Kyle's hand. "I really appreciate this, man."

"No problem." Well, maybe shifting would be, but at least the old-fashioned shift was on the steering wheel instead of the center console. His arms tucked tightly against his sides, Kyle maneuvered the big old car out of the parking lot and onto the street. He drove a bit more slowly than usual so none of the boxes would shift.

When he arrived at the Hesses', Esther came out on the porch. "You can pull into the garage," she called, "and I'll turn on the heater. We sometimes keep medical supplies in there."

Once the car was stowed and Kyle had washed up, Esther sent him into the living room to wait for dinner. Again, a delicious aroma perfumed the air, making Kyle hungry. He relaxed on the couch, relieved he'd soon be headed home.

After dinner, Esther asked, "Would you mind taking those boxes back to the shop before you and Martin leave for the airport? Martin needs to run out to see a patient. I don't know if I could see over such high stacks."

"Sure." Kyle welcomed any distraction from composing his no-thank-you-I-can't-take-the-offer explanation. He comforted himself with the thought that plenty of young doctors like him would gladly take the offer. But the idea of driving over to the store switched his thoughts to Leah. If she worked as a midwife, most likely others in the family ran the store. Part of him hoped he wouldn't see her again, but a small part, one he tried to squash, hoped he would.

Chapter Ten

By the time Leah arrived at the Groffs', Sharon had already completed the checkup. "I've already explained that turning a baby may result in premature labor, but Matthew and Rachel have agreed to take that chance."

Leah followed the other two women into the bedroom, and Sharon showed her how to use her hands to turn the baby to a head-down position. Moving firmly, but gently, she coaxed the baby into place.

Leah pictured Kyle's face if he found out about this procedure. He'd probably think it was dangerous and recommend that Rachel have a caesarean at the hospital. She imagined the two of them arguing over the best choice.

When Sharon finished, she cautioned Rachel, "Some lively babies flip themselves over again during the next few weeks, so we'll keep an eye on you. Also let us know if the baby starts kicking anywhere other than your ribs or upper abdomen. I'll stay a few hours to be sure labor doesn't begin, but once I leave, call me right away if you have any pains."

Rachel turned shining eyes to Sharon. "I will and thank you for everything." She insisted on giving Sharon and Leah each a coffee cake she'd baked that morning.

"Would it be all right if I spend some time discussing the procedure with Leah?" Sharon asked.

Rachel nodded and gestured to the kitchen table. "Make yourselves at home. I need to go down to the basement to do laundry."

Sharon brushed damp wisps of hair from her forehead and smoothed them back into the bun at the back of her head. A white lace prayer veiling covered her bun, much smaller than Leah's heart-shaped *kapp*. "The procedure I did in there is called *ECV*, or *external cephalic version*. You'll also hear it called *version*. I want you to look it up in the textbooks when you get home."

Leah wrote down the names so she could read more about the procedure. Sharon believed hands-on demonstrations followed by book learning would cement the lessons in her assistants' minds, and Leah had found she was right.

"I wanted to wait until thirty-seven or thirty-eight weeks," Sharon explained, "because ECV is best done when the baby can still move freely in the fluid. But the pregnancy needs to be close to term in case the procedure causes labor to begin. We want to be certain the baby is fully developed. If we do the procedure any closer to delivery, though, the baby doesn't have much room to move."

She paused to give Leah time to record the information

before continuing. "There are a few risks, but I think they outweigh the danger of a breech birth. Read up on the possible complications so you can explain them to the parents. Give them an informed choice. I've found most Amish parents are willing to take the chance of an early delivery."

An early delivery? Kyle would certainly not want to take a chance on that. He'd use that as an argument for a hospital birth. For some reason, his voice kept echoing through her mind.

Jotting notes as fast as she could, Leah tried to get down as much information as possible.

"It's also important to know where the umbilical cord is. We can't take a chance if it's around the baby's neck or likely to be. Rachel had an ultrasound yesterday so I knew it would be safe. I recommend having the mother do that so I know exactly what I'm dealing with."

"What if the umbilical cord isn't in the right position?"

"Depending on where it is, I might recommend a hospital birth."

Kyle would approve of that. Leah couldn't seem to keep her thoughts from straying to his reactions.

"Or if it doesn't appear to be dangerous," Sharon said, "I'll take charge of the breech delivery. I've had very few of those in my twenty-five years as a midwife. If I do have one, I'll call you to help me. You should learn how to do it."

As much as Leah would like to see how Sharon did it, she wouldn't wish a breech birth on anyone.

Sharon went on to list many other ways women used to turn breeches. Most of this information wouldn't be in her textbooks, so Leah took detailed notes, ever conscious of how Kyle would glower if he heard some of these backcountry and unscientific methods.

Leah's hand cramped, and she stretched it before resuming her copious pages of notes. By the time Sharon finished, Leah had filled a thick section of her notebook with information, and the sky had darkened. Ben would be back home milking the cows and feeding the horses by now. Leah sighed. He'd be upset to miss her two days in a row, but she had to admit she was more relieved than sad. She wasn't looking forward to their conversation. How did you explain to someone that you'd completely forgotten about them?

Truth be told, she'd spent more time thinking about Kyle than she had about Ben. That should never be. Ever since she'd met him, Kyle kept popping into her mind, evaluating her every decision, following her everywhere she went.

On the way home, sharp twinges in her abdomen alerted Leah that her once-a-month bout with intense pain was about to begin. She'd take a spoonful of that calcium-phosphorous supplement after dinner and hope it helped. She'd also drink some of the herbal blend they sold in the store for cramps.

She arrived back at the shop to find the door unlocked and the lights on. Surprised, she stepped inside and met her *daed*'s glare.

"*Daed*," she faltered, "what are you doing here?"

"Doing your job and trying to find out what happened to our big shipment."

"*Ach*, I forgot all about that." Lately, her midwife calls

pushed everything else from her mind. Yesterday, Ben. Today, the order. "I'm so sorry."

"*Jah, vell*, according to the company, their driver dropped the shipment off between three and three thirty. Those boxes have vanished."

They couldn't have lost the whole shipment. They'd prepaid for it, and if the company insisted they'd delivered everything, they'd not only lose that money, but also all the customers who had placed orders would be upset. *Daed* couldn't afford to replace this order. "Is it possible they made a mistake? Maybe delivered it elsewhere?"

Daed shook his head. "They can track the truck from their headquarters, and they verified his stop here. All the rest of the driver's deliveries arrived as scheduled. The only discrepancy they found was how long he was at this spot. I'm guessing that's because he was waiting for someone to open the shop."

His glower made it clear who should have been there to open the shop. "They tried to talk directly to the driver, but he's not answering. He has off until Monday."

"I'm sorry." Her apology wouldn't bring back the missing merchandise. "Is there anything I can do to help?"

"Stay where you belong and stop running off during store hours." *Daed* stalked toward the door that opened into the kitchen. "If your *mamm* is feeling up to it, we'll have a family meeting to decide whether or not you can continue to help Sharon if it's going to take you away from your duties here. Meet us upstairs after you've closed the shop." His tone brooked no argument.

When six o'clock came, Leah closed out the cash register, locked the store, and pulled down the blinds. *Daed* and *Mamm* would have already eaten the meal her sister brought over tonight. Wishing she had time to grab a bite to eat and take something to ease the pangs shooting through her, Leah scurried upstairs. *Daed* valued punctuality, and she didn't want to do anything to cause further upset.

As she mounted the stairs, *Daed*'s worried voice carried down the hall. "How will we ever afford to replace this shipment?"

The loss was all her fault, but how could she ever repay him? From time to time, people slipped her a little money when she assisted Sharon. Money that she turned over to *Daed*, as all unmarried children were expected to do until they turned twenty-one. The only way she could repay him was to work in the shop during the posted hours, a duty that she'd failed at twice this week. If she'd been where she should have been, she'd be checking in boxes of products right now, and Ben wouldn't be upset with her either.

"Did you have a good day, *dochder*?" *Mamm* asked when Leah entered the room.

How should she answer that? It had been a wonderful day up until she'd arrived home. Now it had turned into a disaster. "Earlier I did," she mumbled. "I'm so sorry, *Mamm* and *Daed*."

"*Jah*, it worries me how we'll make up these losses." *Daed* pinned her with a serious look. "I'm also concerned about the shop being closed so often. I understand it was shut most of the day yesterday."

"I received an emergency call, and Sharon wasn't available."

"She has other assistants. They should be helping her during the day."

"Enos Fisher called and asked me to come. I couldn't turn down his request for help." Her *daed* always stressed helping others. Surely he'd understand she not only wanted to go, she also could never ignore a plea for assistance.

Daed's pursed lips conflicted with the softness in his eyes. "I suppose not," he conceded.

"And the Fishers have a healthy new son," *Mamm* reminded him. "Leah needed to be there."

Actually, Caleb had jaundice, but that would be gone soon. She didn't contradict *Mamm*—not the way she'd contradicted Kyle. Her fists curled at her sides remembering his insistence on taking both babies to the hospital. He'd taken up residence in her mind, and she couldn't seem to shake his voice or comments.

"Leah, did you hear me?" *Daed* stared at her, his brow creased.

"I'm sorry. What did you say?" She'd been so busy combatting Kyle's arguments from yesterday she'd missed *Daed*'s comments.

He blew out an exasperated breath. "I said I'd like you to tell Sharon—"

Mamm interrupted him. "I wonder if we should come up with an alternate solution. I believe Leah is needed in the community. Sharon isn't able to handle all the work."

"That's what she has assistants for," *Daed* snapped, but immediately looked contrite. "I'm sorry. I didn't mean to be so short-tempered."

With a gentle smile, *Mamm* kept her response soft. "I understand Leah is the assistant she trusts most, so Sharon calls on her more than the others. I also think

Leah wants to learn as much as she can. Maybe we could make different plans for the store."

"You want to close it?" *Daed* asked incredulously. "I thought we'd already decided to keep it open for the community even if we barely make a profit."

"I didn't mean we should close it, but we could come up with an alternate plan." *Mamm* held up a hand when *Daed* started to protest. "I don't mean cutting the hours. I know how you feel about that." She hesitated a minute. "Maybe it's time to mend fences with Joel."

Daed's face darkened, and he stood for a few minutes, his chest rising and falling rapidly. Leah wished *Mamm* hadn't brought up Joel. The one issue that roused *Daed*'s ire was his only son who'd left the family and the Amish community. Although he'd never forbidden them to talk about Joel, his anguish—and often his fury—when the subject came up made *Mamm* and Leah hesitate to mention Joel's name.

Mamm leaned back against the pillow and closed her eyes. The fire left *Daed*'s eyes, and he stood staring helplessly at her.

Poor Mamm. They shouldn't have tired her out.

Mamm opened her eyes and said in a shaky voice, "I blame myself. Working in the shop should have been my job. Leah should be free to be a midwife."

Leah rushed over to the bed and took *Mamm*'s hand. "No, *Mamm*. Please, please don't blame yourself. It's my job, and I'll do it, even if it means giving up midwifing."

"If God is leading you to be a midwife, then we should support you in that decision." Her *mamm* glanced over at *Daed*. "Don't you think so?"

He harrumphed but didn't answer.

"You know," she said in a quiet voice, "Joel's been struggling financially. He lost his job a few weeks ago. He'd probably be willing to..."

Daed's glower silenced her. "If he chooses to live in the *Englisch* world, then he must pay the consequences."

"I know you don't mean that."

Under *Mamm*'s steady gaze, he lowered his head and stared at the floor. "Perhaps we should save this discussion for another time." Shoulders slumped, he walked over to the window and gazed out at their back pastures as dusk turned to night.

Daed blamed himself for Joel leaving. If only there were some way she could comfort him. The best way would be to help her family in the store. Swallowing hard, Leah said, "I won't leave the shop again during business hours."

A distressed look crossed *Mamm*'s face. "What about helping Sharon?"

"I'll tell her I can do it only after hours."

"That would be best." *Daed* didn't turn around. "Especially as we'll have to pay for this shipment. If you find working with Sharon in the evenings is overtiring you, I expect you to put the shop first."

Daed had laid a heavier yoke on her shoulders than the one he used for the oxen in the field. If she set aside time after hours to be with Ben and to study, she'd have little opportunity to accompany Sharon. With babies being so unpredictable, how likely was it they'd be born during her free hours? *Daed* hadn't forbidden her to be a midwife, but his requests curtailed her chances.

* * *

Kyle pulled into the parking lot beside the store. He'd forgotten how dark Amish houses became at night. A dim solar bulb hung over the door to the shop, barely illuminating the hours. The blinds on the windows indicated the business had closed for the night. No lights shone in the house, either upstairs or down.

Wishing he hadn't agreed to do this favor, he circled the lot to turn around. A glow from a back window sent a faint patch of light onto the fields beside the barn. Someone must be there. He hated to disturb them, but he needed to get rid of the boxes before he took the red-eye that night. He pulled the car close to the store entrance and emerged into the frigid air. He knocked on the door, shivering as he waited. Hands thrust deep in his pockets, he paced the sidewalk. When nobody answered his second knock, he strode toward the back of the house, where he'd seen the light.

The window was dark. Maybe he'd mistaken that glimmer of light. Esther or Martin would have to bring the delivery back tomorrow. Kyle hurried to the car, eager to turn on the heater and get out of the cold. He unlocked the door and was stepping inside when a small beam of light bobbed inside the store. A flashlight. Someone was coming.

The bells jangled on the door, and Leah raised the blinds and peeked out. How pretty she appeared in moonlight.

Enough, Kyle. Unload the delivery and get out of here. Go back to the city. You'll forget this attraction soon enough.

"Kyle?" Leah's voice wavered. "What are you doing here?"

He stepped from the car. "I, um…" Why did seeing her drive all other thoughts from his head?

She glanced behind him, and her eyes narrowed as they focused on him. "Are those boxes in your car yours?" Without waiting for an answer, she plunged on. "You took our delivery. I thought you didn't believe in herbal medicines. Why did you take them?"

Kyle was uncertain which question to answer first, but she gave him no chance to explain.

Sucking in a breath, Leah put her hands on her hips. "You took them so we couldn't sell them, didn't you? You planned to destroy them."

Kyle held up a hand, but he couldn't stop Leah's words.

"I know you think they don't work as well as your medicines, but are you trying to bankrupt our family? *Daed* paid a lot of money for them. Please let us have them back."

"Leah," Kyle said, managing to wedge a word into her nonstop accusations. "Wait a minute. You're not being fair here. You haven't let me answer even one question. Let me explain."

"Fine." Leah pinched her lips together, but her eyes still condemned him.

"Earlier today Esther Hess asked me to come by to pick up a few things." Kyle reached into his pocket and pulled out the wrinkled list.

"Like you'd agree to come to a natural products store for anything."

"Leah?" He used a low, sharp tone. "Are you going to let me tell you?"

"Sorry," she muttered, and she remained silent as

he described the delivery and how he had rescued the boxes.

"You did it to help us?" Leah appeared to be struggling to accept his version of the story. "But, but—"

Kyle couldn't help being a little hurt. "You don't believe I'm capable of doing something nice?"

"No, I mean, yes. Of course you are. I just didn't expect you to do it for me."

"Why?"

Most of the fight leaked out of her, and her words, when they came, were tinged with sadness. "I thought you hated me and everything I stand for."

"I don't hate you." *Quite the opposite.* "Just because I disagree with you about treating patients doesn't mean I'd let that affect what I do. You wouldn't hold a grudge like that, would you?"

"Of course not."

"But you thought I'd be petty enough to destroy your merchandise?"

"I'm so sorry. I do have a bad habit of jumping to conclusions. Please forgive me."

Kyle nodded. "Now, do you want me to bring the boxes in?"

Leah hung her head. "This is my fault." She headed toward the car. "You don't have to carry them in. I'll take care of it. You've done enough already."

"Now we're going to argue over who carries in the boxes, and meanwhile they'll all explode if they're out in the cold any longer."

Leah burst out laughing. "I told you I'm argumentative."

"No, you didn't. You said you jump to conclusions."

Leah reached the car door before Kyle. "I do both,

and I'm also stubborn." She yanked the door open and grabbed a box.

"Maybe you've met your match." Kyle reached in and hefted two boxes. "Because I'm not going to let you do this alone."

After Leah hung her battery-powered lantern in the store so they could see, they unloaded the car in silence, with Kyle bringing in two or three boxes for every one of Leah's. Twice, he noticed her bend over and wince.

"Are you all right?" he asked. "I can get the rest of the boxes if these are too heavy for you."

Leah crossed her arms over her stomach and turned away from him. She sounded as though she were speaking through clenched teeth. "I'm fine."

Kyle wasn't sure whether or not to believe her. She slowed down, made several stops, and bent over with her hands gripping the boxes when she thought he wasn't looking. He unloaded the boxes even faster to keep her from having to do so much when she appeared to be in pain.

He walked through the door with the last two boxes to find her hunched over, her eyes squeezed shut. The minute the door jangled shut behind him, she forced herself to a standing position and managed a stiff smile.

"You're hurting." He could be as stubborn as she was, and he refused to take her denials as truth when his practiced eye had detected a problem.

Leah waved a hand to brush away his concerns. "I'll be fine." Her cheeks, already rosy from the cold, deepened to scarlet.

He had a suspicion about what was wrong. If he guessed right, she'd never admit it to him as a man and an *Englischer*. "Do you want me to help you unpack the boxes?" He hated to leave her alone to cope with all these cartons.

"No, no, I'll do it tomorrow."

Kyle racked his brain for an excuse to stay longer. "It's pretty chilly outside. Would it be all right if I wait until my hands warm up?"

Leah looked as if she wanted to say no, but she said, "Certainly. I should have"—she took a deep breath—"asked if you wanted…some tea or coffee…to drink." A quick indrawn breath revealed she was fighting a sharp pang.

He disliked asking her to do anything when she'd be better off in bed, but he wanted to keep an eye on her. "Tea would be great." That would give him time to see if he'd diagnosed her correctly.

Chapter Eleven

Leah turned her back so Kyle couldn't see her face scrunch up as the hot stabbing inside her sent needles radiating through her. If only she'd taken that supplement earlier, it would have reduced some of the aching. That needed to be taken after a meal, though, and she hadn't eaten since lunchtime. One of the herbal blends she made for the shop helped to lessen her discomfort. She'd drink some of that, but what could she offer Kyle?

She forced herself not to wince as she pushed out words. "I have a mixture of calming herbs for tea, if you'd like that?"

"That would be fine."

He sounded less than enthusiastic, but she didn't offer any other options. She had to have her own tea as soon as possible. She also needed to get away from him and into the kitchen.

Biting back groans, she limped down the aisle as

quickly as she could, lifted the lid of one of the jars, measured out a precise amount of the herbal blend, and staggered into the kitchen. She turned on the gas lamp, then leaned over and pressed her stomach hard against the sink edge as she filled the kettle. After she put the kettle on the burner of the propane stove, she went into the living room to curl up around some pillows. A hot water bottle usually helped, but she'd wait until Kyle left to huddle up with its soothing warmth.

When the water was ready, she made herself a cup and took a few sips before turning out the lamp and carrying the two mugs out to the store, where Kyle was prowling the aisles. She hoped the sips of tea would give her enough relief to carry on a conversation.

Kyle settled on a stack of boxes and studied her intently while he sipped his tea. His eyebrows rose, and he took another drink. "Hey, this is pretty good."

Leah pushed her lips into a semblance of a smile. "Thanks. I'm hoping to sell that calming blend in the store."

"It tastes good, but I'll let you know if it works."

"My friend Ada said it did, but I'd be glad for other opinions." Especially his. If he liked it, after how critical he'd been of her other herbal remedies, she'd know it was good enough to sell in the store.

"I promise to be honest."

No doubt he would be. He certainly hadn't shied away from expressing his opinion on any of her other herbal concoctions.

"I can't believe how cold it is outside," Kyle said. "I really appreciate the tea and the chance to thaw out. Why don't you sit down too?"

Leah started toward the stack of boxes he'd indicated near him. Partway there, her insides felt as if they were being attacked by a pickax. All she wanted to do was hunch into a ball and moan. Her eyes welled with tears, and she turned to hide them from Kyle. Leaning against the counter, she pretended to look for a pen.

To defend herself against his intense stare, Leah forced out an explanation between the attacks inside her body. "I need to...write down...the amount I took...from the jar. We deduct personal use...from inventory." The jabbing decreased slightly, but her eyes filmed over again as she jotted down the amount on the tablet near the register.

"Look at me," Kyle commanded.

When she ignored him, he stood and stepped around the edge of the counter until he could see her face. Leah ducked her head and concentrated on forming numbers despite the pain shooting through her.

Putting a gentle finger under her chin, Kyle tilted her face up until he looked directly into her eyes. "Are those tears? You're hurting. I can see it in your face."

Leah tried to turn away, but he cupped her face in his hands and continued to examine her. "Where does it hurt? Did you pull something when you lifted those heavy boxes?"

"No, no." She couldn't explain to a man, an *Englischer*, no less, about her severe cramps. The very thought made her cheeks burn.

"You're flushed too," Kyle said. "Do you have a fever?" He laid his hand against her forehead.

"No, please," Leah begged, unsure whether she wanted him to remove his hand or continue touching her.

Ben had never touched her like this. Their hands had brushed from time to time, and once he'd helped her down from the wagon so she'd avoid a large muddy spot, but Kyle's gentle fingers created strange sensations that zinged through her, making her pulse gallop. Could he hear her thumping heartbeat? She had to get away before she did something foolish.

With a quick jerk, Leah untangled herself from his fingers, but the warmth and tingling he'd started continued even after she stepped back. "Do you...um, want another cup of tea?" Making one would allow her to flee to the kitchen.

"I haven't finished the one I have."

Leah moved even farther away, though part of her longed to step closer. "I want another cup." She picked up her partly filled teacup and lurched toward the kitchen, hoping he wouldn't notice her unsteady gait.

Feeling her way around in the dark, she added some warm water from the kettle to her cup and walked back out to the store, where Kyle stood by the shelves of glass jars. If he figured out which one she'd used, he'd realize why she was in pain.

*　*　*

Kyle started. He hadn't heard Leah come into the shop. Tearing his gaze from the glass jars on the lower shelf, he pretended to study the array of vitamins at eye level. That reminded him. He still had Esther's list stuffed in his pocket.

"Would it be all right for me to get the things Esther

needs?" He hoped the question would distract her from what he'd been doing.

"I've already closed out the cash register for today, but if they're putting it on their bill, I can record it as a sale for tomorrow."

"Yes, Esther said it's to go on their personal account."

Leah headed to the aisle where he was standing, her gait steadier than it had been when she'd walked away. Maybe the tea did help. He planned to look up the effects of some of the ingredients when he had a chance. Mentally, he went over the long list. *Black cohosh, raspberry leaf, burdock root, slippery elm…*

"Maybe I can help you find things more quickly." Leah almost brushed his elbow as she reached for the list.

With her standing so near, the rest of the ingredients disappeared from his mind. He forced himself to repeat the name of the tea to control his racing pulse. *Female Disorders.* The name had confirmed his suspicions. Now he had to find a way to talk to her about her problems without making her uncomfortable.

She stretched past him to take a vitamin bottle from the shelf, and her sleeve whispered past his face, setting off a cascade of emotions—a longing for closeness, for caring, for a loving relationship. Why did this woman who made him so irritated raise those desires? Perhaps his subconscious mind was confusing her with Emma. Kyle shook his head. No, every cell in his body recognized this was Leah.

"Are you sure?" Leah asked. "This is the kind the Hesses usually buy."

"What?" Confused, Kyle looked at her. A big mistake.

He drowned in those blue eyes. The smoky shadows between the shelves made the space feel intimate.

She broke their intense gaze but appeared flustered. "You shook your head, so I thought you disagreed with my choice."

Shook my head? Oh, I was trying to clear thoughts of you. He tried to put together a coherent response. "No, give her whatever kind you think is best."

Leah gave him a questioning look, and he schooled his face into a neutral expression, but he couldn't control his reactions to her nearness. He relaxed a little when she moved to a different aisle. He longed to follow her, but that would be a mistake.

Using the large metal reflector at the front of the store, he followed her progress down the next aisle. As soon as she turned the corner and thought she was out of his sight, she winced. Several times she squeezed her eyes shut and leaned her forehead against the shelf. She must have incredible stamina, if she was suffering from what he believed she had.

Clenching her fists, she resumed hunting for products. Several times she disappeared from view when she moved down aisles the light didn't illuminate. How did she manage to find things when she could barely see?

After she emerged from the last aisle, she headed for the counter. "I'll ring this up tomorrow, but let me calculate a total for Esther." She jotted prices beside the items on Esther's list, then she punched numbers into the small battery-powered adding machine.

She sucked in her lower lip and clamped her teeth down on it. As much as he'd like to stay, he needed to let her rest.

Leah scribbled the product names next to the prices on the adding machine tape. Then she recorded the total on Esther's list and handed it to Kyle along with the bag.

"Thank you," he said. Now that he had the package, what excuse could he make to stay? To talk to her about her health?

Leah turned her back to reach for the lantern she'd hung overhead. Her signal it was time for him to exit?

A tiny whimper alerted him. Because she'd hunched over, the light was now out of her reach.

He set his bag on one of the stacks of boxes. "Let me help." He hurried over and lifted the hook of the light to remove it from the ceiling. Instead of handing it to her, he set it on the counter and took her hands. "You don't have to pretend with me. I've been studying medicine for years."

Leah dipped her head, trying to hide her face. He longed to lift her chin again but restrained himself. If he did, he worried he might do something he'd regret. Instead he ran his fingers lightly over the back of her hands, intending to soothe her, but the softness of her skin combined with the darkness of the store made it hard to concentrate.

"I'm concerned about you. You're in a lot of pain, although you've done a good job of pretending otherwise. Do you have this much pain every month?"

She hung her head even lower and mumbled, "Usually."

"You don't need to be embarrassed around me. Pretend I'm your doctor. Do you ever faint?"

Keeping her head down, she answered in a barely audible voice, "Only once or twice."

"Do you get tired or nauseous?"

Her startled gaze flew to his face, then immediately she ducked her head. "Sometimes, but how did you know?"

As he ran down the list of symptoms, his certainty increased. "Leah, please look at me." When she didn't respond, he said, "Please?"

She lifted pain-glazed eyes, and when they stared at each other, Kyle realized he'd made a mistake. She appeared as mesmerized as he felt. Maybe it was the intimacy of being alone in the shadows with only the small circle of light surrounding them, spotlighting them. Maybe it was holding her small, soft hands trembling in his. Maybe it was his foolish heart longing for connection. But he never wanted to let go.

Outside, a horse's hooves clattered into the parking lot. Leah jumped, but Kyle didn't let go of her hands. He needed to tell her something. Something important.

Act professional. He steeled himself against the urge to pull her into his arms. "This is only a preliminary diagnosis, but I think you should be checked for endometriosis."

"What?" Leah jerked her hands from his as heavy boots clomped along the sidewalk outside.

"From your symptoms, I'm concerned you may have endometriosis. Your pain may be a symptom of that."

She stared at him. "Are you sure?"

"As sure as I can be without an extensive checkup. Will you please make an appointment?"

The door banged open, sending the bells into a jangled frenzy that matched Kyle's nerves.

"Promise me," he said.

But she'd turned toward the door, and her face blanched.

* * *

"Ben! What are you doing here this time of night?" The shock in her voice made her sound less than welcoming. Leah corrected her mistake. "I'm glad to see you."

Kyle backed away from her as Ben approached, fire in his eyes. "I'll just get Dr. Hess's bag and go," Kyle said. "Thank you for getting these items for them."

Ben's narrowed gaze followed Kyle's rapid stride to the stack of boxes holding the bag. Ben blew out a breath when the door closed behind the *Englischer*.

Dizziness overtook Leah. Between the severe cramps, Ben's sudden arrival and clenched jaw, Kyle's diagnosis and his departure...

She plopped down on the nearest pile of boxes and put her head in her hands until the nausea and swirling grayness subsided. Then, clutching the edges of the box until her fingers hurt, she eased her eyes open. The world still whirled around her. All she wanted to do was curl up in bed with a hot water bottle. She'd expended so much energy trying to act normal around Kyle that she had little left. And his suggested diagnosis had been a bombshell. But she couldn't exactly ask Ben to leave, considering the way they left things.

Ben stood with his back to her, clutching his suspenders the way he did when he was agitated, watching Kyle pull out of the parking lot. He didn't turn around until the car turned onto the highway and the growl of the engine faded into the distance.

Her nausea increased when he whirled around, his face set in angry lines.

"Do you often open the store for customers during the evening?" In contrast to his irate expression, Ben's tone remained deadly calm.

Leah shook her head, sending colored dots dancing before her eyes. "Not usually. Once or twice during emergencies."

"You considered this an emergency?" Ben's gaze drilled into her as he waited for an answer.

"No, of course not. Under the circumstances, though..."

"What circumstances were those?"

Leah rubbed her temples. Could she plead a headache and escape up to bed? She didn't want to explain about the missed delivery. Heat rushed into her face as she re-called accusing Kyle of stealing the boxes. After that, he'd not only helped her unload all of them, but he'd cared enough to notice her symptoms and offer a diagnosis. He'd placed his hand on her forehead so gently...

Ben cleared his throat.

Leah jumped. She'd forgotten Ben. Again. This time when he was right in the room with her. What had he asked? Something about circumstances? "I'm exhausted tonight. It's been a long day. Could we talk about it later?"

"You didn't look tired when *he* was here."

"I had to take care of a customer."

Ben's face fell. "You're not too tired to take care of a customer, but you're too tired to spend time with me. With everything that's happened recently, I'm beginning to wonder if you want to spend time with me at all."

"Oh, Ben, that's not true."

"I don't know about that. Two missed dates were bad enough, but then I saw how you looked at him." He gestured toward the door, indicating he meant Kyle.

"How?" *Nervous? Shell-shocked?*

Ben's steady stare indicated he'd interpreted the look quite differently.

Leah crossed her arms. "What are you implying?" Her sharp tone didn't quite cover the guilty note in her voice.

"I'm not blind, Leah. And he seemed as reluctant to let go of you as you were to disentangle yourself from his arms."

"That isn't true." Was it? They'd both been startled and...

Ben only gazed at her with sad eyes. "I understand he's here because he's going to be replacing Dr. Hess."

News traveled fast in the Amish community. "Yes, he is."

"I also heard he's only here for three days. In those three days you missed two dates with me. Now I come here at night to find you alone with him in the shop, close together. Touching even." Ben closed his eyes and rubbed his fingers over them as if trying to erase the image.

"You're misinterpreting something completely innocent." Leah hoped she didn't sound as defensive as she felt. "Besides, Kyle is an *Englischer*. I'd never fall for someone who isn't Amish."

A muscle in Ben's jaw quivered. "I should hope not."

Leah had never been attracted to *Englischers*. Ever.

Until now? her conscience whispered.

She shook her head. Of course not. This was ridiculous. By dating Ben, she'd committed to possibly marrying him someday, a commitment she took seriously. Perhaps she should reassure him of her loyalty.

Before she could say anything, Ben hung his head. "I'm sorry, Leah. I've been struggling with jealousy, and seeing you with the *Englischer*, seeing him hold you..." He shook his head. "It added to my worries that I'm not a priority in your life. Tending the store, being a midwife, and studying take up so much of your time it seems there's none left for me."

"Oh, Ben, I'm sorry. I didn't mean to make you feel like you weren't an important part of my life. It's just that I have so many responsibilities right now."

"I understand." But the stiffness of his posture, that muscle still working in his jaw revealed a different story. "What I don't understand, though, is why you weren't here yesterday when I arrived."

"I got a call from the Fishers. They needed me because Sharon wasn't answering her phone." She wanted to add she'd already explained that in her note today but didn't want to sound defensive.

"And you couldn't have left me a note explaining where you went? How long you expected to be gone?" The hurt underlying Ben's words only increased her shame.

"I'm so sorry, Ben. It's no excuse, but when I thought a baby might die, I rushed off." Leah clenched her hands in her lap to prevent herself from reaching out and running a soothing hand over his white-knuckled fists. As a healer and a midwife, she had a tendency to touch people. A tendency that had shocked Ben during their first months of dating. He'd discussed her forwardness once, and Leah had worked to keep her natural touchiness hidden when they were together. Kyle seemed to have similar tendencies. He'd reached out several times tonight. She shouldn't misread his touches. He'd meant to be reassuring, but the warmth of his fingers remained imprinted on her skin. She forced herself to tune back in to what Ben was saying.

"I understand you had an emergency then." His words didn't sound quite convincing. "But what about earlier today? You knew I was coming back this afternoon to talk."

Leah bit her lip and averted her eyes. Silence stretched between them as Ben waited for an answer. She couldn't tell him, in her excitement to learn more about breech deliveries, that meeting him had taken second place. "I left you a note."

"But I drove all the way over here, only to be disappointed again."

"I'm sorry. I didn't have any way to let you know. Can I do something to make it up to you?" Her gaze strayed to all the boxes piled up beside the counter. She wished he'd propose a date later in the week so she could go to bed. The stabbing inside had dulled to a continuous ache, as if a hand were squeezing her insides.

She bit back a sigh when Ben suggested they spend the rest of the evening together. "Would it be all right if I unpack—" She broke off at the hurt in Ben's eyes. He needed and wanted her undivided attention. She'd have to come down to the store at four or five tomorrow morning to get everything counted and shelved. She hoped Ben wouldn't stay too late. She still needed to catch up on her sleep.

After Ben had stayed an hour, Leah couldn't stop yawning. She tried to swallow her yawns, then hide them behind her hand, but he noticed.

"I guess all my talk about cows and milking is boring you."

"Not at all. I'm only a bit overtired."

"I know. I worry about you. You shouldn't be doing the midwifing and trying to care for the shop."

They'd had this discussion before, and Ben's solution to her dilemma was for her to give up her dream of being a midwife. Leah was much too tired to argue tonight, so she clamped her mouth shut as Ben pointed out the various reasons why becoming a midwife wasn't practical.

"The main reason, though, is that it's rather foolish to train for a career."

Why? Leah longed to retort, but Ben had made it clear his wife would not work outside the home. Not even before they had children.

Ben stopped speaking and stared at her. "I'd like to think we're finally seeing eye-to-eye on this topic, but I suspect you really are tired. You haven't argued with anything I've said."

"It's been a long week. Maybe we could spend some time together over the weekend."

"Shall I pick you up for the hymn sing on Sunday evening?"

"That sounds *wunderbar.*" Even if Sharon called about a delivery, she'd turn it down. And Kyle would be gone by then, although that was no guarantee he wouldn't be taking over her thoughts.

With a grateful heart, Leah locked the shop door and turned out the lantern after Ben left. Spending time with him had driven the crippling cramps from her mind, or maybe the tea had taken effect. The pain had been almost manageable for the past hour or so. As soon as he walked out the door, though, the spasms returned with a vengeance. With a moan, she closed the kitchen door behind her before she heated the kettle to fill a hot water bottle.

Too late she realized she'd left the lantern in the shop. Used to finding her way in the dark, she climbed the stairs to bed without a light. Hugging the hot water bottle to her, she fell into a restless sleep, dreaming about a man who wasn't Ben.

Chapter Twelve

Several times, as the car sped to the airport, Kyle opened his mouth to decline the Hesses' offer. Each time, no words came out. He was still struggling with what to say when they exited the highway and followed the DEPARTURE signs.

After he pulled up to the curb, Dr. Hess laid a hand on Kyle's arm. "Son, you don't need to tell me now. I understand it's a huge, life-changing decision. Just pray about it, and we'll talk when you're finished covering for Dr. Patel."

The tightness in Kyle's chest eased slightly. A reprieve. Unfortunately, he'd be done in two weeks.

Kyle reached out and shook the doctor's hand. "Thank you and your wife for your hospitality, and I'll let you know my decision." As soon as he could compose a polite letter of regret.

"Take your time, son. This decision will determine the

course of your future. Be sure it's what God is calling you to do." The doctor motioned toward signs saying unattended cars would be towed. "Wish I could walk you inside, but..."

With a quick nod, Kyle got out of the car. Grabbing his bag from the backseat, he thanked the doctor again for the visit and the wonderful offer before saying a quick good-bye and dashing off. Guiltily, he turned to wave, but the doctor had already pulled out into traffic.

Kyle dozed on the brief flight and woke disoriented when he landed. On the drive back to his apartment from the airport, he went over his conversation with Leah in the store. He worried about her health. Her boyfriend—or at least Kyle assumed it was her boyfriend from the jealousy gleaming in the man's eyes when he'd spotted the two of them together—had interrupted them before Kyle could secure Leah's promise to go to a doctor. He hoped she would. No one should endure such agony. He couldn't help wishing he could check on her from time to time. Only as a physician, of course.

* * *

Staring into Kyle's eyes last night had driven all rational thoughts from Leah's mind, but now in her early morning haziness, one memory from the past resurfaced. That long-ago time she'd seen Kyle, which caused a ball of dread in her stomach. As she shook off the last vestiges of sleep, reality calmed her. Perhaps she'd been mistaken he'd seen her back then. She could have sworn he'd stared right into her eyes that night, but the past few days he hadn't shown any signs he recognized her. Nevertheless, she breathed a sigh of relief knowing he was gone. She hadn't counted on him interfering with her life in other ways, though.

Taking a spoonful of the calcium supplement after breakfast and drinking her special tea relieved some of the sharpest pains, and Leah headed into the shop before dawn to unpack boxes. The lantern on the stack of cartons brought back vivid details from last night. Kyle carrying in piles of boxes, holding her hands, offering advice. The memory of his touch lingered as she opened the cartons he'd sat on, took inventory, priced items, and put them on the shelves. He not only helped, but he'd seen her pain and tried to help. He even tried to make it comfortable for her to talk about it despite her embarrassment. Ben didn't even see her pain.

Leah went back to work. She needed to erase Kyle from her mind and stop comparing him to Ben, but that proved almost impossible.

She worked until just after sunrise, then went to gather eggs and do morning chores. After *Daed* headed off to work, Leah carried a breakfast tray upstairs, but *Mamm*'s bed was empty. *Mamm* rarely got out of bed. Puzzled, Leah searched the house but found no sign of *Mamm*. She wouldn't have gone outside in this cold snap, would she? Leah hurried to the windows. The front yard and backyard were empty. Only one other place to check. The shop. But why would *Mamm* have gone in there?

When Leah opened the door to scan the aisles, a low groan came from behind the counter. She rushed toward the sound. *Mamm* lay on her back, stiff, frozen, and helpless. The phone, off the charger, beeped on the floor beside her. Her overturned walker had fallen just out of arm's reach. "What happened? Are you all right?"

"*Ach*, I'm so glad you're here." *Mamm*'s weak voice barely carried.

Leah knelt beside her and helped her to a sitting position. "How did you get down the steps?"

Mamm closed her eyes. Now wasn't the time to question her. The only time *Mamm* could have walked through the kitchen without them seeing her was when Leah and *Daed* were both outside doing chores. *Mamm* must have been lying here helpless all that time. Leah needed to get *Mamm* upstairs, but she couldn't lift her alone.

Pounding on the door startled Leah. The shop didn't open until nine. Who would be here this early?

Mamm motioned with her eyes to the door. "Answer…it."

"But we aren't open yet." And boxes still blocked the aisles. But at *Mamm*'s pleading glance, Leah headed for the door. The rapid banging began again. She moved the blinds aside a fraction of an inch to peek out and sucked in a breath. *Joel.*

Leah unlocked the door, and her brother barged in without a hello.

His head swung from side to side, scanning the store. "Where's *Mamm*?" he demanded. "She was in the middle of a sentence when I heard a thud and a loud crash. She stopped talking, but she didn't hang up."

"She's over here." Leah led him behind the counter to where she'd propped *Mamm* against the wall. "Can you help me get her upstairs?"

Joel glanced around. "Is *Daed* home?"

Leah shook her head. "He left for work."

"Good." Joel assisted *Mamm* up the stairs, and Leah marveled at his gentleness.

Once he'd helped *Mamm* into bed, Leah turned to both of them. "What's going on?"

"I have no idea." Joel appeared as baffled as Leah. "*Mamm* called and said she needed my help. Then a crash, followed by silence. She didn't answer when I asked what was wrong. I didn't know what to do except rush over here."

They both turned to *Mamm*, who smiled at Joel. "Thank you. Leah never could have managed to get me up the stairs."

Joel dipped his head in acknowledgment but said nothing. He waited for her to continue.

"The reason I called you is that Leah needs help in the store."

Thrusting his hands into the pockets of his parka, Joel shook his head. "*Daed* would never agree."

"If you offered to help, he wouldn't say *no*," *Mamm* said.

Joel shuffled his feet and looked away. "You know I'd do anything for *you*, but *Daed* made it clear I wasn't welcome in this house. Or in the store unless I joined the church."

"He let his anger get the better of him that day. I'm sure he regrets issuing that ultimatum. Maybe if you give him a chance to apologize?"

Leah suspected *Mamm* of being overly optimistic. *Daed* hadn't changed his stance so seeing Joel would set off sparks.

"If not for me, please do it for your sister. She's trying to train as a midwife and court Ben. And now that I have fewer and fewer good days, she's taken over all my household chores." *Mamm* lowered her eyes and plucked at the bedcovers. "She's also taken on the burden of caring for me."

Leah rushed to reassure her. "You're not a burden. I'm happy to take care of you."

Joel shuffled his feet. "I didn't realize. I'm sorry I haven't been here for you, *Mamm*. You never mentioned anything in your letters."

They'd been writing letters? So that's how *Mamm* had learned of Joel's job loss. Leah had assumed someone from town had passed along gossip.

Mamm waved away his apology. "You couldn't have known. Now that you do, will you help?"

"Only if *Daed* asks me."

Leah tried not to let her disappointment show. Joel would be the perfect solution. He'd run the store from the time he was sixteen, so he'd need no training. She could easily explain the new product lines they carried. The only obstacle was *Daed*'s anger. Leah doubted *Daed* would unbend enough to allow Joel to take over.

"I'll see what I can do," *Mamm* assured him.

Daed only worked half days on Saturdays. After he came home, Leah mentioned *Mamm*'s fall, although she didn't give the reason. He rushed upstairs and stayed closeted with *Mamm* in the bedroom for several hours. When he came downstairs, he had tears in his eyes.

"Why don't you take a break for a few hours, *dochder*? I'll mind the store."

Grateful for a chance to drink more tea, Leah hurried

into the kitchen. She'd been fighting off the awful pangs for the last hour or two. After pouring boiling water over the herbs in her teacup, she filled a hot water bottle. She should study her midwifery books, but instead she clutched the hot water bottle to her and fell asleep.

Soon she and Kyle strolled together hand in hand, while she explained the benefits of herbs. He listened to, and agreed with, every word she spoke.

A hand shaking her shoulder almost dragged her from dreamland. "Kyle?" she begged, stretching out a hand to prevent him from disappearing.

"What?" *Daed*'s voice startled her awake.

Leah opened her eyes to find him standing over her. Had she spoken Kyle's name aloud? Her face burned at the thought, but her heart longed to return to those fleeting moments. The fantasy that she and Kyle were enjoying a meaningful conversation about herbs without arguing. That alone signaled it had been a dream. If it had been real life, Kyle would have argued every point.

Dragging herself back to the present, she sat upright. Nobody ever napped in the middle of the day. *Daed* would consider her lazy. "I'll be right out." She jumped up, and the hot water bottle tumbled to the floor at his feet. Leah scrambled to grab it and tuck it behind her skirt.

Daed studied her. "Are you feeling ill?"

How did she answer that? Leah avoided *Daed*'s eyes. "No." She wasn't sick, just enduring the pain she faced every month. "I'm sorry I didn't come back to work."

"No need." *Daed* stared down at the wooden floorboards as if the pattern of the whorls fascinated him. "Your *mamm* made other arrangements."

"Joel?" Leah blurted out.

Daed winced. "Yes. I've made my peace."

Despite her pain, Leah's heart danced. It would be wonderful to have her brother back in their lives. She'd missed him so much.

His head bowed, *Daed* cleared his throat. "Will you forgive me for my anger toward him and for setting a poor example? Pride dictated my actions rather than forgiveness."

A lump in her throat, Leah nodded. "Of course." Her brain still foggy from sleep, she struggled to comprehend what this meant. Would Joel come to family meals? Be welcome to visit any time? Would she still need to work in the shop, or would she be free to pursue midwifing?

"I'm sorry for making you work so hard. *Mamm* warned me I was running you ragged. I see she was right."

"Don't blame yourself." She couldn't explain why she was napping, so she changed the subject. "I'd better go help Joel with the unpacking." Before she went into the shop, she fixed a cup of tea for herself and a calming one for Joel. He'd probably need it.

When she entered the shop, the stacks of cartons had dwindled to only a few, and Joel was waiting on a long line of customers. He appeared competent with the cash register but uneasy around the shoppers, because many of them grilled him about his life. Quite a few saw it as a sign Joel planned to rejoin the church. He deflected their questions.

Leah had hoped reconciling with *Daed* might bring Joel back to the church, but evidently not. She pushed aside her sadness to unpack boxes, direct customers to the correct aisles, and answer the phone. After the last shopper of the day exited, Leah locked up and turned to Joel.

What did you say to a brother you hadn't seen in years? How did you express all the feelings in your heart? "Welcome back," she said shyly.

"Thanks." In contrast to his genuine smile, Joel's voice sounded gruff, but maybe he was struggling with pent-up emotion too.

"I'm so happy you're here."

"I bet you are, so you don't have to work." The twinkle in his eye revealed he was teasing.

His joking broke the ice and put them both back on familiar footing. "Of course." She tossed her head, then broke into giggles. "Seriously, I'm glad you're back. In the store and in our lives."

"I know you are, sis. And I feel the same." Joel's eyes were damp. "If you don't mind handling the closing, I'll run up to spend some time with *Mamm*."

After Joel headed upstairs, Leah closed out the cash register and went through the order book to prepare for Monday pickups.

Hmm. Naomi would need a refill on her prenatal vitamins. Because Naomi couldn't afford them, Leah usually paid for them out of shop profits, but sometimes the Hesses bought them for her. Kyle had purchased that brand last night. Maybe the Hesses planned to give them to Naomi. Leah picked up the phone and called Esther.

"Yes, they were for her," Esther said.

"All right, then we'll cover the next order."

"She's going to need a lot of help, especially after the new baby comes," Esther said. "Taking care of two children with special needs is a lot to handle with a newborn."

Naomi was part of the group of friends who'd joined the church with her. "Our buddy bunch will be there for her. We're planning to take over casseroles, and some of the others have been babysitting to give her a break. With my work schedule, I haven't been able to help with that."

"I've been praying for you. You work much too hard."

"Actually, Joel's going to take over the store. That'll free me up to work with Sharon, assist Ada with wedding planning, and help Naomi." And find time for Ben. He shouldn't have come last on her priority list.

"I'm so glad to hear that. Martin and I can't wait for Kyle to take over the practice."

Leah drew in a quick breath. "So he's decided to come?"

"Well, he hasn't given us a definite yes, but we're praying."

Inside, Leah's feelings warred with her common sense. As much as she hoped Kyle would return, she wasn't sure she wanted to argue with him over remedies. Last night, they'd had a good time together, though. And in her dreams, he listened to her. If only he would do that in real life.

Chapter Thirteen

During the whirlwind last days of covering for Dr. Patel, other opportunities for his future pushed Dr. Hess's offer from Kyle's mind. All the possibilities he considered would move him closer to his dreams, and he weighed the pros and cons of each. While comparing advantages and disadvantages, he never included the Lancaster practice on the list, although from time to time the pull of Leah's presence filled him with longing and the debt of gratitude he owed the Hesses filled him with regret.

After days of deliberation, he settled on his final fellowship choices, and he accepted another position as a covering physician at one of the top hospitals in the country beginning in January. Now he needed to let Dr. Hess know his plans. That call weighed on him. How could he explain his decision? Instead of feeling lighter and relieved by his choice, guilt gnawed at him. He cared about the doctor and his wife. Hurting them troubled his conscience, but his most important consideration had to be for his future.

Not a day went by, though, that he didn't think of Leah. Of course, he assured himself he was only concerned about her health. Several times he picked up the phone to call Dr. Hess to see if he'd check on her, but then he'd also need to give the doctor an answer about taking over his practice.

A few times Kyle even toyed with the idea of calling the natural products shop to hear Leah's voice. He even programmed the shop number into his phone. He could ask if she'd gone to the doctor and say he wondered if his diagnosis was correct. He jerked his thoughts from Leah. What was wrong with him?

After Kyle finished his final day of work, he went back to his apartment and crashed. Eighteen hours later, he woke, groggy and hungry. He'd give himself a few days off to relax, and then he'd start on the fellowship applications.

The phone rang in the middle of the night. He fumbled around on his bedside table to find it in the dark and caught it right before his answering machine clicked on.

"Kyle?" The woman sounded close to tears.

He managed a *hmm*, but his brain hadn't kicked in yet. Who would be calling at this time of night?

"Martin had a heart attack. I'm at the hospital with him now. Is there any way you could fly here and take over his practice while he recovers?"

Martin? Kyle fought to process the name, the request. Slowly, the fog in his brain dissipated, and answers kicked in. *Lancaster. Dr. Hess. Leah. No, not Leah.* "The doctor had a heart attack?"

"Yes, he's in the ICU. We'll pay whatever it costs if you can fly here to help."

The last thing Kyle wanted to do was go back there, but how could he say no? Now was not the time to inform her he didn't plan to take over the practice. She had enough to deal with. "I'll catch the first flight out."

"Thank you. You don't know what this means to us. I'll ask our neighbor to unlock the office, and I'll pray for safe travels."

Kyle hesitated. He wanted to comfort her by saying he'd be praying for her husband, but he had no business asking God for favors. "I hope everything goes well for Martin."

"It's in God's hands."

Kyle's stomach clenched remembering praying for his mother. He'd hate to see that outcome for the doctor. He hurried through the good-byes and flicked on the light. So much for getting a good night's sleep. And there went his vacation.

For now, though, he needed to book a flight and pack. He reached for his computer and found a flight leaving in three hours. If the doctor had patients first thing in the morning, he'd be late, but he should be able to handle appointments from ten o'clock on.

After throwing his things into a suitcase, he texted Esther his arrival time and said he'd get a rental car. Then he sped to the airport and made it in time to check his bag, wind his way through security, and board.

Too tense to sleep, Kyle sat rigid in his seat. He'd been working with skilled doctors, so he always had someone he could ask about his diagnoses if he was uncertain. How could he handle the office on his own? What if he made a mistake? Misdiagnosed someone? Gave out the wrong prescription? Perhaps most of his patients would be Amish and would check with Leah for herbal remedies.

Kyle didn't want to admit to himself that the main reason he couldn't sleep wasn't only fear. His logical brain told him he was making a mistake, but his emotions refused to listen. Part of him danced with excitement knowing he'd be seeing Leah again.

* * *

Now that Joel had taken charge of the shop, Leah could spend more time making breakfast, so she whipped up batter for pancakes, her brother's favorite breakfast. She opened the kitchen door to hear when he came in. She'd finished serving *Mamm* and *Daed* when the phone in the shop rang. She rushed to answer it, hoping Joel wasn't canceling.

Esther Hess said a quick hello before plunging into her reason for calling. She explained about Martin's heart attack and added, "I've been with Martin all night. I need to cancel the appointments before ten o'clock, and I remembered your next-door neighbor has an early appointment. Could you let Barbara Beiler know?"

"Of course." Barbara didn't have a phone, so they were used to taking messages for her. "I'll run right over now. Is there anything I can do for you? If you want to stay with Martin, I could have Joel drive me to the office, and I could cancel the rest of the appointments."

"Oh, would you be able to do that?" The relief in Esther's voice made Leah glad she'd offered.

"I'd be happy to. As soon as Joel arrives, I'll head over. And I'll be praying."

"Thank you, dear. We both appreciate that. Mary Esh next door has a key, but the records room also has a keypad." After giving Leah the code to open that door, Esther hung up.

Joel usually arrived early. If he did, maybe he could drive her over to the office to give her enough time to warn the morning patients. Leah went into the house to inform her parents and ran next door to let Barbara know. Then she waited by the shop door for Joel to pull in. Before he could turn off the engine, she waved and hurried over. He agreed to take her, and she arrived at the office before eight thirty.

She had no trouble canceling the *Englisch* patients, but she was unable to reach some of the Amish ones. She'd wait for them and tell them in person. Esther had sounded so worried Leah hadn't thought to ask her what arrangements had been made for the patients who were coming in after ten.

While she waited, she sorted through the files Esther had stacked on the table in the long, narrow file room. Leah matched them to the appointment list from the reception desk. The first stack held the morning's patient files. The one next to it contained afternoon records. Each one had been placed in order.

A car pulled into the driveway, and someone banged on the back door. Regular patients always came to the front door. Leah hesitated to answer. Perhaps it was a delivery, though. She lifted the blind enough to peek out, and her heart stuttered. Kyle stood on the doorstep. Why hadn't Esther mentioned him?

Kyle appeared as stunned to see her as she was to see him. Their eyes locked, and Leah might have gazed at him all day if he hadn't mouthed, *May I come in?*

She couldn't believe she'd left him standing in the cold while she stared at him. Her face burned, and with stiff, nervous fingers, she fumbled to unlock the door. "I'm sorry. I, um, wasn't expecting you."

"I wasn't expecting you either. I assumed one of Esther's neighbors would be here." He didn't sound too happy.

"I volunteered to come over so she could stay with Martin." Leah hastened to assure him, "Don't worry. I won't be here long. I only need to wait for two more Amish patients I couldn't reach."

"Oh. I, um…" Kyle hesitated, then said abruptly, "I need to hang up my coat."

Was she mistaken, or did he look disappointed? Was he counting on some assistance for the day? She wasn't a nurse, but she could act as a receptionist. She followed him into the hallway as he headed for the doctor's office. "If you need help, I could stay."

"I appreciate that, but I don't want you to close up the shop on my account." Kyle kept his back to her as he set his suitcase on a chair, removed his coat, and hung it in the small closet.

The muscles rippling under his sweater distracted her so much Leah struggled to put together a coherent sentence. "The shop?" Oh, right. Kyle didn't know about the changes. "I'm not working at the shop anymore."

"You're not?" Kyle turned. "You closed it?"

Leah couldn't decide which was more unnerving—staring at his back or meeting his eyes. Definitely his eyes. She broke contact and took a deep breath to calm her fluttering nerves. Her conscience needled her. She had no business entertaining feelings like this for another man, when she'd committed to courting Ben. Being attracted to Kyle was wrong, but him being an *Englischer* only made things worse.

When she didn't answer, Kyle repeated his question.

Leah pushed her attraction to him from her mind to focus on the conversation, but she had trouble coming up with more than a one-word answer. "No, no."

"So you didn't sell it?"

"No." Now she was sounding like a parrot. She needed to get a grip on herself. "My brother is running the store now."

Kyle leaned over and clicked the locks on his silver metal suitcase. Leah turned her head as he opened the lid. Although she was curious, she shouldn't be looking at his clothing or other private items. Plastic crinkled, but she fought the temptation to peek until the locks clicked into place.

Kyle donned his white lab coat before speaking again. "I guess that allows you more time for being a midwife?" He didn't sound particularly happy about that.

Leah tried to tune back in to the conversation instead of watching his strong, competent hands button the lab coat. "Yes, yes, it does."

"I'm not sure about this." Kyle motioned toward his chest.

Nothing wrong with his broad, muscular chest that

she could see. "It looks fine to me," Leah blurted out and then wished she could stuff the words back into her mouth.

"Well, some hospitals banned these because of germs"—he tugged on his lab coat—"but I noticed Dr. Hess wears one in the office, so I figured patients here would prefer it."

"Germs?" Leah's voice squeaked. Her thoughts hadn't been on medicine. Or lab coats, for that matter.

"Don't worry. Some recent studies have refuted that, and I had all my coats packed in plastic to keep them as germ-free as possible after they're laundered. But they can pick up germs during exams."

Leah swallowed hard before answering to keep her tone normal. "I'm sure they'll be fine." One look at him, and the last thing on anyone's mind would be germs. Or was she the only one he affected that way?

A buzzing filled the hall. The front door. Someone had entered the waiting room. Leah hurried out to greet the patient. But Kyle's voice followed her down the hall. "If you could stay for a short while until I get set up, I'd appreciate it."

"Of course," Leah called back. But was she making a big mistake?

* * *

Kyle sat at the desk, taking deep calming breaths. He'd been nervous enough about doing this solo, but seeing Leah again…

He had to compose himself before the first patient. Deep breathing didn't help. Why had he asked her to stay? He'd have enough to handle with seeing patients without having to fight his attraction to Leah.

Jumping to his feet, he paced back and forth in the small office. Even that didn't reduce the tension. Why had he agreed to come back here? What if he harmed a patient?

He jumped when Leah tapped on the door. "I put Elmer Jones in exam room one. He's had a sore throat for two weeks."

"Thank you." With an effort, Kyle slipped a prescription pad into his pocket, put on his professional doctor expression, and strode toward the room, trying to project confidence.

Ahead of him, Leah swished down the hall. He stopped for a moment and closed his eyes until she returned to the waiting room. Shutting thoughts of her from his mind, he opened his eyes, put his hand on the doorknob, and entered the exam room.

The first diagnosis was easy. "I'll just swab your throat and do a rapid test here. Should have some results for you in ten minutes or so. I'll be right back."

Leah had put another patient in the next exam room. He crossed the hall to do a well-baby checkup. Another easy one. Leah had already weighed and measured the baby, which helped. Watching her cradling a baby set his heart thumping. He avoided brushing against her as she held the baby on the exam table.

"Your son is very healthy," Kyle reassured the young mother, who smiled at him. "I take it he's a good eater. He's gained weight well since the last visit." He glanced at the chart again. "Zander does need one shot this time."

When the mother grimaced, Leah asked, "Would you prefer to hold him here or shall I?"

The mother stood. "I can do it. Thank you."

Kyle wouldn't have thought to ask, but Leah's caring nature had made the mother feel more comfortable. She'd make a good nurse. Too bad she didn't have her training.

After he gave the infant the shot, Leah and the mother redressed the baby, and he ducked back into the first exam room to check the results. "It's strep throat, Mr. Jones. I'll write you a prescription." He scribbled a prescription for antibiotics on the tablet.

As they passed in the hall for the next few patients, Kyle imagined Leah was one of the nurses at the hospital. He adopted a brusque tone to keep his distance, but even that barrier didn't hold back his feelings. He was grateful for her assistance, but keeping his interest hidden was proving difficult.

By lunchtime, Kyle couldn't wait for a break. Although he'd been there only two hours, he'd seen seven patients, and he still had all afternoon to slog through. He should send Leah home, but she'd been invaluable all morning. How would he manage without her this afternoon?

He sank into the office chair and lowered his head into his hands. If only he could take a quick nap. Being up most of the night—plus the tension of the morning—had drained him.

"Are you all right?" Leah's soft voice behind him startled him.

He nodded but didn't turn. Looking at her when he was so vulnerable would destroy the façade he'd built of a professional doctor.

"I'll make you some lunch. I found the key to the house in Esther's desk drawer. I'm sure she won't mind if I make you a sandwich."

"You don't need to do that."

"You can't keep going at this pace without something to eat." Leah walked out the door before he could reply.

She returned a short while later with a thick slice of meatloaf between homemade wheat bread slices slathered with mustard and mayonnaise. She'd loaded the plate with coleslaw, chips, and pickles. A large portion of berry cobbler with whipped cream completed the lunch.

Kyle's eyes lit up when she carried the food into the office. "Thank you. That looks delicious, but if this is what the doctor's been eating, no wonder he had a heart attack."

"I'm guessing the heart attack came from stress. He works much too hard."

Was that a dig at him? Kyle dipped his fork into the coleslaw so he didn't have to meet her eyes. Would the doctor have been less stressed if Kyle had accepted his offer earlier? He chewed slowly to avoid responding. Even if she hadn't meant it as a criticism, he carried the guilt of knowing he planned to turn down Dr. Hess when he needed to retire.

When he lifted his gaze from the plate, Leah seemed to be studying him, but she glanced toward the window. If he hadn't been mistaken, she'd blushed. He checked to see what had caught her interest behind him, but the blinds were closed. Was she as interested in him as he was in her? If so, it would make it much harder to keep his distance.

Leah reached for his plate as soon as he finished. "I'll wash that and be right back. The one o'clock patient may come early."

She planned to stay for the afternoon? Kyle tried to tamp down the happiness flooding through him.

You can't fall for an Amish girl. It would be a major mistake.

* * *

Leah rushed to the kitchen to wash the dishes. Her hurry to return to the office had less to do with early arrivals and more to do with wanting to be around Kyle.

Dipping her hands into the sudsy water, she scolded herself. Allowing herself to spend time with a man who attracted her betrayed her promise to Ben. She should leave as soon as the first afternoon patient arrived. The less time she was around Kyle, the better.

But who would check in the patients and explain Dr. Hess's absence? Who would lead them back to the exam rooms, file their charts, and answer the phone? Kyle had too much to do. Leaving him here alone with all this work on his first day would be unfair. No matter what it cost her, she'd help him. After all, she owed Esther and Martin more than she could ever repay. The doctor made frequent house calls now that *Mamm* couldn't get around much. And when money was tight, he'd accepted eggs and milk as payment. Helping to keep their practice running would serve as a tiny repayment. She just had to keep Kyle from discovering her feelings.

The afternoon went even more smoothly than the morning, but Leah breathed a sigh of relief when she escorted the last patient back to an exam room. She tidied the waiting room, straightened the reception desk, and pulled files for the next day and placed them in two neat stacks the way Esther had. Then she waited for the final patient to settle his bill and exit. She locked the cash box in a drawer in the file room and used the codes Esther had given her to lock that door and the storeroom that held sample medicines.

Kyle remained holed up in the doctor's office. Joel would be here soon. Leah overcame her eagerness to get away—to escape, really—from her fascination with Kyle, but she had to make sure he had the codes to the building.

She tapped on the heavy mahogany door, and a faint *come in* drifted out. When she entered, Kyle had his back to the door. He lifted one of the wooden slats in the blinds to peer out into the backyard. Through the slit, trees lifted leafless branches to the overcast sky.

"Are you all right?" she asked.

"I'm fine." His clipped tone indicated he'd rather not talk.

Leah couldn't go without assuring herself he'd be all right. "Esther has a few leftovers in the refrigerator. I could heat something for your dinner."

"I'll be fine. I know how to use a microwave. All I've been eating most days for the past few years are containers of reheated leftovers."

"That's a shame." Leah couldn't imagine what it would be like to eat rewarmed food almost every night. "Don't you ever have home-cooked meals?"

Kyle made a sound that resembled a snort. "Other than the delicious meals I had here at the Hesses', I can't recall any. Few of us make it through med school and residencies without relying on takeout, cafeteria meals, and leftovers."

Leah started to reply that it was sad, but she closed her mouth. He didn't seem to be the type to appreciate pity. Maybe she could bring him a meal tomorrow. Nobody should work hard all day and not have a hearty supper afterward. "Joel's probably waiting, so I need to go. Would you like me to come tomorrow?"

Kyle dropped the blind slat he'd been holding but stayed facing the window. "I don't think—"

"Someone should be in the office to greet patients and answer the phone." Why was she pushing this when he clearly didn't want her here? Still, she couldn't leave him alone. She'd been busy the whole day, and so had he. He might not realize everything she'd done today, but no way could he handle all those responsibilities in addition to seeing patients.

"I suppose." His response was so lackluster Leah regretted offering. Still, it wouldn't be right to let Dr. Hess's patients down. She should do this for his sake.

Leah tried to ignore the niggling question in the back of her mind. *So you aren't doing this to spend more time around Kyle?*

Chapter Fourteen

Kyle stayed facing the window until the door clicked shut behind Leah. As much as he wished to have one last glimpse of her, the rational part of his mind overruled his desires. He'd be glad when he finished substituting for Dr. Hess. Keeping his feelings hidden would be difficult if Leah came in every day.

Heaving a sigh, he stood and headed for the office door. He'd just stepped into the hallway when the side door burst open and Leah dashed in. Racing too fast to stop, she barreled into his chest. Instinctively, he reached out to steady her and wrapped his arms around her, drawing her close to his chest.

She relaxed against him for a second and lifted her arms. For a moment, he dreamed she was about to wrap her arms around him. Then, her eyes wide and round, she pressed her hands against his chest and wriggled backward.

Reluctantly, he released her and stepped a safe distance away.

Her cheeks had turned a becoming shade of pink. "I—I'm sorry. I, um…forgot to tell you…the code."

Was she out of breath because she'd been running? Or had she had the same reaction to him that he'd had to her?

"The code?" Still tantalized by her nearness, he could barely concentrate. He thrust his hands into his lab coat pockets to prevent himself from reaching out.

"The code…to the door."

"Oh, right."

She rattled off the code so rapidly the numbers ran together.

Kyle held up a hand. "Wait a minute. I'd better write this down." Before thoughts of holding her crowded out the random digits she was reciting. Before he did something he'd regret, like stepping closer. Or enfolding her in his arms again.

He ducked into the office to regain his composure and emerged holding a tablet and a pen. Leah repeated the code, and he kept his head down as he wrote. "Thanks." His gaze remained glued to the paper even after he'd finished writing the final number.

"Joel is waiting." Leah turned and scurried down the hall.

This time Kyle didn't have the safety of the office to prevent him from watching her leave. After the door closed behind her, he walked the short distance down the hall to click the lock into place but couldn't resist lifting the blinds to peek out.

Leah was getting into a car with an *Englischer*. She'd

said Joel was picking her up. Was she dating an *Englischer*? What about the fiery-eyed Amish man— Ben, wasn't it?—who'd entered the store the night Kyle had returned the boxes? He'd assumed from Ben's jealousy he was courting Leah. Had they broken up?

As the car pulled away, Kyle shook his head. If she chose to date *Englischers*, it was no business of his. Except it made the attraction he'd been struggling to suppress even harder to resist. After the car lights disappeared in the distance, he let the blinds drift back into place. Those retreating taillights reminded him of his life. Everyone he loved ended up leaving him.

Warning himself not to fall for another woman who could only bring heartache, he trudged down the hall and into the house to microwave leftovers and spend the evening alone. While his food heated, he called the hospital for an update on Dr. Hess. Then he rang the doctor's cell phone but got no answer. He left a message, letting the doctor know the day had gone well.

If only he had someone else he could call to fill the silence. But working long hours a week as a resident and then traveling to different states to work as a covering physician had left him little time for friendships. And with his past, he had little desire for relationships.

Maybe the combination of more leisure time here in the Lancaster area and Leah's constant presence might explain his attraction. Or maybe not. He'd been drawn to her during his earlier visit, when he'd been bone weary and irritated with her natural remedies. He'd been surprised she hadn't contradicted him today when he handed out prescriptions, but maybe she'd done that later while the patients paid their bills. It should upset him, but for some reason, it made him smile. Had he become so besotted with her he'd endanger his patients? Kyle shook his head. He had to find some way to get her off his mind.

After he finished his solitary meal, he wandered through the downstairs rooms. What would it be like to settle in one place and live in a house like this? After moving to several cities to fill in for other doctors, he'd become used to empty apartments, take-out meals, and reheated food. Somehow, though, being in the Hesses' warm, cheery home—perfect for a large, loving family—added to the longing in his heart for closeness and connection.

Instead, he faced another lonely night, warmed only by the memory of holding Leah in his arms.

*   *   *

Leah woke the next morning with Kyle on her mind. Not only had she been dreaming of him, but last night before she fell asleep, she'd decided to be sure he ate some decent meals. She had no idea how long he'd be here, but if he spent all day with patients, he needed nourishing food. While she fixed breakfast, she prepared two meals to put in the Hesses' refrigerator.

Joel arrived early to drive her to the doctor's office, and she appreciated the warmth of the car and her brother's willingness to take her. She'd have frozen if she'd driven the carriage in this wintry weather. Joel seemed glad for the opportunity to chatter about his plans for expanding and improving the shop. Leah didn't want to deflate his eagerness by asking if he'd run his ideas by *Daed*, so she murmured encouragement. Many of his suggestions would attract new customers. Leah hoped *Daed* would step back and let her brother manage the shop.

"All those sound great," she said. "I hope you can do them."

Joel's face twisted. "You mean, will *Daed* let me try them?"

Although *Daed* had asked Joel's forgiveness and welcomed him back into the family, their father remained wary about trusting his non-Amish son with major decisions.

A touch of bitterness in his tone, Joel said, "I may not be with the church, but that doesn't mean I've changed my morals."

A buggy pulled out in front of them, and he slowed to its pace but craned his neck, evidently watching for a clear stretch of road so he could pass.

Leah reached over and laid a hand on his arm. "Give him some time. He believes your decision to leave the Amish means you've turned your back on all our teachings."

"It doesn't." Joel almost shouted the words. Then he glanced over at her. "I'm sorry. I didn't mean to yell at you. Not when you and *Mamm* seem to understand."

"It isn't easy, but if you give *Daed* some time, he'll come around."

"I hope so," Joel muttered, zipping around the buggy. When they neared Dr. Hess's office, he took his foot off the gas and flicked on his turn signal. They coasted into the driveway, and Joel pulled into a parking space. "Thanks for listening."

Leah smiled at him. "You're welcome. And thank you for the ride. And even more importantly, thank you for taking over the shop. I'm looking forward to having more time to train with Sharon."

Joel tipped his head toward the doctor's office. "How do you plan to do that when you're here every day?"

"I called Sharon yesterday to let her know I'd be here for a few days until Esther can come back. I just pray we aren't both needed at two different places at the same time again."

"I'll pray too." When her eyebrows shot up, he protested. "Just because I didn't join the church doesn't mean I don't believe in God or prayer."

Leah regretted her automatic response, but Joel's admission eased her worries. "I'm glad you still have your faith. If you reassured *Daed* about that, it might smooth things over."

"Maybe," he said, but he sounded doubtful.

"At least try." She got out and slid her heavy bag from the backseat. "Have a good day," she said before she shut the car door.

A curtain on the second floor of the house fluttered into place as she crossed the parking lot. Had Kyle been watching them? Perhaps he'd only been checking to see if a patient had arrived early.

Leah punched in the code and entered. She locked up behind her and headed down the hall. She'd reached the reception area when the door to the house creaked open and Kyle stepped out, his hair still damp and slightly tousled, as if he'd just emerged from the shower. His white lab coat highlighted his crisp appearance and...

She lowered her gaze. "Is it all right if I put a few things in the Hesses' refrigerator?"

"That looks awfully heavy. Do you need some help?" Kyle reached for the bag.

Leah drew back the bag before he touched it. "I can manage." Her tone was sharper than she'd intended, because Kyle's offer had started a strange fluttering in her heart. No one had ever coddled her before. That's what Ben would call it. He'd expect her to handle it herself.

"If you're sure." Kyle opened the door to the house and held it for her.

Leah released a pent-up breath when it swung shut behind her. She unpacked the food and hurried back to the office. As long as they had no emergencies to take them past lunch, she'd slip into the house right before their scheduled lunch break to fix Kyle a hearty meal. Kyle had retreated to his office, so she could breathe easier. At least until the first patient arrived.

The brisk pace of the morning appointments kept Leah's thoughts from Kyle, except when she'd announce a patient's arrival or assist with appointments. Then she spent a few moments waiting for her pulse to slow to a normal level before answering the phone or greeting new arrivals.

While Kyle was in the exam room with the last patient of the morning, she headed into the house to heat her homemade chicken corn soup and make Lebanon bologna sandwiches on potato rolls. She added red beet eggs, canned pickles, and broccoli slaw. She'd just managed to sneak the food into the records room when Kyle emerged from the exam room with the patient, Mr.

Garcia. She hurried into the hallway and shut the door, but Mr. Garcia sniffed the air.

"Something smells good. Can I join you for lunch?" His eyes twinkled.

"Of course," Leah said. She'd give him her plate. She could cobble together a few things for her own lunch.

Mr. Garcia laughed. "I was only teasing. I have my own lunch waiting for me back at the office."

"I hope it's a healthy one."

At Kyle's stern tone, Mr. Garcia looked sheepish. "Not today. I promise from now on I'll do better."

"Until we get those numbers down, no sugar and limit your carbs." He turned to Leah. "Does Dr. Hess have any pamphlets or printed diet sheets for managing diabetes?"

The soup would get cold while she rummaged through drawers looking for information, but the patient's health came first. "I'll check at the desk."

Mr. Garcia and Kyle followed her out to the reception area and waited while she opened drawers. In the bottom drawer, neatly lettered folders listed various health conditions. She removed a handout from the one marked DIABETES and handed it to Mr. Garcia.

"I expect you to follow that." Kyle folded his arms across his chest, looking every inch a commanding doctor, and Leah's heart fluttered.

She turned her attention back to the paper. *Ben*, *Ben*, she repeated to herself. She shouldn't allow another man to affect her like this. Not when she and Ben were courting.

Mr. Garcia glanced over the paper. "It won't be easy, doc, but I'll try. You do know you're taking away all my favorite foods."

"You'll just have to make some new favorites," Kyle suggested. "Like vegetables."

Wrinkling his nose, Mr. Garcia nodded and reached for the door. "Enjoy your lunch," he said, closing it behind him.

* * *

Kyle's stomach rumbled at the warm, homey smells coming from the other room. "Your lunch does smell delicious," he admitted, heading for the door to the house.

Another meal of leftovers for him, though. At least the food in the Hesses' full refrigerator was more appetizing than the usual take-out containers he pulled from the refrigerators in his temporary apartments. And Esther had told him to help himself to anything.

"Wait. Where are you going?" Leah stepped toward him. "I brought lunch for both of us."

"You did what?" Kyle couldn't keep incredulousness from creeping into his voice. She'd made him lunch yesterday, but feeding him every day wasn't part of her volunteer duties. "You don't need to do that."

She hung her head as if he'd scolded her. Had his tone sounded that way?

"I just thought... well, you might be hungry."

"You thought right, and I'm not upset with you. It's just that you don't have a responsibility to feed me." Although deep inside, he was grateful—more than grateful—she had.

Leah headed for the records room, and he followed, his stomach growling. She opened the door and handed him a full plate and a bowl of soup. "The Bible says we're to feed the hungry. A doctor who doesn't eat breakfast probably qualifies."

"How did you know I didn't eat breakfast?" he demanded as he inhaled the rich chicken-scented broth and the vinegary tang of the pickled eggs.

Her cheeks darkened to deep cherry. "Well, when you came down this morning..." She waved in the direction of his hair, then lowered her eyes.

So she'd figured out he'd rushed down here straight from the shower when he saw her in the parking lot. At least she wasn't looking at him, because the color of his face probably matched hers.

"I'm afraid the soup is probably cold by now."

Kyle didn't care. He'd eat it at any temperature. He set his plate down on a nearby shelf and tried a spoonful. "It's the perfect temperature." His spirits rose at her faint smile. "We can't stand here to eat, though." He almost invited her into the house but stopped the words before they left his lips. The two of them at the table in a house made for loving families...

"Maybe we could eat at our desks."

No, he wanted to shout, although it would be the wisest course of action. "Why don't we eat in Dr. Hess's office?" Perhaps the solemnity of the mahogany-paneled room would dampen his desire to cup her face in his hands and thank her by pressing a kiss on her lips.

He motioned for her to precede him down the hall and then regretted it. Following her didn't reduce the temptation to take her in his arms.

After he'd settled into the old-fashioned oak chair with rollers, Leah took the hard-backed chair nearby and set her plate on the edge of the desk. Somehow, the office that had seemed massive earlier today now shrank until it seemed claustrophobic, and he could barely draw in a breath.

Kyle forced himself to concentrate on each spoonful overflowing with carrots, celery, corn, chicken, and noodles that he lifted to his mouth. Hearty and tasty, and so much like his mother's. "Delicious," he murmured. He could have eaten several bowls of soup if he didn't have a full plate waiting for him.

He took one bite of the sandwich and closed his eyes, letting the sweet and smoky tang of Lebanon bologna linger on his tongue.

"Are you all right?"

At the alarm in Leah's voice, he forced his eyes open. "Just reminiscing. It's been years since I had this." He held up the potato roll stuffed with Lebanon bologna, cheese, and mustard. After he left Pennsylvania for college and med school, he had no place to buy his favorite lunch meat. "My mom used to make this for my school lunches."

Leah's smile invited him to confide more.

"Mom's been gone since I was in high school, but I still miss her." Kyle glanced toward the ceiling, but his eyes hardly registered the brass-and-glass light fixture overhead. Instead, he stood at the kitchen counter while his mom made and packed sandwiches for three lunches—one for him, one for his dad, and one for his brother, Caleb. If only he'd known that night would be the last one he'd ever spend with her . . .

Kyle's throat tightened. He'd gobbled the two sandwiches from his brown paper lunch bag the next day.

If only he'd known the news that would greet him after school, he would have savored every bite rather than scarfing them down.

"Kyle?" Leah's soft question broke through the mist of pain.

"I'm sorry." He swallowed hard. "The last sandwiches she made me were ones like this. I sat in the school cafeteria eating them, never realizing she'd be gone by the time I got home from school."

"Oh, I'm so sorry. I didn't mean to bring back bad memories."

Kyle shook his head. "You had no idea. And I still love the taste." Even if the memories accompanying it were bitter. "I just wish I could go back and relive the night before. She'd forced me to sit in the kitchen to do my homework so she could keep an eye on me while she prepared our lunches for the next day. I fumed and complained. If only I'd known"— he choked back the lump in his throat—"I would have told her I loved her."

"Oh, Kyle…"

"When she lay unconscious in the hospital hooked up to a ventilator, I told her again and again. But could she hear?"

If only I'd known…

Those words had followed him every day since then.

If only he'd known the destruction his careless driving would cause…

If only he'd known how much pain he'd go through because he dated an Amish girl…

Leah leaned forward and placed a hand on his arm.

The warmth of her touch spread down through the tips of his fingers. The images of his past slowly faded until they were replaced by her caring expression. It hit Kyle with a jolt—he'd fallen for her. And fallen hard. But this time there'd be no *if only*s.

Chapter Fifteen

Lunch was so intimate Leah struggled to eat. Maybe making meals for him had been a mistake. No, that part was fine. Where she'd made her mistake was sitting in the office with him. He was much too close for comfort. And after hearing his heartbreaking story, the urge to comfort him had been strong. She never should have touched his arm. Her only goal had been to ease his distress, but the jolt that went through her...

She should have insisted on sitting at the reception desk. That's what she'd do tomorrow. Or better yet, she wouldn't come in tomorrow. That would be wiser. But how would Kyle handle the desk and the patients alone? She shouldn't leave him without any office support. For the next few days, she'd be professional and helpful but keep her distance. As much as she enjoyed his company, she'd avoid being alone with him in the future.

The minute she finished her meal, she stood. "I'll take the dishes to the kitchen."

Kyle removed the plate from her hand. "No. In this house, the doctor washes the dishes. I plan to follow his example."

"You have patients coming," Leah protested.

"Won't take long to rinse them and load them in the dishwasher. Although Martin and Esther enjoy washing them together." His face flushed. "I didn't mean you had to help." He gathered the plates and fled.

She must make him as flustered as he made her. Maybe he'd sensed her attraction, and it made him ill at ease around her.

To keep from focusing on him, she prepped the files for the afternoon appointments and made a note about the diet handout before she filed Mr. Garcia's thick folder. The afternoon became a blur of answering phone calls, greeting patients, taking them to the exam rooms, filing records, and assisting Kyle.

Most of the time she managed to scurry into and out of exam rooms without running into him. And when she had to speak to him, she did her best not to look at him but couldn't help sneaking peeks while he was occupied. His height and broad shoulders could be intimidating, but his gentle, reassuring touches calmed each patient, and he always squatted to talk to the children. He patiently explained his diagnosis in words they could understand and made sure they knew what the medicine would do. The more she assisted him, the more she admired him.

She only hoped Esther would be able to come back soon. Very soon. Before her feelings for Kyle spiraled out of control.

During a late afternoon lull, Leah hurried into the house to prepare the oven-fried chicken and slip it into the stove along with potatoes. She'd turn the chicken for its final browning once the office closed.

When she returned to the waiting room, two new patients had arrived. She smoothed her hair and apron before going over to greet them. After checking them in and answering questions about Dr. Hess, Leah finished the rest of her afternoon duties. While Kyle saw the final patient, she rushed into the house to finish cooking the meal. She opened the canning jars she'd brought and put green beans on to simmer while she slid a peach half onto the plate with some coleslaw and buttered several slices of homemade bread. Then she turned off the burner and the oven. The food would stay warm until Kyle was ready to eat.

The door to the house opened, and Kyle entered. He stopped short when he spied her by the stove. "Leah? What are you doing here?"

"Fixing you dinner." She motioned toward the plate on the table. "Everything's ready."

A confused look on his face, Kyle stared at her. "I thought you went home. I took care of the payment and locked up."

Had she been in the kitchen that long? "I'm sorry. I intended to get back in time to take care of the billing and files. I just wanted to be sure dinner was ready by the time you finished."

His disbelieving look softened into gratitude. Then tenderness. "You made dinner for us?"

Not us. You. But as she gazed into his eyes, she couldn't form the words.

"You have such a kind heart. Eating here alone last night—" He broke their connection to stare off into the distance. "I should be used to solitary meals, but last night the loneliness was overwhelming."

And he'd be here alone tonight. "I, um ..." How could she tell him she had no intention of staying?

"You don't know what this means to me. No one's taken care of me like this, not since Mom ..." Kyle's Adam's apple bobbed up and down. "Caleb tried, but my brother and I had very little experience in the kitchen. Most meals were a disaster."

Leah's heart went out to him. To lose both their parents and have to fend for themselves.

"If it weren't for Esther, we would have eaten peanut butter sandwiches for every meal. By the time Caleb learned to cook well, I'd headed off to college, and then it was cafeteria food or takeout."

Oh, Kyle.

"And that's pretty much all I've eaten since. Except for now." He gestured toward the single plate on the table. "You did plan on staying, didn't you?"

After what he'd just said, how could she leave him here alone? "I'll call Joel and ask him to come later."

* * *

Joel. The name hit Kyle in the gut. Of course—she had a boyfriend who'd be expecting her company. The fantasy he'd constructed of the two of them sharing a meal crashed down around him. He'd allowed the sentimental side of him to take control.

While he'd been busy sorting out his thoughts, Leah

had already called Joel. "Yes, if you could pick me up at—" She glanced over at Kyle.

"I'd be happy to run you home," he said.

Her brilliant smile and mouthed *thank you* sent his spirits soaring. Already he was planning ways to keep her here after dinner to fill the lonely evening hours.

"What can I do to help?" he asked when she got off the phone.

"Nothing. It's all ready." She opened a few drawers until she found two potholders. "Why don't you sit down?" She slid a pan of crisp chicken and two baked potatoes on the table. Then she set a small, round casserole dish in the hot oven.

Kyle sank into a chair and inhaled the aroma wafting from the pan. Sitting in a room warmed by home cooking and Leah's presence was the closest to heaven he'd been in a long time.

After she'd set out a plate for herself and served both of them, she slid into a seat across from him. Then she bowed her head, and Kyle's gut clenched.

He'd done his best to block every detail of his time with Emma from his mind, but when they ate together, she'd always insisted on praying silently before each meal. Kyle had respected her wishes and bowed his head the way he'd been taught to do as a child.

But look how that ended. Once again, he was risking getting entangled with another Amish girl. He couldn't repeat that devastating mistake.

* * *

Leah lifted her head to find Kyle staring at her with a strange expression on his face. Had her prayer offended him? She hadn't meant to upset him, but she couldn't eat without thanking God first.

When he noticed her looking, Kyle turned his attention to his plate. "Everything looks delicious." His words sounded stilted, as if he were forcing them out.

What had happened? A few minutes ago, he'd been confiding about his life and asking her to stay for dinner. Or had she misunderstood his invitation? Maybe he'd asked her out of politeness because she'd made the meal?

His shuttered expression and refusal to look in her direction made her long to leave, but she couldn't. He'd be taking her home.

A sharp, stabbing pain in her abdomen made her draw in a breath. Not now. It hadn't even been a month. Often those twinges served as an early warning sign.

"What's wrong?" Kyle switched on his caring doctor expression, the one he used when he was seeing patients.

The pain subsided, and Leah waved away his concern. "I'm fine." But she might not be tomorrow or later this week. She picked up her fork and knife to cut a bite of chicken.

He appeared unconvinced, but he followed her lead and began eating. Only the scraping of forks, sawing of knives, and faint sounds of crunching broke the silence between them, punctuated by an occasional murmur of delight from Kyle.

Leah racked her brain for something to say. They'd been having such a good conversation, but now he was acting cold and distant. He'd indicated he wanted company, but he might as well be dining alone. Did he regret confiding in her? How could she get things back to a friendly footing?

She plunged in. "I was surprised to see you back here so soon. Dr. Hess said you were working at another hospital."

Without looking at her, Kyle answered, "I was. I finished up a few days ago." He forked a bite of potato into his mouth.

"It was perfect timing, then."

Kyle frowned. "I wouldn't say that." He dug the tines of his fork into the chicken and concentrated on slicing off a piece.

"Why not?"

"I'd been planning to take a vacation for several weeks. Since I finished my residency and passed my boards, I've been taking positions as a covering physician."

It was almost as if he were speaking a foreign language. Leah disliked interrupting him, but she wanted to understand. "What does that mean?"

"It means I've been filling in temporarily for doctors at different hospitals. It's a good way to see what their programs are like, meet people, and see if I'm well suited for the work there. It's helped me decide where to apply for my fellowship."

When she shot him a questioning glance, he explained, "The fellowship will provide additional training in the specialty I chose—rare diseases. Applications have to be in by the end of this month, so I planned to use these next few weeks to work on that."

"I see. But if you're going for more training, you won't be able to help Dr. Hess. He and Esther must be so disappointed." And so was she.

Kyle didn't meet her eyes. "I haven't told them yet."

"Oh no. They're counting on you."

"I know. That makes it so hard, especially when they've been so good to me, but I have dreams. I want to make important medical contributions."

"And you can't do that here?"

"I don't see how."

Leah's spirits plunged. She tried to tell herself it was because of the burden it put on the Hesses, but deep inside a small whisper contradicted that.

After staring into space for a few moments, Kyle asked, "What about you? You said your brother is running the store now?"

"Yes, *Daed* and Joel reconciled."

"Joel?" Kyle's voice held an odd note.

*   *   *

Kyle sat there dumbfounded. "Joel's your brother?"

"Yes." Her eyes questioned him.

How could he answer? He shrugged and tried to make light of it. "I don't know. I just assumed you were, you know, dating him." How lame was that?

"You thought I was dating an *Englischer*?"

The shock in her voice indicated she'd never consider doing anything like that. Which was just as well. It prevented him from acting like a fool.

He tried to get the conversation headed in a different direction. "With your *brother* running the store, you'll have more time for your training."

"Yes. Once Esther is back, I'll be spending as much time as I can with Sharon and studying."

"That's good." Maybe with more medical training, she'd be less inclined to rely on herbal treatments. "You'd make a good nurse. Have you ever considered that?"

Her faint smile faded. "I really enjoy the work here and wish I could help you more." A blush spread across her face. "I mean, I wish I could learn more about medicine. Reading books and becoming a noncertified midwife is as close as I'll get to that, though."

"Why? You have the time. Why not pursue your interests? If money's the problem, you could get scholarships and loans."

Leah shook her head. "We don't do that."

"By *we*, I'm guessing you mean the Amish."

She nodded. "I finished my education."

Memories of the past surfaced. Emma arguing with him about continuing his education. The Amish went to eighth grade, so Emma didn't understand his desire to go to college. He'd almost given up his dream of being a doctor to be with her. And then...

Kyle jerked his thoughts away from those dark days. The only thing he'd salvaged from the wreckage of his life had been his career. That kept him going through the long, lonely nights. Perhaps if he saved lives, he could atone for his guilt.

A soft voice drew him back to the kitchen table. "Kyle?"

"Sorry. I—"

"It's all right, but you looked so sad, so far away," Leah said.

The compassion in her eyes invited him to confide his troubles. The offer was tempting, but he kept his lips sealed. Only his brother and Emma's family knew this secret. Kyle could never tell anyone else.

When he didn't respond, Leah stood and headed for the oven. She took out the round casserole dish and carried it to the table. "Would you like blueberry cobbler? We have a small patch of blueberries at our house, so they're organic." Steam rose from the dish in her hand.

Kyle inhaled the sugary, fruity aroma. "Yes, please. It smells delicious." He had no idea when she found the time to can fruits and vegetables while running the store and studying to be a midwife.

"So you're content to be a noncertified midwife?" She could do so much more with her life.

Leah set a small plate of bubbling blueberries with crumb topping in front of him. "Why wouldn't I be?"

"You could do so much more with your life. If you went on for further education—"

"That would be *hochmut*. We shouldn't put ourselves above anyone else."

Kyle winced. He'd heard the word *hochmut* many times. Emma had complained about her older sister's attitude of self-righteousness and pride. "But if you weren't Amish, would you consider it?"

Settling into her chair at the table, Leah pinned him with a serious look. "No sense in speculating about things you'll never do."

Kyle tried to imagine his reaction to restrictions like that. Would he have railed against them and broken with his faith or taken on her attitude of calm acceptance? He had a feeling he might have rebelled. "So you have no regrets?"

She didn't answer his question directly. Instead she

said, "I'm grateful I can work with Sharon. At least for now."

"For now? What does that mean? It sounds as if being a midwife is only temporary."

"It is." Leah didn't meet his eyes. "I'll have to give it up when I marry."

Had he detected a deep sadness in her eyes before she said that? "Why would you do that?"

"Well, Ben—" Leah lowered her head and appeared to be intensely interested in rocking her fork back and forth to cut a small piece of cobbler.

Kyle winced. He'd been so elated to hear Joel was her brother he'd forgotten about Ben. What did it matter? Leah remained off-limits to him. For more reasons than one. "Surely Ben"—the name rolled uneasily off his tongue—"wouldn't expect you to give up your profession after you'd studied so long and hard, would he?"

While he waited for her answer, Kyle slid his fork into his dessert. The scent of the juice wafting from his plate proved irresistible, but he waited. He didn't want to have his mouth full, in case he needed to rebut Ben's arguments.

"Well..." Leah toyed with her fork. "He doesn't want his wife to work."

Kyle's anger burned hot toward this Ben. And not only because of jealousy. And the thought of them being married. Ben clearly didn't deserve a wonderful person like Leah, and he had no right to force her to give up a career she loved.

Kyle struggled to tamp down his fury, but some of it leaked into his question. "Why on earth would you have to give up midwifing when you marry? Plenty of women combine families and careers."

"In the *Englisch* world, maybe."

The resignation in her tone doused his fighting spirit. His disagreement wasn't with her. It was with Ben, with her culture. It might be a battle he couldn't win, but he wanted to try. Maybe Dr. Hess could help him convince her. But right now, he didn't want to ruin his time with her by starting an argument.

The heady aroma of the dessert on his plate beckoned to Kyle. He lifted a bite to his mouth, and flavor burst on his tongue. The slight tartness of blueberries mingled with the sugary sweetness of the crunchy topping. He closed his eyes to let his taste buds savor the full experience. *Mmm.* If only he could eat like this every day.

When he opened his eyes again, Leah was staring at him. "It sounds as if you like it."

Had he made that *mmm* sound aloud? So what if he had? She deserved credit for the delicious meal. "I'm sorry I didn't say it earlier, but the chicken was awesome. Everything was. And this"—he pointed his fork at the dessert—"is scrumptious."

Leah beamed. "I'm glad you enjoyed it."

Kyle finished his last few bites and set his fork down on his empty plate. "It's going to be hard to go back to cafeteria and take-out food after this." He flashed her a smile to convey his gratitude. "I can't tell you how much I've appreciated these meals." *And the company.*

Kyle pushed back his chair and stood. "I'll take care of the dishes later."

"I can do them now." Leah picked up their plates and

carried them to the sink. "No one should have to face dirty dishes when they're tired."

She sounded as if she had firsthand experience with that. Kyle hurried to intercept her before she reached the sink. "Exactly, so I'll handle it. Why don't you sit at the table and relax?"

While Kyle squirted dish detergent into the sink and ran the hot water, Leah carried the pots and pans to the counter. Then she picked up a towel.

"I can't stand by idly and let you do all the work."

As he scrubbed the plates and handed them to her, they chattered and laughed. Kyle let his imagination soar. In his dreams, he and Leah worked together in the office all day and spent their evenings sharing meals, doing the dishes, and cuddling together on the couch afterward.

The click of a key in the front lock brought him back to reality. Esther opened the door and walked in. When she spied them in the kitchen together, the small overnight case in her hand hit the floor with a thud.

Her eyebrows arched so high they almost touched her hairline. "Leah? What are you doing here?" Disapproval flowed from her in thick waves. "I never expected...I don't think..."

The buoyant mood in the kitchen popped faster than the soap bubbles in the sink.

Esther stopped speaking, obviously flustered and visibly upset at finding the two of them in her kitchen together. Perhaps the fact they were engaged in sharing the dish washing—an activity of love that she and Martin bonded over—made the scene appear more intimate than it was in reality. Or had it been innocent?

If Esther could read Kyle's mind the past ten minutes, she'd be convinced she had something to worry about. His face burned, although outwardly they'd done nothing wrong. Leah's fiery-red cheeks, though, made her appear guilty. Kyle longed to defend her, to protest that she'd only been drying dishes.

Esther sank into the nearest chair and fanned herself with her hand. Kyle hoped they hadn't caused her to have a heart attack or stroke.

"Are you all right?" The doctor part of him kicked in, and he evaluated her rapid breathing and flushed face.

"I'll be fine." She set her clasped hands on the table and closed her eyes. Her lips moved soundlessly.

Kyle almost rushed over to her before it dawned on him she was praying.

When she opened her eyes, the serene expression on her face didn't match her clipped tone. "It didn't occur to me we needed to set ground rules for the use of our house." She muttered something under her breath about history repeating itself.

The change in Esther's demeanor, when Kyle had only ever seen her softness and kindness, shocked him. The sternness of her jaw and worry in her eyes didn't fit with her usual personality.

"I know you may consider me old-fashioned, but I don't believe men and women, especially young unmarried ones, should ever be left alone together. I know Leah was brought up that way, so it never occurred to me something like this might be a problem."

"We weren't doing anything wrong." Kyle had to defend Leah. "We ate a meal and were cleaning up."

"I'm not accusing you of anything." Esther's gentle

tone had returned, but a note of resolve indicated she intended to have her say. Turning toward Leah, she asked, "What would your parents think if they knew you were alone here with a man? And what of Ben?"

Leah hung her head, and her lips trembled. Kyle wanted to gather her into his arms, to shelter her from Esther's criticism. She didn't deserve any reproach. She'd set the table with only one plate; he'd been the one who'd convinced her to stay.

"It's my fault." Kyle couldn't bear seeing Leah shoulder the blame. "I asked her to stay. I took advantage of her kind heart after she made me a meal. I told her how lonely I've been."

"Loneliness can lead to temptation. I've seen it happen before."

So had Kyle, but that wasn't true in Leah's case. "I don't mean to be rude," Kyle said, "but it isn't fair to judge us, especially Leah, by someone else's behavior when we've done nothing wrong."

"I'm sure I can trust you two. It's just that after what happened with your mother and father..." She snapped her mouth shut, lowered her head into her hands, and rubbed her forehead. "Forgive me. I'm so exhausted after all I've been through with Martin I'm speaking out of turn. I never should have said that."

Esther had been looking at *him* when she said *mother and father*. "What did you mean about my parents?"

Esther shook her head. "I flashed back to a scene many years ago. It has no bearing on this situation. I'm sorry I even brought it up."

Now that she had, though, curiosity got the better of

Kyle. He wanted to hear the end of that sentence. "Tell me, please."

"It's not my story to tell. Besides, this has little to do with my present-day concerns."

Kyle wanted to beg her to tell him the story, or at least tell him whose story it was to tell. Not Caleb's, he hoped. Facing his estranged brother was the last thing Kyle wanted to do while he was here. And how did Esther know about his parents? Maybe they had to get married before they had Caleb? But Esther wouldn't have known them then. His parents had only moved to this area after Caleb was born.

Mom often told the story of the first time she'd taken Caleb to Dr. Hess. Caleb had been two, and he'd taken the doctor's stethoscope and insisted on checking Dr. Hess's heart. The doctor had assured Mom that Caleb would make a good doctor someday. Instead, Caleb had to give up his medical training when their parents died. At the time, Kyle hadn't realized what a sacrifice his brother had made to raise him. Now Caleb had become Amish, so he'd never be a doctor. Kyle had taken his place in the profession, which meant he had an obligation to do an outstanding job for both of them.

Kyle tuned back in to the conversation swirling around him. The worry lines around Esther's mouth had softened back into pleasant lines, but her eyes still held a hint of concern.

She turned to Leah with a genuine smile. "I'm so grateful you were able to take my place in the office. Martin should be coming home in two days. I hope you'll be able to stay until then."

"I'd be happy to," Leah assured her. "How is the doctor doing?"

Kyle had been planning to ask that question. He hoped Dr. Hess was recovering well.

"He's doing well. We were both taken by surprise because he's always been so healthy. It made us realize we need to give up the practice as soon as possible. Martin needs to lower his stress levels." Her gaze moved to Kyle. "I can't tell you how thrilled we are to have you here."

He really should make it clear his time here was temporary, but he couldn't add to her burdens when she was already under so much stress. He should give Dr. Hess some time to recover and then explain, although the longer he stayed, the harder it would be to leave.

She rose. "I need to get some fresh clothes and a few things for Martin. I don't want to leave him alone too long." She started up the stairs, then leaned over the railing to look at Leah. "Perhaps Kyle could finish the dishes alone, and you could keep me company upstairs."

With an apologetic look, Leah handed him the towel and hurried toward the landing. Kyle hoped she wouldn't have to endure a lecture while Esther packed.

By the time they descended, Kyle had finished the dishes, put them away in, and set the pots and baking dishes on the counter.

"I didn't know who these pans and dishes belonged to," he said, as they descended the stairs.

Leah hurried into the kitchen and picked up the casserole dishes. "These are *Mamm*'s." She stowed them in the bag on the counter. "I hope you don't mind that I used your pans, Esther." She bent and slid the cookie sheet into the drawer under the oven. Then she hung the pots and pans on a round wrought iron holder over the kitchen island.

"That's what they're for." Esther waved a hand toward the cabinets and swept it toward the living room and stairs. "Feel free to use anything you need in the kitchen or the rest of the house, Kyle."

Then Esther pinned Leah with a stern gaze. "It was thoughtful of you to make meals for Kyle, but I'd rather you give him the casseroles to heat. I'm sure he can handle turning on the oven."

At her questioning glance, Kyle nodded.

"Good." She turned her attention back to Leah. "I don't want the two of you in the house at the same time. I also want you to avoid being alone together in the office without patients around. Until I return, I'd like you to leave as soon as the last patient goes out the door. Will you promise me that?"

"Yes, of course." Leah's answer was barely a whisper. "I'm so sorry. I didn't mean to . . ."

"I know, dear. I only want to protect you and your reputation. I'm sure your parents would agree."

Leah nodded. "They would."

Esther made it sound as if being alone with him was dangerous. Before Kyle could express his indignation, Esther looked him in the eye.

"I know I can trust you, Kyle. I only want to ensure no gossip starts. I know you understand how important Leah's reputation is. And so is yours. Once your reputation is tarnished, it's extremely hard to recover it."

Kyle had firsthand knowledge of that. In the past few days, he'd mainly seen *Englisch* patients. Most of them had no idea about his past, although he'd encountered several raised eyebrows and some hesitancy from a few people after he introduced himself. But everyone in the Amish community would remember his name, and they'd know he'd left years ago with his reputation in tatters.

Chapter Sixteen

After Esther tucked a few snacks into her purse, she picked up her suitcase and insisted on driving Leah home. Although she should be grateful for Esther's concern, Leah struggled to mask her disappointment. Kyle mouthed an apology before they walked out the door. He must blame himself for inviting her to stay, but she could have said no. She'd been as eager to spend time with him as he'd been to assuage his loneliness.

While she drove, Esther returned to her usual cheerful self, and they chatted about Leah's midwife training, Joel taking over the store, and Martin's recovery. Yet Leah sensed her underlying disapproval. Her stomach in knots, she worried Esther might insist on talking to *Mamm* and *Daed* when they arrived at the house. If she did, they'd forbid her to assist at the doctor's office.

When they pulled into the parking lot, she released a silent sigh for two reasons. One, she could drink some of her special herbal tea for the cramps. But even better, all the upstairs windows were dark. Her parents had gone to bed already. Perhaps by the time Esther saw her parents again, she'd forget her concerns from this evening. Leah determined not to spend any time alone with Kyle for the next few days to avoid giving Esther anything to worry about.

Several times during the ride, Leah had gritted her teeth to keep from groaning and pressed her feet hard against the floorboards of the car to stave off the shooting pains in her abdomen. She had an even worse attack as she opened the car door. Gripping the old-fashioned car handle so tightly her palm hurt, Leah kept her back to Esther and squeezed her eyes shut until the assault on her insides ended.

"Are you all right, dear?"

Glancing over her shoulder, Leah managed a wan smile. "Just some twinges, but they've passed."

"Take care of yourself," Esther said as Leah reached over to close the car door. Her tone implied more than physical health.

"I will," Leah promised. Eating dinner with Kyle tonight had been foolish. She was grateful Esther had interrupted them. Leah had needed someone to bring her back to her senses. They'd been having too much fun doing the dishes. She almost let herself fall for Kyle's charm. From now on, she'd guard her heart.

But she couldn't keep Kyle from her dreams. In her early prewaking haze, she clung to him, begging him not to leave. Reluctantly, she opened her eyes to the icy, gray dawn, but remnants of the images wrapped around her like the frosty haze that clung to the ground when she gathered the eggs. Wisps floated with her as she cooked breakfast, drank her herbal tea, and carried eggs and toast up to *Mamm*.

"Are you all right, *dochder*?" *Mamm*'s brow crinkled as she studied Leah. "Is working at the doctor's office going well?"

"Yes, it is." *Very well.* In fact, Leah enjoyed it so much she wished she could be a nurse so she could do it every day. She loved the opportunity to heal people with herbs, but what if she could do both? So far, she'd resisted the urge to suggest alternative medicine for the prescriptions Kyle gave out. Often herbal remedies worked equally as well and were less expensive.

"You enjoy helping people, don't you? You'd make a good nurse."

Had *Mamm* read her mind? Leah's surprise must have shown on her face.

Mamm smiled. "You glow when you talk about healing, and you've been an excellent nurse to me."

Oh, right. Mamm didn't mean a trained nurse. Leah had misunderstood. But would *Mamm* understand if Leah confessed her longing? "Yes, I love training to be a midwife, and taking Esther's place at the doctor's office has been *wunderbar*." She pushed aside the thought that some of the excitement included being around Kyle. She'd love the work, even if he weren't there. But he made it even more special.

"I can tell by the way your eyes shine."

What would *Mamm* think if she knew Leah's glow

also came from another source? "I sometimes wish..."
No, she wouldn't say that and hurt her mother.

"You wish what?" *Mamm* wiped the last drips of
dippy eggs from her plate with a piece of toast. Her eyes
bored into Leah's as she popped it into her mouth.

With a quick head shake, Leah took the tray and prepared her mother for the morning massage.

"It doesn't hurt to dream," *Mamm* said, as she lay
facedown on the bed.

That was a relief, because Leah had plenty of dreams,
including one this morning she still struggled to shake
off. She suspected *Mamm* wasn't referring to those
dreams. Maybe if she confessed some of the other long-
ings in her heart, *Mamm* would give her some wise
advice.

"You're right about me having dreams," Leah said, but
she hesitated to continue.

Mamm's quiet *hmm?* opened the floodgates, and
words flooded out.

"I enjoy learning all about herbs and making mixtures
to help people, but I'd love to go on for more training.
And not just with natural products. I can't tell you how
much I wish I could be a certified midwife. I'd also love
to take nurse's training."

Mamm lifted her head and glanced over her shoulder
to meet Leah's eyes.

"I know, I know," Leah said hastily. "It's not right."

"It goes against the *Ordnung*." The finality in *Mamm*'s
voice chastened Leah.

Leah hung her head. "I'm sorry."

Mamm set her head back on the pillow with a light
groan. "Don't ever be sorry for the dreams God has put

in your heart. He must have a reason for them. Why not pray and ask Him to show you what He intends for you to do?"

One thing Leah hadn't done was pray about her desires. She had no idea how to pray about the feelings Kyle stirred in her, except to ask God to keep her from temptation. As for the rest, she'd hand them over to God.

"*Danke, Mamm.* I'll do that." Leah moved quickly through the rest of the massage. "I have to hurry. Joel will be here soon."

Despite the tea she'd sipped earlier, Leah had to stop several times to suck in a breath and breathe through the worst of the pain.

"Are you in pain?" *Mamm* asked.

"I'll be fine." Leah had too much to do. She couldn't give in. Last month she'd pushed Kyle's suggestion about seeing a doctor to the back of her mind. She managed to cope during most of that week despite the pain. Today would be difficult, but she'd get through it, and the office was closed on Thursdays, so she'd have tomorrow off. Perhaps some of the aching would abate by Friday, and Esther would be back next week.

Though it shouldn't, the thought made her sad. She'd only see him a few more days, and then he'd head off. Maybe that was God's answer to her dilemma about Kyle.

After she'd settled *Mamm* in bed with tea and a snack for later, Leah interspersed packing a bag of food for Kyle with hugging a hot water bottle. She prepared a second bag for herself with some tea, a mug, a hot water bottle, and a spoonful of the supplement for after lunch. She hoped Esther wouldn't mind her using the kitchen to heat water and prepare lunch as long as Kyle didn't enter the house at the same time.

When she reached the doctor's office, Kyle hadn't come out of the house yet, so she set his bag near the door and tucked hers under the roomy reception desk. Then she went into the file room to organize folders for that day's patients. She'd just completed the first stack when the killer cramps began. She pressed against the waist-high counter and sucked in breaths.

"Leah?" Kyle called. His footsteps passed the file room. Doors opened and closed farther down the hall. He called her name several times as he made his way up the hall. He must be peeking in every room.

Exerting tremendous control, Leah sank onto the stool and turned her back to the door right before it clicked open. She gripped a file in a death grip, hoping she wouldn't tear it.

"Oh, there you are," Kyle said. "Didn't you hear me calling you?"

"Sorry. I was... getting files." Forcing out each word was agony.

"I won't stay in here with you, not after Esther's lecture last night, but I saw the bag you set by the door. Should I put anything in the refrigerator?"

Leah nodded. "I marked... everything."

"OK, I'll take the bag into the kitchen." He stepped into the hall. "You don't have to make me meals, you know. But I really appreciate it." He let the door swing shut, leaving her alone.

What a blessed relief not to have to pretend. Leah

clenched her teeth together until the worst of the interior explosions passed. Then she managed to stack up the afternoon files. Only three patients. That meant she'd have to leave early. If she'd been feeling normal, she'd be disappointed. Today she was grateful.

By the time the first patient arrived, she'd walked to the desk and sat there with a hot water bottle concealed under a small knitted throw. She slipped them both onto the chair as she led patients back to the exam rooms. Several times she clutched at the doorjamb before entering a room or telling Kyle where the next patient was waiting. A few times, she winced just before she turned her back. Twice, while Kyle was checking someone, she went into the kitchen to heat water for herbal tea or to warm the water bottle.

Right before lunchtime, she let Kyle know she planned to head into the house so he wouldn't come in. She had filled both plates when another pain shot through her. She gripped the edge of the counter until it passed. Then she picked up the plates and staggered to the records room. Shakily, she placed the plates on the shelf beside the three files for the afternoon appointments.

After the last patient left, she'd give Kyle his meal. He could have lunch in his office, and she'd eat at the reception desk. One good thing about Esther's rule was that Kyle wouldn't see her hunch over whenever the cramps came. Today they were much worse than usual.

Red-hot stabbing radiated from her center and down her legs. Leah lowered herself onto the stool in the records room, her head woozy. Spots dotted the grayness floating past her eyes. She grabbed the counter and fought to keep her tilting world upright, but blackness closed around her.

*   *   *

A loud crash from the records room sent Kyle scurrying down the hall. No one should be in there. His last patient would be gone by now, and Leah had gone to the kitchen. He hoped nothing had fallen.

He turned the knob, but when he tried to push open the door, he met resistance. Whatever had fallen now blocked the door. Kyle pictured huge stacks of file folders scattered on the floor. He didn't want to risk dislodging more contents. How would they ever match everything up with the correct files? It would take hours of work.

He inched the door as gently as he could until he could reach one hand through, and then he squatted down to push some of the files out of the way. Instead his hand encountered a warm body.

Even though he was a doctor, Kyle recoiled. He forced himself to insert his hand again. Whoever was in there needed his help, but he had to move them away from the door.

If only Leah hadn't gone into the house to fix dinner. He could use her help.

With one last push, he managed to create an opening wide enough to fit through. He squeezed into the room and groaned.

Leah lay on the floor. What had happened? Kyle knelt beside her. Her breathing was slow but rhythmic. He felt for her pulse. Normal. To be on the safe side, he reached for the stethoscope around his neck. Her steady heartbeat reassured him. She must have fainted. And he was pretty sure he knew why.

*   *   *

Gentle hands lifted her head. Limp and boneless, Leah allowed the hands to push and pull her into position. Everything around her remained foggy. Her thoughts floated in the air around her, detached, muddled, vague.

As if from a distance, a familiar voice flowed around her, much too slippery to catch or understand. A man. Calling her name over and over.

She drifted through the ether toward the sound. Pinpricks of light pierced her eyelids, stinging her eyes. And her back hurt. As if she were bent in two. Her head dangled down. Arms wrapped around her, supporting her.

"Leah," the voice whispered near her ear. Her name echoed around her, growing fainter and fainter until it disappeared in the haze.

If only she could stay in this place forever. Cocooned in softness. Warm and comforted.

"Can you hear me?" The deep voice vibrated the air around her.

She wanted to turn toward it, but her limp muscles refused to cooperate. Her mouth, stuffed full of cotton wool, remained slack, but deep in her throat, a gargled groan escaped.

"Are you all right?" Kyle's face floated in front of her.

If he'd keep supporting her, she would be.

She drifted closer to the surface. Broke free from the murky depths. Her head ached. Her eyes burned. And the pain that had sent her into oblivion returned with a vengeance. She clutched at her stomach. A moan pushed through rubbery lips.

Kyle squatted in front of her. "Are you in pain?"

Could she reach out and smooth that frown from his face? But where were her hands, and why didn't they work? Why was she on the floor? Nothing made sense. Waves of nausea swept over her, and she closed her eyes again.

"I'm taking you to the hospital. You need to see a specialist." Kyle's tone brooked no argument. "I'm going to leave you for a minute, but I'll be right back."

Leah tried to protest, but he set a gentle hand on her head to keep her from getting up. "I need to cancel the afternoon patients and lock up." Then he let go of her and stood.

Leaning over, he slid the files from the counter far above her head. "And I'll put our lunch in the refrigerator for later." Plates clinked together before the door clicked closed behind him.

Time oozed past until the door creaked open. Through blurry eyes, she noted he'd donned a coat and carried a fluffy afghan. He knelt beside her to wrap her in cloud-like softness. Then he lifted her. Cradled in his arms, Leah leaned her head against his chest the way she had in her dreams.

Was she still dreaming? If she was, she never wanted to wake up.

Though he cushioned her from shocks, each stride he

took bounced her on a wave, and her insides followed the motion. After he maneuvered her through the door, an icy chill seeped through the afghan. Tipping her closer to his chest and balancing her weight on his muscular forearms, he freed his fingers so he could bend to punch in the door code.

She shivered and burrowed her face in the blanket as he crossed the parking lot, unlocked his car, and placed her on the backseat. His movements tender and gentle, he tucked the blanket around her before shutting the door.

Her eyelids slid shut as the car purred down the roads, and she drifted off to sleep.

Strong arms lifted her from the car and set her on her feet. "We're at the hospital. Can you walk?"

Freezing-cold winds slapped her face, blowing some of the mistiness from her mind. But a tsunami of pain washed over her, drowning her.

Clinging to him and hiding her face against his chest, she staggered beside him through the doors. He seated her in a chair, and she clutched the metal chair arm to keep herself upright. Then he stepped away, leaving her alone and adrift in a tilting world.

Through pain-glazed eyes, she followed his progress as he stood in line, inching closer to the desk. She longed for him to come back, to hold her.

When he returned, he wrapped an arm around her, and she let her head sink onto his chest where the rapid staccato of his heart soothed her. She gasped as the pain crescendoed, then ebbed.

"I'm so sorry. I should have given you something for the pain." His voice tight and angry, he muttered, "I don't know what I was thinking. This is why doctors should never treat family and friends."

"It's...all right." Her voice came out so whispery weak Kyle leaned closer to hear her, and his cheek brushed the top of her head. If it weren't for the knife carving out her insides, she'd be in pure bliss.

"My *kapp*." She lifted a hand to straighten it.

"It's fine," he assured her, and the low rumble of the words in his chest sent tingles through her.

"Leah, before they call us back, I need to know: Did you do what I asked you to do last time I was here? Did you see a doctor or a specialist?"

Leah was so focused on the rise and fall of his chest it took a while for his questions to register. "No," she finally admitted.

He sighed. "Would it be all right if I come back with you? I won't stay for the exam. I'll just tell them what I suspect."

She didn't want to leave the comfort of his arms, so she bobbed her head up and down slightly.

When their turn came, Kyle assisted her down the hall, spoke to the doctor, and turned to her. "I'll wait for you right out here."

The doctor called Kyle in after the exam, and the rest of Leah's visit passed in a blur, with the doctor scheduling tests and scans with names Leah barely recognized. She left with a prescription and a laparoscopy appointment with a specialist Kyle had contacted.

Kyle helped her to the car. "I'll take you home, but our first stop will be the pharmacy. You will take the pills they prescribed, won't you?"

Too groggy to argue, Leah nodded. She'd take them

only if the pain got too bad to cope. "What were the tests the doctor insisted on?"

"They did an ultrasound and MRI to rule out other reasons for your pain, but a laparoscopy's the only way to check for endometriosis."

He was pretty sure that would confirm his diagnosis.

Chapter Seventeen

Kyle had just finished washing his breakfast dishes on Friday morning when a car rattled into the driveway. He recognized the engine and hurried to the window to pull back the curtain. He'd been right. Joel's car.

He rushed from the house and hurried down the office hallway to the side door. He yanked open the door as her brother drove off. "What are you doing here?" he demanded.

At the gruffness of his voice, she stepped back a few paces. "Don't you want me?" She sounded close to tears.

Of course he wanted her. More than she'd ever know. "You should be home resting."

"I'm taking the painkillers. I should be fine." She was carrying a large bag.

"Let me get that." He hurried across the parking lot and took the handles of the bag. "You need to stop worrying about my meals. As much as I appreciate your thoughtfulness, I'd much rather you take care of yourself."

The sweet smile Leah gave him set his heart thumping. "I can't bear to think of you...or anyone...eating leftovers or fast food all the time. You work hard so you deserve healthy meals."

Kyle shook his head. She always thought of other people rather than herself. He had to find a way to take care of her in return. He pushed aside the desire to extend that care far into the future. He had other plans that didn't include small towns and an Amish girl. But as hard as he tried to focus on big-city hospitals and fellowships, his attention—and his heart—kept being drawn back to Leah. When he moved on, he'd have a hard time getting her out of his mind.

Concentrate on the work, he warned himself as he opened the door for her. She brushed past him, and electricity jolted through him. Keeping focused on the job would be difficult. As much as he disliked Esther's rule, it would protect them both from his growing attraction.

As she preceded him down the hall, Kyle hefted the bag into his arms, wishing he could replace it with Leah's softness. When they reached the waiting room, he cleared his throat. "I'll, um, just take this into the kitchen and put everything away."

Leah reached for the bag. "Let me do it."

"Absolutely not." Kyle moved the bag out of her reach. "You will sit at that desk and relax. I'm sure I can figure out where everything goes."

"Most of it's marked," she admitted.

He smiled when he reached the kitchen and pulled out the containers. Small notes had been taped to the top of each dish, indicating whether it belonged in the refrigerator or on the counter. Had she anticipated he'd insist on doing it? His dinner casserole had cooking instructions on top. He lifted the foil to peek. Ham chunks in scalloped potatoes with onions and peas. It smelled delicious even cold. He could hardly wait to inhale the aroma while it baked.

Once he'd sorted everything, he headed back out to the office. When he reached the reception area, the desk stood empty. *Where is Leah?*

His mind immediately flew to Wednesday, when he found her crumpled on the file room floor. He rushed to that door and eased it open in case she was lying behind it.

"Kyle? Are you all right?" Leah looked up from the files she'd arranged into two neat stacks. "You look a bit sickish."

Kyle clenched the doorknob, waiting for his heartbeat to return to normal. Or as close to normal as it could be whenever he looked at her. "I'm sorry. I panicked when you weren't at the desk. I pictured you collapsed in here, the way I found you the other day."

"I'm so sorry. I didn't mean to worry you." Leah's cheeks flushed a pretty pink. "I also need to apologize for all the trouble I caused."

"It wasn't a problem. I'm used to dealing with emergency situations." And holding her close would have been wonderful if he hadn't been so concerned about her. He'd spent the long, lonely evening last night remembering her in his arms.

"Yes, but your receptionist shouldn't end up as a patient."

The door to the waiting room opened, and Leah grabbed the top folder on the nearest pile. "It sounds like the first appointment is here. I'd better get out there."

He stepped back far enough to avoid accidentally grazing her when she passed. Just being near her had already disturbed him enough. He didn't need any accidental touches turning that fire into a conflagration.

When Leah reached the end of the hallway, her cheerful greeting to the first patient floated back to him. Then she turned and called to him, "I'll reschedule the three patients you had to cancel Wednesday."

He nodded, but then she flashed him another one of her sweet smiles, undoing his attempt to douse the flames.

* * *

After she'd checked the last patient out at noon, Leah went back and tapped on Kyle's partially open office door. He looked up from the file where he was making notes. When their eyes met, Leah forgot why she'd come.

She forced herself to look down and break the connection. With Esther's warning ringing in her ears, she avoided stepping into his office. "I'm heading into the kitchen now to make lunch."

"No, you're not. You're going to sit at the reception desk while I prepare the meal."

"But I—" The rest of Leah's sentence died on her lips as Kyle stood and headed toward her.

"The desk. Now." His deep, commanding voice accompanied by a caring look sent thrills through her.

He waved a hand to indicate she should go first. On wobbly legs, Leah led the way down the hall.

"You look a bit shaky," Kyle said, after they reached the waiting room. He reached for her arm and escorted her toward the desk.

His gentle touch made her gait even more unsteady. She was relieved to sink into the chair but was disappointed when he removed his fingers from her arm, leaving behind only the warm imprint of his hand on her skin.

After the door shut behind him, Leah called to reschedule the appointments. When she could walk normally again, she went to the records room to store the morning's files and double-check the order of the afternoon folders. She set the first two on her desk and then rummaged in her coat pocket for the painkillers to take one with her lunch as directed. They weren't there. She'd dropped them in the bag of food she'd given Kyle.

She went to the door of the house, intending to call him. Instead, he'd been leaning over to turn the knob, balancing two plates of food. Caught off balance, he almost tumbled forward. Leah grabbed for a slipping plate before it tipped. She managed to keep it upright, but her other arm had shot out to prevent Kyle from falling.

"I'm sorry," she said breathlessly, but didn't remove the hand that had grasped his forearm. Then she made the mistake of glancing up, and she was drowning in his eyes.

The door to the waiting room clicked open, and Leah jumped back, almost spilling her plate. No patients had appointments until one thirty. Tearing her gaze from Kyle's, she turned to greet the new arrival.

"Ben?" Did her face look as guilty as her voice sounded?

"Leah?" Ben's gaze ricocheted back and forth between her and Kyle. "Dad and I got back from the horse auction in Ohio late last night, and your brother said I'd find you here. I didn't expect—" His eyes filled with hurt. "Where's Dr. Hess?"

"The doctor had a heart attack." Leah couldn't meet Ben's eyes. She'd forgotten the big auction was this week. Even worse, she hadn't even realized he'd been away.

"I'm sorry to hear that. Will he be all right?" Once she'd nodded, he glanced around the room. "Where's Esther? I'd like to send a get-well message to him."

"She's, um, at the hospital with him. I've been taking her place." Leah rushed her words out, wishing she had a different answer for Ben.

"So you and he"—Ben gestured to Kyle with his chin—"are here *alone*?"

At the emphasis Ben placed on the final word, Leah's cheeks flamed. "It's not like that."

"What is it like? Maybe I'm mistaken, but it looks as if the two of you have been in the house together and intended to eat lunch together."

What would he think if he knew they'd had dinner together the other night and that Kyle had taken her to the hospital two days ago? Esther had been right that they shouldn't spend time together.

* * *

Kyle took a deep breath and interrupted their discussion. "Actually, I was in the house by myself," he told Ben.

"And I planned to eat in my office while Leah ate out here."

He walked over and set his plate on the reception desk. "In fact, why don't the two of you eat together here, and I'll have lunch in the house?"

Then he turned his back on them. "Enjoy it, you two." He made himself cross the room, leaving Leah behind with Ben. Before he closed the door to the house, he said, without turning around, "I'll be back a little before one thirty to get ready for the first afternoon appointment."

As much as it bothered him to encourage the two of them to spend time together, he had no right to drive a wedge between Leah and the man she'd chosen to date. While he fixed lunch for himself, he ran over the cases he'd seen that morning, but they did little to distract him from what was happening in the waiting room. Sitting alone in the kitchen, he tortured himself with pictures of the couple enjoying a cozy lunch together.

Did Ben enjoy Leah's company as much as he did? Did Leah make Ben smile and laugh? Would their conversation die when they stared into each other's eyes?

Kyle had gulped down a quick lunch and had started washing his plate, when the door opened.

Leah called in, "If you come out whenever you're finished, I'll do the dishes."

Had Ben left already? Kyle's spirits soared.

"I'm done already. Be right there." He hurried to the door. This time he inched it open to be sure they didn't collide, although he wouldn't have minded if they did.

Leah stood well away from the door, holding two empty plates.

"Is Ben still here?" Kyle checked out the waiting room.

"No. He had to get back to work. He only stopped to find out if we could do something tomorrow."

"So you ate both those meals?" Kyle raised an eyebrow, and his lips quirked.

Leah giggled. "No. Ben managed to find time to eat. Thank you for doing that."

"You're welcome." Kyle reached for the plates. "I can do the dishes."

"I'll take care of them." Leah headed for the house door, and Kyle stepped to one side to let her pass.

That reminded him—he'd put her pain pills in his pocket earlier, but he'd forgotten to give them to her. He pulled them out. "I'm sorry I didn't give these to you earlier. You were supposed to take one at lunchtime."

"Thanks." Leah stacked the plates so she had a free hand to take the container. She reached tentative fingers to grasp only the lid of the pill bottle without touching his hand. Being around Ben must have reminded her of her commitment.

He needed to get his feelings under control. In a clipped, businesslike voice, he said, "I'll be in my office when the first patient arrives."

Had disappointment flickered in her eyes, or was it only wishful thinking on his part?

"Of course." She opened the door. "I'll let you know when Laban Zook is ready."

Another Amish patient? Will he follow my advice or ask Leah for herbal remedies?

Leah had agreed to filling the prescription two days ago, and she'd brought the pills with her rather than relying on her homemade tea. She'd almost closed the door behind her, but Kyle wanted to satisfy his curiosity. "Could I ask you a question?"

A startled expression on her face, Leah glanced over her shoulder. What was she expecting him to say?

For a moment, as he met her sparkling blue eyes, he had a bit of trouble recalling what he'd planned to ask. Then his gaze dropped to the small pill bottle clutched in her hand. He waved toward it. "When we first met, you championed only natural remedies. I wonder why you're willing to take those."

"I don't want to faint."

He wouldn't have minded. Holding her in his arms, having her lean against him for support had been a chance to be close to her, but he wouldn't ever want her to be in that much pain again. He was happy she'd agreed to take some traditional medicine. "You will be going for the follow-up appointment I made, right?"

"I guess," she mumbled, turning away.

He had to impress on her how important it was to keep that appointment. Perhaps he could enlist Dr. Hess to convince her once he got home. "If you tell me when it is, I'd be happy to drive you there."

"Thank you for offering, but I can find a way." She closed the door behind her with a click of finality.

*   *   *

Leah leaned her head against the door and blew out a breath. Her frazzled nerves sizzled throughout her body. Being around Kyle kept her off balance and on edge. And his offer to drive her...

Imagining sitting in a car beside him brought back memories of being in his arms the other day. She struggled to banish the touch of his hands, the comfort of his embrace. Before dinner, she'd been mesmerized, staring into his eyes when Ben walked in.

Soothing Ben's jealousy had drained her. And in feeling guilty about her attraction to Kyle, she agreed to spend tomorrow with Ben after the office closed, when all she wanted to do was rest. She hadn't planned to take this prescription after today unless the cramping became unbearable.

Leah hurried into the house to clean the dishes and straighten the kitchen. That also brought back memories of laughing and talking with Kyle, sharing a meal together.

They'd had so much fun together. Dr. Hess would be discharged tomorrow, so Esther would be taking over the office duties. After that, she'd probably never see Kyle again. That thought made her ache inside.

Leah treasured each minute she had with Kyle the rest of the afternoon, tucking them away in her heart. She did the same the next morning, watching the clock tick down the seconds until she'd have to say her final good-bye.

Around ten thirty, the door to the house opened. Startled, Leah glanced over to see Esther standing in the doorway, beaming.

Several people in the waiting room jumped up and hurried over to her. Soon she was surrounded by a buzzing crowd. She held up a hand to stop the flow of questions.

"Martin's fine. He's home now. They suggested a month's rest before he eases back into his work schedule, so we're grateful to have the new, young doctor to fill in for him."

Esther hadn't noticed Kyle standing in the entryway to the hall, but Leah couldn't keep her gaze off him. She held up a finger to let him know she'd be sending the next patient back shortly. After a brisk, impersonal nod that contrasted with the intensity in his eyes when he looked at her, Kyle stared at the chattering group with Esther at its center.

Once again, Esther waved a hand to quiet the noise. "If you'll all wait a minute, I need to speak with Martin's assistant for a moment; then I'll have another announcement." She hurried over, took Kyle's arm, pulled him near where Leah was standing, and whispered, "You will be joining our practice, right?"

"Actually, I'm—" Kyle swallowed hard.

Leah's heart went out to him. How would he tell Esther the news with all these people watching? No doubt he'd planned to have this conversation in private, to let the Hesses down gently.

"That is…" Kyle stumbled along. "I'm very, very grateful to you and Martin for offering me this opportunity. It's quite an honor…"

"Wonderful." Esther clapped her hands and moved to the middle of the room. With everyone's attention riveted on her, she declared, "We'll be making a formal announcement soon, but Dr. Kyle Miller, who's been working here this week, will be taking over the practice so Martin can retire."

The commotion around Esther intensified as well-

wishers thanked her and Martin and expressed their regret at losing them.

Kyle shifted in the doorway, his expression like that
of a trapped animal. With a sickish look on his face, he
ducked back into the hallway, letting the door swing
closed behind him. Leah longed to go after him to
comfort him, but that would be a mistake. When—
and how—would he tell the Hesses his plans for the
future?

After the furor died down, Esther approached the
desk. "I'm so grateful you could take my place here this
week. I don't know what I would have done without
you."

"I'm happy to help. You and the doctor have done so
much for our family. All the house calls for *Mamm...*"

Esther waved a dismissive hand. "Martin loves that
part of his work. If he had his way, he'd probably be on
the road all day." She lowered her voice. "I didn't mean
to cause such a disturbance by coming in here, but would
you and Kyle be able to come into the house for a short
while after the office closes at noon?"

Leah hesitated. She'd promised Ben she'd meet him
as soon as she was done working.

"I don't want to disrupt your plans."

"No, no," Leah assured her. "It's not a problem. I
don't know if Kyle's plans, though."

"I didn't expect you to." The slight frown on Esther's
forehead and the tartness in her voice served as a rebuke.
"I'll check with him."

During Leah's next break between patients, she
slipped into the file room to call Joel. "Could you tell
Ben that the doctor—Dr. Hess, that is—needs me to

stay longer? I'm not sure when I'll be done. Also, can I call you for a ride after I finish talking to him and Esther?"

"I don't mind coming for you at lunchtime—customers know we're usually closed then—but I'd rather not leave the shop unattended on a Saturday afternoon. That's our busiest time."

Leah smiled to herself. Her brother had been back at the store for only a short while, but he'd already committed to improving the business. *Daed* would be happy that he let Joel take over.

Her brother's voice came through the phone. "Are you there? I don't want to leave you stranded."

"It's all right, Joel. I'll find another way home."

"It's freezing out there, but maybe Ben could come for you?"

Why did her gut clench at the thought? "I don't want to make him run all the way over here, especially not in this weather. Besides, I have no idea how long I'll be." Leah had to get back out to the desk. "I'll call if I change my mind."

She hung up and hurried into the waiting room. Two patients had arrived. She'd just finished checking them in when her cell phone buzzed.

Sharon's excited voice came over the line. "I know you have to work until noon today, but if you can come to the Grabers', I'd like your company. It's their first baby, so Merv called a little early. I expect we'll be here for several more hours."

"I'd love to, but..." She had no way to get there, and she'd promised Ben. She couldn't break another date.

"You can't come?" Sharon sounded disappointed.

"I've missed you this week. I had several prenatal exams and two deliveries. You could have learned a lot."

"I wish I could have been there, but Ky— the doctor who's filling in for Dr. Hess needed help." Help she was quite willing to give.

"I understand. So you have other plans this afternoon?"

"Yes, unfortunately." Leah shook herself. *Unfortunately?* What a thing to say about a date with Ben. Had being around the temptation of Kyle soured her relationship with Ben? If so, she needed to get her priorities straight.

Chapter Eighteen

After Esther's announcement, Kyle struggled with guilt. How could he tell her she'd made a mistake? Why hadn't he been upfront with them from the start? Coming back here a second time only confirmed to them that he planned to take over the practice. He should have mentioned the fellowships he intended to apply for this month. With the deadline for those looming, he needed to send off his applications. Instead he spent his evening hours mooning over Leah, reliving every word, every touch.

To be honest, daydreams about Leah hadn't been the only distraction. He'd been procrastinating because every time he thought about leaving her, he couldn't take that final step of submitting the documents.

His hesitation made no sense. Not only was Leah Amish, but she had another relationship. No way could he overcome either of those obstacles. Did he really want to relive his past heartbreak?

Leah tapped at the partially open office door. As soon as she appeared, his heart answered an emphatic *yes*, but his brain and conscience shouted a stronger *no*.

"Abel Hochstetler is in room one."

The smile she flashed at him set his nerves zinging. Once again, his emotions overrode common sense.

"OK." Kyle rose from the desk, and Leah scurried away, perhaps remembering Esther's instructions. Or maybe Ben had asked her to stay away from him, which would be for the best.

Right now he had patients to see, and then he'd have to meet with the Hesses. He hated to dash their hopes, but he needed to make his plans clear.

After the last appointment, Kyle made notes in the file and carried it out to the reception desk. Leah had her back to him as she locked the door. The heart-shaped *kapp* on her head was a good reminder to rein in his interest.

"Where do you want this file?" he asked her.

She turned and took it from him, avoiding his eyes and only grasping the edge of the folder as if to stay as far from his fingers as she could. "I'll file this and be right in."

He'd hoped to walk with her. "I can wait for you."

"It would be better if you don't," she said, as she headed down the hallway to the file room. "I'll lock up the other rooms."

A flicker of disappointment ran through him, but she was right. And Esther would prefer that they arrive at different times.

Kyle opened the door to the house and went in. Esther sat on the couch near her husband, who was leaning back in the brown leather recliner, covered with one of his wife's knitted afghans. As soon as he noticed Kyle, the doctor reached for the lever to pull the chair into an upright position, but Esther stopped him.

Dr. Hess sighed and ran his hands over the chair arms. With a touch of exasperation in his tone, he said, "If Esther had her way, I'd be tucked up in bed."

His wife put her hands on her hips and scolded, "You've spent years healing others so you can let me coddle you for a short while."

Kyle smiled at their affectionate squabbling. The caring that underlay their words showed neither of them was as exasperated as they pretended to be. Would he ever have an opportunity to share affection like this? Leah's face came to mind, but he shook his head to banish that thought as he sank into the chair Esther indicated.

As if he'd conjured her up, Leah tapped at the door. "May I come in?"

Her soft voice started his blood racing. He kept his attention on the variegated green squares of the doctor's afghan. The last thing he needed was for the Hesses to see his interest in Leah. Esther had worried enough the night she'd found them in the kitchen together.

"Of course, dear. We're all in the living room."

Even without looking in her direction, Kyle sensed the minute Leah walked through the doorway. The atmosphere shifted and vibrated around him. Despite his promise to himself not to look her way, his eyes were drawn to her. She brightened the room with her warm, sunny presence.

Esther patted the sofa cushion beside her. "Why don't you sit here with me?"

Leah complied, and Kyle noted Esther had seated them so they were as far from each other as possible. As much as he wished they were closer, the distance might help him keep his mind on the conversation, although it hadn't slowed the rapid pounding of his heart.

"First of all," Esther began, "we want to thank you for taking over for us on such short notice." She removed envelopes from the table beside her, handed one to Leah, and stood to pass one to Kyle.

Across from him, Leah opened the envelope and pulled out a flowered thank-you card. A check fluttered into her lap. "*Ach*, no. I can't accept this. I came to help, not to work." She tried to return the check, but Esther pushed her hand away.

"If we had to hire someone to come in, we would have paid them."

"But I didn't do it for pay."

Esther picked up the check Leah had set down beside her. She reached over and returned it. "You will keep that. If it bothers your conscience, please donate it to charity."

Leah looked as if she was about to cry. Kyle shifted in his chair and cleared his throat to draw everyone's attention away from her. He also felt guilty about accepting a check from the Hesses, especially because he had no intention of taking over the practice. Now that they both had turned in his direction, Kyle's mouth went dry.

* * *

Grateful for Kyle's interruption, Leah faced in his direction. She'd have to find a way to return the money, but right now, Kyle looked as if he needed help. His face had that sickish expression she'd seen earlier. Was he getting ready to tell them what he'd confessed to her? That he had no intention of staying here? Esther and Martin would be devastated.

Dr. Hess didn't seem to pick up on Kyle's distress. "The reason we asked you both to come in here is because I've been ordered to take a month's rest from my practice." His voice wavered.

Esther reached over to place a hand over his. "It's only a month, Martin, and you were planning to retire. Why not consider this a trial run?"

"It'll be a trial, all right." The doctor's attempt at humor fell flat because he couldn't manage a light-hearted tone, and his face betrayed him.

"Oh, Martin, you make it sound as if spending all your time with me will be a hardship."

Dr. Hess turned startled eyes to his wife. "Not at all. It's just that..."

"You don't like being sidelined," Esther said.

"Exactly. You know me too well, dear," Dr. Hess replied.

Then he nodded at Kyle. "I've been praying God will send you a wonderful wife and helpmeet like mine. Going through life with such a treasure is the greatest blessing you'll ever have."

Leah winced at his words. What kind of a helpmeet would she be for Ben? Rather than caring for him and meeting his needs, she kept pushing him aside. Often, she'd rather be anywhere than in his presence. Even today, she'd had no qualms about postponing their date for this meeting with the Hesses. She wasn't being fair to

Ben. Or to herself. She had no idea what her priorities were. Unfortunately, the one item occupying her mind day and night shouldn't be on the list at all.

Esther drew her out of her musings. "Leah? I'd like to spend more time with Martin while he's recuperating"— she held up a hand to stop her husband's protests—"so I wondered if you'd be willing to work part-time for the next month. We'd pay you, of course."

"I...I don't know. I'd have to talk to my parents." Her *daed* might be grateful for the money to pay bills. "And Sharon and..."

"About Sharon." Esther smiled at her. "Martin and I both think you should continue your training. Because I'm right here in the house, anytime Sharon calls, you could let me know, and I can take your place."

What a generous offer. She could help her parents with the finances and still have time to be a midwife. Her heart full of gratitude, she made the mistake of looking up and beaming. Right at Kyle. The smile he sent her way almost proved her undoing.

Esther must have noticed. "I did want to mention we'd keep the same ground rules I established the other night."

Dr. Hess glanced from one to the other. "Esther told me about that, and I hope you don't think she came down too hard on you." When his wife sputtered in protest, he held up a hand. "I didn't say you did. I thought these young people might believe that."

"I don't want you to think..." Leah had been about to tell him she and Kyle didn't have those kinds of feelings for each other, but could she honestly admit that?

Again, the doctor held up a hand. "Please let me finish. I'm not questioning you or even implying anything is going on between you two."

Kyle stared at the floor, and Leah pleated the fabric of her apron into small creases to avoid meeting the doctor's searching gaze.

"Esther and I have our reasons for being concerned over what might be an entirely innocent friendship. Some of it may be because we're both old-fashioned, but our fears date back to a situation from many years ago."

"Martin, I don't think..."

"Relax, dear. I don't intend to give anything away. I just want them to know that we had a young girl staying here, and unbeknownst to us, she'd been meeting a young fellow behind our backs. She ended up having a child, and—"

"Martin!" The sharpness of Esther's voice halted his flow of words. "I thought we agreed not to..." She waved her hands in the air.

"You're right, dear. I'm sorry. I do tend to ramble on." He turned to Kyle. "We both don't ever want something like that to happen on our watch again. I know Leah is courting Ben, so I'm sure we have nothing to worry about."

"We'll just keep the rules in place for propriety," Esther added. "Better safe than sorry, I always say."

Kyle and Leah both nodded, and Dr. Hess beamed at them both. "I'm so glad we understand each other, and that we had this conversation. Thank you both for taking over at the office. Kyle, I can't tell you how happy I am that you'll be joining us."

Kyle shifted in his chair. He rubbed at the back of his neck, and a look of dismay spread across his face.

Deep inside, Leah felt his distress as if it were her own and wished she could comfort him.

* * *

Kyle cleared his throat. It was now or never. "I'm happy to help out while you recover, but I accepted a position as a covering physician in January, and"—he took a deep breath—"I actually took off November to prepare fellowship applications." He hastened to reassure the doctor. "I didn't mind coming here to help out." He didn't mention that coming here meant giving up a long-awaited and much-needed vacation in December.

Dr. Hess's face crumpled. "I don't suppose working here changed your mind."

Kyle shriveled inside. How could he hurt this couple who had always been so kind to him? But wouldn't lying to them or letting them believe an untruth be more harmful?

He forced himself to say the words he should have said a long time ago. "I've always dreamed of doing research, perhaps finding a cure for a rare disease. I've chosen hospitals on the forefront of discovering ways to fight cancer or inherited diseases. I want to make a contribution to the world." *And make a name for myself.*

He didn't say that aloud because the Hesses and Leah would never understand that desire. He had to admit being around them had made him question that motivation but not enough to give it up entirely. And definitely not enough to tempt him to stay in a small, backwater town.

The only draw for him here would be Leah. A dream that never could be.

They all sat in silence for a few minutes, and Kyle tried to tamp down his guilt. Across from him, Esther's eyes filled with concern as she stared at her husband. Dr. Hess had lowered his head and massaged his forehead, and his large hand shaded his eyes from view.

Leah shot Kyle a sympathetic glance. He appreciated her support, but his heart was too heavy to thank her with a smile.

"I thought…" Dr. Hess said in broken voice. "I thought blood…heredity…would overcome any objections."

"Hush, Martin." Esther's tear-choked voice twisted a knife in Kyle's gut. "You promised not to use that as leverage."

Blood? Heredity? Leverage? Kyle had no idea what the doctor and his wife were muttering about. Did they know something about his family they'd planned to use as blackmail?

"Maybe he should know the truth before he makes his decision." Dr. Hess's low, frantic whisper to his wife carried across the room.

Esther shook her head. "It's not fair to put him in that position."

Kyle longed to ask, but something about their whispers convinced him he'd be better off not knowing. Particularly if the information might cause him to change his mind.

"I do want to thank you for your generous offer," he told them. "I can't believe you'd be willing to give up your home and practice to someone you barely know. Many new doctors would jump at a chance like this, and I'd be happy to provide some recommendations of friends or colleagues who might be a good fit."

His head bowed, Dr. Hess, who'd fixed his gaze on his knobby fingers clasped on his lap, only shook his head. "You don't understand. We chose you for a reason."

His wife leaned over to set a hand on his. "We agreed to leave it up to God. If this is His will, we need to accept it."

"Doesn't Kyle deserve to know?" The doctor's harsh whisper was barely audible.

His wife's equally quiet response was not intended for Kyle's ears. "She begged you never to tell."

"But she's dead. They both are."

"Are you talking about my parents?"

The doctor and his wife turned startled eyes toward him.

Esther turned to her husband. "We never should have started this."

"Started what?" Kyle demanded. "If you know something about my family that I don't know, I think it's only fair you tell me."

"He's right," Dr. Hess said.

"But we promised Hannah..."

Kyle's gut clenched. Hannah was his mother's name. "What did you promise my mom?" Maybe they'd promised to take care of him. That would explain their generous offer. Why would they feel obligated to do that, though? It didn't make sense.

The doctor and his wife were shooting secret messages back and forth with their eyes. Esther's seemed to be begging her husband not to tell, and he appeared to be asking her to break their promise.

"When I was in the hospital and realized how close I'd been to death," Dr. Hess said to his wife, "I worried about taking this secret with me to my grave. What if Kyle has an emergency and needs to know his medical history?"

"You're right, dear," Esther agreed tearfully. "I just don't feel right about breaking a promise."

They seemed to have forgotten Leah was in the room. She sat with one hand pressed to her mouth as if holding back the same dread snaking through Kyle.

His eyes glinting with tears, Dr. Hess took off his glasses and polished them. "This is a hard story to recount, so please bear with me. It begins with my youngest sister, Arlene. As a late-life baby born to parents who were both in poor health, she caused a lot of trouble at home."

Esther reached out and took his hand.

"Arlene rebelled against my parents and God. Esther and I had been married for quite a while by then, and it seemed we'd never have children." His wife's lips trembled, and he squeezed her hand before continuing. "We offered to take Arlene in and parent her."

Kyle had no idea how this story connected with his parents, and he hoped Dr. Hess would get to the point. For as long as he could remember, the doctor and his wife had been childless. Arlene must not have lived with them during his childhood.

"We tried our best to set a good example and give Arlene plenty of love, but we struggled with her the same way my parents had. She broke the rules, sneaked out at night, skipped school, and acted defiant when we grounded her. Then we discovered she'd been meeting her boyfriend in our house while we were working in the office."

Esther chimed in. "I discovered the two of them together in the kitchen, which is why seeing the two of you there upset me so much." She turned to her husband to continue.

"Several weeks later she announced she was pregnant. Her boyfriend deserted her, and she settled down. Having a baby at sixteen turned out to be a sobering experience for her. We helped her through that, but we wanted her to continue her education and have a normal adolescence, so we offered to adopt little Timothy. She agreed, and once we'd signed the papers, she went back home to finish school."

Tears rolled down Esther's cheeks. "I struggled so hard to be a mother and keep up with the office duties. I refused to get a nanny or babysitter. I wanted to do it all myself, despite all the sleepless nights. One afternoon, I broke down in the office."

Dr. Hess interrupted her. "I should have been more of a help. Looking back, I can see ways we could have made it work, but we were so overwhelmed with the practice. Adding childcare, well..."

Esther nodded. "Anyway, only one patient remained in the waiting room when I broke down that day. Hannah Miller."

Kyle sucked in a breath. "My mom."

"Yes, your mother. When she came over and hugged me, I blurted out the whole story. She came over every day for the next few weeks to help care for Timothy."

Now Kyle was confused. If his mom had disappeared every day for several weeks, he would have remembered.

He started to ask when this happened, but Esther went on with her story.

"Your brother, Caleb, was about six, and like us, your parents had struggled for years to have a baby. Hannah begged to adopt Timothy." Esther squeezed her eyes shut and sobbed into a hanky she pulled from her sleeve. "In the end, I gave up my darling baby boy because I believed he'd have a better life with a stay-at-home mom. There's never been a day I didn't regret that decision, Kyle."

Kyle's head spun as he tried to connect all the threads. *Timothy? I had a brother about the same age as me? But that doesn't make sense.*

Dr. Hess cleared his throat. "We've always loved you, Kyle, and kept a close eye on you from afar. Even though your parents changed your name, we still often call you Timothy in private when we talk about you."

What? He was adopted? *He* was the Timothy they were talking about? His parents weren't his birth parents? Kyle sat there shell-shocked.

What did you do when your whole world caved in?

Chapter Nineteen

Leah ached inside for Kyle. She yearned to go to him, to comfort him. If only she could erase his pain.

His face a mask of shock and betrayal, Kyle stood and staggered from the room. With every fiber of her being, Leah longed to chase after him. She wished the two of them were alone. But Esther and Martin were in the room, so she gripped the sofa arm to keep herself in place.

Sobs shook Esther's body after Kyle walked out the door. "Will he ever forgive us?"

Dr. Hess hung his head and shielded his eyes with his hands.

"Give him some time," Leah suggested. She couldn't even begin to imagine how it would feel to discover your whole life, as you'd always known it, no longer existed. You weren't the person you thought you were. Your parents weren't who you thought they were.

Esther dabbed at her eyes with a sopping-wet hanky. Leah reached for a box of tissues on the nearby side table and handed it to her. The small china clock on that table showed it was almost two o'clock. Ben had been expecting her to get home soon after she finished work at noon.

"Would you excuse me while I make a phone call?" When Esther nodded, Leah stood and headed for the kitchen. She paced toward the staircase leading to the bedrooms, wishing she had the right to mount those steps, to be with Kyle while he sorted out all his emotions.

Instead she hit the button to call Joel. And talk to Ben.

"No," her brother said when she asked. "Ben's not here. He waited an hour, then left."

She'd done it again. "Was he angry?"

"Depressed, I think. Do you need me to come and get you? Dad's home now, so he could watch the store."

"I'm not sure." She couldn't leave Esther when she was so distraught. "Maybe in thirty minutes?"

"Will do. We have customers. Gotta go." Joel hung up.

Leah returned to the living room. Not knowing what else to do, she bowed her head and prayed. By the time her brother arrived, Martin and Esther had joined her in prayer for Kyle.

In the car, Leah asked him to drop her at the Grabers'. She hoped she wasn't too late, but Sharon had been right about a first baby taking its time. She and Sharon chatted with the parents while they waited another two hours, but Leah's thoughts kept straying to Kyle. How was he coping? If only she could do something to help.

When the baby finally made his appearance, Sharon let her handle the delivery alone. Her mentor stepped back and watched. After holding the newborn, weighing him, and handing him to his mother, Leah's eyes filled with tears to think newborn Timothy's mother had left him behind. Even the Hesses had given him up. Poor Kyle.

Would every baby she delivered from now on remind her of Kyle?

*   *   *

Kyle had slipped upstairs to the room alone. He needed time to process everything he'd been told. In one afternoon, his whole life had turned upside down. It hadn't been his parents who died in the car crash. He'd lost his parents—his birth parents—long ago. So long ago he couldn't remember them. He didn't even know who they were.

Had Caleb known? He'd been six. Surely he'd remember his mother bringing home a new baby. Had they presented the baby brother to him as a surprise? Would six-year-olds know about pregnancy? Nowadays parents told their children all about expecting a baby. But the Amish didn't. And his parents had grown up Amish. But why did they choose to hide his adoption?

As dusk faded into darkness, question after question whirled through his mind. He arranged and rearranged facts, trying to make sense of it all. So many details from the past fit into the puzzle perfectly, yet others seemed to belong to a different puzzle entirely. He tossed and turned throughout a sleepless night as his dreams dredged up bits and pieces from the past.

As morning light filtered through the window, Kyle

squeezed his eyes shut. He couldn't bear to face another day. Downstairs, the Hesses prepared to leave for church. They'd tiptoed around all morning, trying not to disturb him, but he hadn't slept. Once they were gone, he'd have the house to himself—the house that had once been his home. The house that his birth mother had lived in. The house that he'd lived in with the Hesses, his temporary parents. They might not be his parents, but they definitely were his uncle and aunt.

What did it mean as far as his heritage? Unlike his brother, Caleb, he had no Amish ties. His birth mother had been Mennonite.

Kyle's thoughts whirled in circles, a tilting, ever-changing kaleidoscope of ideas, each one connected to the previous one but creating a different pattern each time, depending on the angle from which he viewed them.

The hardest question to reconcile was why all of them had lied to him for years—his parents, the Hesses, perhaps even Caleb.

Over the next week, he wrestled with the news that had rocked his world. He worked long hours in the office so he wouldn't have to sit at the table with Martin and Esther. He waited until they'd gone to bed before he tiptoed into the house. He couldn't avoid Esther on the days she filled in as the receptionist, but he kept his interactions crisp and professional. Although her eyes often revealed her hurt, he couldn't bear to let down his guard around her. Not yet.

He much preferred the days Leah sat at the desk and tapped at his office door. He only wished she didn't always appear to be tiptoeing around as if afraid he'd been permanently damaged and the least little thing might set him off.

"Kyle, are you all right?" she asked him the following Saturday after the last patient had left.

One week had passed since the Hesses had told him he'd been adopted. "I'm still processing the news."

"I can imagine. It must be so hard." Leah stayed in the office doorway, keeping to Esther's instructions not to be in the room together. "If you want to talk about it, I'm happy to listen."

At her caring expression, the questions churning through Kyle's mind flooded out. "Who are my *real* parents? My birth parents? If it hadn't been for them, I wouldn't be here. But what about the people I called Mom and Dad?" He squeezed his eyes shut to block out the memories. "I believed them, but they lied to me about my true identity."

"I wouldn't say they lied, Kyle. They neglected to tell you the truth, but perhaps they planned to."

"When? I was already sixteen when they died. And where do Esther and Martin fit in? Are they my parents, or aunt and uncle, or both?"

"Maybe that's a question you should ask them. It's obvious they love and care about you."

As they talked, the chaos inside slowly untangled. He still had many unanswered questions, but with Leah's gentle encouragement, he drained much of the poison and the pain.

"I'd better go," she said when he finished. "We shouldn't be here together."

"Thank you for staying and listening." Words were inadequate to express his gratitude for all she'd given him. "I can't tell you how much talking to you helped me."

"I'm so glad." She flashed him a beautiful smile before she left.

Kyle sat in the antique wooden chair, one that had held several generations of doctors, pondering several still unanswered questions.

Was his birth mother still alive? Did he want to meet her? Who was his father? Was there any way to find out? Did he even want to search for him? What if he never found him?

Right now, he had no answers to those questions, but one thing had become clear. He might never know his birth parents, but the word *father* conjured up images of the man he called Dad while he was growing up. He'd always known his dad loved him. So had Mom. They'd taken care of him, made sacrifices for him, raised him. Didn't that make them his real parents?

From the tears in Martin's and Esther's eyes, they'd loved him too, and they'd given him up because they thought he'd have a better life. Maybe he was looking at this all wrong. Rather than seeing himself as abandoned, he could choose to view himself as lucky. Despite not knowing his birth parents, he'd been loved not by two, but by four parents.

* * *

Leah closed the office door behind her and punched in the code to lock it. Kyle's resilience amazed her after he'd had his whole life upended. Most people would have been knocked down by that unexpected blow, but he'd come out stronger. He still had things to work out, but she had every confidence he would.

She was grateful he'd trusted her enough to share his deepest thoughts and feelings. It brought them closer emotionally. Buoyed by that thought, Leah practically floated to Joel's car.

"Wow, you're looking cheery," her brother remarked. "Ben will be happy to see that."

"Ben?" Leah's spirits plunged with a thud. "Is he waiting for me at the shop?" They'd gone on a brief make-up date last week, but he hadn't mentioned stopping by today.

"Not yet," Joel said. "You kept him waiting too long last weekend, but he did indicate he might stop by later."

Was it wrong to hope he wouldn't? What was the matter with her? She'd dreamed of marriage for years, envying her friends who had husbands and families. Now she had a wonderful Amish man who wanted to court her, yet the only man who filled her thoughts was an *Englisch* doctor.

When they got back to the shop, Ada's buggy was parked near the door. "Josiah's watching the children for a few hours while I run errands," her friend said. "I was hoping I'd get to see you. Your *daed* said you're working several days a week at the doctor's office."

Pulling open the door, Leah said, "Yes, I'm alternating days with Esther Hess. I have off Tuesdays and Thursdays, which works well for attending weddings."

"I hope you're planning to come to one this Thursday," Ada said with a teasing smile.

"Hmm. I'm pretty sure Joel scheduled me for the shop that day."

A worried look crossed Ada's face. "You'd better not be working."

"I'm only teasing. I'd close the shop for a whole day rather than miss my best friend's wedding."

"Good, because your best friend is counting on you to be by her side when she marries the man of her dreams."

Leah's heart overflowed with joy for Ada. "I'm so glad you found Josiah."

"I am too." Ada's eyes sparkled. "I never imagined I'd find a man who'd want to take on all seven of my siblings and love them as if they were his own."

"You opened your heart to his son," Leah pointed out.

"That was easy." Ada's face softened. "Nathan is so dear. I love him as if he were my own child."

Leah's eyes misted. Had Kyle's mom felt that way about him? She hoped so.

"Enough about me," Ada said. "Let's talk about you. What's been happening?"

"Not much." Now was not the time to spoil her friend's happiness by mentioning how rocky her relationship had been with Ben. Kyle's problems were private and so were her feelings for him, and Leah hadn't told anyone about her health problems. "Oh, I did deliver two more babies on my own. Sharon observed, of course, but she let me do all of it."

"That's wonderful! Your face glows when you talk about it." Tiny frown lines wrinkled Ada's forehead. "Have you come to an agreement with Ben about it yet?"

"Not exactly." The subject hadn't come up when he'd stopped by the doctor's office, because Ben had been too upset about her being alone with Kyle. But on their brief date the other night, Ben had revisited his concerns about her continuing to work with Kyle part-time.

Ada studied her. "What's the matter?"

"I don't want to burden you so close to the wedding." Besides, Leah couldn't confide most of her secrets.

"It's never a burden to listen to a friend."

"I'm not sure Ben's right for me," Leah confessed. "I don't seem to have the dreamy feelings for him that you have for Josiah." How could she admit she felt that type of attraction to an *Englischer*?

"Not everyone falls in love at first sight. Sometimes people start as friends, and their romance grows."

"Perhaps." Leah worried her romance might never grow. Once Kyle left for his fellowship, eliminating that temptation might help. Maybe then her feelings would change. "I hope that's the case."

But if Ben knew the truth, would he even want to marry her?

Using wedding preparations as excuses, Leah managed to avoid Ben until Thursday. He sat on the men's side of Ada's living room, directly across from her. Leah tried to avoid looking at him as she wondered if Ada was right. Would love blossom if she and Ben married?

When the congregation began singing the opening hymn, Leah joined in, her heart bubbling over with joy for Ada and Josiah, who were downstairs being coun-seled by the bishop. A year ago, she and Ada were the last of their buddy bunch to remain unmarried, and they'd despaired of ever finding true love. Now Ada was marrying the man of her dreams, and Leah was courting Ben. For now, at least.

After a half an hour, the bride and groom entered and took their places. Leah rejoiced in their shining faces and the tender looks Josiah gave Ada. The Scripture reading and sermons seemed especially meaningful because Ada would now be a part of this sacred tradition.

Then Ada and Josiah stepped forward, and the congregation surrounded them as they exchanged vows. As they answered the bishop's questions, Leah tried to picture herself going through this ceremony with Ben but struggled to feel the same joy and lightness she felt as Ada and Josiah responded.

When they reached the final question, Leah's eyes welled with tears. "Do you both promise together that you will, with love, forbearance, and patience, live with each other and not part from each other until God will separate you in death?"

Could she and Ben answer the final question in unison with the same enthusiasm and love as Ada and Josiah? Another face intruded, and Leah tried so hard to erase it she almost missed the bishop's closing statement. But she didn't miss the couple's clasped hands, the symbol of their union. Ada was married to a man she loved with all her heart. Leah's eyes misted at their beaming faces. God had joined them together, and they'd go through the rest of their lives as partners, walking side by side.

Because she was in the bridal party, Leah sat with the bride and groom at the *eck*. Her seat at that corner table provided a welcome relief from being around Ben, who gazed at her longingly throughout the meal. They'd be partners for the evening meal, but right now, she enjoyed spending time with Ada.

Following the meal, the men went to the barn to talk, and Leah joined the other girls upstairs. Chatter flowed around her, but she barely heard it. Her mind remained on the promises Josiah and Ada had made in church. Every time she tried to imagine herself and Ben in their places, Kyle's face intruded.

At a scream from downstairs, the babbling ceased. Everyone stampeded toward the sound. Amid the rushing crowd, Leah was jabbed by elbows and bumped so hard from behind she almost fell headlong down the stairs. She grabbed for the railing to avoid tumbling. A gaggle of girls entered the kitchen.

"What happened?"

"Rose reached up and grabbed one of the knives from the table." Emma sat on the floor, holding her two-year-old daughter on her lap. She'd wrapped a dish towel around the cut.

Leah stopped suddenly. She had no idea Emma would be here. Although Emma had forgiven her, old twinges of guilt squeezed Leah's insides, and she struggled to put on a friendly and calming smile as she knelt beside the little girl. "Can I see it, Rose?" One quick glance revealed that a bandage wouldn't stop the bleeding. "She's going to need stitches." Leah applied pressure.

Behind her, people murmured, "It's too far to take her to the emergency room," and, "Call Dr. Hess. He's close by. He'll come."

"Dr. Hess is no longer—" Other voices drowned out Leah's words. She panicked.

Evidently, some of the women hadn't heard about the

doctor's heart attack. They couldn't ask Kyle to make this house call. Not after all he'd just been through emotionally. Maybe he no longer had feelings for his ex-girlfriend, but it would be awkward for both of them. And many in the crowd would recognize Kyle and remember the past.

Leah tried to protest again, but a teenage girl had already passed over her cell phone, and someone at the back of the crowd made the call.

"I called the doctor's office. Esther said he's not working right now."

"Didn't you hear he had a heart attack?" one woman asked.

"His wife told me that," the caller said, "but she said if they can spare him, she may send his new assistant. It was a bit too noisy to hear, but I think she said his name's Dr. Miller or Muller."

One of the women who'd been a patient announced, "Yes, it's Miller. Kyle Miller."

"Not the Kyle Miller who..."

"Yes, that's the one," the woman confirmed.

Several people gasped, and most eyes focused on Emma.

Emma paled. "I don't think..."

"I could hold Rose," Leah volunteered.

"She's shy and usually won't go to anyone else." Emma's voice betrayed her distress. "Besides, if she's getting stitches, I want to be there to hold her."

"I understand." Leah wished she could offer some comfort.

Emma lifted her eyes to the staring crowd surrounding them. "Could someone go out to the barn and get Sam?"

Had they told Esther the name of the patient? If so, perhaps she'd send Dr. Hess. Putting in stitches wouldn't be too taxing for him. Leah hoped Kyle would be too busy. As much as she'd love to see him, she'd do anything to spare him this.

Her stomach roiled. Seeing Emma again might revive all those old memories of the accident. If it did, would Kyle remember Leah's connection to the past?

*　*　*

Esther entered Kyle's office and handed him a note with an address neatly printed on it. "A child needs stitches right away."

"But I have more patients coming in."

"Only two more. Martin can handle them. One's here for some bloodwork. I usually draw that, so I think he can manage."

The last thing Kyle wanted to do was make a house call, especially to this Ada Rupp's house, which most likely was an Amish farm. But he had to help a child.

By the time he'd grabbed his coat and medical bag, Esther had set out the necessary supplies. He put them in his bag and rushed to his car. The Rupp house wasn't far. When he pulled into the driveway, buggies filled the yard. Must be a funeral or a wedding.

Kyle hesitated. How could he face all these Amish people at once when most of them probably knew what he'd done? He steeled himself to endure their censure.

Freezing air stung his cheeks as he raced across the lawn. Leah pushed the door open as soon as he reached the porch. He smiled, happy to find one friendly face, but after he entered the house, he kept his eyes down. He avoided looking at people. He had no desire to see the recognition—or blame—in their eyes.

"The little girl is right over here." Leah led him to a spot on the floor where an Amish mother held her daughter on her lap. A man sat beside her, one hand resting on the small girl's head.

Kyle mumbled a greeting without looking up. He kept his attention fixed on the small hand wrapped in a dish towel. When he sank onto the floor in front of the child, Leah lowered herself to the floor beside him. How would he concentrate with Leah so close?

Focus on the child. Tuning out everything else in the room, he flexed his hands, stiff from the cold, and slid on disposable latex gloves. Then he reached for the child's hand.

"Her name's Rose," Leah told him.

"Hi, Rose. Can I see your cut? I'll fix it for you." The little girl cooperated, but her mother was shaking. Kyle glanced up to reassure the mom her daughter would be all right, and froze.

Emma?

She appeared as upset to see him as he was to see her. No wonder she was trembling. She had no reason to believe he'd help her daughter. Not after what he'd done to her.

His throat parched and his nerves stretched taut, Kyle longed to mumble an apology. But what could he say to someone who'd paid a terrible price for his mistakes?

While he dithered, Leah opened the bag and set out the supplies. "I can hand things to you as you need them."

Trapped between the woman he'd destroyed and the one he'd fallen for, Kyle struggled to concentrate on his work.

The cut, Kyle. The cut. He clicked his mind into doctor mode, blocking out Leah's soft presence and Emma's frightened face.

He unwrapped the towel and was relieved to see that, although the cut was deep, it was clean. It would be easy to stitch and should heal well. "This will pinch a little." He repeated the lie most doctors used.

The small girl surprised him by remaining still throughout, which was more than he could say for Emma. Not that he blamed her. If she had her choice, she'd probably snatch her daughter and run as far from him as she could.

Leah passed him supplies as he needed them, and their fingers brushed. Being in Emma's presence somewhat dampened those jolts of electricity, but Kyle still struggled to concentrate on his work, rather than Leah's nearness.

While he finished the stitches and bandaged Rose's hand, he parroted the care instructions. Leah helped him clean up and pack his supplies. But as Emma rose, Kyle's conscience wouldn't let him leave without an apology.

As her husband reached for their daughter, Kyle stood and faced them both. "I'm so sorry. For everything."

Emma's eyes filled with tears, and her husband set a hand on her shoulder. "We all forgave you long ago."

Kyle shook his head. He had a hard time believing that.

"God has a reason for everything that happens." Emma smiled up at her husband. "If it weren't for the accident, I'd never have married Sam, and you wouldn't have become a doctor."

Emma was right. Who knows where they might have ended up if things had continued the way they had, but that didn't absolve him of the damage he'd done.

As if she'd read his mind, Emma said softly, "You need to forgive yourself, Kyle. And also believe God can forgive you."

Before he could turn and bolt, Leah set her hand on his arm as if she sensed his need for comfort. Kyle longed to interlace his fingers with hers. If only he had that right. She handed him his bag, and he turned to smile at her. The sympathy in her eyes touched his heart, made him want to enfold her in his arms. He forced himself to reach for the bag and head to the door before he acted on that impulse.

Leah's eyes and smile stayed with him, but Emma's words echoed in his ears as he crossed the lawn to his car. He wasn't sure he could ever forgive himself. But maybe it was time to try.

Chapter Twenty

As Kyle turned on the engine, someone shouted his name. A man, holding one hand on his black felt hat to prevent it from flying off, jogged toward his car.

No...not Caleb. If only he'd driven off, Kyle could have put this whole nightmare behind him. He was tempted to throw the car in gear and push the gas pedal to the floor, but his brother had already reached the car.

Gasping for breath, Caleb asked, "May I get in?" Without waiting for an answer, he rounded the car and slid into the passenger seat. "When they told me you were here, I couldn't let you leave without seeing you. How have you been?"

Kyle kept his expression stony and his tone chilly to hide the turmoil inside. Learning he was adopted, seeing Emma again, fighting his growing attraction to Leah, and now facing his estranged brother. Too many emotional encounters had hit him this past week; his head hadn't stopped reeling. "I've been better."

"I'm sorry to hear that." Caleb tilted his head as if inviting Kyle to confide in him. When Kyle didn't respond, Caleb waved a hand toward the porch. "There's Lydia with the twins."

Kyle glanced in the direction his brother indicated. One six-year-old stood on each side of his sister-in-law. Or was she his sister-in-law? Now that he'd discovered he'd been adopted, family relationships had become murky.

He turned back to Caleb. "Why didn't you tell me the truth about my birth?"

"What?" From the confusion on his brother's face, Caleb had no idea about the truth.

As Kyle recounted the story the Hesses had told him, Caleb's expression changed to shock, then pity. "I had no idea. I remember Mom bringing you home, but I never questioned it. She only said you were my brother, and that hasn't changed."

Kyle started to protest, but Caleb interrupted him. "Did either one of them ever treat you differently than they did me?"

"No, but—"

"Exactly. They loved us both. To them, the circumstances of your birth didn't matter. You were their son the same as I was."

Kyle had come to that conclusion earlier, but to have his brother reinforce it made a much bigger impact. If Caleb hadn't seen a difference, then it must be true. That only made Kyle's teenage rebellion doubly shameful.

He'd spent years trying to tamp down the guilt. The

main reason he'd avoided Caleb had been to evade the truth.

He turned to his brother. "Caleb, I owe you an apology. I made your life miserable after"—he forced himself to continue—"Mom and Dad died." Would he ever be able to say the words *Mom* and *Dad* again without choking up? "Can you ever forgive me?"

"I forgave you a long time ago. I know what it's like to be a teenager. *I* rebelled against *our* parents when I was that age."

Kyle noted the emphasis on *our*. Caleb must have been trying to reassure him of his place in the family. "I don't remember that."

"You were what? Maybe nine or ten at that point? Mom came down hard on me." Caleb's eyes held regret. "All you had at age sixteen was an older brother who had no idea how to parent. I blame myself for not doing a good job. The truth of the matter is I should be asking for your forgiveness."

"It's not your fault I went wild."

"Like many teenagers, you had a rough time. It's over now, so let's put all that behind us. Look what you've done with your life now. I'm so proud of you."

Becoming a doctor had been Caleb's dream. A dream that he'd set aside to parent Kyle. Not only had Kyle dashed his brother's dreams, he'd damaged Emma's life. They both seemed to have recovered, but how different their lives would have been if it weren't for Kyle.

Caleb reached out a hand to shake Kyle's. "Let's start fresh and leave those teenage years behind."

Kyle shook his hand, and Caleb knuckled his head like he used to do when they were kids.

* * *

Watching Kyle treat Emma's daughter brought terrible memories rushing back. Kyle shouldn't be blaming himself for that accident. Leah had to tell him the truth. The first time she'd seen Kyle, she'd been afraid he'd look into her eyes and remember. So far, he'd shown no signs he recalled that connection. And when their gazes met, Leah forgot everything. Past, present, and future condensed down to one heart-stopping moment in time.

But today, she'd go out to the car and avoid looking at him—staring, actually—so she could confess. Maybe then he could forgive himself.

Leah had been about to dash out to talk to him when Caleb pushed past everyone in the living room, murmuring, "Please, God, don't let him drive away before I can talk to him."

Stepping aside so Caleb could dash outside, Leah went to the window to watch their interaction. She hoped Caleb wouldn't say anything to hurt Kyle. He'd been through so much.

As soon as Caleb stepped from the car and slammed the door, Kyle revved his engine. Praying the same prayer Caleb had, Leah dashed out the door. The car had already started down the gravel driveway, stones spitting out from beneath the wheels, by the time she reached the lawn.

"Kyle," she called.

She worried the roar of the motor had drowned out her voice, but Kyle slammed on his brakes. The locks clicked as she neared the car. Was he unlocking the door or keeping her out?

Reaching for the door handle, Leah tried to assess Kyle's mood. "I didn't want you to drive away while you were upset." And she had something to tell him.

"I'm not upset. But why does it matter if I were?"

Before she could stop herself, Leah blurted out, "Because I care about you." She couldn't believe she'd just said that. What had she been thinking? "I mean…"

"I know what you mean," Kyle said dully. "As a friend."

The feelings roiling inside Leah were anything but friendlike, but she nodded anyway. "Of course. I wouldn't want anything to happen to you."

Kyle pinched his lips together and stared straight ahead through the windshield as if fascinated by the quiet country lane.

"It must have been hard coming here today. Facing everyone."

Tight-lipped, Kyle's curt, "It was," indicated he didn't want to talk about it.

But Leah couldn't let him go without letting him know about her part in his past heartache. "About the accident…"

"I'd rather not talk about it, if you don't mind."

"There's something you should know." Leah pleated her apron with her fingers. Once he knew, he'd probably never forgive her. How could he? She'd let him take the blame all these years and carry all the guilt.

"Maybe you'd better tell me another time." Kyle waved toward his rearview mirror. "I'm not sure he appreciates you being alone with me in the car."

Ben stood in the doorway of the house, waiting for her.

* * *

He regretted hurting Leah's feelings, especially after she'd been so kind, but he had to gain control of his emotions. His attraction to her had grown so strong he'd almost blurted out his feelings when she'd laid her hand on his sleeve. He wanted to reach out and pull her into his arms. Resisting that impulse had taken all his willpower.

He was glad he hadn't, because as he pulled away, he glanced in the rearview mirror for one last glimpse of her. Ben stood in the doorway, waiting for her, looking as if he'd been betrayed.

What if Ben broke up with Leah? The possibility set his heart singing, but he'd never wish for anything that might hurt her. She wouldn't leave her faith, and she deserved a good Amish man.

Unlike his brother, Kyle could never become Amish. He would have to give up his profession. Could he do that?

It still bothered him to see Caleb dressed in plain clothes. He'd probably never adjust to his brother with a beard and bowl haircut wearing suspenders and a broad-brimmed hat. Although if Caleb had fallen for Lydia as hard as Kyle had fallen for Leah, he could understand his brother's motivation.

He shook his head. What was he doing imagining such far-fetched scenarios? Leah already had a relationship, and even if Ben were upset with her, he'd be a fool to give up someone as wonderful as Leah.

Rather than heading straight back to the office, Kyle drove around for a while. With everything that had happened this past week, his head was whirling. He needed to unwind and regain some peace of mind before he returned to the Hesses'.

Seeing Leah and Emma together today revealed how childish his infatuation with Emma had been. His schoolboy crush on Emma paled in comparison to his budding love for Leah. All the more reason to stay away from Leah, stay out of her life. Emma claimed everything had worked out for good, but she'd failed to mention she'd lost several years of her life recuperating from the accident he'd caused. And that hadn't been the worst of it. Every time he worked with a child, he remembered.

As Kyle wound down country lanes past chopped-down fields of corn, fields lying fallow, it reminded him of the emptiness of his life. Ever since the accident, he'd been desolate. Emma's words came back to him. He needed to forgive himself. But how?

How could he ever forgive himself for what he'd done? The Amish community had, but only a few people knew the whole truth. Yet Emma and her dad both knew everything, and they'd both forgiven him.

Perhaps the reason he couldn't forgive himself or let it go was because he'd closed himself off from God's forgiveness. Accepting that meant asking for forgiveness for all the things he'd done in the past, not just to Emma. Kyle wasn't sure he could reach that place right now. But he could apologize to two people he'd hurt.

He turned the car around and headed back to the Hesses' house. When he walked in the door, Esther was reading the Bible to her husband, who was ensconced in the recliner with an afghan tucked around him. A mug and a glass of water sat on the table beside him, along with a small plate of fruit.

Kyle smiled to see that the doctor had acquiesced to his wife's preferences. She loved to care for him, bring him drinks and treats, and read to him. Kyle usually tried to avoid their reading times because they preferred the Bible or spiritual books.

Esther waved to him. "Come in and join us. I'm almost done with this passage. Then you can tell us about the stitches."

Kyle wished he could slip upstairs and come down later, but he felt obligated to be polite, and he did have things he needed to say to them. He sat on the edge of the chair, ready to flee as soon as he could.

"We're reading First John, chapter one," Esther said. "I'm on verse eight. I can go back to the beginning if you'd like."

"No, no." Kyle motioned for her to continue. He tuned out as she began to read. A few words penetrated. Something about *sins*. He had plenty of those. He didn't want to hear more about that, but the first part of the next verse stood out.

"'If we confess our sins, he is faithful and just and will forgive us...'"

Esther finished the rest of the verse, but Kyle mulled over those words. To hear the same message twice in the same day? He'd grown up in the church and heard that section many times, but today it seemed he couldn't escape.

His shoulders relaxed after Esther closed the Bible and set it on the table beside her, only to tense again when she and the doctor bowed their heads for prayer.

To be polite, Kyle followed suit, but he kept his eyes open.

His mom's whisper floated through his mind, warning him as she had in childhood that a rebellious attitude would only bring heartache. She'd been right. He'd had so many heartaches since his teen years. Mom would say he needed to get right with God. But Kyle still balked at that idea.

The Hesses raised their heads, and Kyle lifted his head in relief.

"So how did things go at the Rupps'?" the doctor asked.

"Fine." Well, the doctoring part did. The rest of the visit had left him in emotional turmoil. "A little girl needed stitches in her hand."

"*Aww*, poor thing." Esther's compassionate voice revealed her love of children, reminding Kyle of his plans. Before he could speak, her face switched to alarm. "Oh, I hope it wasn't one of Ada's siblings."

"No, it was"—Kyle didn't want to subject himself to the Hesses' sympathy—"one of the other guests."

"Do you know her name by any chance? If she's a local, she'll be coming here to get her stitches out."

"Rose," he muttered. "I'm pretty sure she's not from around here."

In fact, he was positive she wasn't. Caleb had moved to Upper Dauphin County after he married Lydia, and Emma had married their next-door neighbor, Sam. A place he'd avoided at all costs ever since that day he and Emma had their painful confrontation, and she'd broken his heart.

"Are you all right?" Esther sounded alarmed.

"Just remembering the past."

"It looks to be a rather upsetting memory."

Kyle had no idea how to answer that. Most of his memories were equally as disturbing.

"You know, son," Dr. Hess said, "you could take some of those burdens to the Lord."

The doctor had often called him "son," but he'd assumed it had been a generic term. Now that he knew the truth, he wondered if the term had a deeper meaning behind it. He couldn't meet Dr. Hess's eyes. "I know," he mumbled.

"Knowing and doing are two separate things." The doctor's kind tone took much of the sting from his words.

Bowing his head slightly so Dr. Hess couldn't see into his eyes, Kyle managed a nod. He'd been getting slammed from all sides by spiritual lessons. Lessons he wasn't ready to apply to his life. Not yet.

Time to change the conversation to something a bit less distressing. Or maybe not. He had to make a confession.

His mouth dry, he began the apology he'd planned in the car. "When you told me about being"—he choked back the tightness in his throat—"adopted, it stunned me. I needed time to process it."

Now came the hard part. "I know I haven't been very polite or friendly to you since, and I'm sorry. I've been trying to wrap my mind around it, but I'm still struggling to accept the fact that I built my whole life around a lie."

"Oh, Kyle." Esther appeared close to tears. "I wish we could start over and do things differently. We're the ones who should be apologizing. We didn't supervise your mother closely enough, we gave you up when we should have persevered, and we kept a secret we should have told you many years ago."

"I'm not blaming you for any of that." Somehow this conversation had gotten derailed. He was supposed to be asking for forgiveness. Instead, they were saying they were sorry.

"I hope you'll find it in your heart to forgive us," Esther said in a shaky voice.

"You weren't to blame." The two of them had taken in his mother and offered to adopt him. "I'm the one who needs forgiveness." The words came out like a cry from his heart. And he realized he'd not said it only to them, but also to God.

* * *

Ben's sad gaze followed her as she crossed the lawn. "Everyone's already heading down to the basement for the evening meal."

Leah's face burned. She had made a fool of herself in front of everyone by running after Kyle, getting in the car alone with him. It would have been embarrassing enough if she'd done it in front of Ada or a few friends; instead, she'd humiliated Ben in front of more than two hundred wedding guests. What had she been thinking? Actually, she hadn't been thinking about anything except comforting Kyle. And confessing.

"I'm sorry." After she stammered out a lame excuse about not wanting Kyle to blame himself for the past, Ben's questioning stare made her squirm inside.

His tone was calm and reasonable when he asked,

"Wouldn't it have been more appropriate for Emma or one of her family members to tell him that?"

Leah hung her head. "You're right." Actually, Emma had made that message quite plain. At least Ben hadn't heard that part of the story. The men had been in the barn, but whoever alerted Caleb to Kyle's presence must have let Ben know.

Ben waved a hand toward the basement steps. "We should get to the table, but we need to meet and discuss our relationship and our priorities. Why don't I plan to stop by this week?"

"The week after would be better."

"I'd rather settle this as soon as possible. Do you have plans for this week?"

"I, um, that is…" Leah did have plans, but she couldn't tell Ben. The specialist she'd seen a couple of weeks ago confirmed Kyle's diagnosis and scheduled surgery for this coming week. Esther had already agreed to take her place while she recuperated.

"Either you have plans, or you don't." Ben's face darkened. "Unless you'd prefer not to tell me what you intend to do, which makes me wonder if those plans include Kyle."

That she could answer truthfully. "Definitely not." She hadn't told Kyle about the surgery, and she'd asked Esther not to tell anyone except her husband. *Mamm* and Sharon were the only other ones who knew. "You have nothing to worry about with Kyle. He's *Englisch*. Besides, he'll be leaving in a few weeks for a big-city hospital."

"And how do you know that?" Ben's narrowed eyes made it seem as if he suspected she and Kyle shared personal secrets.

"He told the Hesses when we met with them last Saturday."

"I see." Some of the tension drained from his face. "Let's hurry. We can discuss this when I stop by."

Following the usual tradition, they filed in oldest to youngest. By weaving in and around people, she and Ben managed to slip in near their buddy bunch right before they headed downstairs. The *youngie* followed them. Leah's cheeks flamed as she and Ben took their places at a table. How much of the low buzz of conversation around them was gossip about her?

Chapter Twenty-One

The haziness in the room slowly drifted into focus. A nurse bustled around checking the tube snaking from Leah's arm. Her cheery patter barely registered while Leah struggled to shake off her grogginess.

The nurse's instructions on how to use the PCA, a button to release pain medication, slid past Leah. Why would she need that? Nothing hurt while she floated along like this. She concentrated on the instructions.

"Don't push that button if you're sleepy," the nurse said. "If the medication doesn't help or you feel nauseous, push *this* button."

Too many buttons. Too many instructions. What if she pushed the wrong button? She wanted to ask, but her mouth was too cottony to form sounds.

"Also check with us before you get up for the first time." After a few more directives, the nurse headed out the door, leaving Leah alone in the room.

Leah dozed off and on for a while as nurses popped in and out to check on her. The empty bed beside the door made Leah wish for a roommate, someone she could talk to. If only *Mamm* were well enough to visit.

When the door opened, Leah turned to it, eager to have company. The surgeon entered and headed toward her bed.

"The surgery went well." He described what he had removed and detailed the expected steps for her recovery. Most of the time rather than meeting her eyes, he read from the clipboard.

Leah followed along with his explanations. Studying to be a midwife had given her a good understanding of the terms he used, and she mentally pictured the diagrams in her textbooks. Then he dropped his bombshell.

"The surgery was more extensive than we anticipated. Unfortunately, there's a good likelihood you may never have children."

Leah lay stunned. He'd warned her before the surgery that it might be one possible outcome, but she'd been hoping and praying...

"You're not ready to have children yet, are you?" When Leah shook her head, he said, "Too bad. You have a very narrow window of opportunity. To be on the safe side, I'd say a year. Maybe a little more."

Courting Ben would most likely lead to marriage, but she and Ben hadn't discussed their future together yet. Ben had hinted at it when he encouraged her not to be a midwife, but they'd made no commitments. Even if they did get engaged, most likely they wouldn't get married until next year.

Her throat constricted, and she struggled to speak. "Only one baby?"

"I wouldn't recommend more." The rest of the doctor's words faded to a stream of noise. Babbling that made no sense.

Leah focused on his mouth opening and closing, but her brain refused to translate the sounds into sentences. Once his lips stopped moving and he raised a questioning eyebrow, she nodded, hoping that was the correct response to what he'd said. Inside, though, numbness bloomed in her heart. A deadness. An emptiness that nothing could fill.

The only words her mind could form were *Why, God? Why?*

Once the surgeon exited, Leah kept her back to the door and let her tears run down her cheeks. Cool wetness soaked her pillow. She'd always dreamed of being a mother, of having a big family. Now she'd have no children. Not even one baby.

And what about Ben? He wanted a large family too. Any Amish man would. It wouldn't be fair to marry him. Or anyone.

The surgeon's words, along with his knife, had destroyed her future. She'd not only lost her dreams of a home and family, but she'd also lost any chance for a husband and marriage.

* * *

Footsteps crossed the threshold of the room, and Leah closed her eyes. She had no strength left to talk to a nurse.

The person rounded the bed. "Leah?"

No. What was Kyle doing here?

He dragged a chair close to the bed, so close his breath feathered against her face as he leaned over to wipe teardrops from her cheek with a gentle fingertip. "Are you in a lot of pain? If you press that button, you'll get more meds to ease the worst of it."

Leah's eyes fluttered open, and she shook her head. Her insides felt like ground glass now that the anesthesia had worn off, but no medication could ease the pain tearing her apart.

"What's wrong, then?"

Kyle's soft question, combined with the caring in his eyes, started a fresh round of tears. Leah squeezed her eyes shut to hold them back. But when Kyle took her hand and stroked it tenderly, those tears flooded down her cheeks.

Her conscience warned her to pull her hand away when his touch started an exquisite ache inside. But she wanted—needed—this tenderness. No man would ever hold her hand like this.

"Leah?" Kyle leaned closer again.

His soft whispered breath close to her ear sent shivers through her. If only she could live in this fantasy world for a short while. But she had no right to dream of a life with any man, and certainly not an *Englischer*.

He tilted her chin and tenderly brushed away each teardrop. "Look at me," he said, his voice low and husky.

When she did, his eyes pleaded for an explanation. Yet talking about pregnancy and childbirth around men was *verboten*. But Kyle was a doctor, and he'd first diagnosed her. He'd also taken her to the clinic and waited for her there. The rules shouldn't apply to him.

"Is there anything I can do to help?" he asked.

Too shy to look at him, Leah lowered her eyes and blurted out, "No one can." Then she took a deep breath. "There's a good possibility"—she bit back a sob—"I can never have a baby."

* * *

As a doctor, Kyle had trained himself to detach, to treat every patient dispassionately, so he tried to keep his voice neutral, doctorlike, and professional. "That sometimes is the outcome."

As soon as he said the words, he regretted them. They sounded cold and callous. This was Leah, not some unknown patient. She was someone he cared about. He tamped down the longing to enfold her in his arms. Besides not having that right, he could hurt her because she'd just had surgery.

He did the only thing he could and squeezed her hand. "I'm so sorry."

"What am I going to do about Ben?"

The anguish in her voice tore through Kyle. He wished he could erase the misery from her face. Even if he could, he had no power to remove it from her soul.

"We can't get married if I'm unable to have children."

Kyle winced inwardly at the thought of her marrying Ben. "If he loves you, he'll understand." He wished he could say something to ease her sadness, but all that came to mind were the happy, childless-by-choice couples he hung around with. "Plenty of couples don't have children. Look at the Hesses."

"I know some *Englischers* choose not to have children, but not the Amish. Having children is important to our families and our community."

Another option he'd offered to some patients came to mind. He winced, remembering how cavalierly he'd suggested, *There's always adoption.* Little did he know his childhood home hadn't been his first home, and the people he'd called Mom and Dad weren't his birth parents. But you could love an adopted child the same as a child you bore. He choked out, "You could adopt."

"Oh, Kyle..." Despite her own grief, she reached out and touched his hand. "I'm sorry."

"I'm not. I had wonderful parents who raised me. I never realized I was adopted"—he swallowed hard—"although I don't recommend hiding that from your children. Mom and Dad treated me the same way they did Caleb, and I never once questioned their love for either of us."

Her hand lay atop his, and Kyle flipped his hand over to weave his fingers with hers. He told himself he was offering her comfort, but he liked being connected with her.

Leah squeezed his hand, setting his pulse racing. Despite her own devastating news, she was more concerned with his feelings than her own. What a thoughtful, giving person she was. If only he could help her the way she'd helped him.

"I wouldn't mind adopting," she said, "especially if I could get a child who'd turn out as *wunderbar* as you."

"I wouldn't mind if you adopted me."

Leah giggled. "Thank you for making me laugh on one of the worst days of my life."

Kyle loved her light, airy laugh. He would have given anything to be close to her, to be part of her family. Although he had no desire to be her child.

"As much as I'd like to adopt if I can't have children of my own, I'm not sure Ben would agree. I don't even think it's fair to ask him. He might say he's all right with it but not mean it."

"It doesn't sound like you trust Ben to be a loving parent."

Leah sucked in a breath. "*Ach*, I didn't mean it that way. It's just that he cares for me..."

So do I, Kyle wanted to say, but clenched his teeth to prevent the words from passing his lips.

"He might not want to hurt my feelings."

"I can understand that. You should give him a chance. He might feel the same way I do. I'd be happy to adopt children."

"You're different," Leah said. "And not just because you were adopted. You have an open heart."

Kyle had no idea how she saw that in him. He'd always tried hard to put on a remote, detached, professional demeanor. He hadn't succeeded with her, though. Warmth flowed through the places where their hands connected and filled him to overflowing. If only he had the right to hold her hand, pull her into his arms, hold her close.

"Are you all right?" she asked.

More than all right. "I should be asking you that question."

"I feel like someone blasted a gaping hole right

through me, but having you here has made the bad news much more bearable." Leah winced.

"Are you in pain? From the surgery, I mean."

"Yes. The nurse told me about buttons and rules, but I didn't pay close attention."

Kyle demonstrated what to do, and Leah thanked him. Then she lay back and closed her eyes. He should leave, but he didn't want to go. Nor did he want to untangle their fingers.

* * *

Leah could barely keep her eyes open. They kept drifting shut. She wanted to stay awake to feel the pressure of his fingers on hers. To talk to him.

But when she woke again, Kyle was gone. Darkness had descended, and loneliness overwhelmed her. She'd never spent a night alone, or away from her family.

In the stillness of the night, she wondered at God's purpose for this. She and Ada had prayed so long and hard for husbands. Ada had found hers. Leah thought she had Ben, but it wouldn't be right to marry him when she couldn't have children.

Although she was devastated about not being able to have children, deep inside, part of her was relieved to break up with Ben. Her conscience had been bothering her ever since she realized she'd been falling for Kyle. Ben had never aroused the same emotions as Kyle had, so it wasn't fair to go ahead with a marriage when she felt lukewarm about him. Nothing could ever come of her feelings for Kyle, but she had to do the right thing for Ben.

The next day before she was discharged, Kyle arrived and offered to drive her home. She'd been planning to call Sharon for a ride, but going with Kyle would be easier. Most likely nobody would question the fact that the *Englisch* doctor brought her home; the Amish sometimes used *Englisch* drivers when they traveled longer distances.

Leah felt fragile, achy, and hollowed out inside as she stepped gingerly over to the wheelchair. The aide took her down in the elevator to settle the bill.

Although the hospital was used to dealing with Amish patients and charged them less because they didn't have insurance, Leah cringed at the total. How could a one-night stay cost so much? And how would they afford this on top of *Mamm*'s medical expenses? Often the Amish community contributed toward hospital bills, but *Daed* refused to ask for help. Instead, he would put down a deposit and work out a payment plan with the hospital.

The aide wheeled her out to the car, and Kyle helped her in.

"You're going to think I'm always helpless and weak. I've always been strong and healthy."

Kyle laughed. "I know. You were quite a fierce opponent when we fought about hospitals versus herbs." He sobered. "I'm glad you had this taken care of, so you can go back to your feisty self."

"I wasn't really that bad, was I?"

"I like you just the way you are—fiery spirit and all."

When they arrived at the shop, Kyle insisted on helping her out. As much as she wanted him to keep his arms around her, supporting her, Leah moved away from him to cross the parking lot alone.

Joel's eyes widened as Kyle held open the door. "Where have you been, Leah? Ben stopped by twice this week asking for you. I had no idea what to tell him."

"*Ach*, I asked him to wait until next week." What did he think when she wasn't here? That she was deliberately avoiding him?

"You should be resting," Kyle said. He looked as if he were about to take her arm and help her into the house.

If Joel hadn't been watching, she would have let him, but reluctantly she moved out of touching distance. Thank goodness her overnight things fit into her hand-bag. No need to give her brother ideas he might convey to Ben. She also hoped Joel wouldn't mention that Kyle had brought her home.

Her brother examined her closely. "You do look pale. Are you all right?"

"I'll be fine."

"Do you need anything from the store?"

Leah headed toward the house. "Not right now, but I'll let you know if I do. *Danke*, Joel." She kept her attention on turning the doorknob so her eyes wouldn't meet Kyle's. "*Danke* for bringing me home, Kyle."

Joel stopped her as she walked through the door. "If Ben stops by, should I call you?"

Leah wasn't ready for a confrontation with Ben. Not yet. Not when she was feeling so fragile herself. She needed time to prepare.

Behind her, Kyle said, "If Leah asked him to come next week, then he should at least wait until then. Even longer would be better."

Bless Kyle for supporting her. She longed to turn and thank him with her eyes, but she'd struggle to break the connection if she did, and Joel could guess her secret. A secret she'd been denying. She'd fallen in love with Kyle.

Too choked up to respond, Leah only nodded. After she shut the door, she couldn't resist one last peek. She turned to wave, but Kyle's back was turned as he headed out to the parking lot. Suddenly not caring what Joel thought, she stared after him until he drove away.

The following Friday, Joel stuck his head in the door and called, "Leah, Ben's here to see you."

Leah was no more prepared for a confrontation with Ben now than she had been last week. Still fragile physically and emotionally, she wished she could avoid meeting him, but maybe it was best to get this over with.

Ben frowned when she entered the shop. "Have you been away? You weren't in church yesterday."

"I, um…" How should she answer that? "Would you like to come into the kitchen for a cup of tea?" They could both use some of her calming herbal tea.

A smile lit Ben's face, and he followed her into the house. She busied herself with filling the kettle and measuring out herbs. When everything was ready, she placed a cup in front of Ben. Then she sank into a chair opposite him and wrapped her hands around her mug, hoping the heat seeping into her hands would warm her ice-cold body and heart.

Ben took a long swallow. "That's good." After one more drink, he set his cup down. "You never answered my question."

Leah sipped at her tea to avoid answering, while her brain raced to find an acceptable response. Maybe she should get straight to the point. Lowering her mug to the table with shaky hands, Leah said, "You asked me to think about our relationship, and after much soul-searching, I've decided I should never marry."

Ben gaped at her, and she wished he'd drink more of the tea. He'd need its calming effects.

"Have you prayed about that?" he asked.

"God made His answer very clear to me last week." Leah choked back a sob. "You've often said I couldn't combine midwifing and marriage." Midwifery was now her only choice, though she had no idea how she'd cope with delivering babies when she couldn't have a child of her own. Holding each newborn, seeing the parents' joy, watching families grow...

"You're choosing midwifing over me?" The hurt in Ben's eyes tore at her.

"I'm not choosing it over you. I don't plan to marry any man. I believe God has called me to dedicate my life to...to..." Leah choked up. Why had God given her this dream when every birth would be a painful reminder of her own loss?

Ben's chair scraped the floor as he shoved himself back from the table. "I wanted to meet to straighten out our differences." His voice shook. "I thought we'd come to an agreement about courting and spending time to-gether." He turned his back to her and walked toward the door. "I never expected this."

Leah's heart echoed his parting words. *Neither did I.*

Chapter Twenty-Two

Kyle headed out to the waiting room at the end of the day. His spirits always plummeted to see Esther at the reception desk rather than Leah. He hoped Leah was recovering well. At least physically. It might take a long while for her to heal emotionally. He only hoped Ben had been understanding.

Esther stopped him. "Every year in December, we close the office for two weeks so Martin and I can visit his sister in Florida. I didn't mention this before because I wasn't sure about his health, but I'm convinced the visit will do Martin good."

"I see." Kyle would have a vacation for the first time in years. What would he do with himself all alone? His fellowship applications had been submitted.

"You're welcome to come with us, of course, but Martin was hoping you'd be willing to be on call while we're gone. We usually refer everyone to Dr. Mitchell when our office is closed, but it's quite a drive, especially for our Amish patients."

"I'm fine with being on call." Although he appreciated her invitation, he wasn't ready to meet other family members yet. He'd barely had time to adjust to his own circumstances.

"Oh, thank you." Esther beamed at him. "That will relieve Martin's mind."

After Esther and Martin left on Saturday afternoon, Kyle wandered through the downstairs rooms, lonely and at loose ends. He hadn't realized how much he'd come to appreciate their company. If he'd let himself, he'd fill his mind with daydreams of Leah, but he cut those off before they started.

Would it be appropriate to stop by the store and inquire about her health? It didn't seem Joel had been aware of her surgery, so how could he ask? By the time he'd decided to stop by, using the excuse of buying some vitamins, the shop was closed. He'd have to wait until Monday.

* * *

On Monday morning, Leah's phone rang as she cleaned up after breakfast.

"Leah? Matthew Groff. Rachel needs you. Sharon isn't answering her phone."

"She may still be at Anna Troyer's."

Sharon had called Leah soon after daybreak to invite her to the delivery, but Leah couldn't drag the buggy from the barn and hitch up the horse by herself. The surgeon had warned her not to do any heavy lifting yet. *Daed* had left early to put in extra hours for all the Christmas orders at the woodworking business where he worked in town. Unlike the Amish, *Englischers* bought many expensive gifts for the holidays, which meant *Daed* worked overtime hours.

"My brother should be here soon." Leah headed out to the shop. "I'll have him drive me over."

The minute Joel arrived, Leah ran out to the car. "Could you take me to the Groffs' house right away? Also, could you put my bag in the car for me?"

Her brother looked startled. "I guess so." He lugged her heavy midwife bag out to the car and hefted it into the backseat. "I've never known you to ask for help carrying things before. Has hanging around that *Englischer* made you soft?"

"*Neh*, of course not." But she couldn't explain why she wasn't carrying her own bag.

When they arrived at the Groffs', Joel said, "Do you want me to take the bag inside for you?"

"If you wouldn't mind."

Matthew opened the door, and as soon as he saw Joel lifting the bag from the backseat, he rushed over to take it. He carried it into the bedroom while Leah went to wash up.

Rachel, her face a bit worried, greeted Leah. "I think the baby turned again. All the kicks have been down low."

Sharon and Leah had turned Rachel's baby several weeks ago. Perhaps Rachel was mistaken. Leah examined her, and the baby definitely had flipped again. At least it wasn't coming feet first. Sharon had explained how to deliver breech babies. But if Sharon didn't get here soon, Leah would be doing it for the first time, and she'd be alone.

Leah tried to ignore the nervous fluttering in her stomach. She needed to convey a calm, professional attitude. The last thing she wanted was for Rachel to panic.

"Your baby's in the best position for a breech birth," she assured Rachel as Matthew entered the room.

"Thank the Lord," he said.

The worry lines on Rachel's face smoothed out. "That's good to know."

Even with the baby in this position, complications might arise. They could be dangerous, so she should have backup in case anything went wrong. As much as she disliked asking Kyle to come out when he was so busy in the practice, she couldn't risk Rachel's life or the baby's.

Luckily, he answered on the first ring. With Rachel and Matthew listening, she addressed him formally. "Dr. Miller, I'm at Rachel Groff's for a delivery. A breech birth."

He sucked in a breath. "I'll call an ambulance and meet you there. We'll get her to the hospital for a C-section as fast as we can."

"I don't think that'll be necessary. At least I hope not. I'm hoping to deliver the baby."

"Deliver the baby?" Kyle's voice rose. "That mother needs to be hospitalized."

"Maybe not. The baby's heart rate is normal, and it's a frank presentation." If it had been a feetfirst presentation, she would have recommended a hospital birth.

"I'm praying all will go well, but I'd like you here for backup."

"How far along is she?"

"She's almost ready to push."

Rachel groaned, squeezed her eyes shut, and panted. Her husband cradled her close and wiped her forehead.

"Don't waste any time. Call an ambu—"

Leah clicked off her phone. She didn't have much time.

"My cousin Johnny's volunteering at the fire station today," Matthew said. "If I call him, he can alert the EMTs in case we need them."

"Yes, we should have them here on standby, just in case." She tossed her phone in his direction, and it bounced on the bed in front of him. Meanwhile, she'd pray. Pray that everything would go well. Pray for a healthy baby. And a healthy mother.

"Our second one was a breech," Matthew informed her after he'd hung up the phone. "Turned out all right. Everything is in God's hands."

Matthew's stolid acceptance of the situation calmed some of Leah's anxiety. Still, her hands trembled. Whispering another quick prayer, she tried to remember everything Sharon had taught her.

* * *

Stunned, Kyle stood still for a second, staring at the phone in his hand. He shook it a few times and held it up to his ear to check. It had gone dead. Had Leah hung up on him?

Surely she hadn't been serious about delivering a

breech baby. He must have misheard. *Who did she say? Groff. Rachel Groff. Why didn't I ask for an address?*

Kyle redialed the phone, but it rang and rang until her voicemail kicked on. He tried again. Pacing impatiently, Kyle grabbed his coat from the hook and put it on. Still no answer. If she was in the middle of an emergency delivery, she might not answer. Maybe Sharon would answer.

Flicking his finger to scroll through the numbers on his phone, Kyle's anxiety increased. Every minute he wasted equaled a minute that a baby's life could be draining away. There it was. Sharon Nolt. Kyle pushed the button as he grabbed his bag and rushed outside. He was punching the code on the office door when Sharon's cheery voice answered. He hated to waste time locking doors, but with the sample drugs they kept in the office, he needed to be safe.

"Hello, Dr. Miller. How are you?" Sharon sounded a bit tired but upbeat. Not at all concerned about the medical emergency that was worrying Kyle.

"I wanted to call the ambulance for the baby," Kyle said, "but I don't have the family's address." A fine layer of snow drifted down on his head and jacket. Early morning flurries had dusted his car and the roads. As fast as he brushed off his windows, snowflakes coated them again. He got into his car and started the engine. As soon as she let him know where to go, he'd send medical help and head there himself.

"Ambulance?" Sharon sounded puzzled. "What for? Everything went fine. Anna and her new son are resting quietly."

Anna? He was positive Leah had said Rachel. "I, um, thought the mother was Rachel. Rachel Groff."

Sharon didn't answer for a second. A second that stretched into an eternity. A second that could make the difference between life and death.

"Rachel Groff? Let me check my messages and get back to you."

"Just give me the address," Kyle barked, but the phone had gone dead. Drumming his fingers on the icy steering wheel, he flicked on the wipers as he waited for the car to warm and the phone to ring. If anything happened to that baby...

The ringtone sounded, and Kyle immediately tapped the button.

"I missed a call from Rachel earlier." Sharon sounded out of breath. "It was while I was here at Anna's. Leah's there."

"I know. She called. It's a breech birth. I need the address."

"Oh, it'll be her first alone. Don't worry, though. She's done a good job with her other deliveries."

Those weren't breech births. "The address," Kyle said through gritted teeth.

"Of course. Matthew Groff lives out beyond Esh's Cabinet Shop. It's the first right. Sorry I can't think of the name of that road. I've been up all night with Anna, and my brain's a bit foggy."

Kyle gripped the phone so hard the edge bit into his hand. He couldn't send an ambulance there if he didn't have an address. He stepped on the gas and backed down the driveway while he waited for the rest of Sharon's directions. He could at least head toward the cabinet shop.

"Matthew's house is the last house on that lane. The pale yellow one."

"Do you know the house number?" he asked as he shot down the road, going a bit above the speed limit.

"Not offhand. Sorry, but it should be easy to find."

The car slid a bit on the slippery road, and Kyle slowed down. He'd be no help at all if he was in an accident. "I want to send an ambulance. I can't tell them to look for a yellow house."

Sharon laughed. "Some of them might know if you tell them Matthew Groff's, but why don't you head out there first to see if an ambulance is needed. I've only ever had one emergency with a breech birth, but that was only because there were other complications with that delivery."

Kyle gritted his teeth. Why were these midwives so antihospital?

"Tell you what," Sharon said. "Why don't I meet you out there? I'm only a few miles down the road. We can both provide Leah with backup, although I doubt she'll need it."

"If you could get there as soon as possible, that would be good. Be sure to check the house number and call an ambulance if you get there first."

"If it will ease your worries, I'll do that, but we may find everything has gone well." Sharon's voice faded in and out a bit.

He stepped on the gas. Despite promising himself he'd never speed again, a baby's life might depend on him getting help in time. If a cop stopped him, he'd have the police lead the way and call an ambulance. If the police knew how to find the house with no address.

By the time he reached Esh's Cabinet Shop, though, he'd slowed to a crawl as drifting snow blew across the road. He turned at the first right, but snow obscured the street sign. He prayed he'd found the correct turn, and he followed Sharon's directions to the end of the lane.

He rushed to the porch of the yellow house, but no one answered his knock.

Kyle took a chance and turned the knob. The door opened, and he called out, "It's Dr. Miller."

"We're in the back bedroom," a man called out.

Kyle rushed down the hall and stopped in the doorway. He forgot all about calling an ambulance because Leah appeared so calm and relaxed, as if she'd gotten into the rhythm of Rachel's contractions. She was urging Rachel to push.

"One more time." Leah assisted with the shoulders, and the head slipped out.

She blew out a loud breath as the newborn let out a lusty cry—the only sign she'd been more tense than she'd let on. Her face glowing, Leah met Rachel's questioning eyes. "You have a beautiful daughter."

Kyle stood back, admiring Leah's proficiency. She'd delivered a breech baby, handling a dangerous delivery with a skill and a calmness many doctors would envy. In swift but gentle motions, she delivered the afterbirth, cut the cord, checked the baby, weighed her and footprinted her, and noted the Apgar, which was nine. After she'd taken care of the routine duties, she wrapped the baby in a blanket and handed her to the mother, who cuddled her close, while the father sat beside her, one hand smoothing the damp strands of hair back from his wife's forehead, the other on his daughter's head. It amazed Kyle that the mother kept her prayer *kapp* on her head during the delivery.

"We'll be naming her Emily Beth," Matthew said, and his wife nodded.

While Rachel attempted to feed her newborn, Leah cleaned up and then washed and sterilized her equipment. Kyle helped when he could, but she seemed to have a routine, so he mainly avoided getting in her way. After she'd packed her heavy bag, he offered to take it.

"You shouldn't be lifting this," he said.

"I know. Joel carried it for me."

"Good." Kyle set the midwife bag by the front door. "Do you have a ride home?"

"I don't think Joel will come out yet." She headed for the kitchen, where she spread her paperwork on the table. "He doesn't like to leave the shop during the hours it's open." Her mouth twisted into a rueful expression. "Unlike me, he won't miss customers or deliveries."

Kyle smiled. He hadn't minded picking up that delivery. It had given him a chance to spend time with her, get to know her, and diagnose her.

He leaned closer. "How have you been feeling?"

She grimaced. "Better than I was, but it's still painful sometimes."

"That's normal. Many times it takes a month or more—even as much as ninety days—to feel better. I hope it happens much sooner for you." Common sense told him to leave, but after sharing the miracle of birth with her, he was reluctant to go. He settled in a chair that allowed him to look at her.

As much as he'd admired her serenity during the delivery, it must have been difficult. "Was this your first delivery since your operation?"

Glancing up with damp eyes, she met his gaze. "Yes,"

she whispered. "I didn't think about it at all during the delivery. My attention was so focused on doing everything right. Plus, with it being a breech, the delivery was trickier than usual. Now, though..." Her voice wavered.

Kyle reached out a hand and placed it over hers. "This is a difficult job to have when you're hurting over your loss."

"It is," she agreed. "I'm trusting God has a reason for this."

He shouldn't ask, but he did anyway. "How did Ben take the news?" At her obvious wince, he tightened his grip.

"Not well."

He'd like to confront the man who'd hurt her that way. How selfish he must be. "Any man who can't accept that doesn't deserve you as a wife."

"Actually," Leah admitted, "I never told him. I, um, just broke up with him."

Torn between elation for himself and sadness for her, Kyle said, "That must have been painful."

"It was, and it still is, but it wouldn't be fair to him when I—well, never mind." Her cheeks grew rosier than the bowl of apples on the scrubbed wooden tabletop.

She bent her head over her paperwork again. She allowed him to continue holding her left hand as she filled in information about the baby with her right. When she'd completed the forms, she slid her hand out from under his and stood.

He missed the softness of her hand, the serenity of her presence. He followed her into the living room, where she tucked the paperwork in her bag.

The sadness in her eyes when she stood left Kyle

fighting an impulse to draw her into his arms. Before he could reach out, she rubbed her forehead, and her expression changed to a smile.

"I can't go in there looking glum and spoil their excitement."

Kyle admired her courage and caring in putting other people's feelings above her own heartbreak.

Chapter Twenty-Three

Leah wished she could stay here in the kitchen with Kyle. It had been so hard to pull her hand from the warmth of his. The protection and compassion in his gesture meant so much to her, and it brought her comfort. A comfort she sorely needed and missed.

Going back in that room would be hard. A beautiful baby and a happy couple normally brought Leah great joy, but today, with her insides scraped and sore, and no longer courting Ben, she dreaded holding the baby, knowing she could never have one of her own.

When she and Kyle reached the room, Matthew was holding the baby over his shoulder and patting her back.

"She didn't suck well, but maybe she's as tired as I am." The love shining in Rachel's eyes as she gazed at her husband and tiny daughter twisted Leah's insides.

Not only would she never have a child of her own,

she'd never have a husband. She wanted to turn away to hide the wetness in her eyes, but she pushed herself to do her duty.

"I'm sure she'll do better later," Leah reassured her. "Babies sometimes have weak sucking reflexes at first."

The front door banged open, and Sharon rushed down the hall. She stopped in the doorway and assessed the room. "Looks like you managed a breech birth. So how'd everything go?"

Leah told her and added the important stats: "Emily Beth. Seven pounds, two ounces. Nineteen inches. Apgar nine at five minutes."

"Good, good," Sharon said. "Not sure why we've been having so many back-to-back deliveries, but you coped well." She studied Kyle. "I see you made it, and I'm glad you had no need for an ambulance."

Matthew broke in. "I had one on standby, just in case."

"That was sensible," Kyle told him. He turned to Sharon. "Leah did a wonderful job, very calm and professional."

His words warmed Leah from head to toe. That was high praise coming from someone who'd insisted she call an ambulance.

"But," he continued, "I still think it would be safer to deliver breech babies in a hospital. So many complications could have occurred."

"But they didn't," Leah pointed out.

"There's always a possibility they could. You might not be so lucky next time."

"We don't believe in luck. What happens is God's will."

The passion and concern shining in Kyle's eyes flickered out, leaving behind bleakness. Leah longed to reach out to him, to assure him of God's love. She had no idea how he had made it through his life without the assurance of God's strength and the power of prayer.

With a brisk nod to everyone, Kyle said, "Congratulations, everyone, on a good delivery. I should get back to the office. I'm on call while the Hesses are away."

"Thank you for coming," Matthew said, and his wife echoed his words.

"I'm so glad you were here." Leah hoped her words didn't reveal anything beyond professional interest.

"Impressive delivery, Leah. Take care of yourself." Kyle's clipped words had the neutral, professional edge Leah had been trying to achieve, but the burning intensity in the glance he sent her way conveyed a different message. Leah sucked in a breath. With one brief look, he'd set her pulse quivering. Then he turned abruptly and exited, taking a part of her heart with him.

* * *

A frantic phone call sent Kyle rushing back to the Groffs' house the following Thursday afternoon. Heavy, dark clouds hung low in the sky, and snowflakes pelted his head and jacket as he locked the office door.

A full-fledged storm trapped him in a snow globe of whiteness. He slid into the car, and turned on the windshield wipers as the snow grew heavier. Winds buffeted the car and whipped snow into eddies, lowering visibility, and Kyle fought to keep the car on a road he could barely see. Patches of black ice could be hidden under the drifts blanketing the roads.

Memories of that long-ago snowy night constricted his breathing. His chest ached and his eyes burned. He'd vowed never to drive in icy weather, but a baby's life depended on him. He gripped the steering wheel and drove on.

Without actually being aware of it, he murmured a prayer over and over until it became a litany. *Lord, please help me to get there safely, and watch over baby Emily.*

He turned into the Groffs' driveway, and the car slid down the hill.

With an audible sigh, he turned off the engine, which shuddered to a stop, and in the silence, he repeated the words he'd been saying. They echoed around him. He'd been praying? Was it a prayer if you didn't directly intend to address God? If God had been listening, He'd already answered the first part of the prayer. Kyle had made it here.

This time, he directed the words heavenward. "If You're listening, God, please protect and heal baby Emily." Uncertain if his words had been heard, Kyle slid out of the car into the whirlwind of flakes and grabbed his bag from the trunk. Already almost eight inches had fallen, and gusts blew loose snow into drifts several feet tall. Frigid winds penetrated his overcoat, chilling his bones, and iced his cheeks as he rushed to the front door.

He knocked once to warn them he'd arrived, but because they'd insisted it was an emergency, he opened the door and entered. A murmur of voices came from the back bedroom. He headed that direction.

He stopped in the doorway, taken aback to see Leah.

Emily lay in Leah's arms, limp and barely responsive. Kyle's heart clenched. He wanted to elbow Leah out of the way and snatch the baby from her, but an internal voice urged him to wait.

Leah placed Emily on the makeshift changing table Rachel had created on the top of a low dresser. She unwrapped the newborn, undid her diaper, and sniffed. "I smell..." Her voice trembled.

"*Ach*, no." Rachel squeezed her eyes shut. "We were afraid of that. My sister's baby..."

Matthew met Leah's gaze, his eyes fearful. "Is it—?"

Leah turned back to the baby and sniffed again. "I'm afraid so." She glanced back at Matthew. "What time is it?"

He glanced at the small windup clock beside the bed. "Three thirty."

"There's still time," Leah said. "We'll have to hurry. The clinic closes at five." Her fingers moved rapidly to change the little girl's diaper and wrap her in a blanket. "Do you have more blankets?"

Matthew headed to a chest under the window. "How many do you need?"

"As many as you have."

"What is going on here?" Kyle's voice cracked around the room like a whip. He needed to take control of the situation. "I want to examine the baby."

"There's no time," Leah insisted. "The faster we get her to the clinic, the sooner they can start feeding her the special formula." She glanced over at him, her eyes begging him to understand.

But understand what? They all seemed to have come to a silent consensus on a diagnosis. "What do *you* think is wrong?"

"Her urine has the distinct odor of maple syrup. There's no mistaking that smell. We have to get her to the clinic."

MSUD. Maple syrup urine disease. Is that what Leah had smelled? But no clinic would be able to help with that. Rushing out the door into a snowstorm was foolish. No, it would be much worse than that. Downright dangerous. The roads were much too slippery for travel.

Kyle racked his brain to remember the fleeting lesson he'd had on MSUD in med school.

"Emily should be fine. We caught it fairly early." Leah's wan smile belied her comforting words. "They can do wonders at the clinic."

What clinic were they talking about? The one where he'd taken Leah wouldn't have the facilities to care for this inherited disease, common only to Mennonite children. Its effects were devastating. The poor baby.

Matthew's gaze landed on Kyle. "*Ach*, it's a blessing you're here to drive us. We'll get there much faster than in the buggy."

"But I haven't even examined the baby," Kyle protested.

"We don't have time for that," Leah insisted. "The main symptom is the maple smell. Emily's also lethargic, hasn't been eating well, and has lost weight. We have to get her to the children's clinic."

What? They called him over here, didn't give him a chance to check the child, and expected him to accept a midwife's diagnosis and drive them to a clinic in a snowstorm. And he never drove on icy roads with anyone else in the car. Never. Not since...Kyle swallowed hard. But how could he refuse to take the baby to the clinic?

"But I can't..." The words died on his lips at Leah's pleading glance. She knew about his past. His whole life had been ruined by one patch of black ice.

But if he didn't take this baby to the clinic, he'd be responsible for harming another baby. "Where are you taking her?" he asked Leah.

"To Strasburg. The Clinic for Special Children. They've done a lot of research on these hereditary diseases. If we get her there, they have a formula to help mitigate the symptoms."

"If we don't leave now," Matthew's panicked voice said behind him, "there's a good possibility we won't be able to get her there at all. This storm's only going to get worse."

"And the faster we get Emily to the clinic, the sooner she'll get help." Leah's sympathetic glance assured him she understood his fears. "Please, Kyle," she begged.

Her pleading voice propelled him through the deep snowdrifts to his car. He turned it on to warm it while he cleared the snow from the roof and windows with Matthew's assistance.

As soon as she'd helped Matthew get the baby situated in the backseat, Leah slid into the car, and Kyle inched out of the driveway. Leah sat next to him, but his panic overrode that pleasure. Memories of the last time he'd driven on icy roads flooded his mind, choking him. His hands clenched on the steering wheel, he hunched forward, trying to see through the blinding snow. What if he had another accident like that and hurt the woman he loved? Or killed another baby?

* * *

Leah clutched the car armrest as Kyle's car crawled along the winding country roads. If only they could move faster. They needed to get to the clinic before it closed. She'd had firsthand experience with how treacherous patches of black ice were on these roads, so she appreciated his caution, but an infant's life hung in the balance.

"Maybe I should call the clinic to let them know we're coming." Surely someone would stay if they knew a baby was on the way.

"*Danke*," Matthew said as he laid a protective hand over Emily's chest.

After the clinic assured Leah they'd wait for them, she relaxed a bit. But poor Kyle held the steering wheel in a death grip, and his jaw was so tense she wondered if his teeth hurt. Driving in these icy conditions had been a real act of courage. She wanted to reach out and touch his arm to calm him but worried she'd startle him and cause an accident.

She didn't want to be responsible for another accident. Because Kyle seemed not to recognize her, Leah tried to bury her guilt over that accident, but her conscience insisted she needed to confess.

Please, Lord, give me the right opportunity and the strength and courage.

Leah added prayers for their safety and for Emily's health when the eight-mile car ride turned into an hour of inching along on slippery roads.

When Kyle pulled up in front of the timber-framed building, he blew out a loud breath.

"*Danke* for getting us here safely," she whispered.

His *you're welcome* came out shakily, and Leah wished she could reach out to ease the tension lines around his eyes and mouth.

When they got out, gale-force winds and driving snow nearly blew them over. Kyle took Leah's arm, while Matthew cradled Emily. Leah used the winds and snowy sidewalk as an excuse to cuddle closer.

"You go first," Kyle said to Matthew. Bending to put his mouth close to Leah's ear, he whispered, "Let's stay right behind him in case he slips. I don't want anything to happen to him, and especially not to the baby."

As they bent against the winds, Kyle held her steady. "Be careful," he said as they reached the part of the walkway that had been salted. "This slush can be slippery."

One of the doctors waited for them just inside the door. The doctor pushed it open, but a huge gust yanked it from her hand. Kyle let go of Leah to grab the door before it slammed, and Leah missed his warmth and comfort.

The doctor directed them down the hallway. "Hello, I'm Dr. Sensenig. Take her right back there to the first exam room on the right."

They all crowded into the room, and Matthew, his face

anxious, unwrapped Emily and handed all the blankets to Leah. "Will you be able to help her?"

"We'll do our best." The doctor turned toward them. "One of you thinks she has maple syrup urine disease?"

"I smelled it quite distinctly," Leah told her.

The doctor studied her. "And you are?"

"I'm Leah Stoltzfus. The midwife at the delivery last week. I'm working with Sharon Nolt."

"Ah, yes. Sharon has sent us several babies with inherited diseases," she said as she bent over the examining table and sniffed. "I'll do an amino acid analysis right away." After taking a blood sample, she hurried from the room.

Leah clutched the extra bundle of blankets against her chest, and beside her, Matthew stood rigid, holding Emily in place on the table until the doctor returned.

* * *

"We should have the results shortly, but—"

Kyle stared at her. "You can get results that quickly?" He hoped he hadn't offended her by acting skeptical, but he'd been expecting it would take a few days.

Dr. Sensenig didn't seem bothered by his question. "We have the equipment here to do the testing. Most places have to send out for results, which can take a while. Many local doctors send their blood samples here for amino acid analysis."

"That's impressive," Kyle murmured. "Would it be all right if I looked around? I'm scheduled to start a fellowship in rare diseases in January."

The doctor undressed Emily. "Why don't you stop by

for a tour sometime? You can get an in-depth picture of our work. We do many kinds of genetic research."

Kyle's eyes lit up. "You do research too?"

Dr. Sensenig nodded. "Our main focus is researching various inherited diseases in the Amish and Mennonite communities—conditions like Crigler-Najjar syndrome, Byler disease, and what the Amish call chicken breast disease," she said as she weighed and measured Emily. "We practice transitional medicine, so we combine research with clinical care."

"The best way to do it," Kyle said. He had no idea this clinic even existed. Of course, if he'd run across information on it earlier, he wouldn't have read it once he saw the word *Amish*. He'd have to find out more about it. He liked the fact that they treated patients here.

Then the doctor turned to Matthew and questioned him about Emily's birth weight and the baby's symptoms.

Dr. Sensenig frowned as she jotted down the information on Emily's chart. "She's lost quite a bit of weight. We'll need to get her started on the formula immediately." She handed Matthew a container.

Kyle's gut clenched. Babies usually lost some weight in the first month, but not a lot.

Matthew sat on one of the chairs and tipped the bottle of formula to Emily's lips, coaxing her to eat. Leah sat beside him, holding the blankets and running a finger along the baby's cheek as if to encourage her. How could Leah be so giving when she'd just faced such a devastating blow? Kyle could already hear her answer to his question: Every situation—good or bad—is God's will. At times, he wished he had her unshakable faith. But that would mean accepting his parents' deaths as God's will, something he couldn't do.

Once again, Leah had diagnosed a patient correctly. Would he have even thought of MSUD? Maybe not at first, although the maple smell probably would have jogged his memory. He'd buried that information in the back of his mind after med school, figuring he'd never need it again. He had no plans to have anything to do with an Amish community. Being around Leah made him rethink that.

The other thing that surprised him about Leah was that, although she championed natural remedies, she had no hesitation about bringing the baby to a clinic for help. And she'd gone to the hospital herself for surgery and even consented to take pain meds. It seemed she had a more balanced view of medicine than he did. Maybe it was time for him to be more open-minded about herbal remedies.

After she checked the analysis results, Dr. Sensenig's face looked grave. "We need to admit Emily to the hospital right away."

"Can I stay with her?" Matthew asked. When the doctor nodded, his face relaxed slightly. "I need to let Rachel know."

Fumbling under the pile of blankets filling her arms, Leah managed to extract her cell phone. She handed it to Matthew.

Matthew clicked the button, talked to his wife for a few minutes, and held the phone out to Leah. "*Danke.*"

"Why don't you keep the phone for now?" She dug in her pocket and pulled out the charger. "That way you can keep in touch with Rachel tonight."

*   *   *

Darkness had fallen by the time the doctor led Leah and Kyle down the hall and let them out the door. The clinic lights, shining dimly through the layers of snow piled on them, lit the slushy walkway.

Once again Kyle held out his bent arm to escort her to the car, and Leah tucked her hand into the crook of his arm and clung to him tightly. Perhaps more tightly than she should. But she was grateful for their closeness when they reached the parking lot and she slid on a patch of ice.

A deep frown on his brow, Kyle studied the ground. "That's black ice. If it formed on the parking lot, the roads will also be icy. It's not safe to drive tonight."

"We can't stay here, though."

"I know." He wrapped an arm around her and supported her the rest of the way to the car. After he helped her in, he tucked the baby's extra blankets she carried around her, making her feel warm, cozy, and coddled. Then he shuffled around to the other side, feeling for hidden ice.

Once he got in and hooked up his seat belt, he turned on the engine. Only cold air blasted from the vents. He flicked off the heater. "I'll wait until the engine warms up to turn it on. I hope you're warm enough."

"I'm fine, but what about you?"

Kyle's teeth chattered as he shivered, but he waved away her concerns. "I'll be fine, but I'm worried about taking you all the way out to the store when the roads are so treacherous."

He pulled out of the parking lot and slowed to a crawl.

Snow pelted the windshield, coming down in sheets, covering the road and hiding the black ice underneath. Even with the windshield wipers going at full speed, visibility was minimal.

Leah longed to talk to him about the accident, but he had such a look of intense concentration on his face she didn't want to be a distraction. She'd wait until he stopped. He hunched over the steering wheel, trying to peer through the thick white powder that coated the windshield faster than the wipers could clear it. His white-knuckled grip on the steering wheel revealed his tension. If only she could calm him down.

* * *

They should never have come out in this weather. Fear held his stomach in a vise grip, one that tightened as they inched along. Blizzard-force gales shook his compact car, shoving it first to one side and then the other. It grew harder and harder to see through the squall.

The car fishtailed, and Kyle hyperventilated. *No!* He couldn't repeat his worst nightmare. *Please, God, please save Leah! I don't care about myself. Just keep her safe.*

Time slowed down as the car spun in a circle. The blackness of the past loomed over him. Invisible hands closed around his neck, drew tighter, cutting off his breath, choking him.

No other cars were on the road. They were alone. Unlike the night he'd driven Emma.

He slipped back into the past. *Anger consumed him.*

Emma was leaving him, returning to the Amish. Desperate words had burst from his lips. "You can't leave me. I won't let you go. This baby is mine too, and I have a say."

Rage coursed through him, and he stomped on the gas. He always drove fast, but even he sensed his speed was reckless. Especially on a winter night. But he didn't care. Whatever it took, he had to make her change her mind, come back to him.

Kyle took his eyes off the road to shoot a furious glare in her direction. Emma stared at him with tear-filled eyes, and he regretted his harshness. But he'd never let her get away.

A horse, his eyes wild, galloped straight toward them, dragging a buggy behind him. They were going to collide.

He wrenched the steering wheel hard. Not hard enough. He met the eyes of the terrified girl inside. Another jerk on the steering wheel. The buggy careened past only a hairsbreadth away. The gray boxy carriage whooshed past his window, its wheels clattering.

And then he made his fatal mistake.

The car slid sideways. Hit a patch of ice. Spun toward a tree. He raised his foot from the gas pedal. Too little, too late. They sped toward it.

Then sounds filled his ears. Sounds that still woke him in the dead of night.

Emma's screams. Crunching metal. Splintering glass. Ragged breathing.

His. Not Emma's.

Because she lay crumpled and bleeding on the snow.

* * *

Ragged breathing filled the air around him. *Not Emma. Leah.* She sat beside him, gripping the armrest, her body rigid, gulping for breath, staring at him with panic-filled eyes.

Those eyes. The same eyes from that long-ago night...

Chapter Twenty-Four

Leah sucked in a breath as the car fishtailed, then spun out of control. She bowed her head and prayed for their safety. *Lord, give Kyle the wisdom to pull out of this.*

They were headed straight for a tree.

When he'd turned and met her gaze, recognition had dawned in his eyes. He knew.

She squeaked out, "I'm sorry."

But Kyle had already turned his attention back to the sliding car. He eased off the gas, turned the wheel in the opposite direction, and then righted it before lightly pumping the brakes.

The car shuddered to a stop inches from the tree.

Kyle leaned his head against the steering wheel. "Forgive me," he whispered.

They both trembled from the near miss. Adrenaline still raced through her, making her jittery, and blood pounded in her ears.

"This"—Kyle waved his hand toward the snow—"happened before."

She nodded. "Only this time no runaway buggy forced you off the road." Her voice was as shaky as his.

"It was you," he said dully.

Leah hung her head. "Yes. I saw your car swerve, but I didn't realize I'd caused an accident until days later when people at church mentioned what had happened to Emma. I apologized to the Eshes immediately, but it was a long time before Emma was well enough for me to ask for her forgiveness." When Kyle winced, Leah laid a hand on his arm. "Please don't blame yourself."

Kyle opened his mouth to protest, but Leah rushed on. "I never had a chance to confess my part in the accident because you left town right away. Ever since you returned, I've been trying to find a way to tell you the truth. That accident wasn't your fault. It was mine."

He looked over at her with tortured eyes. "You aren't to blame for my reckless driving. I was livid and driving much too fast for the conditions. Too fast even for normal conditions. Plus, I'd taken my eyes off the road."

"You'd never have skidded off the road if my horse hadn't gone out of control," Leah pointed out.

"Maybe not at that spot, but I certainly would have hit a patch of ice somewhere, and maybe with more deadly results. Although they were..." His face scrunched into a mask of agony.

"It's all my fault. The guilt has been eating away at me ever since. I came out to your car at Ada's wedding to ask your forgiveness."

"There's nothing to forgive you for. It was my foolishness, my pride, my temper. I destroyed so many lives that day."

"You didn't destroy anyone's life. Everything's over now, and Emma recovered." Leah understood how he was feeling. She'd wrestled with her own guilt while Emma spent months in a coma and even longer recovering from amnesia. Not until she'd apologized to Emma and been forgiven did she experience closure. "Emma doesn't seem to have suffered any lasting damage."

"You don't understand," he said in a broken voice. "I didn't only hurt Emma. I killed our baby."

Leah sat stunned. *A baby?* Sick with guilt, Leah clenched her hands together in her lap. *I killed a baby. An innocent baby.*

Kyle rubbed his fingers hard over his closed eyelids. Leah's dad and brother often did that to hold back tears.

She wished she could comfort him, but what could she say? The words *I'm sorry* seemed so inadequate in the face of the tragedy she'd caused. "I-I didn't know…"

"Nobody did." His words, low and husky, added to her guilt. "We'd only recently learned she was pregnant."

An unborn baby. Poor Emma. To lose her first child. And Kyle too. How awful to feel responsible for your child's death.

He shouldn't blame himself, though, when she was the cause. How could she get him to understand that?

* * *

Kyle had just blurted out a secret that he never should have shared with anyone. He trusted Leah, but suppose she let it slip to a friend or family member, and the story got back to Emma's dad? He'd know who'd started the gossip. "Listen, what I just said—it's private. I never should have told you about it."

"I'll never share that with anyone." Her expression revealed how seriously she took that promise.

Deep inside, he trusted her, and he held her secret about never having a child in strictest confidence. Leah impressed him as loyal, and as a midwife, she'd know many families' private matters. He'd never heard her divulge any of them. He appreciated her discretion, and it was such a relief to finally be able to talk to someone about the baby.

Although both of them had stopped shaking after the near miss, Kyle's anxiety levels remained high. No way could he get Leah home safely on these roads. Each bend in the road, each hidden patch of ice posed grave danger. Even though he'd only been inching along, the car had spun out of control and almost slammed into that tree. Another foot or two, and Leah might not be sitting here right now. He shuddered to think what might have happened.

"The Hesses' house isn't too far from here. I know Esther set strict rules about us being alone together in the house, but I don't want to take a chance of another accident." He promised himself he'd stay away from her. Though his attraction to her remained as strong as ever, her safety meant even more. He had to take care of her.

Leah stared at the snow blanketing the windshield in the short time they'd been here. "I don't want to take any more chances than we have to on these roads. I can sleep on the couch in the office, and we can keep the house door locked, so we're still following Esther's rules."

"The couch in the office is large enough for me, so I can take that. I'm sure Esther won't mind if you sleep in the guest room." He held up a hand to stop her protests. "You had surgery not long ago. You should be taking care of yourself." Though he was pretty sure delivering babies had not been on her surgeon's list of approved activities.

Leah didn't contradict him, but from the steely glint in her eyes, she planned to dispute the arrangements he'd suggested. He'd fight her, though. But they could discuss that once they left this storm behind.

His heart tripping with trepidation, Kyle grasped the steering wheel and tapped the gas pedal. He blew out a breath as the tires bit into some gravel under the snow. He'd been worried he might have to dig them out of a ditch on the side of the road, but the car gained enough traction to move forward through the drifts.

Beside him, Leah's lips moved silently. No doubt she was praying. He should offer up a prayer of his own. One of gratitude to God for saving them from an accident. He'd wait until he got home to do that. Right now, he needed all his concentration for the road.

By the time they'd crept a few blocks, Kyle's hands ached from gripping the steering wheel, and his teeth throbbed from clenching his jaw. Foot by foot, they inched closer to the Hesses' house.

"What's that?" Leah pointed into the trees at the side of the road.

Kyle jumped. Her sudden sharp exclamation startled

him so badly he jerked the wheel, sending them sliding, but he brought the car under control.

"I'm so, so sorry." Leah looked as if she were about to cry. "I didn't mean to alarm you." A confused look on her face, she peered out the window. "A light bobbed over there in the trees. I hope nobody is caught out in this storm."

No houses lined this stretch of road, so the person— if it was a person—would have to travel quite a distance to reach any shelter. As much as he disliked driving in this weather, he had to assist a person stuck in the blizzard.

"Could it have been animal eyes?" he asked.

"It disappeared now, but I don't think so." Leah scanned the dark woods. "I'm fairly sure it was a flashlight. I last saw it right over there."

As much as he'd like to believe it was her imagination or the headlights glinting on a piece of metal, Kyle had to check. What if a person had collapsed in the snow?

He opened his car door. "I'd better take a look. Where did you see it again?"

"Between that huge oak and the small sapling." She pinpointed the direction for him.

He shuffled through the calf-deep snow toward the trees she'd indicated. A quick rustling nearby caught his attention. He'd been right—Leah had seen an animal. The scrabbling stopped. Kyle turned to go, when a slight movement off to the right caught his attention. He stepped nearer.

Cowering behind the oak, a young girl wrapped in a huge black cloak, wearing a black Amish bonnet, crouched back against the tree trunk as if trying to make herself invisible. Her eyes squeezed shut, she clutched a penlight in her hand. It amazed Kyle that Leah had spotted such a tiny light. No glow came from it now. Had the girl turned it off, or had her battery run out?

"Are you all right?" Kyle asked. "What are you doing out in this storm?"

The girl didn't answer. Instead, she straightened from her hunched position, and her wide, fearful eyes darted from side to side as if seeking an escape route.

"I won't hurt you," he assured her, but the anxiety didn't leave her face.

"Where are you heading?" Kyle asked. "We can drive you there."

"I don't need help," she rasped out.

"I can't leave you alone to find your way in a blizzard like this. Why don't you—?"

The girl groaned and doubled over. Her cloak hid her movements, but she seemed to be clutching her middle. His first thought was appendicitis.

"You need help." Without waiting for her consent, he swept an arm around her as soon as she stood upright. "Let's get you to the car." He had no idea if an ambulance could come out on such treacherous roads, but if she did have appendicitis, he'd have to get her to the hospital, even if it meant driving her there himself.

The girl struggled to get away, and she was stronger than he'd expected from her petite height. Kyle kept a firm hand on her arm. She might not realize what danger she was in, but he was well aware of the complications if her appendix burst.

They'd made it only halfway to the car before she

doubled over again. Her face contorted, and low moans came from her lips. The way her arms were puffing out her cloak seemed odd, though. Almost as if . . .

Before he could complete that thought, Leah hopped out of the car and hurried over. "What's wrong?" Her practiced eye homed in on the problem immediately.

The girl groaned and clutched at her middle. This time, in the faint light of a streetlight, her pregnancy became obvious. What he'd thought was her arms tenting out her cape when she stood among the dark trees turned out to be a baby bump.

Leah stepped closer, slid her hand under the cloak, and placed it on the side of the girl's protruding belly.

Alarm in her eyes, she glanced up at him. "I'd say she's in active labor. That contraction was strong." She waited until it subsided before asking the girl, "How far apart are your contractions?"

The girl stared at her with terrified eyes. "Let me go. Please. I can't . . ." She moaned and doubled over.

"She's almost ready to deliver." Leah used a calm voice, evidently hoping to soothe the edgy teen.

Neither of them wanted to frighten her, but they had little time. He had to get her into the car.

Once they reached the vehicle, Leah turned to Kyle. "We need to get her somewhere safe. How quickly can we make it to the office?" She opened the back door to the car. "If we get stuck, at least the seat is lined with blankets. Thank the Lord for small miracles."

Kyle was grateful for an even larger miracle. Leah's presence. He could have done this alone if he had to, but having her here with him made it much easier to cope with everything that had happened in the past few hours.

She'd likely be a calming influence on this agitated young girl.

Kyle kept his arm tightly around the girl. From the tension in her body, she intended to bolt the first opportunity she got. "Can you get into the car now?"

The girl pinched her lips together and shook her head.

"So you'd rather have me carry you?" She obviously hadn't expected that to be her other option.

With a shaky *no*, she appeared to cooperate by taking the last few steps toward the backseat, but her gaze flitted toward the narrowing gap between her and the car. Kyle loosened his grip slightly as she bent over as if with another contraction. But when she tried to twist away, he hung on. She'd faked a contraction. She couldn't deliver a baby out here in this weather. A newborn wouldn't stand a chance of survival. Unless that had been what she'd intended?

If so, he'd do everything he could to thwart her. Never, ever would a baby die under his watch.

* * *

As Kyle turned the car around, Leah swiveled in her seat to study the girl, who appeared to be about sixteen. "Where were you headed in this storm?"

A sullen look crossed the girl's face, and she crossed her arms, her lips tight.

Could she have made it any clearer that she didn't want to communicate? She almost seemed angry they'd picked her up. Where could she possibly be headed during a snowstorm? Especially with no houses nearby. And why had she ventured out when her labor had started? If her parents discovered her missing, they'd be frantic.

Kyle slid to a halt at the next intersection. "I guess I should obey this stop sign in case someone whizzed through." His attempt at a joke fell a bit flat because of the tension lines etched into his face.

Leah's heart went out to him. He'd been through a horrible accident with Emma, where he'd lost his child. Then he'd come close to crashing into a tree a short while ago. Yet he continued to drive to get her and this teen to safety.

While he was stopped, she said, "Maybe our friend might want to phone her family or a neighbor who can let her parents know she's safe."

"Good idea." Kyle pulled out his phone and handed it to Leah. "You gave your phone to Matthew. Do you need to call your family to let them know you're safe?"

"Um, no. Thank you for thinking of it. With all this snow falling, Joel had suggested I stay overnight at Matthew's place tonight. He promised to stay at my parents' house to keep an eye on them and to shovel out the parking lot tomorrow. It's probably better not to worry them."

Besides, Leah would rather not endure the grilling she'd get if she told her parents or Joel she'd be spending the night at the Hesses'. Everyone in town, including her parents, knew the Hesses took their annual vacation this time of year. With the blinding snowstorm, she only hoped their arrival might pass unnoticed by any nearby neighbors.

Leah held the phone out to the girl as Kyle crossed the intersection and headed down the last block. The teen's quick intake of breath, followed by a long, low cry, indicated she was having another contraction. Leah prayed they'd make it in time. She assumed this was the girl's first baby, so hopefully it might take its time.

As they turned into the snow-covered driveway, the car fishtailed. Leah sucked in a breath and held it until Kyle regained control. Then she blew out the air to release the pent-up anxiety she'd held since they'd started this journey. It had been a long day, but this delivery would soon begin.

"We're here," Kyle announced. "I'll try to get as close to the door as possible, but the drifts by the house may make that difficult."

"Thank you, Lord," Leah whispered. He'd answered her prayers. Now she had one more. A safe delivery for the teen in the backseat.

Kyle hopped out of the car and opened the girl's door. "I don't want you to fall. We also need to take good care of that baby." Then he wrapped an arm around the girl and supported her to the door. Over his shoulder, he called to Leah. "I'll come back for you as soon as I get her inside so she can warm up."

Leah wasn't about to wait for him to return. That girl needed help, and she needed it now. Leah opened the car door and stepped one foot outside. Snow closed over her shoe and ankle and reached the hem of her dress. Thankful Kyle had his back turned, she lifted her skirt and apron slightly to keep them from dragging in the drifts. Then she stepped from one of Kyle's footprints to the next to keep icy, white crystals from sliding into her shoes.

The snow that had already crusted on her shoe melted

from her body heat and slid in freezing rivulets inside
her shoe to puddle under the arch of her foot. Inside,
her shoes squelched, while outside, they crunched. She
squelched and crunched her way to the door, which had
slammed shut behind Kyle.

She quickly grabbed the handle and made her way
inside. She had a baby to deliver.

The teen stood in the hallway, her mouth set in mutinous lines. Leah puzzled over her attitude. It almost
seemed she didn't want their help. She certainly didn't
plan to have her baby alone. Did she?

"Let me take your cape and bonnet," Leah said. If they
didn't hurry, the poor girl might deliver her baby standing here in the hallway.

The teen appeared reluctant to part with either, but
Leah coaxed them from her. Under her black bonnet, the
girl wore a *kapp* without strings. Either she worked in
a shop where *kapp* strings might be hazardous, or she
was signaling her rebellion from the Amish faith. Judg-
ing by the girl's condition, Leah suspected her second
guess was probably correct.

"Please don't worry," Leah said as she escorted the
girl into an exam room. "We should have introduced
ourselves sooner, but with the harrowing conditions out
there on the road, things were a bit nerve-racking. I'm
Leah Stoltzfus. I'm studying to be a midwife."

The girl's eyes rounded more in fear than surprise.
Was she afraid of having an unskilled midwife attending
her?

As if sensing that might be the case, Kyle introduced
himself. "I'm Dr. Hess's new assistant, Dr. Miller, and
I've attended several of Leah's deliveries. She's quite

competent. You have nothing to fear." Then he turned to Leah. "I'll get your bag out of the trunk."

The girl doubled over again. Leah waited until the contraction had passed before asking, "What's your name?"

The teen stood there stone-faced.

She didn't want to give them her name? What was she running from? "We won't hurt you. I promise. Or tell anyone you've been here if you don't want us to."

Still no answer.

"We'll need a name for the birth certificate."

The girl looked off into the distance. "I'm...Mary. Umm, Mary Esh."

Leah had a sneaking suspicion that she hadn't given her real name. Perhaps after the baby was born, they'd convince her to be honest.

"I'm going to wash up," Leah told her.

"Hang on a minute." Kyle lugged in her bag. "I need to get something from the storage closet. I'd like you to check it." He returned in a few seconds. "See if these are all right." He stood in the doorway with an arm full of rubber sheets.

Why wouldn't they be all right? "They look fine to me." She headed to the door.

As she passed, he leaned close to whisper, "I think she wants to escape."

Leah nodded. That fit with the girl's refusal to give her name. Where did she think she could go in this storm that would be better for a delivery than here?

Leah scrubbed up and put on latex gloves. Then she entered the room and, as Kyle had just done, guarded the door as he went to wash up.

Mary moved closer to the exit but then doubled over.

"Panting sometimes helps," Leah suggested. She waited until the contraction had passed. "Now, let's get you on the examining table so we can check how far along you are."

While she'd been gone, Kyle had draped the rubber sheeting over the usual paper covering on the examining table and spread the other sheeting on the floor around the table.

But Mary balked at climbing onto the table.

"Would you prefer the floor?" Leah asked.

When Mary nodded, Leah assisted her to sit on the nearest sheet. Kyle returned to the room, allowing Leah to relax her vigil. Soon neither of them would need to block the door. By the time Leah convinced Mary to let her do an examination, the baby's head had almost crowned.

They'd barely made it here in time. Leah whispered a prayer of thanks for God's protection. If she and Kyle had passed by that spot in the woods a few minutes later, this child might have been born outside in the blizzard. Leah forced that dire thought from her mind and concentrated on the delivery.

"Could you give me the massage oil from the bag?" Leah asked Kyle.

Kyle rummaged through the bag to find it. "What for?" he asked.

"This is her first baby. If we're patient, I can stretch her skin to avoid tearing."

"That's what episiotomies are for."

Leah sighed. "Those are rarely necessary if we're

careful. Most doctors don't want to take the time to do things the natural way." She took the oil and applied it while Mary panted between contractions. When the next contraction began, she said, "Now push, Mary. The baby's almost here."

Her face red and eyes bulging, Mary shook her head. "I can't."

"Yes, you can," Leah encouraged. "Wait for the next contraction and bear down."

Mary's *no* turned into a whimper, then a howl. With gritted teeth, though, she cooperated with her body's urges and pushed.

"Again," Leah said. She murmured encouraging words until the baby's head and shoulders appeared. "Now, one final push." The baby slipped out into her hands.

"You have a lovely little girl," Leah announced.

Kyle added his congratulations to the new mother.

With sweat rolling down her forehead, Mary collapsed back on the floor, shivering, and tears rolled down her cheeks. While Kyle covered her with several blankets, he kept a close eye on the baby and Leah's procedures. Then he took the baby from her.

Seeing him with a baby in his arms did strange things to Leah's insides. Then her spirits plunged. She'd never have a child of her own. Any fantasies of Kyle with a child made her heart ache. She shook herself. If he had children, it would be with someone else, not her. She had no business entertaining thoughts like that. None at all.

First of all, he was *Englisch*. Besides, she made her choice to remain single and be a midwife. She'd get to hold babies, rock them, feed them sometimes. What difference did it make if they weren't hers? She could love them the same as if they were.

Once Mary had stopped shivering, Leah helped her into the house to get cleaned up. When they returned, she seemed more docile, relieved almost. Perhaps her earlier desire to flee had been connected to the pain of childbirth. Maybe she'd been confused and upset when her labor started.

While they were gone, Kyle had fixed the small table with low sides they used for examining babies into a makeshift bassinet, and he'd dressed the baby in an adult-sized T-shirt and tucked a small knitted blanket around her.

At her raised eyebrows, he defended himself. "The doctor has formula samples and disposable diapers in case of accidents, but they don't keep baby clothing here. This was the softest thing I could think of to cover her." He lifted the blanket so she could see he'd knotted the shirt at the bottom to form a sleep sack. The extra-large neck and one sleeve had also been knotted to keep the soft cotton close to the baby's chin.

Leah hadn't thought about clothes. They'd only wrapped the newborn in a blanket at first. "That was a good idea."

Kyle had his knuckle in the baby's mouth, and she was sucking hard. "This little one is ready to eat," he said to Mary.

She backed away, her hands crossed in front of her, a look of horror on her face.

Leah had hoped she'd been coming to accept her role as the baby's mother, but maybe her youth and inexperience caused her to feel inadequate. "I've helped plenty of first-time mothers," she assured her.

Mary shook her head and refused to look at the baby.

Kyle sighed and turned to Leah. "When I got the diapers from the supply room, I noticed a few new-mother kits on the shelf. From the advertising photo on their covers, they seem to include a bottle, a pacifier, a box of baby cereal, and a few other infant supplies inside."

"I'll go see." If they didn't have a bottle, she'd have to find a way to make do. During an emergency when she was young, she'd helped her neighbors feed baby goats by poking a hole in a latex glove. They had plenty of gloves here, but it seemed a shame to feed a newborn human that way.

To her relief, the kits contained bottles. She felt guilty raiding them and taking the supplies the doctor kept for needy patients. They had to care for this infant, though, if the mother refused.

How could any mother reject her sweet newborn? Leah's eyes filled with tears as she reached for a sample can of formula. *Why, God? Why can't I have children, but this young girl turns her back on her child?*

She leaned her head against the shelf edge and tried to compose herself. The baby's wail in the background urged her to hurry back, but Leah needed a few moments alone to deal with her grief.

"Leah?"

Kyle's voice behind her made her jump. She hadn't heard him come into the room. Perhaps because she'd been so lost in her own world, so full of self-pity.

"Are you all right?" His gentle tone opened the flood-gates.

Leah tried to bite back her sobs. "It feels so unfair. I wanted children more than anything in the world. Yet Mary has an adorable baby and turns her back on her newborn."

Chapter Twenty-Five

Ignoring all his internal warnings and clamoring alarm bells, Kyle reached for Leah and drew her into his arms. She needed comfort, and he couldn't walk away, leaving her alone at a time like this. "I'm so sorry. If anyone deserves to have children, it's you." She'd be a wonderful mother.

She leaned her head against his chest, and he feared she'd detect the rapid hammering of his heart. He cradled her face, wishing for a way to ease her heartache.

The door to the room banged open, and they jumped apart. Pale and wan, Mary leaned against the doorjamb. "The baby's screaming," she said as if caring for the infant was their responsibility.

"You could feed her," Kyle pointed out, trying not to let exasperation creep into his tone. He shouldn't be taking his annoyance out on her because she'd interrupted his time with Leah. He should be berating himself for holding Leah in the first place.

A series of expressions crossed Mary's face. Uncertainty, fear, and then defiance. Right before she turned away, Kyle glimpsed grief in her eyes.

Leah grabbed one of the bottles. "I'll go sterilize this. Be right back."

Kyle clenched his fists to keep from reaching out to wipe the traces of tears from Leah's cheeks. Those moments he'd held her in his arms had erased years of loneliness. If only he could ease some of her sorrow the way she'd alleviated his.

After grabbing a small stack of diapers, Kyle closed the storeroom door and locked it. He offered Mary an arm in case she needed support and escorted her back to the room, but now that the baby had arrived, she didn't seem ready to flee. Perhaps she was too drained after the delivery, but the fight seemed to have gone out of her.

She sank onto a chair and winced. Wriggling around, she made herself more comfortable. He needed to get her upstairs and into bed. First, though, the baby needed to be changed and fed. He put the diapers near the makeshift bassinet and changing table, then turned to find Mary staring off into the distance.

"Look over here," Kyle said in the authoritarian tone he sometimes needed to use as a doctor. "You need to learn how to hold your baby properly."

Mary's eyes widened, and she shook her head.

"Now." His command left no room for argument. If she was afraid, knowing some basics would help her overcome some of her fears. "This is important."

As soon as he had her attention, he changed his voice

to soothing as he described the baby's soft spot and the importance of supporting a newborn's neck. Then he lifted the baby to demonstrate, but when he walked over and tried to place her daughter in her arms, Mary fixed her eyes on the floor and shrank back.

Leah entered with the bottle, and after one look at Mary, she said in an upbeat voice, "Let's feed this beautiful little girl."

She must have dried her tears while she prepared the bottle. Maybe she'd also prayed, because her face was serene. He admired her inner strength and courage.

Despite her own heartbreak, she reached out to Mary, trying to encourage the young mother to participate in the process. With a blank face, Mary barely registered Leah's gentle explanations about feeding and burping, and whenever Leah attempted to hand over the baby, Mary balked.

It seemed Mary was doing everything possible to avoid bonding with her baby. That didn't bode well for the child's future. He hoped she had caring relatives who would step in to care for the little girl.

Once the baby had been fed and diapered, Kyle suggested an early bedtime. Most new mothers barely got out of bed the first few days, but Mary hadn't had stitches. And some of the teen mothers he'd seen at various hospitals seemed to bounce back pretty quickly. She had to be exhausted, though.

"Let's get Mary up to bed and make sure all three of you settle in for the night. Then I'll sleep down here in the office." To forestall Leah's protest, he pointed out, "I can't very well sleep upstairs. What would Esther think?"

Kyle had no idea how he'd explain these arrangements to Esther and Martin when they returned, but at least he and Leah could say they'd kept their agreement. And now they had two chaperones.

Upstairs, they made a makeshift bassinet from one of Kyle's dresser drawers and layers of blankets. Kyle carried it into the room where Mary would sleep and set it on the hope chest at the foot of the bed. "If you get tired of caring for her in the night and need a break, just call me. I can take her downstairs and use the makeshift bassinet."

"I'll be right next door," Leah assured her. "I'm happy to help with anything. I can run downstairs to heat her bottles."

After they left Mary's room, Kyle whispered, "I'm concerned because she seems to have no interest in caring for her daughter."

"I noticed that. Don't worry. I'll take care of the baby if she doesn't." She flashed him a tired smile. "Thank you for everything today."

Kyle held up a hand to stop her. "You're the one who was a hero today. You brought two babies into the world and saved both of their lives." He swallowed hard. "You're an amazing woman."

Leah ducked her head, but the pink suffusing her cheeks revealed she appreciated the compliment.

"Do you need anything else before I go?"

She glanced up at him with shining eyes. "I think we'll be all right."

"I'd better go downstairs," he said abruptly, fighting the urge to take her into his arms. If he didn't leave now, he'd forget Esther's rules entirely.

* * *

The next few days flew by in a blur. Outside the snow piled up, trapping them inside. Leah called Joel to let him know she'd be staying with a new mother for a while and would call him when she was ready to go home. Her brother didn't subject her to the inquisition her parents would have. She also explained about Matthew having her phone so they wouldn't try to call her.

Mary stayed in bed and refused to hold or help with the baby. Leah took the night shift, and Kyle cared for the newborn during the day. But with Leah making meals and cleaning during the day, and Kyle making dinner in the evenings and sleeping restlessly on the sofa, they sleepwalked past each other and shared weary smiles.

The snowplows came through late Thursday night, scraping the roads clear. When Friday dawned sunny, Kyle knocked at the door to the house. Despite being drained, seeing him sent her pulse pitter-pattering.

"Would you be able to watch the baby for a few hours this morning?" he asked. "That way I can go to the store for groceries and baby supplies. I want to replace everything we used and get a few things for the baby to wear."

Leah had been counting on a morning nap, but they'd run low on everything. "That's fine. I'll work on cleaning the house before the Hesses get back. Tomorrow, right?"

Kyle nodded.

"I don't know what to do about Mary," Leah said. "She refuses to name the baby. Now that the snow is cleared, I'll need to mail the birth certificate forms."

"I'll see if I can get her to cooperate." Kyle had observed her closely for postpartum depression, but other than avoiding the baby, she showed no signs of the baby blues. "With Esther and Martin returning, we need to take her home today."

"If you can get Mary to tell you where she lives. I haven't gotten that information from her." Leah rubbed her eyes, which were gritty from lack of sleep. Kyle tried to speak with Mary before he left, but he got no further with her than Leah had.

Leah sighed. "Until we find out her information, I guess I'll have to take her and the baby to my house. *Mamm* won't mind. She loves babies."

After Kyle left, Leah gave the baby her first bottle of the morning. Then she sank onto the bed. She should clean up, but she could hardly keep her eyes open. Caring for a newborn wore her out, but she'd fallen in love with the tiny infant. She'd do anything for the little one, including sacrificing sleep. Being exhausted meant she had little time for daydreaming about Kyle. Anytime she relaxed, rather than drifting off into fantasies, she drifted off to sleep.

She woke with a start. Disoriented, she stared around the room. How long had she been asleep? The baby hadn't cried. Rustling downstairs in the kitchen meant Kyle had returned with the groceries. Though it went against Esther's rules, she should help him. It would also be one of her last chances to spend time alone with him. First, she should check on the baby.

She eased open the door to Mary's room. It surprised Leah not to find Mary in bed, but the baby still slept soundly. Leah tiptoed over to enjoy the rise and fall of the newborn's chest with each breath. She could stand here all day, but Kyle could use help. She headed for the door, one quiet step at a time. A note on the nightstand drew her attention.

Leah and Kyle,

I'm leaving my baby in your care. I can see how much the two of you love each other. You'll be good parents. Please don't try to find me.

P.S. My real name is not Mary Esh.

* * *

Kyle had slipped into the house with the groceries and stowed them in the refrigerator and cupboards, trying not to wake Mary, the baby, or Leah, if she was napping. An image of her cuddling and smiling down at the newborn caused his stomach to flip. He wished their time together didn't have to end.

Upstairs, Leah shrieked. Kyle pounded up the stairs. Had something happened to the baby?

Leah stood trembling beside the unmade bed in Mary's room, holding a sheet of paper in her hands. "Mary left. She took off." Leah held out the note for him to read.

Kyle skimmed it. "I thought she was settling in."

Leah stared at him. "Where could she have gone in this weather?"

"She can't have gotten far. I'll drive around and see if I can find her and talk some sense into her."

Snowplows had cleared most of the streets, but they'd

left huge mountains of snow along the shoulders. "If she cut across fields, you'll never see her."

"I have to try. Maybe she left footprints I can follow."

Leah wished she could go with him, but someone needed to stay here with the baby.

The door opened downstairs, and Kyle smiled and set the note down on the nightstand near the door. "Maybe she changed her mind and came back."

Leah basked in the sunshine of his smile and in the hope that Mary had decided to accept some responsibility. "It would be hard to leave such a darling baby."

Sharp footfalls clacked up the steps.

Leah leaned toward Kyle and whispered, "Should we act like we haven't seen the note?"

"I thought I heard voices up here." Esther walked to the doorway of the room and blinked.

Leah straightened and moved away from Kyle but not quickly enough to prevent Esther from seeing how close she'd been standing. Esther's gaze roamed from the two of them to the unmade bed right behind them with its covers dangling on the floor. Her eyes widened, and her eyebrows arched up so high they almost disappeared into her permed gray bangs.

"I can explain," Kyle said.

"I'd rather not hear any justifications for this . . . this betrayal of our trust." With sadness in her eyes, she turned to Leah. "I'll wait until you've gone downstairs to talk to Kyle. Then either Martin or I will drive you home."

"But I can't leave—"

Before she could explain about the baby, Esther cut her off. "You can, and you will. I'll talk with you downstairs."

Leah should respect her elders, so she closed her mouth and headed down to the living room. She hoped Esther would allow Kyle to explain about the baby. Then she'd show her Mary's note.

* * *

Still in shock at Esther's early return, Kyle blurted out, "I thought you were coming home tomorrow."

"Martin and I decided we'd prefer to rest for a day before attending church on Sunday. We caught an early flight back." Her eyes sad, she shook her head. "So you thought you'd have one more day together before we got here?"

"It really wasn't like that." Kyle didn't know how to begin. "It's a long story. Maybe we could all sit in the living room so Leah and I could explain."

"I really don't think, under the circumstances, I can trust any explanations—or justifications—of your behavior." She turned to leave.

"Please, Esther..."

"I came up to ask if you'd help Martin with the luggage, but I forgot."

"I'll go now." Kyle took the stairs two at a time so the doctor wouldn't be stuck carting in the heavy suitcases. Perhaps he could explain everything to Dr. Hess.

The doctor stood in the garage beside two large suitcases. "I got them in from the driveway after the cab dropped us off, but wheeling them in winded me."

"I'm sorry I took so long. I'd like to discuss a misunderstanding I had with Esther," Kyle said, as he picked up both suitcases.

Dr. Hess held up a hand. "I made it a policy years ago I'd never listen to anything negative about my wife."

"I meant with both of you together, but first I need to do something urgent." Kyle rushed up the stairs with the suitcases. Then he came back down and poked his head into the living room. "I don't want to leave you to face Esther's wrath alone, but the sooner I go after Mary, the more likely I am to find her."

"Don't worry," Leah said. "I can handle things here. Once Esther realizes the truth, she'll calm down."

A thin wail came from upstairs, and Leah rose. "I'd better take care of the baby. Go ahead and search for Mary."

*   *   *

Leah hurried upstairs and ran into Esther in the hallway.

"What is going on?" the doctor's wife demanded.

"That's what Kyle and I need to explain, but first I need to take care of the baby."

A confused frown etched between her eyebrows, Esther followed Leah into the bedroom and stood to one side staring while Leah picked up the newborn to comfort her.

"That's not…that can't be yours." Esther shook her head.

Leah longed to say, *Yes, this baby is mine.* Then joy exploded through her. She'd left the note downstairs on the table, but Mary had given her the baby. This child was hers. *Her own child.*

"Actually," Leah said with a smile, "she is. And I need

to feed her." She cuddled the squalling baby close and headed down the stairs.

"But, but..." Esther sputtered behind her.

When she was partway down, it occurred to her the house belonged to Esther and Martin. Her cheeks heated. How rude she'd been! For the past few days, she'd been living here as if it were her own home, freely using the kitchen and bedrooms. And now she was just waltzing down to the kitchen as if she had every right to be there. What must Esther think of her? Well, she already knew one answer to that question.

"Is it all right if I use the kitchen to fix the baby a bottle?" she called up to Esther.

Esther's voice floated down the stairs, her tone bemused. "Of course."

When Leah reached the kitchen, she stopped short. Martin sat at the table drinking a glass of water and sorting through the mail that had accumulated while they were gone.

He looked up, startled, at the bawling infant in Leah's arms. "I thought I heard a baby, but I assumed it was in the office. My hearing must be getting worse."

"I need to fix her a bottle if that's all right."

"Go right ahead, but whose baby is it?" He didn't add, *What are you and a newborn doing in our house?* Yet his tone implied the question.

The baby is mine, she longed to answer. *All mine. Well, and Kyle's too.* Instead, she said, "That's what Kyle and I need to talk to you about."

The doctor looked as puzzled as his wife had moments ago. "Is that what Kyle was nattering about before he ran off?"

"I imagine so. Esther seems to have gotten the wrong impression about us." A flush of heat swept up her neck and splashed across her face. "I hope you'll both let us explain."

"Why don't we do that while you're feeding the baby? I'll get Esther." He went to the foot of the stairs and called up to his wife.

"I-I'd been hoping for more time," Esther replied in a shaky voice. But a few minutes later, she descended the stairs as Leah removed the baby bottle from the pan of water on the stove.

"Are you all right, dear? You're quite pale." Martin rushed over and put an arm around her shoulders to lead her into the living room.

"I'm still in shock, I think. It came as quite a blow to find out I couldn't trust Kyle."

Yes, you can, Leah longed to tell her. The faster she went into the living room, the faster she'd clear up Esther's misperceptions. Leah tested the bottle on her wrist and slid the nipple into the baby's howling mouth. The little girl latched on and began sucking. *Ahh, blessed silence.*

On the counter, Kyle had left bags of baby products. Holding the bottle with one hand, Leah changed the baby's diaper and slipped her into a sleeper. She should have washed it first, but she wanted the little one to be presentable.

When she entered the living room, Esther and Martin, their heads close together, looked up and stopped whispering. Martin's grave face made it clear his wife had filled him in on her suspicions.

Leah sank into the chair across from Esther. Then

cuddling the newborn close, she said, "This is a long story, but it might be best if I start with what happened on Monday." Had it been less than a week ago? Leah's exhausted body clamored that weeks had passed.

From their crossed arms and matching frowns, neither of the Hesses appeared to be in a receptive mood. Leah hoped by the end of her story, they'd wear looks of understanding and kindness.

She began with a brief account of the breech birth. The Groffs' plight of MSUD elicited sympathy from both of them. Leah tried to describe the snow and dangerous roads on the way home but omitted Kyle's suggestion she stay here.

"As we were driving, we found a pregnant teenager and brought her here. With Kyle's help, I delivered this baby in an exam room."

Dr. Hess interrupted with a flurry of questions about the delivery and how they'd managed. Leah fielded all of them, impatient to get back to the story and exonerate Kyle.

"The girl, who claimed her name was Mary, wanted nothing to do with caring for the baby." Leah lifted the infant over her shoulder and patted her back. "We borrowed the formula samples and disposable diapers from the supply room, but we'll replace them."

"Don't worry about that," Esther said. "I'll order more." Her eyes filled with tears after Leah recounted wrapping the baby in Kyle's T-shirts. "The poor little child."

"Anyway," Leah continued, "the roads were too treacherous to drive, so Kyle insisted the young mother and I stay here. He slept in the office. I hope it was all right for us to use the bedrooms."

"Of course. Our home is always open to those in need."

"It's been a rough few days. I hoped I'd convince the young mother to love and care for the baby, but I failed."

"I assume that means you've been doing it all." Esther's eyes grew distant. "I remember those days. The bone weariness, confusion, trudging through each day half-awake." As if realizing she'd begun rambling, she snapped her mouth shut and motioned for Leah to go on.

"Kyle helped." At Esther's raised eyebrows, Leah hastened on. "We made sure we were never alone together. Until today."

Esther's brow furrowed, and she nibbled on her lower lip.

"I went in to check on Mary and found this." Leah reached for the note she'd left on the table and passed it to Esther and Martin.

They read it in silence, and Leah waited until they looked up again. "I must have screamed, because Kyle raced upstairs. I showed him the note, and we were trying to decide what to do when you arrived."

From Esther's steely gaze, she was weighing Leah's words, searching her eyes and body language to be sure she was telling the truth.

Leah needed to clear up one more thing. "About the bedcovers...I'm sorry they were so messy, but Mary slept in there, and she refused to clean up after herself or make her bed. I would have done that if I'd had time."

Esther glanced at Martin, and he nodded and took her hand. Was that a sign he believed Leah's account?

Esther bent her head and reread the note. "What does

she mean by this?" She tapped her finger on the paper. "She says she could tell you were in love with each other."

"I expect she mistook our working together in harmony as something more. Or perhaps it was wishful thinking on her part, wanting to have two parents for the baby."

The answer made Leah ache inside. Although she could never have a relationship with an *Englischer*, it hurt that they'd never be able to share the baby or their lives.

Esther studied Leah for a short while before saying, "I owe you both an apology for jumping to conclusions and misjudging you. Will you forgive me?"

"Of course." Leah bent forward to accept Esther's outstretched hand.

Esther squeezed her hand a few times, then let go. "I imagine you're dazed and exhausted. I remember those days from Timothy—I mean Kyle."

The sadness in her eyes as she spoke about the past made Leah ache for her. How hard it must have been to give up the baby she loved.

Martin cleared his throat. "So what are your plans for the baby?"

"I…I don't know." That wasn't entirely true. She longed to keep this baby, love her, raise her. But if the mother changed her mind, she'd have to give up her dreams. The same way she'd been struggling to accept not having any children.

Esther and Martin both stared at her, waiting for her to continue.

"Kyle went out to see if he can find the baby's

mother," she said, trying to conceal her misery at the prospect of finding the young teen.

The door opened, and Kyle entered. Alone. Leah's heart leapt. He hadn't found Mary. But her racing pulse wasn't only relief at that fact. She'd been sleepwalking through the past few days and hadn't had time to even look at Kyle, to admire his rugged good looks, the strength of his jaw, the...Leah stopped herself. She had no right to be thinking things like that. For the past few days, she'd been close enough to see his strength of character, his calmness under pressure, his kind and generous spirit, his love for babies, his tenderness toward her and the new mother...

She forced herself to tune back in to the conversation. Kyle had removed his boots and winter coat. In his stocking feet, he padded to the chair across from her and sought her eyes.

"Leah, I'm sorry. I didn't find her. A few times I saw footprints in the snow and followed them, but they all led to a dead end. I checked the woods where we found her. The snow there remained untouched."

Although Leah prayed Mary was safe, she couldn't help hoping they'd never find her. If they didn't, the baby would be hers, wouldn't it?

"I inquired at several houses, but nobody recalled a pregnant Amish teen living in this neighborhood. I guess it's time to call the police."

Leah gasped. "The police? Why would we do that?"

"They have better search capabilities."

"You can't do that." Leah's shrill voice startled the baby, who whimpered. "She asked us not to search for her. And won't they arrest her for abandoning her baby?"

"Not necessarily," Dr. Hess said. "The state has a safe-haven law that allows new mothers to leave their babies at a hospital or with a police officer within twenty-eight days of birth. A few of my unwed or teen mothers have done that."

"We should definitely track her down before that time is up," Kyle said.

"Won't the baby go into foster care, then?" Leah couldn't lose her only chance to have a child. She hugged the infant close. "I don't want to lose her."

"Oh, honey, you aren't really thinking of keeping her." Compassion in her gaze, Esther leaned forward in her chair. "Caring for a little one is exhausting, and doing it alone makes it even harder. What would you do with her when you're called out to deliveries?"

"I don't know," Leah admitted. "I'll figure it out."

Esther shook her head. "Best to get this child back to her family. If she's Amish, the teen's parents will raise her. Don't worry—you'll soon be married and have plenty of babies of your own."

"No, I won't."

Chapter Twenty-Six

Leah's tear-filled words tugged at Kyle. What if she ended up losing this child because he wanted to do things legally? Yet how could he let her fall in love with a child that might someday be taken from her? What if the mother changed her mind and came back for the baby?

After Leah finished explaining things to the Hesses, he offered to take her home. The Hesses insisted she take all the diapers and formula Kyle had bought. He handed her the package of clothes too. As she thanked them, her eyes misted.

Kyle loaded her midwife bag into the trunk. He'd purchased a car seat, so he took the baby from Leah and buckled the tiny girl in.

Riding in the car with Leah again brought back memories of the other night and seeing the tree so close to Leah's window. He could have lost her that night. His heart stopped at the thought.

They'd had a precious few days together. Days he'd keep tucked close inside long after he left for his fellowship. Before he dropped Leah off, she mulled over baby names.

Kyle tried to discourage her. "If you name the baby, you'll get too attached to her."

"What's wrong with that?"

"It'll make it much harder to give her up when the real mother is found."

"She doesn't want to be found. She asked that we not search for her."

"She's only a teen. One who's been through a scary emotional experience. She most likely was confused and not thinking clearly."

Leah smoothed the note that lay on her lap. "She doesn't sound at all confused here."

Kyle didn't argue. He pulled into the parking lot and helped Leah unload.

Joel's eyes widened as they walked through the door. "A baby?"

Leah smiled her heart-stopping smile as she looked down at the little one in her arms. The picture so mesmerized Kyle that Leah's explanation to Joel didn't register. In that moment, he made a vow. Whatever it took, he'd make sure she could keep that baby permanently.

*   *   *

After they got over their initial shock, her parents went out of their way to care for the little girl Leah named Ruby. Having a baby in the house was good for the whole family. *Mamm* had more good days than she'd had in a long time, so she was able to spend some time caring for Ruby. Even Joel begged to have Ruby in the store from time to time. He claimed she was good for business.

Esther had given Leah several weeks off to care for the baby, so she spent her days and nights feeding, changing, and cuddling Ruby. She loved her baby time, but she missed Kyle. She daydreamed of their meal in Esther's kitchen, working together in the office, driving together to the doctor, and caring for the baby, so she was overjoyed when he stopped by one evening after work. Until she discovered the reason for his visit.

"I've found some clues to Mary's whereabouts, I think."

Leah's heart sank. She assumed they'd settled this. Why had he continued searching?

"Grace Fisher and her husband took in a pregnant niece about six months ago. I understand they're rather reclusive. Often don't go to church and pretty much kept the girl hidden. A neighbor mentioned he'd seen a young teen living with them. He's Amish, so I couldn't really question him about her pregnancy."

Leah clamped her teeth on her bottom lip to hold back a cry. Maybe the neighbor had made a mistake. The timing and a visiting teen matched, but those could be coincidences. Grace had been in their buddy bunch, but after she married a much older man, she stopped attending events and even church.

"I'm going out to visit them tomorrow. Do you want to come along?"

She'd love to spend the day with him. "What about Ruby?" At his puzzled look, she explained, "I named the baby."

"I see." He tapped a knuckle against his lip and appeared deep in thought. "I'd love to have her along, but if Mary is there..."

Ach, that would never do. She might snatch the baby away. By now she'd have had time to think it over and regret her decision.

"I can watch Ruby if you won't be gone long," Joel volunteered.

"Maybe an hour or so," Kyle told him.

"No problem," her brother answered.

Maybe not for him, but it definitely was for Leah.

The next morning Leah's heart skipped a beat when Kyle entered the store. She restrained herself from running over and forced herself to bend and check on Ruby.

Kyle came over and knelt beside her. So much for calming herself.

He reached out and placed a hand on Ruby's head. "Looks like she's grown already. I hope you'll bring her to the office for her well-baby checkups."

"I wouldn't take her anywhere else."

Kyle's face lit up. "Good. Wish I could hold her, but we should leave now while she's peaceful."

He stood and offered Leah a hand. After he helped her to her feet, he didn't let go. "It's slippery in some spots."

That sounded like a lame excuse, especially as Joel had scraped the sidewalks clean that morning and sprinkled salt for extra safety. But Leah didn't care.

Once he started driving, though, knots formed in her stomach and pulled taut. The closer they got, the more her insides hurt. She couldn't lose Ruby. She just couldn't.

Kyle took her hand again as they walked up to the unkempt house. This time drifted snow covered the walk-way, and ice patches dotted the porch. He knocked, and Leah prayed they wouldn't come face-to-face with Mary.

The door opened only crack. A woman's eye peered out at them. "Yes?"

"Grace?" Kyle asked. "May we come in? It's cold out here. We won't take much of your time."

"I don't think—"

"Who's there, Grace?" a man barked from the other room.

Before Grace could answer, Leah said, "I'm from Stoltzfus Natural Products." If she claimed to be a buddy bunch friend, she suspected her husband wouldn't let them in.

"You must want a lot of jams to come out in weather like this." He snickered.

Leah glanced at Kyle. She hadn't brought any money with her. When Kyle nodded, she called out that they intended to purchase as much as they could afford.

Grace led them to the kitchen, where Kyle bought a dozen jars of jam.

"You'll need to pay my husband," she said, and swept a hand toward the living room.

A small girl toddled into the room and clutched Grace's skirt. Her older brother peered out from behind the pantry door.

A frown creasing his brow, Kyle returned to the kitchen. He accepted his bag and then asked, "Did you have a teen girl staying with you recently?"

"Wh-who told you that?" She waved them toward the front door. "You'd better go."

As they headed out the door, Grace caught Leah's

arm and whispered, "Could you ask Sharon to stop by? I think . . ."

"Grace," her husband groused from the other room, "we can't afford to heat the outside."

"I'm sorry," she called to him. *Please*, she mouthed to Leah.

"Of course," Leah said.

When Sharon stopped by to tell her that Emily's prognosis was good, Leah relayed Grace's message.

Sharon looked troubled. "I hope it's a false alarm. Poor Grace has enough troubles."

Leah suspected one of them might be her husband, but she asked, "What do you mean?"

"They're in bad financial straits, and her husband won't let anyone know. He's out of work, depressed, and refuses to see a doctor for his health issues. Grace supports her family by canning jams and jellies for farmers markets and local stores."

"I see." Leah already knew about the canning. Perhaps buying her jams had helped the family a little. Leah hoped so.

"It's not easy for her now," Sharon said, "with working full-time and caring for children."

Was that a subtle hint Leah shouldn't consider keeping Ruby if she also wanted to be a midwife?

* * *

Kyle went home thoughtful. He'd stayed at the store when he dropped Leah off, and enjoyed holding Ruby and giving her a bottle. And spending time with Leah was always a delight, but he needed to focus on getting information from Grace, something he couldn't do with her husband around.

As they drove in earlier, he'd noticed cows in the barn. Someone needed to do the milking, and he bet that someone would be Grace. Her husband, weighing in at more than three hundred pounds and with his red, swollen ankles propped up on a cushioned stool, didn't appear capable of handling many tasks.

After withdrawing several hundred dollars from the bank, he headed back out to her house in the late afternoon. Many farmers milked around then, and Grace would need to finish that chore before cooking dinner and putting the children to bed. He parked the car down the road from their farm and walked toward the barn, trying to stay out of view of the room her husband occupied. He doubted the man could move from room to room. Then he sat on a hay bale to wait.

When Grace came to the barn with her two children dragging on her apron, Kyle stood and called her name softly, hoping he wouldn't spook her.

With large, frightened eyes, she backed away. "Wh-what are you doing here?"

"I won't hurt you. I only wanted to ask you a question. Can you give me the name and address of the teenage girl who just had the baby?"

"I can't give you the address. They paid us money to care for her and keep it a secret, but if anyone finds out she had a baby, we'll have to pay it back. She was supposed to drop the baby at one of the local hospitals. All the hospitals around here have a bassinet inside the door for mothers who can't care for their babies."

Kyle wanted to ask why Mary couldn't take her baby home to her family, but it was none of his business. He was glad Mary chose a better future for her child by picking parents she thought would take good care of her baby. Perhaps she hadn't been as indifferent as she'd seemed. You couldn't ask for a better mother than Leah.

Kyle reached into his pocket. He'd guessed right about the bribe. He hadn't thought the Amish would stoop to that. "Would this be enough to pay them back if you disclose where to find your niece?"

Her eyes widened. "More than enough."

He pressed the roll of bills into her hands. "Keep the extra in a safe place." He hoped she understood he meant to keep it out of her husband's hands.

"I will. *Danke.*"

Kyle had one more concern. "Does your husband hurt you?"

"N-no. He's a bit short-tempered, but he only yells when he's upset."

"He needs to see a doctor as soon as possible." Kyle had seen several worrisome symptoms along with his weight, and he suspected depression might cause the anger.

"I'll try, but I don't know if he'll listen to me."

Kyle could only hope the man would listen to his wife. He left with uneasiness and the address of Miriam Ebersol.

Twenty minutes later, he pulled up to a house with a large garden, bordering a cornfield. To his surprise, Mary—or Miriam?—opened the door. Her eyes bugged out. She started to slam the door, but Kyle stuck his foot over the threshold to keep the door from closing.

"What do you want?" Her voice shook.

"All I want is—"

"Wait!" She reached toward a nearby set of hooks and pulled down a black cape. After she'd wrapped it around herself, she stepped outside and closed the door. "*Mamm* and *Daed* don't know about the baby. You're not going to tell them, are you?"

"I have no intention of telling anyone. But if your parents don't know, who paid Grace?"

"You know about that? I can't believe Grace told anyone. I had to promise not to tell anyone about the pregnancy and not to keep the baby. I couldn't look at her. If I did..."

Kyle ached for her. All along they'd assumed she'd been stubborn and uncooperative. He would have been gentler with her if he'd known she was just trying to not form an attachment to the baby. "I'm sorry."

Miriam drew circles with the toe of her shoe on the slushy porch. "I'm glad she'll have a good home." Then she looked up in alarm. "You are going to keep her, aren't you?"

"That's what I came for. Will you go to the courthouse to sign an official document giving the baby to Leah?"

"No."

"She can't adopt without the paperwork."

The mutinous look she'd had the night of the delivery had returned. "I want my baby to have a *mamm* and a *daed*. I'll sign if both of you adopt her."

Kyle didn't see any way to do that. He never wanted to be an absentee dad. As much as he wanted to spend his life with Leah, that was impossible. "Let me think about it." He already knew he couldn't do that to a child, but he needed to have his argument ready. Perhaps if he brought Leah along, Miriam would change her mind.

That night Kyle wrestled with his answer.

If Leah weren't Amish, he'd marry her in a heartbeat. But after he'd seen how much her faith meant to her, he could never ask her to give up her beliefs, her family, her community. And he could never become Amish.

But if he refused Miriam's request, what would happen to the baby? Ruby would be sent to child protective services and eventually be adopted. Adoptions often turned out well. His had. But what if Ruby's didn't? What if her adoptive parents didn't love her the way Leah did?

And what about Leah? She'd lose the little girl she loved. How could he hurt Leah—and Ruby—that way? Leah was a wonderful mother. He'd searched for Miriam so Leah could adopt Ruby; he couldn't back out now.

Was he being given another chance? A chance to take responsibility for a child's life?

Except he didn't deserve to parent a child. Not after what he'd done.

He fell to his knees beside the bed. *Oh, God...forgive me. For everything...*

All the pain of the past welled up—his anger at God, his failures, his shame, his guilt. He poured it all out to the God of the universe.

When he finished, a huge burden lifted from his heart. For the first time since his parents' deaths, since Emma's accident, he felt clean, whole...and forgiven. And in the early morning stillness, Kyle made one more request.

Please, God, show me what to do. Help me to make the right decision.

After having spent the night on his knees, he rose, his mind and spirit clean and clear. He'd not only gotten his life right with God, but he'd also made his decisions for the future.

Chapter Twenty-Seven

Leah had just run down to the kitchen for Ruby's bottle when Joel called from the shop to say she had a visitor. She hoped it might be Ada. She hadn't had a chance to tell her friend the good news yet. She rushed out and stopped short.

Kyle! Why now? When I'm such a mess?

He smiled at her as if nothing were amiss. "I have a surprise for you. I hate to ask you to leave Ruby again, but I think it would be best to go without her."

Once again, Joel came to her rescue. "Oh, good. Another chance to watch Ruby."

"I'll let *Mamm* know." Leah rushed into the house to smooth back her hair, wash her face and hands, dab at several spots on her dress, and take off her soiled work apron to pin on a fresh one.

As she hurried back downstairs, she called to *Mamm*, "Dr. Miller needs to show me something."

"He couldn't do this when you're back at the office?"

"It sounded urgent." She stopped running right before she reached the store entrance. Taking a few deep breaths to compose herself, she grabbed her cloak, straightened her back, and walked out into the shop with dignity, hoping the effect wasn't spoiled by bloodshot eyes, dark under-eye circles, or stains on her dress.

"You look great for a new mother." The appreciation shining in Kyle's eyes made it clear he meant the compliment.

"*Danke.*" Leah ducked her head so he wouldn't see the heat flushing her cheeks. She could return the flattery but held her tongue to avoid gushing about his handsomeness.

While he drove, Kyle questioned her about how she was healing after her operation and asked how Ruby was doing. He also expressed worry over Leah's lack of sleep. His attentiveness made her feel cared for, almost cherished. She had to keep reminding herself his interest stemmed from his medical concerns.

They pulled into the parking lot of a small pretzel shop, and Kyle turned to her. "Hungry?"

Leah struggled to remember when she'd last eaten. "For sure and certain." Then she backtracked. "Never mind. I didn't bring money."

"This is my treat."

He took her arm to support her over slushy puddles on the heavily salted sidewalk. "Miriam asked to meet us here, so we'll act like regular customers."

"Miriam?" Leah ran through everyone named Miriam from their church district but racked her brain for a reason they'd drive all the way out here to meet anyone.

"Ebersol," Kyle said as he opened the door and reached out to help her over the threshold.

Leah inhaled the warm, yeasty air fragrant with melting sugary icing. She searched the menu board. *Oh good, they have my favorite. Cinnamon raisin.* Leah noted many of the young bakers in the back room had no *kapp* strings. Rebellion or safety? Or perhaps both.

"May I help you?" one of the girls behind the counter asked.

Leah had been so busy staring at people in the back room twisting the pretzel dough she hadn't realized it was their turn. With a smile, she turned to order, then clapped a hand to her mouth. What was Mary Esh doing here?

Kyle stood close beside her, and Leah turned to him in horror, only to find him smiling at Mary.

He knew! He set this up. Had he been grilling her about Ruby for Mary's sake, because he planned to return the baby to her mother?

Heartsick, she whirled around. "You set this up after I told you—?" Brushing past him, she wove through the crowd and pushed through the door. She stood under the small awning, hyperventilating, tears frozen solid in her chest, too numb to cry.

"Leah, wait," he said as he followed her outside. "You don't understand." Kyle set his hands on her shoulders.

Gulping in a breath, she twisted away. "I understand you had to follow your conscience, but Ruby belongs with me."

* * *

Kyle pulled her into his arms, and she collapsed, boneless, against his chest. He'd been foolish to do this. He should have prepared her better for the shock.

"Leah," he whispered against her hair, "I wrestled with this for hours last night. Ever since I learned I was adopted, a hole opened in my life. I strongly believed children shouldn't ever be separated from their birth mothers. I never got to know mine."

Indignant protests rumbled from Leah's lips, but Kyle touched a finger to her mouth to halt the flow of words.

"I also wondered if adoptive parents could ever love a child the same way birth parents could, but after you delivered Ruby, I learned that some birth parents don't want their children, and adoptive parents can love wholeheartedly."

Leah pushed away from his arms and stepped back on unsteady legs. He wanted to reach out and support her, but he kept his hands to himself. "Yes, adoptive parents can and do love their child with every fiber of their beings." In a choked voice, she said, "It'll rip out my heart to give her up."

As she spoke those words, Miriam exited the shop behind Leah. "You really love her that much?"

Leah whirled to face her. "She means everything in the world to me."

Meeting Kyle's eyes, Miriam nodded. "I could see that from the minute she was born." She teared up. "I was forced to give her up, walk away, and never mention her again. I couldn't look at her, so I watched you instead."

"Forced to give her up?"

Miriam stared at the ground. "My boyfriend's parents insisted. His father is a famous preacher, and they'd groomed him for a high-profile role. They don't want anyone to know. I thought he'd wait for me"—she bit back a sob—"but he got engaged to someone more suitable. Another *Englischer*."

"I'm so sorry." Leah reached out a hand to Miriam. "I can see why you'd want your baby back."

"My baby back? I can't take her back. My parents would never understand." Miriam stepped back and turned wary eyes in Kyle's direction. "I thought..."

Kyle held up a hand. "Leah seems to have gotten the wrong impression about our meeting." He set his hands on Leah's shoulders. "I looked for Mary—Miriam— because I wanted to ensure you could adopt Ruby legally. I didn't want you running in fear of discovery."

Leah stared at him uncertainly. "I can keep Ruby?"

"We're heading to the courthouse now so Miriam can sign the papers. She also needs to amend the birth certificate."

When Leah lifted teary, but shining, eyes to meet his, it took all his willpower not to enfold her in his arms and kiss her. He'd vowed to see that she could keep Ruby permanently, and he'd kept that promise, but would she be happy about the rest of the agreement he'd made?

He took a deep breath. "There's just one catch."

Some of the joy on Leah's face dimmed, and she stared at him, her expression apprehensive.

Kyle wished he didn't have to tell her she'd need to share Ruby. "The thing is, well, Miriam wants her daughter to have two parents. She insisted that I adopt Ruby too."

"There's no one I'd rather parent with." Leah, her cheeks crimson, pressed a hand to her mouth.

"You mean that?" A seedling of hope took root in Kyle's heart. Maybe, just maybe...

* * *

Leah couldn't believe she'd blurted that out, but at the chance to spend more time with Kyle, her happiness overflowed. What must he be thinking?

Her burning cheeks revealed her real feelings for the whole world to see. She could barely look at Kyle while they signed the paperwork. Afterward, they dropped Miriam off at the shop.

When they pulled into the parking lot beside Leah's house, Kyle said, "We should probably discuss how we'll parent Ruby. Could we go to a restaurant and find a quiet corner to talk about the future? With our baby, of course."

"I'll run in and get her."

Her heart singing, Leah practically danced into the store. Precious Ruby was hers now and Kyle's too. She'd get to spend more time with him. He'd be a wonderful father. If only they could marry, but he'd been adamant about not becoming Amish, so that was impossible. But with Miriam being Amish, Leah hoped Kyle would agree to raise Ruby Amish.

Joel studied her when she waltzed past him to pick up Ruby. "Wow," he said. "Your eyes are so starry they could light up the whole night sky," Joel said.

If they reflected even a small portion of the delight filling her, Leah could only imagine how brightly they shone. "I need to get Ruby. Kyle and I have to discuss some things."

"She's right here, sound asleep. I just changed her and fed her, so she's all ready to go."

Joel helped her get Ruby bundled up for the cold. Then Leah practically skipped out to the car. Kyle carried Ruby and settled her gently into her car seat.

Leah's heart swelled at how tenderly he held Ruby and adjusted the belts of the car seat, testing each one to make it snug. They'd be doing this parenting together. Her elation expanded to fill her whole body; every cell thrilled with anticipation and delight.

At the restaurant, Kyle requested a secluded corner where they settled across from each other and passed Ruby back and forth between them. When Leah cradled her little girl, her precious daughter, in her arms and met Kyle's eyes, she couldn't imagine ever being happier.

A short while later, he looked up from feeding Ruby her bottle, and a serious expression crossed his face. "I spent the night in prayer, getting right with God and asking for His guidance for my future. I believe I told you I applied for fellowships several weeks ago."

Tears sprang to Leah's eyes. She'd dreamed of being a team, of working together. "You won't be around to see her grow up." Though she tried, she couldn't keep disappointment from coloring her tone.

"Wait, I haven't finished yet." Kyle lifted Ruby over his shoulder and patted her back. "As I was saying, I prayed about it. Miriam refused to sign the forms unless both of us agreed to parent Ruby. I couldn't let you lose the baby."

"You did it for me, so I could keep Ruby?" It touched her that he cared to help her, but much of the joy and excitement fizzled.

"I promised Miriam I'd be a father to Ruby."

"You agreed but have no intention of keeping your commitment?"

A look of hurt flashed in Kyle's eyes. "I thought you knew me well enough to know I always keep my promises."

"It's hard to be a father when you're not around."

"I agree. The fellowships won't be posted until January, but I planned to turn down any offers. I told Dr. Hess I'd take over his practice, but I'd love it if you could work there, so we could both be around Ruby all day."

That would be wonderful, but without the Hesses around, they'd be facing a great deal of temptation.

Kyle continued, "I'd been hoping to get fellowships at hospitals that study rare diseases. After seeing what they do at the clinic here, I realized I could have that opportunity here. What do you think?"

Leah kept her answer to a neutral, "That sounds like a great idea," even though inside she shouted *YES!*

After Ruby had been redressed in her outer garments and swathed in blankets, Kyle tucked the baby into her car seat, and they headed back to the shop. The baby soon fell asleep. As they rode out of town, Kyle veered off onto a different road, one that wound into the country. Leah rejoiced that he'd chosen the long way home so they'd have more time together.

But when he made one more turn onto the road where the accident had occurred, she clenched her hands together as they neared the spot. Kyle startled her by pulling over.

Then he turned to her. "I wanted to come here together because this tragedy—the one that occurred here—shaped both of our lives. Although I've asked for forgiveness, I've struggled with guilt for so long, and I know you have too."

Her eyes brimming with tears, Leah nodded. Her guilt had only increased after she'd discovered he and Emma had lost a baby.

With his thumb, Kyle brushed away a teardrop trickling down her cheek, and the gentleness of his touch started an inner fire.

When he spoke again, his voice was husky. "We can't go back and change what happened, but I'd like us to move forward—together. To start a new life as a family."

He reached for her hand, and as his large, warm fingers closed over hers, Leah's pulse pitter-pattered out of control.

"Dr. Hess once told me if I waited for the special person God has for me, I'd be as blessed as he and Esther are. I believe I've found that special person." Caressing her hand, Kyle looked deep into her eyes. "Being around you, working with you, sharing a child with you means so much to me. I've tried to deny my feelings for a long time, but I've fallen in love with you. Would you do me the honor of being my wife?"

Leah's dream had come true. She almost said yes but stopped herself in time. "Are you considering becoming Amish?"

His eyes registered his shock. "I couldn't. I'd have to give up my profession. I'm planning to go to church with the Hesses. Could you...would you consider becoming Mennonite?"

A hollow emptiness opened inside Leah. How could

he even ask that question, knowing what her Amish faith meant to her? "I can't do that," she whispered.

The sorrow in Kyle's eyes made it clear how deeply she'd hurt him, but she'd made a vow when she joined the church, and she couldn't give up her commitment to God and her community. Even if it meant spending the rest of her life alone. Even if it meant giving up the man of her dreams, the man she'd come to love with her whole heart.

Kyle opened his mouth as if to speak, but then he shook his head. Gripping the steering wheel, he glanced in the rearview mirror before pulling out onto the road. The rest of the ride, they sat in silence. Not the companionable silence that had fallen from time to time while they were at the restaurant, but the painful silence of unspoken thoughts, dashed hopes, and unrequited love.

As soon as Kyle pulled into the parking lot, Leah unbuckled Ruby and barged through the door of the shop with their daughter in her arms.

Joel stared at her. "Earlier you walked through here thrilled and excited. Now you look like you're about to cry. Want to talk about it?"

No, she didn't, but she couldn't keep this heartbreak to herself. While she removed Ruby's winter clothing and changed her, Leah told Joel about the parenting agreement and Kyle's proposal.

"Congratulations! I could tell he's the right one by the way you light up whenever he's around."

Leah bit her lip to prevent tears from sliding down her cheeks. "I turned him down."

"Why? You love him, don't you?"

"With all my heart." A deep sadness choked her, closed up her throat. She could barely get her next words out. "I'm Amish, and I'll never give up my faith. He won't become Amish, so…"

"Oh, sis. That's…" Joel seemed at a loss for words.

His sympathetic look started the pent-up tears flooding down her cheeks. How would she live without Kyle? Her heart had been torn in half. But she could never give up her faith. Remaining true to the vows she'd made to God had to take priority in her life. No matter how wrenching the sacrifice.

"Leah?"

At her brother's hesitant question, she gazed at him through blurry eyes.

"I don't know if this would work, but would you consider becoming Beachy Amish?"

"*Ach*, Joel, what would *Mamm* and *Daed* think?"

"The same thing they thought about me turning *Englisch*. This wouldn't be as bad as that. You'd still be Amish."

Her parents had welcomed Joel back, although *Daed*'s eyes still revealed his hurt from time to time when he glanced at his son. Yet no one could doubt their love for him.

"Think about it, sis. It's obvious you've fallen for him hard, you've adopted a child together, and he wants to marry you. You'd still be keeping your commitment to God."

Leah shook her head. Yes, her commitment to God was paramount, and she'd still be faithful to Him. But leaving the church still wouldn't be right. She'd joined the Old Order Amish. She loved her community and wanted to remain a part of it forever. If she became Beachy Amish, she'd be turning her back on everyone she loved.

Leah hung her head and gazed down at the beautiful little girl in her arms. "We'd be shunned." She loved her daughter too much to make her an outcast from her own heritage.

"I know." The sympathy in Joel's voice touched her.

Her brother had experienced what it was like to be excluded from the family for years. He hadn't been placed under the Bann because he hadn't been baptized and hadn't joined the church, but their father had treated Joel as if he'd been shunned. Leah's case, as a baptized member, would be more clear-cut. Everyone in the community would be required to shun her for leaving the church. Joel and *Daed* had reconciled, but it still broke her father's heart that Joel was not with the church. And they'd all endured the pain of separation— Joel most of all.

"It isn't easy," Joel admitted. "It's a lonely life if you aren't a part of a community. You'll find yourself on the outside looking in, not really a part of anything because the *Englisch* will never quite accept you, and you'll be unable to accept many of their ways."

"And I'd break *Mamm*'s and *Daed*'s hearts…" She couldn't hurt them more than they'd already been hurt by Joel. Yes, they'd forgiven him, but they'd always ache inside. She couldn't add to their sorrow.

"*Jah*, it would," her brother agreed, "but it would also be foolish to throw away the love of a good man."

She wouldn't be throwing away his love. "Kyle will still help me parent Ruby no matter what."

"He's a good man, then. Many men would walk away. But is it fair to Ruby not to have both her parents living in the same house?"

Plenty of *Englischers* did that, but the Amish married for life. When she got old enough, Ruby would question it, wonder why her home life was so different from her friends'. Could Leah put her little girl in that situation?

Yet what were the alternatives? Joining the Beachy Amish meant leaving the community she loved and being shunned.

Joel cleared his throat. "I'm not trying to play devil's advocate here, but if you don't marry Kyle, I assume that means you're both free to marry other people?"

Leah's eyes widened. "I-I don't know. We didn't talk about that." Without a commitment from her, Kyle could marry someone else. He'd still continue to parent, but he might have a family of his own, and she'd have to watch him with his wife. Her stomach churned at the thought. Could she bear to be around him if he fell in love with someone else? She'd have to, for Ruby's sake.

"Why don't you pray about it?" Joel started down the nearest aisle, straightening shelves and putting products back in their proper places, something she did when she was nervous. "I'll pray too," he added. "And maybe you should discuss it with *Mamm* and *Daed*. They might have some ideas."

"Thanks." Leah wasn't sure she wanted to discuss this situation with her parents, especially when she was pretty sure it wasn't the right decision. If she backtracked, she'd only have caused them unnecessary heartache.

After saying good night to Joel and thanking him for his suggestions, Leah headed upstairs to put Ruby in her crib. As she lowered her sleeping daughter into bed, Kyle's face flashed before Leah's eyes. His tender gaze when he held and fed Ruby. He loved their little girl. Was it fair to him that he would never get to see her sleep at night? Never read her bedtime stories? Never wake to the patter of her feet as she grew older?

And what about her own life? Would she be content to leave Kyle each night, spend her nights alone? Joel's suggestion that Kyle might marry someone else made her ache inside. She couldn't ask him to give up his whole life for her and Ruby. Maybe he'd want to have a family of his own, other children.

Even if she gave up her Amish life for him, she'd never be able to give him children. He'd been happy to adopt Ruby, but had he only said that to comfort her? If he truly meant it, could she turn Beachy Amish to marry him?

Joel was right. The Beachy Amish did allow more freedom than the Old Order. Kyle could keep his Mennonite beliefs. He'd be permitted to use his car and remain a doctor. And she could get her certification as a midwife. She could even take nurse's training the way Kyle had once encouraged her to do. They could be together as a family if Kyle was willing to join.

She'd struggle with some of their ideas, so she'd ask Kyle to let her keep most of her Old Order ways. The other major hurdle would be her parents. She hated to hurt them this way, but she should ask for their counsel.

When *Daed* got home from work, Leah asked to talk to him and *Mamm* upstairs. In the bedroom, she poured out her heart.

Daed tugged at his beard the way he did whenever he was distressed. He remained silent and stoic.

Her eyes wet, *Mamm* said, "It seems it might be the best solution, *dochder*. I'd like to see you married, and a child should have two parents."

Leah gave her a grateful glance. *Mamm* knew of Leah's decision never to marry and her inability to have children. Likely, she viewed this as the only chance Leah would have. And she knew of Leah's dreams of higher education.

Daed, his face sorrowful, said, "Parents don't usually have a say in the choice of marriage partners. As much as it pains me, I will support whatever you decide. I only ask that you spend time in prayer before making such a momentous decision."

"I will, *Daed*." Though her heart longed to accept Kyle's proposal, how could she leave the Old Order, knowing she'd be shunned by her community?

Mamm lifted her gaze to meet Leah's. "You will always be welcome in our home whatever choice you make."

They'd still have to keep to the rules of shunning, and Leah would need to eat at a separate table, but knowing she wouldn't lose her parents' love and could still be a part of family gatherings helped. *Daed* hadn't agreed yet, though, and he was the head of the house. If he forbade it, *Mamm* would accept his decision. The way she'd done with Joel.

Daed's grave expression indicated he might contradict *Mamm*, and Leah held her breath, waiting for his response.

He shuffled his feet and stared at the floorboards as if examining each whorl in the wood. Finally, he spoke. "I regret cutting Joel out of the family. I won't be happy with your decision, but I won't turn you away if you visit."

"*Danke, Daed.*" Leah appreciated how hard it had been for him to agree to that.

Her heart lighter, Leah slipped from the room to pray. With her parents supporting her—or at least resigned to her decision if she chose to become Beachy Amish—Leah's spirits were lighter. The road ahead would be difficult, but at least Ruby would get to know her grandparents. And with Kyle getting to know and love his first set of adoptive parents, Ruby would have a second set of doting grandparents. Leah couldn't wait to tell Esther she had a granddaughter. If Kyle agreed, of course.

Right now, though, Ruby needed to be changed, fed, and settled in again for the night. Or for as much of it as she'd sleep through. A few times Ruby had managed five or six hours straight at night, which was a blessing. Leah hoped this would be one of those nights.

She spent time in prayer beside her daughter's crib, praying for Ruby's future and the wisdom to make the right choice. After the baby fell asleep, Leah tiptoed out of the room and slipped into the dark shop to call Kyle.

The sadness in his voice when he answered struck at her heart. "I'll be right over," he said when she asked if he could come over to talk.

Despite her worries that Kyle might not agree to join the Beachy Amish, Leah's heart was at peace. She'd accept whatever happened as God's will.

The minute hand on the battery-powered clock crawled along as second after second ticked by. Would Kyle ever get here?

When he finally arrived, he walked through the door, shoulders slumped. Was she responsible for that haggard look on his face?

"Kyle, first of all, I didn't say what was on my heart earlier. I tried to fight my attraction to you, but I ended up falling in love with you."

He groaned. "Leah, I'm already suffering enough. Knowing you care about me, but we can't be together…"

"Joel had a suggestion. Would you consider joining the Beachy Amish?"

"How would I support you and the baby? Being a doctor is all I know."

"They aren't as strict as the Old Order Amish. You could still be a doctor and drive a car. They're sometimes called the Beachy Amish-Mennonites."

"I'd do anything if it meant I could have you. I spent the past hour wrestling with the idea of becoming Amish, but I don't know the language or anything of the religious commitment. And I'd have no idea how I'd make a living."

"You'd have become Amish for me?"

"I didn't want to lose you."

"Oh, Kyle." Leah flung herself into his arms.

He folded her close to his heart and pressed his lips to hers.

Leah's heart overflowed with gladness and thanksgiving. God had answered her prayer in the most thrilling way possible. He'd not only given her the man of her dreams, a man she loved with all her heart, but He'd given her a child.

After a while, Kyle pulled back. "I love you, Leah. I could stay here forever, but I want you to get your sleep."

Although he was right, Leah would be willing to forgo sleep to spend time in his arms.

His voice thick, Kyle said, "I think we'll make a great team. And I'm sure Martin and Esther will be thrilled to have us both in the office. We can even combine traditional and herbal medicine."

Leah feigned surprise. "What? You'd let me suggest herbal remedies for your patients?"

"*Hmm.* Sometimes. We'll have to work out some compromises."

"But both Fisher boys did recover," Leah pointed out.

"You don't think jaundice and pneumonia would have healed faster and they'd have been safer in the hospital?"

"Most likely they would have, but sometimes you have to think about the family's needs."

Kyle tilted her chin up and met her lips. "*Mmm . . .* You might be right."

She pulled back. "Might?" she asked indignantly.

"OK, OK." He held up his hands in mock surrender. "You *are* right. You know, you're so cute when your eyes flash like that."

"So you were teasing to get a rise out of me?"

"Could be." He lifted one eyebrow and smiled. "Actually, I looked up some of the herbs you carry, and there are plenty of scientific studies on their effectiveness, so I'm open to learning more." Before she could retort, he added, "Even the ones without scientific evidence."

"Good." Leah snuggled against him, resting her cheek on his strong chest, thrilled by his rapid heartbeat, which matched her own racing pulse.

After another kiss, he placed his hands on her shoulders and turned her toward the hallway to the kitchen. "I said you should get some sleep, and I'm keeping you from it."

"I don't mind."

"Neither do I, but I want to take good care of you." Kyle twined his fingers through hers. "Could I kiss my daughter good night before I go?"

Leah smiled. "Of course."

Together they slipped up the stairs and into the darkened room, where Ruby lay curled in the wooden cradle, sucking on her fist. Kyle knelt beside her and stroked her downy hair. Then he bent and kissed her.

"Sleep tight," he whispered.

Then, arms around each other, Kyle and Leah stood by the cradle while moonlight streamed through the window, bathing all three of them in a heavenly glow.

Acknowledgments

I feel very privileged to have had an Amish midwife deliver two of my five children at home. Like Leah in this story, Martha preferred herbal products, and she gave me insight into many Amish ways.

I also owe a debt of gratitude to the wonderful people at the Clinic for Special Children in Strasburg, Pennsylvania, who do genetic research into inherited diseases of the Amish and Mennonites. They graciously gave of their time to show me around the clinic, explain their research, and demonstrate the equipment they use for studying genes. For those who want more information or who would like to donate to their work, please visit clinicforspecialchildren.org.

As always, I'm grateful to my Amish friends, who invite me into their lives and check my books for accuracy.

When Grace Fisher's husband dies—leaving her pregnant and with two small children— she's determined to take care of her family by herself. Elijah Beiler has always had a soft spot for Grace. But can he convince the independent widow to accept his help? And can he overcome his own past hurts to open his heart to a ready-made family?

A preview of
The Amish Widow's Rescue
follows.

Chapter One

Grace Fisher stood staring after the *Englisch* doctor who'd just handed her a huge wad of bills. He left through the side entrance of her barn so he couldn't be seen from the house. She longed to run after him to return his money. But she could never erase the information she'd given him. She'd betrayed Miriam, hoping to save a baby.

The money burned her fingers and her conscience. Judas had accepted thirty pieces of silver. *Have I just done the same?*

Her daughter toddled toward her and grasped a handful of Grace's black work apron to stay upright. Grace reached down and swept Libby into her arms. The comforting scent of her daughter's plump body, the horsey smell of the Morgan stamping in his stall, and the cows lowing to be milked all drew her back to the barn and to her work.

But first she needed to do something with the money.

After checking over her shoulder to be sure her three-year-old son was still playing with the barn cat, she headed to the farthest stack of hay bales. Levi was now at the age where he noticed details and blurted things out at inappropriate times. The less he knew about this, the better.

If her husband discovered she had this money, he'd take it, and Miriam would never see a penny. Rightfully, this money belonged to Miriam. All of it. Perhaps turning it over to their niece would relieve some of Grace's guilt.

She poked a hole in the top hay bale in the darkest corner. Although she was the only one who fed the animals, she still wanted to hide the roll of bills well. After pushing the money into the opening she'd made, she pulled bits of hay down to cover it until no green showed.

She needed to hurry. The encounter with the doctor had made her late for the milking, and Melvin would soon be roaring for his dinner. With Libby clinging to her, Grace fed and watered the animals. Usually she required Levi to help, but right now it would be faster to do it herself.

Then, hugging Libby close, she rushed to the first stall to milk Daisy. After settling onto the stool, she shifted her daughter in her lap. It wasn't easy doing chores with a child in her arms, but she'd learned to do many things while holding her babies. If she'd soon be adding another little one to their family, the practice would come in handy.

Grace dreaded telling Melvin the news. Most Amish men were delighted about having children, but Melvin's moods could be quite unpredictable. He might be non-committal, or he might rage.

After wiping the cow's udder with antiseptic, Grace began the rhythmic motions of squirting milk into the pail. The familiar ping of liquid hitting the pail calmed her nerves. Levi joined her as she prepared to milk the next cow, so Grace put Libby down and placed Levi on the stool in front of her. He was old enough to learn to do chores now. Although it would take much longer, she guided his small hands as he cleaned the cow and struggled to get milk.

"You'll soon be strong enough to do this. Try again," she encouraged him.

To his delight, some milk dribbled into the pail. He giggled. "I did it."

"Yes, you did." She placed her hand over his to strengthen his grip. "That's the way. Keep going like this." She bit her tongue before she praised him too much. Children should not be prideful. Neither should adults, but her spirit swelled with joy at his accomplishment.

After the milking was finished, Grace picked up two pails of milk and, with the children clinging to her apron, headed for the barn door, her stomach queasy. They'd been out here much too long. Melvin would be furious if his dinner was late. When he flew into a temper, he often berated the children.

The barn had been cold, but when Grace opened the door, frigid winds slapped her in the face. She wished she could protect her little ones from the cold—and their father's wrath.

The doctor had questioned her about her husband's

moods and asked if Melvin ever hurt her physically. She'd said no, but the look in his eyes made it clear he hadn't believed her. But she'd told him the truth. Or most of it. With his weight now hovering slightly over three hundred pounds and with all his health issues, Melvin couldn't get up from the couch to touch her. As long as they stayed out of arm's reach, they were safe.

Melvin was no longer the quiet, taciturn man she'd married four years ago. He'd lost his roofing job three years ago when the company folded. Since then, he'd been morose.

Despite being pregnant with Levi at the time, Grace had started to sell jam to make ends meet. She often suspected friends and family bought her jams more to help the family than to serve at meals. Everyone in the community could easily make their own jams and jellies. But that first summer, a few tourists had stopped when they saw her homemade wooden sign by the driveway. They'd bought a dozen jars, and soon orders flowed in from several *Englisch* specialty shops in other states. Grace had gotten a business license and a home inspection, and now she worked long hours filling orders. Most of the Amish shops and tourist spots in the Lancaster area carried her jams too.

But the more successful her business grew, the more Melvin's spirits plunged. He'd been unable to find another job. His health declined, and Grace soon had to take over all his farming chores. The more Melvin sat, the larger he grew. And the worse his temper became. Today, the doctor had suggested her husband needed to see a doctor and had urged her to be sure he had a physical soon. But how could she suggest that to Melvin? He'd have a fit.

The nauseous feeling in Grace's stomach increased as she neared the back door. How much of it was from the baby she suspected she was carrying and how much from anxiety? She was keeping too many secrets. But she couldn't tell Melvin about the baby. At least not yet. And if she told him about the money, he'd know she betrayed his niece. Her roiling stomach might also be from the guilt of concealing things from her husband.

When they reached the back porch, Levi let go of her skirt and raced up the steps. Before she could warn him to be quiet, he banged through the door, letting the storm door slam shut behind him.

As soon as Grace opened the door, her husband's low snarl came from the living room, and she cringed. Levi halted midway through the kitchen. His head hung low as his father berated him. Grace longed to hug him, to cover his ears, to stop the flow of angry words. If she did, they'd all pay. She settled for squeezing Levi's shoulder as she passed, hoping Melvin wouldn't notice. He could only see part of the kitchen from his perch on the couch.

Her son glanced up at her gratefully, and she signaled her love and support with a brief smile. But that was enough to direct Melvin's attention to her.

"It's long past time to cook dinner," Melvin barked. "What took you so long?"

"The man . . ." Levi lisped in his three-year-old drawl.

"Man?" Her husband stared at her accusingly. "What is he talking about?" He waved a hand toward their son.

"I, umm, that is . . ." Grace set Libby at the kitchen table so she could keep her back to Melvin for a few moments to compose herself before turning to face him. She clutched the sides of her work apron to keep from wringing her hands together. If she did that, Melvin would know she was hiding something.

Yet her conscience wouldn't allow her to do something dishonest. She had to tell him the truth, the whole truth, even if it meant he took the money from her, even if he exploded.

"Why was a man in the barn?" he snapped. "Who was he?"

Bowing her head and keeping her eyes downcast, Grace sucked in a quick breath, but her words still came out shaky. "Th-that *Englisch* doctor who bought the jam."

"He came back to return it? It wasn't to his taste?" The sneer on his face made it clear he didn't think much of her jam-making business.

Grace bit her lip. "No, he didn't return it." She kept her voice meek and gentle because the Bible said "a soft answer turneth away wrath." Although it rarely worked with Melvin. "He wanted to ask me a question." How could she tell him about Miriam?

"He couldn't have asked it when he was here in the house buying jam?" His eyes narrowed. "Or was it *private*?"

At the way he emphasized the last word, Grace's cheeks heated, and the words she'd been trying to form died on her lips. Was he accusing her of being unfaithful? She squeezed her eyes shut briefly to hold back tears. Then keeping her tone as measured as possible, she said, "He wanted Miriam's address."

"You didn't give it to him," he said, but his eyes held a question.

Grace froze, and her mouth dried out too much to answer.

Melvin's face purpled. "You did, didn't you?" He pushed himself partway up from the couch, and Grace took a step back. "If they find out, they'll make me pay back the money." Spittle flew from his lips. "You didn't care about that, did..." His voice trickled off into a gurgle, and he clutched at his heart. Then he keeled over, hitting the floor with a thud.

* * *

Elijah Beiler had just helped his father back into bed when someone banged on the back door. He had no wish to speak to anyone. For years, he'd been a recluse, only going to church on Sundays and occasionally meeting the truck driver who collected his milk for the distributor. Most of the time, though, he could leave notes for the driver. If families in the community needed help with a barn raising, he'd attend but try to find a solitary job.

He intended to ignore the light banging, but a shrill child's voice shouted, "Help!"

A child. Elijah's gut tightened. He did his best to avoid children ever since his sister...

The yell came again. Praying it wasn't a prank, he rushed to the door. His neighbor's little boy stood on the doorstep. "Something bad happened to *Daed*. My *mamm* said to call the bu-lince."

Elijah blinked at him. *Bu-lince? What in the world is that?* "Is your *daed* hurt?"

The small boy who had the same reddish hair and long eyelashes as his *mamm*—not that Elijah noticed things like that, of course—nodded vigorously. "He fell on the floor."

Elijah hadn't seen Melvin Fisher outside the house in years, but he'd heard rumors that he'd become extremely overweight. If he fell, his slim little wife could never help him up, although she did seem to manage all the farming chores on her own.

"Call quick," the little boy said.

Then it dawned on Elijah. *Ambulance.* That's what the child had been saying. "Stay right here," he commanded, pointing to the porch. Then he ran to the barn to call 911.

The Fishers didn't have a phone, but Elijah had one in the barn for the dairy business. He made the call, gave the address, and rushed back out. Until the ambulance came, he might be able to help. He'd volunteered at the fire company when he was younger, so he had some emergency training.

Scooping up the small boy, he raced across the side lawn to the house next door. He barged through the back door without knocking. "I called 911," he called out. "They're sending an ambulance."

Through the kitchen archway, the petite redhead was tugging and pulling at a huge inert body. The man, who appeared dazed but conscious, seemed to be struggling against her efforts.

"What happened?" Elijah asked as he hurried into the room.

"I think it's his heart."

Elijah couldn't resist the plea in her soft green eyes. "Let me help," he said, moving to the opposite side. Pulling his gaze from her eyes, Elijah forced himself to meet her husband's. "You didn't hurt or break anything when you fell, did you?" When the man shook his head, Elijah said, "If we all work together, we can prop you up against the couch."

They could worry about getting him back on the couch after the EMTs arrived. Elijah had fought stubborn cows and lifted heavy equipment, but nothing prepared him for the deadweight of the corpulent man on the floor. A man who seemed to be doing nothing to assist them. They'd barely managed to move him a few inches when Melvin gasped and went limp.

Cardiac arrest. Elijah's training came flooding back. Putting one hand on top of the other and interlocking his fingers, he pressed on Melvin's sternum. After each compression, he waited until his chest recoiled and then pressed again. Three, four, five... Elijah counted until he reached thirty.

Then he slid his hand under Melvin's neck to tilt his head back and open his airway. Pinching Melvin's nose, Elijah completed two breaths and returned to thirty compressions. Over and over he silently repeated, *Two breaths, thirty compressions, two breaths, thirty compressions*, until the ambulance siren whirred outside.

Grace rushed to the door to let the EMTs in. Elijah continued his rhythm until one of the men set a hand on his shoulder. Exhausted, Elijah rocked back on his heels and took in a long, slow breath. Then he stumbled to his feet and stepped aside, his heart pounding from adrenaline, as the EMTs shocked Melvin.

Grace stood framed in the kitchen doorway, the children behind her, peeking out from behind her skirt. Her hands were clenched in front of her, and her gaze remained focused on the EMTs bent over her prone husband. Elijah wished he had some way to help, to reassure her.

One EMT stood. "We need to get him to the hospital *now*."

Icy wind blew through the door as the driver wheeled in the stretcher, which left snowy tracks across the polished hardwood floors. Elijah assisted them in settling Melvin onto the stretcher, which groaned and creaked under his weight. Then they whisked him out the door.

Elijah turned to Grace. "Did you want to ride along to the hospital?"

She glanced down at her son and daughter, who were staring after the stretcher. "I-I can't."

"Go ahead," he urged, waving her toward the door. "I'll watch the children for you."

"But they haven't had any dinner or…"

"Don't worry. I can handle everything. You should be with your husband." He motioned toward the door. "You'd better hurry."

She glanced at him uncertainly, and he tried to project an air of calmness and competence. Once she'd snatched up her black bonnet and cape and hurried out the door, all his bravado leaked out. As a confirmed bachelor with no siblings or nieces and nephews, he had no idea how to care for children.

What have I gotten myself into?

ABOUT THE AUTHOR

Rachel J. Good grew up near Lancaster County, Pennsylvania, the setting for her Amish novels. Striving to be as authentic as possible, she spends time with her Amish friends, doing chores on their farms and attending family events. Rachel loves to travel and visit many different Amish communities. She also speaks at conferences and book events across the country and abroad.

When she's not traveling, she spends time with her family and writing. In addition to her Amish novels, she's written more than forty books for children and adults under several pen names.

You can find out more at:

racheljgood.com
Twitter @RachelJGood1
Facebook.com

Fall in Love with Forever Romance

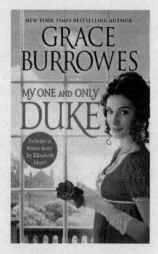

MY ONE AND ONLY DUKE
By Grace Burrowes

A charming Regency romance with a Cinderella twist! When London banker Quinn Wentworth is saved from execution by the news that he's the long-lost heir to a dukedom, there's just one problem: He's promised to marry Jane Winston, the widowed, pregnant daughter of a prison preacher. Also includes the novella *Once Upon a Christmas Eve* by Elizabeth Hoyt, available for the first time in print!

Fall in Love with Forever Romance

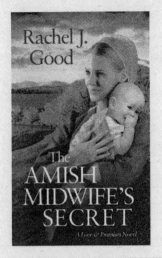

THE AMISH MIDWIFE'S SECRET
By Rachel J. Good

When *Englischer* Kyle Miller is offered a medical practice in his hometown, he knows he must face the painful past he left behind. Except he's not prepared for Leah Stoltzfus, the pretty Amish midwife who refuses to compromise her traditions with his modern medicine...But one surprising revelation and one helpless baby in need of love will show Leah and Kyle that their bond may be greater than their differences.

Fall in Love with Forever Romance

THE STORY OF US
By Tara Sivec

Don't miss this heartbreaking novel about love and second chances from *USA Today* bestselling author Tara Sivec! "One thousand eight hundred and forty-three days. That's how long I survived in that hellhole. And I owe it all to the memory of the one woman who loved me more than I ever deserved to be loved. Now, I'll do anything to get back to her... I may not be the man I used to be, but I will do whatever it takes to remind her of the story of us."

Fall in Love with Forever Romance

TIGER'S CLAIM
By Celia Kyle

Two big-cat shifters go undercover as a couple in love to take down an organization that wants to kill all of their kind. But to survive among so many enemies, they absolutely *cannot* fall in love...

THE CAJUN COWBOY
By Sandra Hill

With the moon shining over the bayou, this Cajun cowboy must sweet-talk his way into his wife's arms again...before she unties the knot for good!

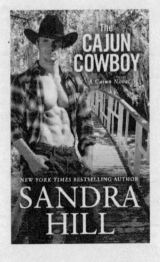